Other books by Jordan Falconer . . .

Knight Predator
Let Us Prey
Dark Elf

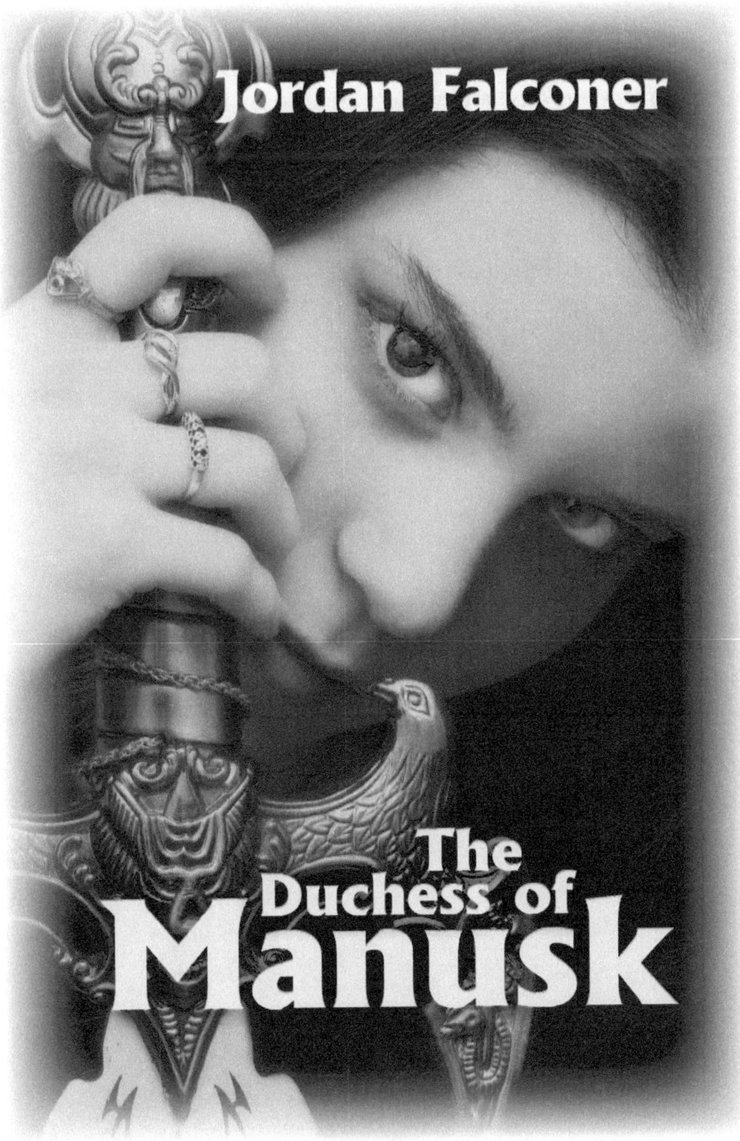

Jordan Falconer

The Duchess of Manusk

Mindancer Press
Bedazzled Ink Publishing Company * Fairfield, California

978-1-939562-90-6 paperback
978-1-939562-91-3 ebook

Cover Design
by

Tree House Studio

Mindancer Press
a division of
Bedazzled Ink Publishing Company
Fairfield, California
http://mindancerpress.bedazzledink.com

For Tammy . . . who never lets me give up . . .

ACKNOWLEDGMENTS

Thank you, as always, to Casey to making me sound much better than I really am. It is always appreciated!

CHAPTER 1

"WHY WEREN'T THE signal fires lit?" Elizabeth demanded as she reined in her horse.

A guardsman with the insignia of a lieutenant jogged up to her and automatically grabbed the horse's bridle as it tried to rear.

Her Highness, Princess Elizabeth St. John—and also Her Grace, Duchess of Manusk—slid easily off the horse and gave him an angry glare. "There are supposed to be fires here, Lieutenant, but I see none."

"Yes, Your Grace," he replied with a quick bow. "We've found wood and bodies, but no signs of any signal fire. We lit another up there." He gestured toward a fire, rapidly growing in size on the headland. "That's the best we can do, but too late."

Elizabeth grimaced at the loud crack of breaking wood mingled with the crashing waves on the beach. She shook her head. "It's my responsibility, not yours, Peter. It's *my* duchy."

An explosion rocked the beach and they ducked. Peter shielded her as another explosion followed close on the heels of the first.

"Powder kegs, Your Grace," Peter said.

Elizabeth eyed a column of flame roaring into the night sky. "So I see." She shook her head. "Have we found any survivors?"

Peter nodded and gestured toward the cluster of shadowed guardsmen a little further down the beach. "Some can walk, some are unconscious, and some won't survive. We are lining up the dead so the living can't see them."

"Do we know where the ship came from?" Elizabeth made her way toward the cluster of survivors.

Peter shook his head. "Their standard doesn't look familiar." He pointed at a pennant carefully laid out in the sand ahead of them.

Elizabeth stopped as they got nearer to it and studied it. It was black and had a red dragon on a yellow star burst on it. *Wonderful. I can't afford any more strife with other nobles. Duke Gilbert of Osk and Duke Clayton of Sandcliff are quite enough.* "It looks familiar. I just don't remember who it belongs to." She bit her lip. "I feel like I *should* know whose it is."

She looked at the people lined up on the beach.

"These ones will survive," Peter said, following her gaze.

Elizabeth nodded, studying the unconscious figures. They were a mixed collection of men and women, old and young. There were no signs of arms or armor amongst them. She bent over, her eyes drawn to a woman with light blonde hair. She was shockingly beautiful, and tall, of a height to the men lying around her. Elizabeth guessed the woman was over her own five foot eleven. The blonde woman's drenched clothes were expensively tailored, of an unfamiliar style, and stained on one side with dark blood.

"Can any of them travel?" Elizabeth gazed at the field surgeon that had come to stand beside her. She waved away his quick salute.

"These ones are the ones with the lightest injury." He waved at the tall, blonde woman. "She's more seriously hurt than the others. She seems to be of some importance, so I am making certain she remains simply unconscious."

Elizabeth nodded, feeling swift relief. She smiled at him. "Thank you, Doctor. You've done well."

The doctor bowed. "Thank you, Your Grace. If you will excuse me, I have other patients to see to."

Elizabeth nodded and he hurried off. She turned back to Peter. "See to it that these ones are taken with us. We'll go on to the city."

"Yes, Your Grace." He tilted his head, studying the row of people. "It's a pity we haven't actually seen the city yet, Your Grace. We have no idea what's waiting for us there."

"Anything is better than out in the open like this," Elizabeth said. "Captain Herbert has been in the city for a week by now. He should have cleared out some space for us."

Peter nodded, his sour expression speaking volumes about what he thought of the Duchy of Manusk. "Yes, Your Grace."

Elizabeth gave him a grin. "Manusk will be ours again, Peter. Sandcliff and Osk will be driven out."

Peter nodded, his expression carefully neutral. "If you will excuse me, Your Grace?"

Elizabeth nodded. "Of course."

Peter bowed and hurried away and Elizabeth turned to the dark sea. The voices of her troops surrounded her, the volunteers who came with her to take back the Duchy of Manusk for her father, King Vincent.

The sound of crashing breakers was interrupted by loud explosions as the last of the powder kegs on the wrecked ship exploded. Some of the survivors groaned softly.

She squared her shoulders. She couldn't do anything about the broken ship—the damage had been done. They could only take care of the survivors and help them get home.

Her horse—who had been trailing quietly behind her—snorted as she mounted. She patted his neck and he quieted. She heeled him around and watched her guardsmen move efficiently around the beach.

The burning wreck caught her eye and she almost unconsciously glanced back at the blonde woman on the beach. Disquiet washed over her. *I really* should *know who the standard belongs to.* The sensation of memory just out of reach maddened her and she shook her head in frustration.

"Guardsman," she said to the small group of armed men standing close to the survivors.

"Your Grace?" a deeply shadowed man said.

"Assemble and prepare to move out." She gestured toward their new guests. "Load them onto the supply carts. We leave now to go to the city."

"Yes, Your Grace," he said.

A quarter hour later the guardsmen were sufficiently organized to move out again, toward the city of Manusk. They formed neat ranks around a few makeshift carts. The survivors had been covered in cloaks and rough horse blankets.

A group of guardsmen remained on the beach in a cluster around the surgeon, who was tending to the needs of the more gravely injured.

"Sean!" she called.

"Yes, Your Grace." Sergeant Sean seemed to materialize beside her, Peter in tow.

She looked up at him. "See to it that the surgeon has what he needs to move the others. We have to get them under cover."

Sean saluted. "Yes, Your Grace."

Elizabeth nodded and turned to Peter. "Let's move out, Lieutenant."

Peter saluted, mounted his horse, and fell into line beside her.

Elizabeth led the way back up to the highway that went into the city of Manusk. The night was very dark and starlight lit the way down the road. Her horse stumbled and she gently soothed him. She heard a soft cry from a wounded survivor behind her.

She glanced around and saw the dim outline of a cart dip and sway as it passed over a rut in the road. She frowned. *Another thing to add to the list. Road repair.* She caught Peter's eye.

His jaw tensed and he shook his head.

She gave him a grim, humorless grin.

They traveled for an hour past flat land—Elizabeth supposed it was fields—which darkness mostly hid from them. She wrinkled her nose at the few things she could see—sagging fences, desultory vegetation, and the occasional outline of a rickety house. They all looked as though they were in need of care. *It'd be nice to know if anyone's living in any of those farms. If they're abandoned we must take that land back to grow food.*

Peter's horse stumbled and he cursed softly.

"At ease, Lieutenant," she said. "We will simply repair the roads."

He grunted.

"You wish to say something, Peter?" she asked.

Peter blew out a deep breath. "This duchy is horrible. I can hardly believe what we've seen over the past couple of days. Neglected roads, starving peasants, murder, and wanton destruction. Why would anyone *do* something like this to their home?"

"I'm certain most of the rabble we've seen are from Osk and Sandcliff," Elizabeth said. "I am guessing that thanks to them, most of the citizens of Manusk have fled. Do you know why the king gave me this duchy?"

"I know, Your Highness," Peter said. "Osk and Sandcliff illegally occupy Manusk and monopolize trade. The Steward of Manusk is dead so their influence increases. We're going to politely ask them to leave."

Elizabeth nodded. "Yes, that's right, but that's not all of it. We won't be going back to the Heartland. This is my new home. It is His Highness's wish that I take and hold Manusk. I'm to put and end to the stranglehold Osk and Sandcliff have on the Heartland by taking from them of their most precious prize—the sea duchy of Manusk." Her knuckles were white from her grip on the reins. She took a deep breath.

"I was wondering why he suddenly decided now was the right

time to finally throw those beggars out of Manusk." He glanced at her. "He wants you to settle down?" He smothered his chuckle with a cough. "*You?*"

"Yes, Peter. Me." Elizabeth accepted the teasing and relaxed her shoulders. She wasn't sure why her father had suddenly decided that was to be her fate, and she wondered if he'd picked someone out for her to marry as well. *No, he wouldn't do that to me, he loves me too much.*

"I never thought you'd settle down."

"I hadn't planned on it. I'm better on a battlefield than I am on a throne."

"I'm sure you'll do well at this as well, Your Highness. Perhaps settling down wouldn't be—"

"Thank you, Peter," Elizabeth said sharply. She looked down at her trembling hands and consciously relaxed them.

"I'm sorry, Your Grace," Peter said. "I don't mean to make light of your situation."

Elizabeth forced a grin. "It doesn't bother me, Peter. I'm more worried about our new guests—the ones we're in no position to care for properly." She gestured back toward the wagons. "I don't know who they are but I'm sure they're going to take—or try to, anyway—a pound of flesh from me. If that's so, they're only one amongst many."

Peter nodded. "Do you think it was Osk or Sandcliff who put out the signal fires?"

"I don't know," Elizabeth said. "It wouldn't be in their best interests since they are hell bent on maintaining their monopoly on trade. Wrecked ships don't make for good trade."

"I don't suppose it really matters, though, does it, Your Grace?" Peter said. "As you so rightly point out, when our guests wake up, they'll see us, they'll find out it's your duchy and you're going to get the blame."

"My thoughts exactly," Elizabeth said.

She surveyed the darkness of the road in front of them. She could see flickers of light from the city of Manusk ahead of them, and a dark shape coming down the road toward them.

"I still think we should have brought more guardsmen," Peter said.

"From my understanding the city can barely feed itself let alone our entire army. We *have* to keep a small force. If we need more men we'll send for them."

Peter nodded but looked unconvinced.

"Is that Captain Herbert?" Peter asked.

"I presume so," Elizabeth said. "I haven't met him. He's my brother's man."

Seconds later, an armed man wearing the insignia of a captain reined to a halt in front of her. He was middle aged and carried himself as though he were a nobleman.

"Your Grace," he said with a crisp salute. "We weren't expecting you until tomorrow."

"You're Captain Herbert?" Elizabeth said.

"I am," the man said.

"You saw the fire by the beach?" Elizabeth said without preamble. "It's from a ship that broke up on the rocks."

Captain Herbert cursed.

"Why weren't the signal fires lit, Herbert? What happened?" Elizabeth said.

"They should have been, Your Grace," Herbert replied. "I sent men up there myself this afternoon. The lighthouse was burned down a few days ago and the keeper did his best to light a signal fire on the headland but armed men attacked him. He came for help and he got it."

"Not really," Elizabeth said dryly. "He and the troops you sent to him are dead. A ship with a standard we don't recognize has broken up on the rocks. We have some of the living with us, the rest are on the beach. We have to go back for them."

Captain Herbert's mouth tightened with displeasure. "There are guardsmen behind me. I'll send them back to the beach."

"Thank you, Captain," Elizabeth said. "We need to get these people to shelter. You will come with us and show us to the house and the barracks."

Herbert hesitated. "Yes, Your Grace."

Something's bothering him. Do I want to know? No, I don't think so. One problem at a time.

"Move out." Elizabeth heeled her horse into motion, Captain Herbert beside her, Sean taking up position beside him, and the cavalcade moved again.

They passed twenty silent and grim-faced guardsmen.

"Go to the beach and help with the wounded," Captain Herbert said.

"Yes, Captain," the guardsman said at the head of the column. He turned around. "Move out."

He trotted passed the other guardsmen, who murmured greetings to one another.

The farms finally petered out and more houses appeared at regular intervals. After another ten minutes they reached the western gate of the city. The city walls reared up before them, dark denizens in the night sky. The doors stood open and there was no sign of the night watch.

"Where is everyone?" Elizabeth asked, looking around.

Herbert cursed. "Our troops are down at the docks minding the warehouses. There are many pests, Your Grace, human and otherwise, that seek to rob us blind. There are still some of the city watchmen in the city and we have made use of them, but it looks as though these have left."

Elizabeth narrowed her eyes. "Is there *anyone* in this city loyal to Manusk?"

"The watchmen and troops are not of Manusk, so their loyalty is uncertain. The true citizens of Manusk are loyal to the bone, Your Grace."

"Good," Elizabeth said. "That should make things a little easier."

"Ahem," Herbert said.

Elizabeth raised an eyebrow at him. "Yes, Captain?"

"The citizens of Manusk are loyal to Manusk, *not* to her Duchess," Herbert said. "Your grandfather, Prince Stephen, is still a bright light in their memories."

Elizabeth's mouth tightened. "I am *nothing* like my grandfather. I am not a thief, a letch, or a bloodthirsty bully. *I* did *not* do this to Manusk."

"I know, Your Highness," Captain Herbert said. "But there are many who wonder why the king would suddenly send a noble in to take control of Manusk. *Especially* a noble related to him *and* one of their former duke's bloodline. They wonder what you want from them and what you will do *to* them."

"I am here to make a home for us *all*, beggars and nobles alike. Manusk will once again become a free seaport and her citizens will live in peace and prosperity."

Herbert smiled at her. "Then perhaps if we keep telling them that they'll begin to listen and believe in us."

Elizabeth nodded. "It's not words that distinguish us, it's deeds." She shook her head. *So no one wants me here. That's no surprise.* It wasn't the first time she had gone into an enemy's territory and taken it for her father. A small, weary part of her, deep inside, cringed.

They rode along in silence for a few minutes, and Elizabeth blinked as she tried to make out stores and houses in the dim light. It looked as though half of the windows in the buildings had been broken, and there were no lights to speak of. They'd passed one or two taverns along the way, but even they had been darkened and almost deserted. It was quiet; the only sound she heard was from her own men.

"Why are there no streetlights?" Elizabeth peered into the darkness. "Are they all broken as well?"

"No, Your Grace," Herbert said in hushed tones. "Osk and Sandcliff have imposed martial law in the city of Manusk. They have toughs roaming around challenging every citizen in the streets after dark."

Elizabeth growled. "Not in my city, they don't. If you run into any men engaged in such activities, throw them in jail and let me know." She waved a hand. "See if you can find one brave soul to come out at dusk tomorrow and light the street lamps. Send a guard with him."

"Which streets do you want lit?" Herbert asked. "Manusk is a large city."

"All the main roads through the center of the city. If any louts dare show themselves to try and stop you, throw them in jail. Understand, Herbert?"

"Clearly, Your Grace," Herbert said with a crisp salute. He gestured ahead of them. "This is the residence of the Duchess of Manusk."

Elizabeth peered around the courtyard, frowning at the broken stones. She looked up at the house. The windows appeared to be made of shattered glass, and the outline of the roof looked ominously jagged against the night sky.

"You're joking, sir," Peter said. "This place is worse than my aged grandmother's midden heap."

Herbert grunted. "I wish I was, Lieutenant." He dismounted as a sudden light from an open door chased away some of the shadows in the courtyard. "Ah, Harriet."

A middle-aged woman lifted her skirts and jogged out to them. Another woman followed close behind, carrying a torch. Shadows waxed and waned in the flickering light.

"Captain Herbert," Harriet puffed as she came to a stop before Elizabeth. She nodded toward Elizabeth. "Who is this one?"

"Show your respect, woman." Peter stepped up beside Elizabeth. "This is Her Grace, Elizabeth St. John, Duchess of Manusk."

Harriet gasped. She opened her mouth to speak but Elizabeth held up her hand, forestalling her.

"It's quite all right, Peter," Elizabeth said, half smiling despite the tension she felt deep inside.

Harriet's cool gaze raked over Elizabeth. "I meant no disrespect, Your Grace."

Elizabeth noticed that Harriet never curtseyed and her tone bordered on insolent. *I wonder if all of the real citizens of Manusk have as much fire as this woman? Perhaps I can claim Manusk as my own after all.*

"None taken," Elizabeth said with a warm smile. "Herbert tells me you've been taking care of my house? I would like to see it. Do we have room for guests?" She briefly considered asking if there was a hospital or barracks close by but decided against it. If there were, they were probably in as terrible condition as her own house.

"The house needs fixing. Half the roof is missing and it's unsafe," Harriet said in clipped tones. "You can use the great hall as barracks— that's what your other soldiers have been doing—and there are one or two rooms on the first floor that can still be used."

"We have wounded with us. We should probably bring them up to the first floor so they won't be disturbed." Elizabeth pulled her saddle bags off her horse and handed the reins to a stable boy who materialized beside her. "See to the wounded, Herbert."

"Very good, Your Grace," Herbert and Harriet said together. They shot each other a quick, unreadable glance.

"Peter, see to the guardsmen," Herbert said, striding away. "Sergeant, you stay with Her Grace."

Sean and Peter snapped off quick salutes and Peter left.

Harriet led them into the house, and Elizabeth grimaced at the foyer's worm-eaten wood, cracked floor tiles, and moldy ceiling. Harriet walked straight ahead toward the broad staircase that led to the upper floors.

"Stay to the right," she called over her shoulder to Elizabeth. "Some of the risers are rotten."

The wood creaked dangerously under Elizabeth's booted feet and she quickly stepped over to the right behind Harriet. Harriet led her along a darkened, musty corridor. She shoved the door of the room closest to the head of the stairs. It opened with a tired creak and Elizabeth winced and looked inside. She quickly stifled a sneeze. It was dusty and empty of furniture and looked as though it could hold ten people. She smiled.

Harriet led the way to the second room. She touched the knob and the door broke off its hinges with a loud squeal and crashed forward into the room. The floorboards groaned mightily in protest.

Elizabeth grimaced and gingerly stepped inside and surveyed the room. It was as dusty and empty as the first. She glanced at Sean, who was already standing the rotten door against the closest wall.

Harriet shook her head and pursed her lips.

"Let's see the third room," Elizabeth said, shaking her head.

"Yes, Your Grace," Harriet said.

Elizabeth trailed behind Harriet as she led them to the end of the dilapidated corridor and opened the end door. It opened silently, much to Elizabeth's surprise. She stepped in and took a cautious breath. This room was much smaller, with an unobstructed view to the port of Manusk, a large, clean fireplace, and a hastily erected four poster bed. The bay window ahead of her was open a crack, allowing clean, fresh air to come in.

Elizabeth took a deep breath. "Excellent. Harriet, this is much better than I expected." She left and led the way back down the stairs, keeping to one side as carefully as before. She spotted Peter waiting for them. "Peter. You can put the wounded upstairs. We have three good rooms."

"Thank you, Your Grace," Peter said. "We're about out of room down here. The great hall is filled to capacity with guardsmen. We're going to have to send some out to the stables."

"Can't be helped. I was going to suggest I take up lodging in an inn but there are none that would take me, are there?" Elizabeth studied the stone-faced Harriet closely.

Harriet remained expressionless and silent.

"I will bunk with the wounded." She turned back to Peter. "Take them all upstairs. Put Her Ladyship in the corner room. There's a bed and I'm sure she'll be more comfortable there."

"The bed was intended for you, Your Grace," Harriet said, sounding scandalized.

"And I appreciate it, but my blankets and cloak will serve me as well as any bed. I am a soldier in good health, unlike some of our guests. The more gravely injured will be joining us soon. We have to have somewhere to house them." Elizabeth gestured at the rotting foyer. "Are there any carpenters in Manusk who would be willing to work on the house?"

Harriet thought for a moment. "I can think of one, but he will need some help," she said grudgingly.

"We will see who we can round up tomorrow, then," Elizabeth said.

Her eyes felt gritty with exhaustion. Despite her words, this was almost worse than living at campsites by the road or on a battlefield. She stepped back as two guardsmen functioning as stretcher bearers began their ascent upstairs. Harriet quickly hurried after them, calling for them to walk to the right.

"Where are *you* going to sleep, Your Grace?" Peter asked. "We could move—"

"None of my men need move themselves for me." Elizabeth thought of the hearthstones upstairs and smiled. "I'll be fine. I saw some comfortable, quiet hearthstones upstairs."

"But, Your Grace," Peter said. "You have no assurances that the wounded we brought here won't slit your throat."

"I know. But I will have to stay where there's free space. Tomorrow we will talk to our guests and find out why they came," she said.

"As you wish, Your Grace," Peter said, looking unhappy but giving her a salute and backing away.

Elizabeth went upstairs and dodged guardsmen carrying stretchers of wounded. The door to the corner room was open, and she went inside. The lady from the beach had been carefully laid out on the bed. Her midsection was covered in bandages and her color was good. Elizabeth sat on the edge of the bed and studied the woman.

She was exceptionally beautiful with angular, perfect features and lush lips. Her pale skin shone with the bloom of youth. She gently pushed her golden hair back off her forehead.

"Sweet dreams, my lady," Elizabeth said.

She got up off the bed with a sigh, trudged over to the hearthstones, and spread out her cloak. She lay down, feeling bone weary. It was hard but no different to the multitude of other times she'd been forced to sleep on the ground, ready to wake at a moment's notice. *This is*

*better than I normally have. At least I'm indoors, out of the weather. I
have a roof over my head, which is more than half my soldiers have.*

That would have to be one of the first things on the list. Fixing the
house and finding food for everyone. Did the neglect and abandonment
she saw in the city extend to the countryside? Did Harriet look in need
of a good meal and care?

Elizabeth drifted off to sleep and her thoughts merged into her
dreams.

CHAPTER 2

ELIZABETH'S EYES FLUTTERED open at the gentle shake of her shoulder. She stiffened. The hand touching her stopped and she heard the rustle of cloth as the owner took a step back.

"Yes?" Elizabeth asked, blinking and slowly sitting up. Her voice cracked.

To her surprise, she felt rested and not sore as the hard stone suggested she should be. She blinked at the bright, early morning sunlight that shone into the room. It wasn't often that she slept past dawn.

Harriet watched her with wary eyes. "Captain Herbert suggested you may wish to go down to the docks this morning. He also said you would want a hot bath and breakfast."

"The bath and breakfast both sound heavenly, so thank you, Harriet," Elizabeth said.

She studied the housekeeper. She was middle aged, with hard lines carved around her mouth and eyes. Her eyes were steel grey, cool and sad, and measuring her.

"Tell me. Have you enough to eat? Is food in short supply?"

Harriet blinked, surprised, but it was quickly hidden behind her impassive façade. "There isn't as much food as we'd like but we get by."

"We know of no shortages in the King's Heartland."

"Perhaps because there are none," Harriet said.

Elizabeth studied her, and Harriet remained expressionless. The silence played out.

"Will that be all, Your Grace?"

"Bath?" Elizabeth said, smiling pleasantly. "I believe I will have breakfast with my soldiers this morning."

"Very good, Your Grace. The bathing chamber is through that door," Harriet said, nodding to a place behind Elizabeth. "Leave your clothing here, Your Grace. We'll attend to it today."

Elizabeth nodded. "Thank you, Harriet."

Harriet bobbed a quick curtsey and backed out of the room.

Elizabeth stood with a sigh and made her way to the bed to study her guest in the daylight.

She was as beautiful as the night before, and her blonde hair shone in the sunlight. Her face had regained some of its color and her breath was deep and even in her sleep.

"You *are* a beautiful one, aren't you? I wonder how many hearts you've broken." Elizabeth smiled. "And I wonder who you are." She smoothed back the woman's hair. "I will see you this evening, pretty lady, and until then rest easy."

She backed away from the bed, shedding her clothes as she went. She dug in her discarded saddle bags for spare breeches and a shirt.

She padded into the bathing chamber and found it much better than she'd expected. It was a large room with a tub of steaming, fragrant water in the center. Thick towels hung over the back of a chair set to one side of it.

She climbed the steps and gingerly stuck one foot into the water. It was perfect and she quickly sank into it with a deep sigh of contentment.

She padded back into the bed chamber twenty minutes later, flicking her long hair back over her shoulder. She pulled on her boots and stopped suddenly at the sound of a soft moan coming from the bed. She quickly stood and hurried to the blonde woman.

The woman turned her head on the pillow and moaned softly.

Elizabeth laid a hand on her forehead, trying to soothe her, and her eyes fluttered open. They were a mesmerizing shade of cornflower blue.

"Safe. You are safe," Elizabeth said.

The woman uttered an unintelligible word.

Elizabeth frowned in confusion. "I didn't understand you. What do you need?"

The woman uttered the word again, and then, "Water."

"Water. Yes." Elizabeth glanced around the room and grinned broadly at the tray of steaming broth and carafe of water a servant had put on the old table by one of the bay windows. She quickly grabbed a glass, poured the water, and hurried back to the bed.

The woman blinked at her and moved around weakly.

"Here, I'll help you," Elizabeth said, putting an arm around her shoulders and helping her to sit up a little.

She held the cup as the woman took a cautious sip. The woman closed her eyes in evident pleasure, and then took another sip. Each sip became stronger until she'd drained the entire glass.

"Good," she murmured and settled back into Elizabeth's embrace.

"More?" Elizabeth asked, but got no response. The woman was unconscious again.

Elizabeth gently lowered her down again, struck by the heavy muscles in her arms and shoulders. It seemed that this exceptional beauty was no stranger to a physical activity. Was she a sailor or a soldier?

The door opened and a young woman rushed in. She saw Elizabeth sitting on the bed next to the woman and stopped.

"Here, who are you?" the serving girl said. "What d'you think you're doing?"

Elizabeth gave her an easy smile. "I'm Elizabeth St. John."

"Oh, lord." The serving girl flushed and dropped into a deep curtsey. "I'm very sorry, Your Grace. I meant no disrespect."

Elizabeth shook her head. She went to the serving girl—who practically had her face to the floor and was still apologizing—and helped her up. "Forgiven. What's your name?"

"Mara," she said, her voice cracking. She cleared her throat. "M-Mara, Your Grace."

"Well, Mara," Elizabeth said. "Our guest woke up long enough to drink water and has now gone back to sleep. Please continue to take good care of her and let me know if she wakes up again and says anything."

"Yes, Your Grace," Mara said, relief shining in her eyes.

"I'll be back this evening. Do you know where Captain Herbert or Lieutenant Peter is?"

"Captain Herbert? Captain Herbert. Yes. Yes, Your Grace. Captain Herbert asked that you meet him down—"

"At the port," Elizabeth finished with Mara. "Thank you."

"I'm sorry, but I don't know where any of your other guardsmen are, Your Grace."

"That's fine, I'm sure I can muddle along," Elizabeth said, waving her away and striding toward the door. "Thank you again."

She opened the door and left without waiting for a response. She trotted down the stairs, keeping carefully to the left. She surveyed the foyer, bustling with guardsman, and saw Peter talking to Harriet.

Harriet spotted her and inclined her head in acknowledgement, and left him.

"Peter," Elizabeth said. "Good morning."

"Good morning, Your Grace," Peter said, bowing.

"Have you eaten yet?" Elizabeth asked.

"Yes, Your Grace," he said. "Captain Herbert has given me strict instructions to tell you to meet him—"

"At the port, yes, I know." Elizabeth gritted her teeth. *Does he think I've lost my wits and my memory?*

"I've been given my own orders, Your Grace," Peter said, properly impassive although his eyes danced with mirth.

"And what were they?" Elizabeth asked.

"I'm to go and assess the city watch. He's given me responsibility for building a perimeter defense of the city."

Elizabeth nodded. "And while you're at it, make sure the signal fires—"

"Are lit," he finished with her. "Yes, Your Grace."

"Thank you," she said.

"Sergeant Sean will escort you to the field kitchen, Your Grace. He will also accompany you to the port." He indicated the tall guardsman who'd appeared behind Elizabeth.

"I think I can find the port. All I have to do is walk toward the water. And I'm perfectly capable of taking care of myself." She patted the hilt of the sword strapped to her hip.

"I am aware of that, Your Grace," Peter said. He leaned forward and whispered in her ear. "Perhaps it's not for you, Your Highness."

Elizabeth gave him a searching look. His face remained properly impassive. What was *that* supposed to mean? She and even a small number of guardsmen were a match for simple merchants at the docks.

"All right," she finally said, gazing at the tall man who towered half a foot over her. "We'll go after we've eaten."

"Very good, Your Grace. If you will excuse me?" Peter said.

"Of course, Peter." Elizabeth turned to Sean. "Sergeant Sean, show me the kitchen."

Sean saluted and they went toward the rear of the manor house. They walked down a dusty, rotten corridor, toward the smell of baking bread and rich stew.

They passed servants and guardsmen hurrying about their business. The guardsmen all offered small salutes to her as she passed by.

Sean opened the door to the kitchen and they were blasted by warm air and the rich smell of fresh food.

Elizabeth immediately went to a stack of bowls and grabbed a bowl and a spoon. She went to the cooking fire and helped herself to a couple of ladles of rich, beef stew. She grabbed a hunk of bread, Sean close behind her.

Rough benches and tables had been set up in the middle of the kitchen and most were half empty. Elizabeth sat in the closest vacant seat so her back was to a wall and began to eat. She smiled. The stew was every bit as tasty as it smelt.

She could only see her guardsmen in the room, and they were relaxed and laughing but on the lookout for trouble, like any good soldiers. She wondered where the domestic staff ate. She looked through the open kitchen doors at the rear of the room, and saw Harriet standing with a group of men and women, gesturing toward the manor house.

Elizabeth got to her feet and approached the doors, curious. She heard raised voices, but they were muffled. She couldn't make out individual words.

She took a step outside and the voices faltered to silence as the group saw her.

"Harriet, what's going on here?" she asked.

"Nothing," Harriet said.

The crowd glared at her and she returned the glare. Elizabeth marveled at the battle of wills before her.

Elizabeth nodded toward the small, thin, ragged boy hiding behind his father's leg. "That hardly looks like nothing. Now, what's going on?"

"Who are *you*?" a man asked.

"These people are here because they are hungry and have no homes," Harriet cut in before the crowd's ugly mood could change to anything worse.

"Why are you homeless?" Elizabeth asked, keeping a careful eye on a tall, thin man who was clenching and unclenching his hands. *These people are not loyal to me.*

"Osk and Sandcliff rob us blind," he retorted. "Bully people. Throw them out of their homes. Burn everything to the ground."

"Where was your home, good sir?" Elizabeth asked. *These people are loyal to Manusk.*

"It is on the outskirts of the city. I am a blacksmith. I wouldn't pay the new taxes so they drove me out."

Elizabeth went to stand beside Harriet, a wary Sean at her shoulder. *These people* must *be loyal to me or there won't* be *a Manusk any more.*

"How many of you are tradesman?" Elizabeth asked.

"What's it to you?" the man said, spitting between her boots. "Plan on putting a good word in with His Nibs the Duke, were you?"

"Duchess."

"Pardon?"

"Duchess. A *duke* doesn't rule Manusk. A *duchess* does."

"Wonderful. A woman in charge. We may as well give Osk and Sandcliff the city now."

Elizabeth's temper snapped and she took a step forward. "It looks to me like you've already given yourself to Osk and Sandcliff." She looked up at the crowd, some of whom apparently guessed who she was and stared at her with fear in their eyes.

"I am Elizabeth St. John, Duchess of Manusk," she said in a loud voice. "I ask again. Are there any tradesman amongst you?"

The crowd stared at her in silence, showing a range of emotion that spanned terror all the way to open anger and defiance.

"Well?" she demanded.

"Your Grace?" a woman said in a faltering voice. "I am a cook, Your Grace."

"I am a seamstress."

"I am a carpenter."

Suddenly all the voices seemed to call at once and Elizabeth found she was talking to several blacksmiths, fletchers, glazers, carpenters, and cooks.

Elizabeth held out her hands. "I am happy to feed and shelter you."

The crowd gasped and was silent for another moment.

"What do we have to do?" the blacksmith asked warily.

"Help me. That's all I ask. I need good men and women to rebuild the city that they are trying to take from us. I need farmers, farriers, thatchers, maids, apothecaries, and doctors. I need anyone willing to help me take Manusk back."

One of the ragged men looked down at the woman leaning into him and put his hand on the cowering boy's head. "I will help you. My wife and son are starving."

"I can also help you with that," another man said, stepping forward. "I'm a farmer. I was driven off my land for refusing to pay higher taxes. My farm was taken from me and given to Osk."

Elizabeth's mouth tightened. "You are exactly the kind of man I seek. What's your name?"

"I'm Jarrod and this is my wife Rebecca," he said, pulling a sallow-faced woman to stand by him.

"Would you be willing to meet me back here this evening, Jarrod?"

Jarrod and Rebecca exchanged a long look. He turned back to Elizabeth and gave her a short, sharp nod.

"I will be back at six. Eat with me and we'll talk."

Jarrod nodded. "Yes, Your Grace."

"*All* of you. You are hungry. Come and eat, then," Elizabeth said to the rest of the curious crowd. She turned to the ragged man with the starving son and held out her hand. "You are welcome to our food." She looked at the rest of the crowd, the sullen, disbelieving faces. "You are *all* welcome."

The man took her hand. She squeezed it, stood back, and pointed toward the kitchen. "Go. Eat."

The crowd didn't need to be asked twice. They descended on the open door. Each looked on the point of tears and several knuckled their foreheads as they rushed past her.

Harriet stayed behind and eyed Elizabeth closely, her expression inscrutable. "You are an unusual noblewoman, Your Grace."

"And you are an unusual housekeeper, Harriet," Elizabeth replied. "Will you help me too?"

Harriet was silent for a moment. "So far you've proven yourself to be unique, Your Grace. I'll do it for now."

"Good enough," Elizabeth said. "Truce?"

"Truce," Harriet replied.

"You must eat with Jarrod, Rebecca, and I. We'll talk this evening. I need to know more about what's happening here. I need to know more about my duchy."

Harriet nodded. "Yes, Your Grace. There are certainly some things you need to know." She studied Elizabeth for a moment. "Your blood is not of Manusk, but it may as well be. Your Grace." She bowed and backed away toward the kitchen where the last of the crowd waited for food.

"Your Grace?" Sean said.

"Yes, Sean?" Elizabeth said. She'd almost forgotten he was there.

"Might I suggest that we send word to Coral Bay to see if good Duke Carter has food to spare? The city is in short supply and half the farmers are gone."

Elizabeth nodded. "Excellent suggestion, Sean."

She made her way back into the kitchen, past a table of ragged peasants silently devouring their food. One—the blacksmith—waved a greasy spoon at her and bobbed his head. She grinned.

The food situation must be much worse than anyone's letting on, Elizabeth thought as she strode through the courtyard, automatically dodging soldiers, Sean at her heels. *What can we do about it?*

Well. We can take some of the imported food from the ships landing at the docks. We can buy from Coral Bay, as Sean suggested. I really need to know what's going on outside the city. I need to know where my farmers are.

They walked down the busy street, side by side. She felt Sean stiffen beside her.

"I know, Sergeant," she said for his ears alone. "We have quite a following, don't we?"

"Yes, Your Grace," Sean replied, his gaze darting around the street, watching for potential problems.

Elizabeth shot a quick look over her shoulder under the guise of glancing in a shop window.

A group of children was trailing behind them, trying to keep up the appearance of playing some nonsensical children's game that involved hiding and calling for one another. Elizabeth would have thought it real if it hadn't been for the furtive glances they cast in her direction. It felt as though they were sizing her up.

Elizabeth glanced around at the adults going about their business along the city streets. They walked close to the shops, well out of the street, and avoided looking at each other. She met the eyes of one young man, but his gaze quickly stuttered away from her face. His face tightened into a frown and he resolutely looked in the other direction.

Suddenly Elizabeth's nerves stood on end as she sensed someone creeping up behind her.

She whirled, catlike, and caught a young girl's hand close to her hip. The girl shrieked and slapped at Elizabeth's hand.

"Now, then," Elizabeth said, holding her in a firm grip. "What do you think you're doing?"

"I was just playing," the girl said in between bouts of struggling and yelling.

"Really?" Elizabeth said and looked up at Sean. "Check your belt, Sergeant, and make sure your coin is intact."

Sean quickly felt for his money pouch and cursed when he found it was missing. "What did you do with it, you little wretch?"

"Now, then, Sean," Elizabeth said, quickly patting the girl down.

She grinned in triumph and pulled Sean's pouch out of her tattered clothing. She tossed it to him and turned her attention back to the girl.

"Who are you? How old are you?"

The girl spat at Elizabeth and Elizabeth shook her. She instantly stilled and regarded Elizabeth coldly.

"Do you know who I am?" Elizabeth asked.

"A dead woman."

"You're not the first person to tell me that. Guess again."

The girl studied her with hard, angry eyes. "When I tell Charles what you did he's going to kill you."

"When I see Charles he'd better keep a civil tongue in his head. Who are you, girl?"

"Who are *you*?"

"Elizabeth St. John, Duchess of Manusk. You won't tell me your name? Then *I* will tell *you* your name. You are four hundred and one."

The girl looked perplexed. "I'm who?"

"Four hundred and one," Elizabeth replied calmly. "That is your number, prisoner, and it's how you will be known until you reach your majority."

The girl went berserk and Elizabeth shook her again.

"Stop shrieking," Elizabeth said coldly. "I have won. I will throw you in prison as a thief unless you start answering my questions. Now, who are you and how old are you?"

The girl studied the ground. "Benton. I don't know how old I am."

"Do you have a place to sleep?"

Benton glared at her and nodded once, sharply.

"Who is this Charles you mentioned earlier?" Elizabeth asked.

"Charles takes care of us."

"What's going to happen to you when he finds out you got caught?"

Benton's eyes flickered and she looked away. "Nothing," she mumbled.

Elizabeth felt her tense up. "I'll bet." She straightened and tilted her head. "I have a job for you, Benton—*and* all of your friends—if you're interested."

Benton looked down at the ground but her body relaxed. Elizabeth knew she'd caught her attention.

"You don't have to do much," she said. "Simply what circumstances have forced you to do."

Benton looked sharply at her. "What? You mean be a cutpurse?"

"Not quite. I want you to be my eyes and ears. Does that interest you?"

"You want me to what?"

"I want you to watch some men. And I want you to keep doing it until I tell you to stop. Does that sound good?"

"What's in it for me?"

"I will look the other way, past your *activities*. But you are not to touch any citizens of Manusk, understand?"

Benton shook her head. "I already do that for Charles."

"How about a roof over your head and safety from my guardsmen?"

"Charles already does that for me."

"Can I even appeal to your sense of civic duty?"

Benton wrinkled her dirty nose. "My what?"

"Your pride in Manusk."

"What's there to be proud of?"

"This is a great sea port and city. The blood that flows through your veins is courageous and honorable."

Benton stared at her and shrugged.

Elizabeth sighed and shook her head. "Never mind. I will leave you alone, then."

Benton grinned, her posture relaxing.

Elizabeth gave her a pleasant smile. "Since you refuse my offer, there is one other thing I have to add to our dialog."

"Our what?"

"Our little talk," Elizabeth said, kneeling before Benton and looking directly into her eyes.

Benton paled a little and pulled back. "Oh."

Elizabeth nodded. "I won't catch you stealing again, will I? Because if I do, you really *will* be four oh one, understood?"

Benton nodded so hard her head seemed in danger of flying off her shoulders.

"On your way, Benton," Elizabeth murmured.

Benton unfroze and sketched a salute and ran back into the street. Children materialized seemingly out of nowhere and they all faded into the surrounding alleyways.

"You're brave, Your Grace," Sean said. "Why did you let her go?"

"Her life is not ideal but she's safe," Elizabeth said. "She at least has a roof over her head and if she is lucky food in her belly. Besides, theft is the least of our problems at the moment. If she's ever caught, I want her brought to me."

Sean nodded, unconvinced. "Yes, Your Grace."

CHAPTER 3

"WELL, CAPTAIN?" ELIZABETH said, pushing her way through the crowd jostling around the docks. Sean stayed close to her, a silent shadow. "What's all this?" She gestured at the crowd, held back by a line of her guardsmen.

The guardsmen stood, grim faced, steadfastly ignoring the taunting and insults from the crowd.

"Your Grace," Herbert said, bowing. "Please come with me." He stood aside and gestured for Elizabeth to go ahead of him.

Elizabeth nodded. "Very well, Captain." She frowned and glanced back at the crowd. "I trust you're going to explain this to me?"

"Yes, Your Grace," Herbert said. "The merchants of Manusk have been complaining of a rat infestation at the docks. I thought we should help them."

That's what you insisted I come down here for? Why don't you just deal with this? "Of course. I'm perfectly willing to deal with rodents."

"I thought so, Your Grace," Herbert said with a distinct air of satisfaction.

"Sean. Go and get ten guards." Elizabeth turned back toward the crowd.

They watched her, most with expressions of frustration and disgust. There were only ten guards holding them back and Elizabeth knew that was shortly not going to be enough.

The crowd was a mix of men and women—mostly men—some well dressed, some poorly dressed, others in serviceable armor. She looked closely at the last. They seemed to be clustered around well-dressed men scattered throughout the crowd and they watched her carefully, hands resting on the hilts of their swords.

Elizabeth picked the closest one, a short, fat man. His clothing was richly appointed in deep maroon with silver trim. His goatee was oiled to a fine point and his dark eyes showed a hint of anger.

"You," she said, pointing to him. "What is your name?"

"Who wants to know?" he said after a moment. His guards shuffled in closer to him.

"Elizabeth St. John, Duchess of Manusk," Elizabeth said.

The man surveyed her for a moment, and then barked a sharp laugh. "Well, Duchess Elizabeth," he said, making the words sound like an insult. "Why do you keep honest merchants from their rightful business?"

Elizabeth looked at Sean.

He nodded almost imperceptibly, lunged forward, and snagged the man by his coat. He dragged him before Elizabeth. The man's guards charged for him, but Elizabeth's troops were ready for them. The suddenly silent crowd watched them closely.

"Kneel before your duchess," Sean said silkily.

He kicked the man to his knees and clutched the back of his neck to force his head down.

"All right," the man ground out. He grimaced as he shifted in Sean's grip so he could see Elizabeth's face. "Your Grace."

"Thank you, good sir," Elizabeth said. "Now, then, what is your name?"

"Richard of Manusk," the man said.

"Please stand, Richard," Elizabeth said and Sean eased his grip.

Richard stumbled to his feet, glaring at Sean. He turned his attention back to Elizabeth, his eyes hot with anger.

"Richard, are you a good man of Manusk?" she asked.

Richard nodded once, sharply.

"What do you do?" she asked.

"I am a merchant, Your Grace," he replied. "I buy and sell timber and stone."

Elizabeth smiled. "Excellent." She glanced at Sean. "Exactly the man I had in mind."

"For what?" Richard asked, hastily adding, "Your Grace," as Sean glared at him.

"Who is in there? Are they men of Sandcliff and Osk?" she asked.

Richard frowned and his mouth tightened. "Yes. We are being driven out of the trading halls. No one wants to deal with us. Import tariffs have tripled in Manusk and our taxes are high. We can't recoup our costs and remain competitive. Osk and Sandcliff traders have *special import exemptions* which allow them to buy at normal prices and sell cheaper than us. We of Manusk—traders, merchants, and citizens alike—are being slowly crippled by these business practices."

"These laws are *not* Manusk laws, nor are they the king's laws. Why are you obeying them? Why have you not sought help?"

"What help? Who in Manusk has the power to enforce the law? The steward of Manusk is long dead and Osk and Sandcliff are free to enforce any laws they see fit on us," Richard said. "The King's Heartland is a long way away and they don't care about us anyway."

Elizabeth frowned. "King Vincent cares, Richard. How long has this been going on for?"

"The steward of Manusk has been dead for two years," Richard said, gritting his teeth, dark eyes flashing with anger. "And all our goods must pass through Osk and Sandcliff to reach the King's Heartland. Any goods shipped out by way of Coral Bay are sent back to Manusk."

"Why have we not heard this?" Elizabeth exchanged a grim look with Herbert and turned back to Richard. "How is this not more widely known?"

"I don't know, Your Grace, but I'm sure I can guess. All roads between Coral Bay and Manusk are under Sandcliff and Osk control, as are those to the north. We pay tolls on the road that further cuts our profits."

"From today your trade—and taxes—will resume as normal. But for now I don't want your coin. I would like your goods and your help. We must rebuild Manusk. Will you help us?" Elizabeth looked up at the other traders in the crowd. "That applies to all of you. I want your help to rebuild and to drive Osk and Sandcliff from Manusk."

The traders eyed her warily and remained silent.

"What is the matter with all of you?" she said, eyeing them severely. "The honor of Manusk is said to be unequalled, as is its courage. What do I see here? A cowering, suspicious people. I offer you the chance to reclaim the glory and honor of Manusk yet each of you quail at the opportunity. Real citizens of Manusk would fight to the last person to keep their homes intact and the name of Manusk unsullied."

"Those are brave words, Duchess Elizabeth," Richard ground out. "Who are you to speak of honor and courage? Who are you to lecture us when one of your blood brought ruin upon Manusk? Now you come back with bluster and demand that we follow you. Why should we do it?"

The crowd murmured agreement, and Elizabeth met each pair of eyes. "It is exactly for that reason that my father sent me here as the Duchess of Manusk. My father cares about each of the loyal citizens in his kingdom. Who best to fix a problem than the one who created it in the first place?" She paused, mind working. *I am a soldier not a statesman, despite my titles. I am content to travel far and wide in the Kingdom upholding my father's laws.* "How about I make a bargain with you. *All* of you. My father has given me the task of driving Sandcliff and Osk from Manusk and I will do it, with or without your help." The crowd gasped and mouths tightened. "But." She held up a hand to still the murmuring. "If, when Manusk is free again, you still don't want me here, I will leave. Is that agreeable to you?" She looked at Richard.

The crowd began to speak and amidst the raised voices, Elizabeth heard cries of *take the bargain.*

"Silence," Richard cried after a moment.

The crowd gradually quieted.

Richard shoved aside Sean's hand and stood eye to eye with Elizabeth. "It seems we have a bargain, Your Grace." He held out his forearm. "If asked, when Manusk is ours again, you will leave."

Elizabeth grasped his forearm. "Agreed."

Richard turned to the crowd. "You heard this. We have a new duchess for the time being." The crowd applauded and Richard bowed low before Elizabeth. "So, Your Grace. We will begin at your convenience."

"Good," she said. "Bring your guards with us. I will need some more swords."

Richard nodded and grinned. "With pleasure, Your Grace." He nodded sharply at his guards and Sean stood aside to allow them to pass beyond the barrier.

Sean went to Elizabeth's side, watching them closely for any signs of hostility. Herbert, who had been silent until now, sidled up to her.

"What are you doing, Your Highness?" he hissed. "Your father told you to stay here."

Elizabeth gave him a sad smile. "You know what'll happen when we challenge Osk and Sandcliff. There is yesterday and today, and there may not be a tomorrow."

Herbert nodded, his expression noncommittal. "I am your man, Your Grace."

"Thank you. Sergeant," she said, turning to Sean. "Go and get Peter. Tell him to bring our best officers of the watch."

Sean saluted. "Yes, Your Grace."

"All right," Elizabeth said, watching his retreating back and trying not to think about how thinly her forces were spread around the city of Manusk. "Let's go."

Richard and Herbert fell in on either side of her, slightly behind her back. Richard's guards—marching with sharp glances at Elizabeth's guards—brought up the rear.

"This way, Your Grace," Herbert said, guiding her toward the largest building on the docks. "This is the import terminal. All cargo must pass through here."

Elizabeth nodded. "And the import agents are in the hall at the rear of the import terminal." She turned to Richard. "How many ships come here simply seeking trade and how many are expected?"

"It used to be that almost all of them were expected. The ones simply seeking to sell their goods more often than not went into Coral Bay since import laws favor occasional visitors." Richard's mouth twisted. "Now all ships come into this seaport and cargos are all open season. I have often ordered goods from my suppliers only to find that they had been *redistributed* or my suppliers had gotten *a better bargain* from another merchant." He snorted. "I don't doubt it would have been at the point of a sword."

"Well, take heart. There will be no more pilfering." She gazed at Richard. "Who is in charge of this place?"

"An easy answer," Richard said. "That would be Lawrence. He holds the post of Chief Import Officer."

"Is he an honest man?" she asked.

Richard gave her a humorless grin. "If honesty can be bought I would have to say yes."

Elizabeth growled. "Are his loyalties to Osk or Sandcliff?"

"They are to the highest bidder," Richard said. "Manusk will never have coin enough for him."

Elizabeth nodded once, sharply, and tried to fight down her outrage. It wouldn't do any good to lose her head in a situation that already teetered on the edge of an armed conflict.

They approached the broad, stone steps of the Import Terminal. They had to push aside merchants and a few mercenaries, who glared at them. The guards standing around idly on the steps watched them closely, as did the ones guarding the doors. They wore livery that did not belong to Manusk. Elizabeth looked at the ships in the harbor.

Almost all of the berths were taken, one by a large, three-masted ship. She had the breadth and depth of a merchant's ship. Her colors hung desultorily from her masts.

The shipwreck had the same standard. I wonder where it's from? She frowned. She nodded toward it. "How long has that ship been there for?"

Richard followed the direction of her gaze. "I'm not sure, Your Grace. I don't recognize her colors."

Elizabeth grimaced. "Wonderful. After we leave here we will return to the house to see if any of our guests have woken up." She ignored Richard's sharp glance.

"Very good, Your Grace," Herbert said.

She leaned close to Herbert. "While we're in there, see if you can find any papers for that ship. Anything. I want to know why it's here."

Herbert nodded.

Elizabeth walked up the stairs. The guards minding the doors to the hall crossed pikes as they approached, blocking their entrance.

"Stand aside," Elizabeth said.

"For whom?" the guard asked. He looked Elizabeth up and down, gaze lingering on her breasts.

Elizabeth frowned. "Elizabeth St. John, Duchess of Manusk."

The guard glanced at his compatriot and they burst out laughing.

"Move. Now," Elizabeth said sharply.

"You have no authority here," the guard said, gaze filled with malice.

"No," Elizabeth said, signaling her guardsmen and drawing her own sword.

The guards at the door quickly stepped forward and pointed their pikes at Elizabeth's chest.

Elizabeth's guards drew swords and crowded around her. Richard's guards, although disciplined, reacted more sharply. One fired a pistol crossbow. The bolt took a liveried guard in the meat of his chest and shoulder. He cried out sharply, dropped his pike, and clutched the quarrel as his blood seeped through his fingers.

"Thank you," Elizabeth said. She raised her sword so the point dimpled the other guard's throat. "Stand aside or we will be less kind to you."

He moved out of the way and watched her cautiously as he sank down to his moaning friend's side.

Elizabeth sheathed her sword and walked into the hall.

"Well done, Your Grace," Richard said, his voice filled with grudging approval.

Elizabeth smiled, her only sign of having heard him.

Merchants and guards milled in the front chamber, which was dominated by a high desk. A man sat behind the desk, his quill moving across parchment stacked up in front of him. He was middle aged and his worn clothing suggested he was a clerk.

Elizabeth approached the desk, Richard close by her side.

"Excuse me," she said, looking up at him.

The clerk showed no sign of having heard her. Elizabeth waited another moment, fighting down irritation. She was not used to being ignored.

"I said, *excuse me*," she said a little louder.

The man continued to write.

Elizabeth waited another moment. *Damn it. Is there anyone at all in this duchy who isn't determined to ignore me or blatantly attempt to infuriate me?* She slapped her hand over the parchment he was writing on.

He glanced sharply at her, then coolly eyed her from top to bottom. "Remove your hand," he said after another moment's study.

"I don't think you want me to do that," Elizabeth said, drawing her sword.

"Excuse me?" the man asked.

"Oh, you meant for *me* to remove *my* hand," Elizabeth said, feigning surprise. "You weren't asking me to cut yours off?"

"Are you mad, woman?" the man asked, his acerbic tone undercut by his pale features.

"Your Grace."

"Pardon?"

"Are you mad *Your Grace*," Elizabeth said and smiled.

"Oh my god," the man breathed. "You are the Duchess of Manusk?"

Elizabeth nodded once, sharply.

"You have no authority here."

Sean's sword dimpled the skin of his throat and he swallowed convulsively.

"No need to be nasty."

"You are Lawrence, are you not?" Elizabeth asked.

He nodded. He looked at the party behind her and his eyes widened.

Elizabeth glanced in the direction of his gaze. Richard watched him and smiled.

"Richard?" Elizabeth asked, gesturing for him to join her.

He did so after a moment.

"This is Lawrence, yes?" she asked.

Richard nodded. "This is Lawrence."

Elizabeth nodded. "Excellent." She nodded at the riot of merchants and guards in the hall. No one seemed to be paying any attention to them. "Who is the reason for the state my import hall is in?"

Lawrence gestured over his shoulder. "I don't know what you mean. This is a place of business and that is what's being conducted here."

Elizabeth looked behind him and saw a tangle of well-dressed men. One immediately caught her eye. A corpulent man sat at a plain, wooden table. His clothes were brightly colored and looked made of the costliest material; his bald head gleamed in the wash of sunlight that spilled into the hall through the vents in the roof. He was laughing with a thin, rat-faced man. Guards surrounded them, watching the interaction with careless grins.

"Who is that?" Elizabeth asked, her irritation increasing at each loud laugh that erupted from the man.

"That is Sen of Osk," Lawrence said. "He is the largest trader."

"Thank you," Elizabeth said, taking a step back and gesturing for her guards to join her. She glanced at Richard. "Are you coming?"

"Oh, I wouldn't miss this for the world," Richard muttered, his hand dropping to the hilt of his sword.

Elizabeth strode toward Sen's table, the milling guards and merchants parting to allow her through.

Sen's guards saw her first and nudged their master as she approached.

"Well, well, well," Sen said without preamble. "And who do we have here?"

Elizabeth stopped before him, Richard and Sean by her side.

"Richard," he said with a quick, rich laugh. "Brought your whore with you, did you?"

Elizabeth drew her sword in a blur of motion and pushed the sharp tip into his throat so a thin line of blood appeared. "Another word out of you, Sen of Osk, and you won't speak ever again. I give you one minute to take yourself out of this import hall."

"Or what?" Sen asked, trying for a swaggering tone.

"Or I cut your throat. Your choice."

"By what right do you do this?" he asked.

"The law of Manusk and of the King's Heartland. You have no license to practice trade in Manusk. Leave or I prosecute you."

"I have a license." Sen leaned back out of reach of her sword and steepled his fingers. He gave her an infuriatingly superior grin.

"Richard?" Elizabeth asked. "Do you have a license?"

Richard gave her a short, sharp nod. He pulled a piece of paper out of his robes and handed it to Elizabeth. His eyes remained on Sen.

Elizabeth unfolded it and looked carefully at it. The seal had the coat of arms of Manusk, a sea eagle on a field of blue and white, but it was unsigned.

"This is not a legal document," Elizabeth said, glancing at Richard. "It must be signed by the head of government of Manusk to be valid."

Richard glared. "Manusk has no government."

"It does now. Can you prove that you were born in Manusk?"

"I am on the register of births for Manusk. You can have your men look me up."

Elizabeth turned to Sen. "You? What about you? I assume your license to trade is as unsigned as his is."

Sen nodded, a small smile playing about his lips.

Elizabeth smiled. "Were you born in Manusk?"

"You know I wasn't," Sen said, his smile slipping.

"Well," Elizabeth said, re-sheathing her sword. "All I see in this hall is another legal mess we have to fix. Sergeant Hunter?"

A bearded guardsman came to attention. "Your Grace?"

"Sergeant Hunter," Elizabeth said. "Clear the hall of all traders. They are to take nothing but the clothes on their backs. We must begin issuing trading licenses in short order since trade must continue."

Richard gasped.

Elizabeth turned to him with a small smile. "We need the registrar, Sergeant." She fixed her eyes on Richard's. "He must check all traders who claim to be of Manusk. Those native to Manusk will be issued licenses as soon as their birthright is proven." She turned to Sen and leaned forward on his desk on her knuckles. Her eyes narrowed. "Those not of Manusk will need to prove their place of birth and provide documentation that they are licensed traders in their home duchies. Then we will begin talking about issuing temporary trader's licenses." She paused for a moment. "And that," she eyed Sen coldly, "could take some time."

Sen turned pale and his mouth tightened.

"Yes, Your Grace," Sergeant Hunter said.

She felt Richard shift behind her. "Your will, Your Grace," he said, amusement in his tone.

Sen's eyes narrowed in rage and he tensed. A split second later he had a dagger in his hand and with a speed that belied his size and girth, leapt over the table toward her.

Elizabeth side stepped him, caught his wrist, and used his momentum to yank his arm up against his back.

"Dear me, that won't do," she said in his ear. "An assassination attempt against a noble."

Elizabeth glanced up at Sean. Her guardsmen and Richard's guards stood shoulder to shoulder holding back Sen's guards. She nodded at Sergeant Hunter and he quickly disarmed Sen's guards with another guardsman.

"Hunter, take these men—Sen and his guards—to the city jail," she said.

"Yes, Your Grace," Hunter said with a bow.

Sen's guards protested, as did Sen. The guards dragged him, struggling furiously, out of the hall.

Elizabeth sighed and turned to Richard. "If there are any problems—*any* problems,—let me know and I will send in my guardsmen again."

"You trust me enough to leave us all alone in here?"

"Trust has to start somewhere," Elizabeth said. "I have your word, that you will help me rebuild Manusk?"

Richard was silent a moment. "Yes, Your Grace You have my word."

"Thank you, Richard," she said. "By the way, you are welcome to eat with me this evening. I will be in my house at six."

"Thank you, Your Grace," Richard said, bowing. "I look forward to it."

CHAPTER 4

"COME WITH ME, Sean," Elizabeth said, striding from the hall. She stopped outside and took a deep breath of the brine air.

"This is good," she said. She nodded toward the ship. "You and I are going to take a look at that trading ship."

"Yes, Your Grace," Sean said, inclining his head.

Richard's guards cleared a path through the ejected Osk and Sandcliff traders, past cries of *bitch* and *whore of Manusk*. Traders from Manusk trickled through the crowd as word spread of Elizabeth's enforcement of licensing law. She was greeted with open, calculating stares, furtively knuckled foreheads, and some open bows. She kept her eyes steadfastly forward, ignoring the raucous shouts of outrage.

Richard's guards held the last of the crowd back and Elizabeth stepped through, Sean close behind.

"Your Grace," the largest guard said, giving her a deep bow, his companions following close behind.

Elizabeth nodded. "Thank you."

The commotion started again when a harried, balding, middle-aged man arrived at the rear of the crowd. Cries of *Registrar* and *Sir* echoed in his wake.

The guards disappeared back into the shoving crowd, while Elizabeth and Sean dodged stragglers to the hall on their way down to the dock. Elizabeth stopped at the edge of the deserted pier, shielded her eyes from the midday sun, and peered at the ship. Her sails were furled, and the single pennant bearing a dragon on a star burst fluttered in the breeze.

"Your Grace," Peter said, jogging to her with three men in shirts and breeches.

Those men must be the watch.

"Peter," Elizabeth said.

"I see the captain finally got you to the docks," Peter said, his lips twitching.

Elizabeth snorted a laugh. "Yes, he did." She nodded toward the crowd, who were milling around under the careful eye of Richard's guards. "I imagine the Registrar will be on the end of the queue of citizens wanting to stick a knife in my back."

"He won't, Your Grace," one of the watchmen said.

Elizabeth surveyed him. He was a grizzled veteran in his mid thirties with a scarred eyebrow and cold, glittering brown eyes.

"I live under no illusions that my presence is welcomed by everyone," Elizabeth said. "And those that don't actively oppose me have no reason to stand with me."

The watchman smiled. "Not everybody thinks a duke or duchess in Manusk is a bad thing, Your Grace. I am Mark and I am your man," he said with a deep bow.

"Thank you, Mark," Elizabeth said, forming a smile that felt warm and genuine. "It's always a pleasure to have good men aboard." She nodded toward the foreign trader. "What do you know about this ship?"

Mark shook his head. "Not much, Your Grace. She appeared in the harbor about ten days ago. I haven't seen the crew."

Elizabeth nodded. "All right. Sean, you take—" She indicated the watchmen with Mark.

"Daniel," a young man with blonde hair and cool, blue eyes said.

"Marcus," the second man said, almost identical to the first. Elizabeth guessed they were twins.

"—Daniel and Marcus and search before the mast. Peter, Mark, and I will go below decks to the hold."

Peter, Sean, and the watchmen bowed. "Yes, Your Grace."

Elizabeth continued on down the pier, looking all around her. Almost all the berths had ships in them, and rough-looking sailors scurried around under the watchful eyes of their captains, loading or unloading cargo. An official trailed by a servant traveled between the ships, inspecting and stamping manifests.

"Just the person I was looking for," Elizabeth said, striding toward him. "You, good sir. May I ask you a question?"

The official ignored her as he walked to the ship across the pier from the trader.

Elizabeth frowned. "You. Official with servant. Stop."

The official glanced at her. "What do you want, woman?"

Elizabeth rolled internal eyes. "I want to know where the manifest to this ship is."

"Which one?" he asked, glancing at her. "Make it quick, girl, I haven't got all day."

"You will give me as much time as I ask for," Elizabeth said coldly. "And it's *Your Grace*."

The man pulled himself up to his full height and stared down his nose at her. He remained silent. "Well?" he snapped after a moment.

"Where is the manifest to this ship?" Elizabeth enunciated each word carefully and clearly and forcibly relaxed her hands.

"I imagine it's in my office." He turned to his trembling servant. "Come along, and try to keep up."

He began to hurry away, but Sean and Peter stepped in front of him. Peter frowned.

"Where is your office?" Elizabeth asked.

The official ignored her and tried to turn away.

"You aren't supposed to be stamping manifests, are you?" she said. "You're not from Manusk, are you?"

The official paled and remained silent. He shifted from foot to foot.

"You there!" a voice shouted from above and to the left of them.

Elizabeth turned to the owner of the voice. He was a tall, well-dressed man with braids on his coat sleeves, proclaiming him to be a captain.

"Yes?" she said.

"This man is *not* the harbor master of Manusk," he said. "Yet he has been going from ship to ship throwing his weight around for two weeks."

"Where is the harbor master?" Elizabeth asked.

"I don't know," the captain called. "Why don't you ask him?"

"A fine idea," Elizabeth said with the trace of a smile. She turned back to the man. "What is your name and where are you from?"

A group of sailors jumped down from the ship and surrounded them.

"His name doesn't matter," the largest of them said. He towered over Elizabeth and she forced herself not to take a step back. His arms were the size of small trees. He smiled unpleasantly at the now shaking man. "My captain would like to speak with you."

Peter stepped forward and took a deep breath. Elizabeth put a restraining hand on his arm. He glanced at her and she shook her head. She glanced up at the rigging and Peter followed her gaze. His eyes widened and he looked around at the other ships.

All the sailors had stopped what they were doing and were watching them and the struggling official closely. They were tensed and ready to move at a second's notice.

The captain who had spoken to her strode down the gangplank onto the dock.

"Your Highness," he said, coming to a stop before her and bowing deeply. "Welcome to Manusk."

Elizabeth bowed. "Captain. Do I know you?"

"No, ma'am," he said. "But my brother Darvis served in your army in the Battle of Surnow. He often spoke of you as a fair and honorable officer. He is alive because of you."

"I'm sorry," Elizabeth said with a grimace, as she remembered the mud, blood, and carnage. "I don't remember him, but I'm sure he was a valiant soldier." She tried to push aside memories of the screams of the wounded and dying. "*All* of my men were."

The captain watched her closely, studying her and nodding. "He walks with a limp but he has a wife and family because of you. I, Delmarco, am your father's man and I am *your* man."

Elizabeth felt genuinely touched and bowed low. "Thank you, Captain Delmarco." She wanted to say more but she couldn't think of a single way to express how much his loyalty meant to her.

Delmarco gave her a warm, genuine smile. He held out his forearm. "If you are ever in need of my services, all you have to do is ask."

"Thank you, Captain," she said, clasping his forearm.

Delmarco cleared his throat and released her arm. "If you will excuse me, Your Highness?"

"Of course, Captain," she said, turning away with Peter, Sean, and the watchmen. "May the wind be at your back."

"And yours, Your Highness."

They reached the trader and Elizabeth strode up the gangway.

"Your *Highness*?" Daniel asked. "What did he mean, Your Grace?"

Elizabeth turned and shot him a quick grin. "Nothing, Daniel. I am my father's daughter and a simple soldier."

Daniel gave her a doubtful look.

Elizabeth peered all around the deck. It was scrupulously clean and all the ropes and lifeboats seemed to be in place. The sails had been neatly tied.

"She came in peacefully, at any rate," Peter said softly.

Elizabeth nodded. "So she did." She made her way to the far rail and ran her hand along the smooth wood. "Neat and clean. No sign of blood." She looked forward toward the bowsprit. "Search, Sean. You are also looking for any logs, manifest, any documentation you can find."

"Yes, Your Grace," Sean said with a quick bow. He, Daniel, and Marcus disappeared into the forecastle.

Elizabeth bent over the open hold amidships. "Peter, check the captain's cabin and see if you can find anything that might tell us something about this ship. Mark, come with me. We're going into the hold." She quickly led the way into the quarter deck and they climbed down a ladder onto the gun deck, down to the orlop deck, and into the hold.

"This is interesting, isn't it?" Elizabeth said, peering around in the gloom. "She's still loaded with cargo."

"Not completely," Mark said. "Look. Some of the boxes have been moved."

Elizabeth frowned and looked closely at where he was pointing. The cargo hold was packed, but the load distribution looked uneven. There was a gap toward the stern where disturbed dust told her something had been placed but was now missing.

They searched the boxes thoroughly and found the barrels to be full of vinegar. The boxes held silk and other material, as well as jewelry and what looked to be farm machinery and leather goods.

"This is interesting, isn't it?" Elizabeth said, about an hour later.

"Why would anyone carry a cargo of such mismatched goods?" Mark asked, sitting on one of the barrels and panting from exertion.

"Easy. You'd bring a selection if you didn't know what the traders on the other end of your voyage wanted." She gestured upwards. "This ship isn't local. It's flying the same pennant as a ship that was broken up on the rocks at the mouth of Manusk Harbor last night." She eyed him. "You really don't know how long this ship has been here for?"

Mark shook his head. "We weren't exactly allowed close to the docks."

Elizabeth shook her head. "How long have Osk and Sandcliff been doing this for?"

Mark was silent for a moment. He finally shrugged and threw up his hands. "I really don't know. For as long as I can remember. The

Steward of Manusk was only a name on parchment. The real people in charge have been Osk and Sandcliff."

"Not any more," Elizabeth said, pushing down a surge of irritation. "Manusk is ours once more."

"Yes, Your Grace," Mark said doubtfully.

"You disagree, Mark?" Elizabeth asked after a moment of silence.

Mark avoided her eyes and rubbed his thighs. "May I speak freely, Your Grace?"

"Of course."

"How many men did you bring, Your Grace? Five hundred? There are only a hundred of us loyal to you on the watch. The people are waiting and watching to see what you will do, and what will happen to you. We have tried to cast off the rule of Osk and Sandcliff before but it's always ended in spilled blood, increased taxes, and too much hanging for any sane person's liking."

Elizabeth nodded and gave him a rueful grin. "Things are different this time, Mark. There may be only five hundred volunteers with me now, but I have my father's entire army standing behind me. Osk and Sandcliff don't dare tweak my nose."

"That's as may be, but how are they going to help? Don't you realize Osk and Sandcliff are going to find out about your desire to restore order? And they're going to try and stop you?" Mark looked closely at her. "This is a *sea duchy*, Your Grace. We have our backs to a wet wall and are surrounded by Osk and Sandcliff."

"And that's what works to our advantage, Mark," Elizabeth said. "You must trust me. I've been in tighter spots than this one and I and my men have survived."

"When will it be the last time, Your Grace?" he asked, clenching his fist. "How many of us are to be sacrificed for this? I have no wife and children but there are other men in this city who do. You are about to turn us into a battlefield. How many of our families will fall for this?"

Elizabeth's shoulders slumped. "Don't you think I know that? Do you know who I am, Mark?"

Mark eyed her and warily shook his head.

"I am Princess Elizabeth St. John, Commander of the Army of the King's Heartland. I am King Vincent's most experienced field general. I have seen more battles and blood than I care to remember, so I know exactly what the stakes are." She blew out a breath. "My father's orders were very simple—take and keep Manusk." She stood in front of Mark, arms crossed and glowering. "I want peace as much as you do. Since this is my new home I have no desire to treat my people as pawns in a bloodthirsty chess game run by a pair of tyrants."

"You don't have to justify yourself, Your Highness," Peter said quietly from behind her.

She looked at him and saw Marcus and Daniel shifting uncomfortably under the onslaught of her glare. Sean stood rigid with tension behind them.

"As I said," Mark said, jumping off the barrel and standing directly before her. "I am your man. I am loyal to you. I want a life and home that I can be proud of. I am sick of living as a cowering dog. My grandfather told me stories of Manusk as it once was and I want my home to be like that—free of bullies and brutality."

Elizabeth nodded. "Then I think we both want the same thing."

Mark's gaze bored into hers for another moment until Peter stepped between them.

"Stand down, Mark," he said softly. "There are limits."

Mark's hot gaze swung over to Peter. He nodded once, sharply.

Sean stepped forward. "Your Grace?"

Elizabeth turned to him, the moment broken. "Yes, Sean?"

"There is no paperwork on this ship. We haven't found any signs of a manifest, the captain's log, any maps, or anything that would tell us anything about this ship."

"What about the crew? Are there any signs of where they could be? Did you find any signs of foul play?"

Sean shook his head. "No, Your Grace. This ship is completely clean."

Elizabeth frowned. She felt uneasy. *We have a trading ship half full of cargo, no crew, no logs, maps, or manifest and no port of origin. What in God's name is going on here?*

"All right," she said. She turned to the watchmen. "Have you heard anything about foreign prisoners in the city jail?"

Mark shook his head. "No. No rumors of note either. There are always people in the city jail, and if we paid too close attention to that fact we were likely to join them, so we minded our own business."

"Then I think our next order of business is to visit the city jail and find out if they were there."

"Yes, Your Grace," Peter said, bowing low. "But first I think you have to return to your manor house. It's almost six o'clock."

Elizabeth growled in frustration. "Yes, I must." She raised an eyebrow. "And I can't be late to my first state function, can I?"

Sean and Peter exchanged a look and grinned. "No, Your Grace."

Elizabeth sighed and headed toward the ladder. She began to climb out of the hold the guardsmen and watchmen close on her heels. When they were out on the main deck, Elizabeth looked down at herself. She wrinkled her nose. She was covered in dirt and sweating freely.

Sean eyed her sympathetically. "I'll just run ahead and tell them you'll be a little late, Your Grace."

"Thank you, Sean," she said as he jogged off. She turned to the others. "First order of business tomorrow is to see if we can find our new guests. For now, go and patrol the city and clear out any rats you see come out after dark."

Peter snapped a sharp salute, followed closely by the more awkward watchmen.

"Yes, Your Grace," they chorused, bowing low.

"Excellent. Peter, you and Sean—report to me at nine tomorrow morning."

"Yes, Your Grace," he said as Elizabeth set off at a jog toward the manor house.

CHAPTER 5

ELIZABETH BURST THROUGH the doors to the chamber she shared with the blonde woman, drawing a startled gasp from Mara.

"Sorry," Elizabeth said, tugging at the laces on her shirt. "I didn't mean to startle you."

Mara curtseyed, staring resolutely at the floor. "That's fine, Your Grace." She colored.

Elizabeth began to pull her shirt off. "Fresh clothes, Mara. Bath."

"Yes, Your Grace," Mara said, grabbing for the tray by the woman's bedside. She looked everywhere but at Elizabeth and fled.

What's gotten into her? Elizabeth glanced down at her chest, almost hidden by her loosened shirt. *Have I grown horns or something?*

"I was going to ask if our guest had eaten but I think I'm too late for that," she muttered to the almost empty room.

She looked at the woman in the bed, who was propped up on pillows. Her color seemed good and her chest rose and fell with her even breaths.

We'll talk tomorrow if you wake up.

"Your Grace," Harriet said, bustling into the room trailed by a series of women holding buckets of warm water. "Your bath."

"What? Oh. Yes," Elizabeth said, tearing her eyes away from the woman in the bed. "Do I have fresh clothes?"

Harriet pursed her lips. "Of *course*, Your Grace."

Elizabeth grinned. "Thank you, Harriet."

She dropped to the hearthstones and pulled off her scuffed boots, followed by her dirty clothing.

She caught Harriet's wrinkled forehead as she surveyed the ruined clothing.

"Don't ask," Elizabeth muttered. "You don't want to know."

Harriet shook her head. "Of course, Your Grace." She turned and steered servants out of the chamber, and then turned back to Elizabeth with a glint in her eye. "If you insist on ruining every set of your clothes, pause to consider that eventually we'll only be able to give you frills and skirts."

Elizabeth gaped at her, unable to form a reply.

Harriet's lips twitched as she turned away. Elizabeth could have sworn she heard Harriet muffle a snort of laughter.

She shuddered and strode naked into the bathing chamber. The tub had been filled with warm, fragrant water and she sank into it with a sigh. As she bathed, she thought about her first day in Manusk.

What do we have so far? We have one sunken warship and a trading ship from the same people sitting in the harbor. The most logical reason that the second ship came is because it was looking for the first ship. We'd better find those sailors quickly—and we'd better start talking to the survivors of the shipwreck.

She stepped out of the tub and quickly toweled off. She dressed in the bathing chamber and then strode out into the bedchamber to pull on her boots. She glanced at the peacefully slumbering woman in the bed and felt a stab of unease.

She pulled her boots on and left.

Sean was waiting for her outside, and they passed Mara coming down the hall. She bobbed a ragged curtsey and studiously avoided looking at Elizabeth.

She's very odd for a servant. I wonder where Harriet found her.

"Everyone's in the kitchen," Sean said quietly.

"Huh? Oh. Yes. The kitchen." She took in his wet hair and damp clothing. "How late are we?"

"Not very, Your Grace. Can't be more than ten minutes."

"Well, that's something at least," Elizabeth said with a sigh as they hurried downstairs. "Hah. No creak." She studied the risers, which looked new. "Replaced. Another something."

Sean nodded. "It's certainly easier to see to the wounded if you don't have a broken leg yourself, Your Grace."

Elizabeth nodded as they dodged guardsmen and servants in the broad corridor that led to the kitchen. The guardsmen quickly saluted her as they went passed and she nodded absently.

They strode into the kitchen and found most of the makeshift tables occupied by ragged peasants, interspersed with silent guardsmen. The large table in the middle of the room was half empty, with Richard, Herbert, Harriet, Rebecca, and Jarrod sitting close to the empty head.

"Where's Peter?" Elizabeth asked.

"Behind you, Highness," he said. "I'm late."

"No more so than we are," she replied, approaching the table.

Everyone stood as Elizabeth took her place at the head of the table. She gestured impatiently for them to sit.

As she sat down, a servant appeared to her left and ladled thick vegetable stew into a bowl before her. She murmured her thanks.

Everyone watched her carefully after they'd been served and she picked up her spoon. "Aren't you all hungry?" She glanced around and met everyone's eyes. "I'm starved. We can talk after we've eaten."

Rebecca and Jarrod immediately began eating, Richard glanced at Harriet and Captain Herbert and ate with an economy of motion that Elizabeth found fascinating. Herbert and Harriet ate more slowly— Harriet looking a little awkward and stiff, Herbert perfectly relaxed and smiling blissfully at each mouthful.

"Oh, this is excellent," Elizabeth said, following a mouthful of hot stew with a portion of freshly baked bread.

Harriet gave her a genuine smile. "Thank you, Your Grace."

"I must say, Your Grace, this is unique," Richard said, idly indicating the kitchen with his spoon.

Elizabeth looked around. "What?"

"It's not often that a noble eats with the commoners, he means," Harriet said. "And in a kitchen no less."

"Oh," Elizabeth said, slightly confused. "Well, I'm more a soldier than I am a duchess. I'm used to living in tents and out in the open. This is luxury, compared to what I'm used to. Besides, I like solid conversation at my dinner table, not frivolous nonsense."

"You hear that?" Peter said helpfully, nodding proudly toward Sean. "She says we actually speak beyond thoughtless grunting."

"Huh," Sean said.

"What? Someone forgot to give you your lines for this meal?" Elizabeth asked, smiling.

"I know what I'm supposed to say, yes. Leather, lace, and chains are to be our main topics of conversation," Peter said, waving a hank of bread at Sean. "This one is as ignorant as ever. He can't read."

Peter and Sean laughed and Elizabeth smiled a little.

"Reading isn't high on my list of duties," Sean said. "You don't need letters to jump in front of arrows aimed toward Her Grace."

"Really? I always thought it was the other way around. Since when have you ever needed to do catch arrows aimed at me?" Elizabeth said. "Or is that how you're trying to pass off your poor excuse for dancing skills?"

"I have to show my mother I learnt *something* in my travels," Sean said imperiously.

"Yes, but that normally applies to *skills* one has learnt," Elizabeth said with a snort of laughter. "Say hello to your mother for me and have a cup of ale for us both when you get home."

The three exchanged a glance and quieted.

"How often do you see your home?" Rebecca said softly into the silence. She ate quietly and studiously avoided looking at Elizabeth.

"Home is where you make it," Elizabeth said. "I haven't seen the walls of my father's house for a few years. I don't know when I'll be going back there. This is to be my new home." She grinned. "Hence the reason for my sudden appearance."

"That sounds like a sad life, Your Grace, having nowhere to call home."

Jarrod tugged Rebecca's arm and quickly shook his head.

"It's all right," Elizabeth said. "It's not all bad. I've seen much of this world and I've made as many friends as I've made enemies."

"Have you been to the Northern Reaches?" Richard asked smoothly.

"Yes," Elizabeth said, grinning. "I spent a winter in the Duchy of Eagle's Reach. It has to be one of the most beautiful places I've ever seen."

"I haven't had the pleasure," Richard said. "I've seen Fotheringill, but had to miss out on Eagle's Reach."

The conversation comfortably slid over into Richard's travels, and he amused them for several moments with a complicated story involving merchant's daughter, a donkey, and cask of ale. They all laughed until tears rolled out of their eyes, including Rebecca who seemed to relax as the meal went on.

Elizabeth relaxed back in her seat, pleasantly full, and the others had finished eating as well.

"So," she began, after their empty bowls had been taken away. "It's time for us to talk. Which of you would like to begin? I want to know what the state of Manusk and her people is."

They all silently exchanged glances. Eventually, all eyes fell to Richard. He smiled and shrugged.

"Well," Richard began smoothly. "Trade so far has gone poorly but will improve thanks to your intervention this morning. Almost all the traders of Manusk are back in the import hall and buying goods to trade and sell at fair prices without interference." He bit his cheek. "The traders from Osk and Sandcliff are somewhat less than pleased with this arrangement."

Elizabeth looked between Herbert and Richard. "Do we have problems?"

"Not yet," Captain Herbert said.

"But I'm reasonably sure we will," Richard finished. "We need more of your guardsmen at the port."

Elizabeth shook her head with genuine regret. "I don't know that I can do that. My forces are spread thin and it's going to get worse." She looked at Peter. "The watch?"

"We don't have enough men. Some of them are guarding the city jail, and the extra guardsmen we have are training the watch and patrolling the city." Peter paused for a moment, eyes troubled. "We're having a lot of trouble with civil unrest and it's not related to your presence, Your Grace. We are seeing troops close to the borders of the city and we will be hard pressed to defend the walls."

Elizabeth nodded, unsurprised. "I think we already know Osk and Sandcliff will attempt some form of retribution for pushing them out of the city. They will be gathering on the plain to try and cut us off."

Peter nodded. "My thoughts exactly."

"We have to keep the highway open," Elizabeth said. "We will need to get word to the rest of the army."

"Army?" Harriet asked hesitantly.

"Yes. The guardsmen I have with me are an advance force. The bulk of my army is behind us. If Osk and Sandcliff attack they will find themselves sandwiched between the city and my forces." Elizabeth turned to Richard. "Back to the docks. I will give you what I can but it won't be much. Each of you merchants have a small armed force, don't you?"

"Yes, Your Grace," Richard said, eyes intense and glittering.

"Good," Elizabeth said. "Would they accept orders from my officers? If all of you agreed, the merchant guards could form a small army and keep the docks safe. One of my officers in command will send Osk and Sandcliff a message that your duchess knows and approves of this arrangement."

"Yes, Your Grace," Richard said. "Who do you propose to put in charge of our men?"

"Sergeant Hunter. He is an excellent officer and an outstanding administrator."

Richard smiled and nodded. "That would be quite acceptable."

Elizabeth stared at him. "No arguments?"

"No, Your Grace. We made a promise to you. We would work with you to rebuild Manusk."

Elizabeth gave him a genuine smile. "Thank you, Richard. I won't forget this." She held out her hand. "To seal our bargain."

Richard clasped her forearm with a return smile that lit up his dark eyes. "To seal our bargain, Your Grace."

"Did you really make that promise, merchant? To help rebuild Manusk?" Jarrod asked. "You are a merchant. You are interested in coin. How do you propose to sell your goods since we have no money to buy?"

"We have to come to an arrangement," Richard said after a moment. He smiled. "Money is only good if it can be gained and spent. So far no one has been able to do either because of Osk and Sandcliff interference. My trade is suffering and it is in all of our best interests for us to be back in business."

"Again, how do you propose to sell your goods when we have no money to buy?"

Richard stared calmly at him. "Trade must resume."

"I'm sure we can come to some arrangement with the king," Elizabeth said just as Jarrod, brow furrowed, opened his mouth. "Richard, what if you were to sell half of your goods at cost to the citizens of Manusk and the other half at your normal rates to your other buyers?"

Richard was silent for a moment. He stroked his beard, leaned back, and drummed his fingers on the table for a few minutes. "All right. I think I could talk the other traders into that."

"But, Your Grace," Rebecca said. "How are we to buy goods off the merchants? We can't even afford to feed ourselves."

Elizabeth smiled. "I buy the goods off Richard and the other traders and give them to you. You repay me in trade and food."

Rebecca and Jarrod bent their heads together and whispered. Hands moved in emphasis of whispered words and Elizabeth waited patiently until they reached an agreement.

"Yes, Your Grace. That's acceptable to us. But if we're to repay you we have to get back to our land. If we began now the first harvests would be ready in a few months," Jarrod said. "But you should know that we were driven off our land by the tax collectors. Confiscated, they said, until we could pay our taxes. We have no land to give anything to you."

Elizabeth stiffened as anger flowed through her. She forced it back and nodded. "How many of you are there that have this problem?"

"Most of the farmers are gone. There are only about twenty or so farms left," Jarrod said.

Elizabeth raised her eyebrows. "*Twenty* farms? To feed a duchy of *ten thousand*?"

"There are only about two thousand Manuskmen left in Manusk," Harriet said. "The rest are of Osk and Sandcliff."

"So whatever food is grown in Manusk is shipped to Osk and Sandcliff?" Elizabeth asked, clenching her fists.

"Yes, Your Grace," Rebecca said hesitantly.

"Well, we can buy it as well, so we're not starving," Harriet said. "Although, as soon as Dukes Gilbert of Osk and Clayton of Sandcliff know you're here it will be too expensive to buy before long."

"This stops *right now*," Elizabeth said, tapping her forefinger on the table for emphasis. Her hot gaze swung between Richard and Herbert. "Who's the record keeper for these improper transactions?"

"The registrar has a land scribe," Richard said after a moment. "If anyone would have such records, I'm sure he would."

"Good," Elizabeth said. "Herbert, at dawn tomorrow, you will go to the registrar's office and begin collecting these records. Drag him out of his bed if needs be."

"Yes, Your Grace," Herbert said.

She turned to Jarrod and Rebecca. "Where did the farmers go after they were thrown off their land?"

"Some went to the King's Heartland or the other duchies. Others are still here living off the land in the hills around Coral Bay," Jarrod said.

"Can they fight?" Elizabeth asked.

Jarrod looked at her, posture stiff, his gaze anywhere other than at her.

"Come now, Jarrod," Elizabeth said after the silence had played out for a moment or so. "They're safe from me. They've lost their land and they want it back. They're staying close to it. I understand why they're doing it. I want to help them." She smiled. "Now. Can they fight?"

Peter and Sean exchanged a glance and watched her with sharp eyes.

"Yes," Jarrod said. "They've learnt how to fight."

"Do they fight well?"

"They're not soldiers, Your Grace."

"Do you keep in touch with them?"

A short, sharp nod from Jarrod.

"Good. I have a job for you—*all* of you, if you've a mind to do it. I need my farmers back on the land so we can feed the citizens of Manusk. I don't have enough guardsmen to guard your farms properly, but what I do have I will share with you."

Another short, sharp nod, this time from Jarrod and Rebecca.

"I will assemble a list of improperly seized farms from the registrar. I will use this list for my guardsmen to ride forth and reclaim the farms for their rightful owners. The farmers must be ready to retake the farms I return to them. I would like those who are waiting to help those who have land to farm their land and tend their crops."

Rebecca and Jarrod sat straight up in their seats and stared intently at her.

"Those than can fight will teach those that can't how to. I'll also teach them as will my officers." She looked at Sean and Peter. "As of now, you will spread word that Her Vacuous Grace issues a call to all fighters, in order to test her sword skills. Avoid any direct questions about it." She turned back to the avidly watching Jarrod. "Send your friends to me in small numbers. We will teach them how to fight. When they return to you, you will all defend your land with the help my guardsmen are able to give you, with the blessing of your duchess. You are not only farmers, you are my militia. Does that sound agreeable to you?"

Jarrod's face slowly creased into a broad smile. "Yes, Your Grace. Yes, it does."

"Excellent," Elizabeth said. "Are we all in agreement with this?"

Richard, Rebecca, Jarrod, and Harriet all exchanged an unreadable glance.

"I think so, Your Grace," Richard said.

"Yes, Your Grace," said Jarrod, Rebecca, and Harriet.

Elizabeth gave them a broad grin and felt a little hope filter into her consciousness. "Then I think we have a workable plan." She held up her cup, filled with weak ale. "To Manusk."

"To Manusk," they chorused as they brought their cups together in a toast.

They all drained their cups.

Jarrod put his cup back on the table and stood. "Thank you, Your Grace. This has been the best meal Rebecca and I have had for some time." He nodded toward the other civilians and soldiers scattered around the room. "I am forever in your debt, Your Grace." He bowed low and Rebecca quickly stood beside him and curtseyed.

Elizabeth stood and returned his bow. "You have a standing invitation at my table for dinner and conversation. Thank you for talking to me, Jarrod."

"You're welcome, Your Grace. You've made us a generous and welcome offer." Jarrod nodded. "Rebecca and I must be leaving if we're to find our friends."

"Yes. We'll expect the first of these in the next two days. We'll wait. Where is your farm?"

"It's on the highway to Coral Bay. It's the first farm after the soldier's checkpoint."

Elizabeth's mouth tightened and she exchanged grim glances with Herbert, Peter, and Sean. "The checkpoint won't be there for long. Travel safely."

"Thank you, Your Grace." They bowed again and left.

"I must leave as well, Your Grace. I've a great deal of work to do with the other traders and merchants." Richard stood and bowed low.

"Good evening, Richard, and thank you," Elizabeth said. "You also have a standing invitation at my table."

Richard regarded her with genuine pleasure. "Thank you for the invitation, Your Grace. I will gladly take you up on it."

Elizabeth smiled. "Excellent."

Richard bowed and left the kitchen. Harriet also stood, curtseyed, and disappeared in the crowd close to the kitchen fire.

Elizabeth watched them go, as Peter, Sean, and Herbert moved in closer to her. Elizabeth glanced around the kitchen. People still sat at the tables, not paying any attention to them. Two small figures at a table in the corner glanced around suspiciously and ate quickly.

Elizabeth nudged Sean. "Look." She nodded toward them.

"Is that the little brat from this morning?"

"I think so," Elizabeth said. "Benton."

"Everyone should be checking their purses," he muttered.

"I wonder why she's here. I thought someone called Charles looked after her."

"That's a good question, Your Grace," he said. "That's interesting."

"I think we should watch her closely."

"I agree."

Elizabeth turned to Herbert and Peter. "Back to business. Your thoughts, gentlemen?"

"If you're talking about Manusk I think we have a chance to rebuild," Peter said. "I've been listening to gossip and it seems most people are interested in what you have to say. You're not being dismissed out of hand. If you keep doing this Manusk will be yours by the end of the season."

"I hope so," Elizabeth said. "And this is all pretty much what I thought. But I'm concerned."

"I think we all are," Sean said. "A force of five hundred is hardly enough to take and keep a city of this size."

"Four hundred and fifty," Herbert said quietly. "We have four hundred and fifty men here."

"We've lost *fifty* men, Herbert?" Elizabeth asked sharply. "My guardsmen are simply not that poorly trained."

"We are thoroughly overwhelmed by numbers," Herbert said. "We lost ten in the debacle with the signal fires. We've lost twenty to patrols outside the city—and now twenty more are missing. That left me with fifty men. Ten more have been lost to injury—they won't be back on their feet for a while. We need the remaining forty on the city walls."

"Herbert," Elizabeth said sharply. "You lost twenty men on patrol, and then sent out another twenty? Why?"

"They were destined for the army, Your Highness," Herbert said. "I don't know whether or not they made it. That's what the second patrol was for—half of which was to go another route."

I wonder if I believe that. Surely no one could be that stupid.

"We are being slaughtered," Peter said. "Why?"

"Taking back the farms might be a near impossible task." Elizabeth sighed. "I brought four hundred men with me. Twenty of those will go down to the docks and begin helping Richard. I will take ten with me to begin opening the highways and returning the farmers to their lands. Send twenty out to teach the farmers to fight. A hundred must go out and keep the highway to the King's Heartland open. The remainder of our troops will help the watch to fortify the city and shore up our defenses. That will include clearing out all the rats in the city. We can't afford to be decimated from inside when fighting breaks out." Her jaw clenched. "We will begin clearing out the city jail tomorrow and evicting those who are not loyal to Manusk."

"What do you want us to do with the prisoners?" Peter asked.

"We will rule by law," Elizabeth said. "And we will have speedy justice. If there is evidence of a criminal act by the citizen of a foreign duchy, then the guilty will be punished. Theft, assault, and murder are hanging offences. All others are exile. For citizens of Manusk, they will be temporarily imprisoned."

"Yes, Your Grace," Herbert, Peter, and Sean murmured.

"Our last order of business," Elizabeth said, "is that ship in the harbor. Herbert, did you find any paperwork for it? Manifests? Any evidence of sailors?"

Herbert shook his head, his eyes troubled. "No, Your Grace."

"We have trouble ahead, don't we, Your Highness?" Sean said.

Elizabeth nodded. "I think we do. I don't know what, yet. I'm going to visit our new guests and see if their leader is up to talking with me."

"At this hour?" Herbert said. "It's late."

"It doesn't matter," Elizabeth said. "Can't you feel the clock?"

Peter regarded her closely for a moment. "Yes. I think we all do."

Herbert and Sean nodded in agreement.

Elizabeth shook her head in frustration and Herbert, Peter, and Sean nodded again.

"All right," Elizabeth said, pushing away from the table and standing. "We'll call it an evening and meet back here tomorrow night for dinner. Sean, report to me as soon as the sun is up. We're going out to the highway."

"Yes, Your Grace," they chorused and stood, bowing.

She returned their bow. "Sean, one moment, please."

Sean stopped and Elizabeth waited until Herbert and Peter left. "Go to the land scribe's office and find the deed for Jarrod's and Rebecca's land. We'll need the information for tomorrow."

"Yes, Your Grace," Sean said, bowing, and left the kitchen.

Elizabeth watched him go, feeling bone weary. Would the misdeeds of Osk and Sandcliff never stop?

CHAPTER 6

ELIZABETH SLOWLY ASCENDED the stairs, more tired than she'd been in a long time. Her exhaustion was undercut by a terrible, droning feeling of dread. *I'm not looking forward to this. I just don't want to deal with this on top of everything else.* She reached the top of the stairs and gently stroked the newel post. *I've faced down armies. I've had more swords and arrows aimed at me than most other people, and yet I'm afraid of walking into a room of sick people.*

Or perhaps it wasn't that, she mused as she slowly made her way to the first bedroom that held the survivors of the shipwreck. Perhaps it was just the questions swirling around the trading ship in the harbor and the shipwreck. The shipwreck. Her father would be much less than pleased that such a thing had taken place at all, regardless of the timing.

She squared her shoulders as she stood in the doorway and surveyed the room. *Brave heart, Elizabeth.* Twenty cots stood together in close quarters. Twenty bodies lay in the cots, covered with rough, clean blankets. Buckets with cold, clean water and dippers were in the center of the room. Most of the people in the bed were senseless, but some moved and whimpered in discomfort.

One grey haired man moved his head restlessly on his pillow, moaning softly. Elizabeth glanced around the room, but saw no servants. She took a step forward, breaking her paralysis, and approached the older man.

She knelt and looked closely at him. He was deathly pale, with a red spot on the bandage around his forehead. She hesitantly touched his face, fleetingly grateful that his skin was cool, but clammy. If he'd ever had a fever, it'd broken.

His eyes widened at her gentle touch and he blinked. His lips moved soundlessly.

"Shh, you are safe," Elizabeth said softly, glancing at the bowl of water and a wet rag on the crate that sat by his bed. She took the rag and wiped his face with it.

He sighed and his eyes fluttered closed. She wiped the sweat off his face and his eyes opened again. He whispered a single, unintelligible word.

"I'm sorry, I don't understand you," she whispered. "But I am going to guess you want water."

"Yes. Water," he whispered back.

Elizabeth nodded. She wasn't surprised. The woman in her chamber also knew their language. This was a good development. "I'll get it."

She hurried over to the bucket, filled a dipper, and brought it back to the bed.

"Drink," she said softly, putting her hand behind his neck as he struggled to sit up.

She held the dipper to his lips and he drank deeply. When he'd finished, he looked at her.

"More?" he asked.

"More," Elizabeth said, nodding. She quickly got him another dipper of water and held his head as he finished it.

"Good," he said, sighing.

Elizabeth nodded. "Can you tell me your name, friend?"

"Isengard," he said softly. He opened his eyes again, unfocussed. He blinked and his gaze became sharp. "The princess? Where is Rowan?"

"Rowan?" Elizabeth asked, struggling to control her shock. "A tall woman with blonde hair and blue eyes?"

"Yes."

"She safe. She's in my chamber. She has a wound to her midsection but she is recovering. Her color is good."

His eyes narrowed in disbelief.

"I will ask her to come to you when she wakes up," Elizabeth said. "Would that be acceptable to you?"

Isengard stared at her, his gaze almost a physical weight. He finally nodded. "Yes." He gripped her wrist in a surprisingly strong grasp. "Know this, woman—if anything happens to her I will kill you."

"All right," Elizabeth said, pushing back a stab of anger. "Who is Princess Rowan? Where are you from?"

"Well and . . ." Isengard began as he slipped into unconsciousness.

Elizabeth sat back on her haunches, wincing. She searched her memory for anything she knew about Welland. It was a kingdom, she knew, across the Markand Sea. Trade with Welland had ceased a century or so earlier, and years earlier they'd heard rumor of a civil war.

She looked at the other survivors in the room. Now it was more important than ever to see to their care and return them to good health. The princess had to be protected at all costs or there would be war with Welland.

Yet, when the initial shock of Isengard's news passed, all she saw as she looked around the room were hurt people. She checked each and every person. She straightened blankets and gave water when requested. She was washing the remnants of blood off her hands when her battlefield surgeon slipped into the room.

He stopped dead when he saw her. He bowed. "Your Grace? What can I do for you?"

"Nothing, Doctor," she said. "I just came into see how our guests were doing. I've been giving out water."

"Did you see the servants I left here to see to their needs?"

Elizabeth shook her head. "No. I was surprised there was no one here."

"I'm very sorry, Your Grace. This won't happen again—"

Elizabeth grasped his shoulder. "It's all right, Doctor. I was here and I could help. No harm done."

The doctor smiled, relaxing. "Thank you, Your Grace."

Elizabeth made her way toward the door. "Good night, Doctor."

"Actually, it's good morning, Your Grace," he said with a half smile as he approached the closest bed to check on his patient.

Elizabeth slipped out of the room and stood for a moment in the corridor, debating. She steeled herself and entered the second room of survivors. This one was empty of servants as well but unlike the other room, most seemed asleep and less gravely injured. Just as she turned to leave, she heard a soft sob.

She frowned and checked the beds. The sob sounded again, and she quickly found a young man, his leg heavily splinted, with tears streaming down his face. She knelt beside him and wiped his sweaty face with a rag.

He gave her a beseeching look and said something unintelligible in his language. He pointed to his leg.

Elizabeth smoothed back his hair. "One moment. I'm going to get the doctor."

She got up and as she moved away, he called for her.

She turned back to him and held up her hand. "You can't understand me but wait. Wait. I'm getting help."

She hurried out of the room and almost collided with the doctor.

"Your Grace?" he asked.

"There's a boy in a lot of pain in there. He's pointing to his leg but I don't understand what he wants."

"Ah, the boy with the bad break. I know him," the doctor said. He held up his bag. "I have some herbs for him to help with the pain but I need to elevate his leg."

"How can I help?" Elizabeth asked. "There's no one in there either."

The doctor colored. "Ah, you could hold him as I shift his leg?"

Elizabeth waved him ahead of her. "After you, Doctor."

The doctor nodded and led the way back into the room. The boy watched them approach, tears streaming from his eyes. The doctor quickly bent over him and checked his splint.

The doctor shook his head. "We need someone to put pillows under his leg while I lift it. You'll have to hold him. He won't like this and I don't speak his language to tell him what I'm going to do." He glanced at Elizabeth. "I need to find a servant."

"No," a soft voice said from the bed beside him. "I help."

Elizabeth looked at a young woman, who was blinking uncertainly at them.

The woman sat up, wincing. She pointed to herself. "What me do?"

The doctor gestured for her to come closer. As she slowly and painfully stood, the doctor hurried over to a stack of blankets and pillows on a small chest in the corner of the room. He came back with several pillows and dropped them to the floor beside the bed.

"Your Grace, please hold him down," he said. He looked at the young woman, who was watching him intently. "When I lift his leg, put these," he patted the stack, "under his knee and shin." He patted his knee and shin.

"You lift and I put," the young woman said, miming lifting and pushing the pillows.

"Yes," the doctor said. He looked at Elizabeth. "Your Grace?"

Elizabeth knelt by the boy and curled her hand around his clammy one. She knelt over him.

"Ready, Doctor," she said.

"Lift," the doctor said and grasped the boy by his splinted ankle and lifted.

The boy groaned and clutched Elizabeth's shoulders. His hot face, streaming tears, was pressed against her neck, stifling the worst of his cry.

Elizabeth held him as he clutched her, until he finally sank back onto the mattress, semi conscious. She glanced back at the doctor, who was busily mixing herbs for him. The girl sat back on her haunches and watched them with wide eyes.

"Help me sit him up a little so he can drink this," the doctor said, gesturing to the cup he held in his hand.

Elizabeth gently put her arm behind the boy's shoulders and lifted him as the doctor pressed the cup to his lips. He drank convulsively. Elizabeth lowered him and he sighed. She wet the rag from the almost forgotten bowl of water by the side of the bed and cleaned his face. He gazed at her, eyes glazing from the strength of the herbs and she stroked his hair. He fell asleep moments later.

She sat back with a sigh, drained.

"Good work, both of you, and thank you," the doctor said, patting her shoulder and giving her a genuine smile.

"You're welcome, Doctor," Elizabeth said.

He got up and began to check his other patients.

"Who you?" the girl said from her place at the end of the boy's bed.

"Elizabeth St. John, Duchess of Manusk. And you, my dear, should be in bed. You're not well." She lifted the blankets of the girl's cot and gestured for her to go back to bed.

The girl's eyes widened at the mention of her title. She scurried as quickly as she was able to back to her cot and dived in.

Elizabeth settled the covers over her and gently stroked her face. "Thank you, stranger, for your help."

"No stranger," the girl said softly. "Me Kellen." She pointed to the boy in the cot beside her. "Him Garvin."

"Well, Kellen, thank you once again. Sleep well."

Elizabeth stood and watched the doctor as he quietly moved around the room. She left and headed toward her own chambers, exhausted.

She slipped inside the room and looked at the sleeping woman in the bed.

Good night, Princess Rowan, she thought as she sank to the hearthstones, deeply asleep seconds later.

ELIZABETH WOKE WHAT felt like a minute later. She opened her stinging eyes and slowly sat up. She looked around and blinked, wondering why she was awake. A low moan sounded from the bed. She blew out a breath and levered herself up, unsteady on her feet as she made her way to the bed and inwardly cursing her exhaustion. She sat heavily on the edge of the bed and reached over to Rowan. Rowan's head moved restlessly on the pillow.

"Safe," Elizabeth murmured. "You're safe."

Rowan's eyes fluttered open. "I was having a nightmare." She sighed.

"Do you want some water?" Elizabeth asked.

"Water. Yes. Good," Rowan said.

"All right," Elizabeth said, looking by the side of the bed. It was empty. "I'll be right back." She quickly got up off the bed and jogged out of the room. She went to the closest room of survivors and peered in, looking for a servant. She spotted Mara and gestured for her to come.

"Yes, Your Grace?" Mara said, quickly approaching Elizabeth.

"Can you please get me some water from the kitchen and perhaps something to eat? Our guest has just woken up," Elizabeth said.

Mara's eyes widened. "Yes, Your Grace." She hurried away.

Elizabeth glanced at the people in the room—they all seemed to be asleep—and quickly jogged back to her chambers.

Rowan was sitting up, comfortably resting on the back board.

"Do you want some more pillows for your back?" Elizabeth asked.

Rowan nodded. Elizabeth held her and carefully pushed more pillows behind her back. Rowan hissed in pain.

Elizabeth sat on the edge of the bed, feeling Rowan's eyes on her.

"Who are you?" Rowan asked after a moment of cool, intense study. "I've seen you on the hearthstones but you don't look like you're a servant."

"I am Elizabeth St. John, Duchess of Manusk," Elizabeth said. "You're in my house. We're short of space so we put you in with me."

Rowan's bright blue eyes widened. "Where are all the people who were with me?"

"We rescued twenty from your ship. They're on this floor in two of the rooms. Would you mind telling me who you are?"

"Only twenty? And Isengard is one of them?" Rowan sighed and her eyes fluttered closed. She relaxed for a moment.

"He's alive and wants very much to see you. I told him you'd visit as soon as you could." Elizabeth paused. "Perhaps they should *all* see that you're alive." She studied Rowan's face. She was classically beautiful and had full, red lips that begged to be kissed. "Would you mind telling me who you are?"

The door opened and Mara quietly snuck in, carefully balancing a tray with a jug of water, clear broth, thick bread, and cheese.

"I'm Rowan Stonecypher, Crown Princess of Welland and Commander in Chief of the Armies of Welland." Her eyes pinned Elizabeth in a cool, bright blue stare. "We came in peace but found *this* instead. I will see you swinging at the end of a rope for this."

Elizabeth inwardly rolled her eyes and sighed.

Mara unobtrusively approached the bed and put the tray on Rowan's lap. Rowan ignored her.

"I understand you're upset. I also understand that this is, in some part, my responsibility. But I only just got here myself," Elizabeth said. "And I didn't know you were coming."

Rowan raised a sculpted eyebrow. "Really? And you expect me to believe that?"

Elizabeth held up her hands. "What could I possibly gain by lying to you?"

Rowan remained expressionless.

"Look," Elizabeth said. "If you don't believe me, why don't you ask your people tomorrow? Isengard, at least, is worried about you so you should probably talk to him. I have nothing to hide."

"I'll do that. I want to see them."

Elizabeth handed Rowan a cup of water from the tray. "Drink. Please."

Rowan watched her carefully and slowly brought the cup to her lips. She sipped. "Good."

Elizabeth nodded. "Eat. You must be starving."

Rowan nodded once, sharply, eyes never leaving Elizabeth's. She took the bread and carefully dipped it in the steaming broth. She took a large bite.

Elizabeth held her gaze, feeling a little like a mouse caught in a snake's sights. "I have to ask. Why are you here?"

"We came in peace to trade with your people. We also came seeking an alliance with your king." She swallowed a hunk of cheese. "But I don't think we will pursue this course of action." She smiled coldly. "Send me—us—back to our fleet and we'll be on our way."

Elizabeth hesitated for a moment. "Is there anything I could say or do that will change your mind? You can't think badly of all of us simply because of an unfortunate accident."

"An *accident*? Is that what you want to call this?"

"I have no other words for what happened to you. I didn't deliberately sink your ship. I don't want hostilities with you."

"You have them."

"Look," Elizabeth said. "This is what happened. I and my men arrived here in Manusk last night. On our way here, we saw a ship breaking up at the mouth of Manusk harbor. Something happened to the signal fires. They weren't burning, despite the best efforts of my advance guardsmen. Your ship was the result of this incident. *My* guardsmen—and hence myself—were responsible for the signal fire and for that you may extract retribution from me as you will. But don't let that destroy neutrality at least between our peoples."

Rowan stared at her. "You admit this about the signal fires?"

"I have nothing to hide," Elizabeth said. "And there is something else you should know. There is a trading ship at the docks in the harbor that isn't from this kingdom. Her markings indicate she's from Welland. We haven't found the crew yet, and some of her cargo is missing."

Rowan narrowed her eyes and her mouth set in a hard line.

"When did she sail into the harbor, Your Highness?" Elizabeth asked.

"What kind of a foul place is this?" Rowan snarled. "Why don't you have better control over your lands?"

Elizabeth's eyes watered and stung with exhaustion. She felt as though she had a millstone around her neck, and her control over her temper slipped. "Who are you to judge me or us? The politics of this duchy is none of your concern. I and my people are none of your concern. Why don't you go back to your threats of seeing me hanged? That would be a much better place for you to begin your attempts at *diplomacy*."

Rowan stared at her, her gaze flickering. She dipped her bread into the broth and carefully chewed and swallowed it. Elizabeth watched her closely.

"All right, Duchess," Rowan said. "My ship sailed into your harbor a week ago. The agreement was that she would drop off her cargo and a diplomatic contingent. The ship was to come back out to the fleet again, and a second trading ship would return. If, on the other hand, there was no word from the first trading ship after three days, my ship was to go in and I would lend my support to the ambassador."

Elizabeth sighed. "Not just missing sailors? A missing ambassador." She turned to Mara, almost forgotten beside them. "Go down and get Herbert, Peter, and Sean."

Mara gave her awkward curtsey and slipped out of the room.

"Who are Herbert, Peter, and Sean?" Rowan asked.

"Herbert is the captain of the guardsmen of Manusk, Peter his lieutenant, and Sean is my sergeant."

"Did you think to consider if I wanted to talk to them in my present condition?" Rowan asked.

"Who do you think fished you out of the water?" Elizabeth gave her a broad, genuine grin. "I didn't think you'd mind. You are clearly quite concerned about your people, and I want to find the crew of the trader. I have to give orders before I leave for the day."

"Where are you going?" Rowan asked.

"To open the highways around Manusk. I must send word to the king about what's happened here and give you safe passage out of here since I'm no statesman."

"You are the Duchess of Manusk, are you not?"

"In name. I'm a simple soldier." Elizabeth eyed Rowan carefully. "Not unlike yourself, I think, Your Highness."

Rowan colored. "Diplomacy between us isn't going well, is it?"

Elizabeth snorted a laugh. "No, it's not."

"I want to return to my fleet."

"The only way we can do that is to send you on the trading ship. And you have only twenty to man the ship, and half of those must not be moved."

"Can't you spare anyone?"

"If you intend to leave and not return, how will I get them back? If you don't take your ship it'll be stuck in the harbor until you come in for it."

"Take me to my fleet. We will return for my people. That would be acceptable to me."

"All right," Elizabeth said. "We will send you back to your fleet. You can leave in peace."

"Without the friendship we'd hoped for but with no hostilities."

"I can't change your mind about that?"

Rowan shook her head.

"Then neutrality it is, Your Highness." Elizabeth held out her forearm. "To seal our bargain."

Rowan clasped her arm. "Yes, Your Grace."

A knock sounded on the door.

"Enter," Elizabeth said.

The door opened and Herbert, Peter, and Sean entered the room. All three were in simple breeches and shirts, unlaced at the throat. They saw Elizabeth sitting on the bed with Rowan and stopped dead.

"Your Grace?" Herbert asked.

Elizabeth inclined her head with a half smile. "Captain Herbert, Lieutenant Peter, and Sergeant Sean, this is Princess Rowan Stonecypher, Crown Princess of Welland."

Herbert's eyes widened and he dropped to one knee. Peter, looking dismayed, dropped to one knee, while Sean remained expressionless and followed a heartbeat behind.

"Your Highness," they chorused.

"Gentleman," Rowan said, blue eyes cool.

"At ease," Elizabeth said. "Take a seat. I—or we, rather—have something to tell you."

Herbert, Peter, and Sean seated themselves on the hearthstones, and Elizabeth told them about the trading mission and about Rowan's plans to leave.

Herbert regarded her thoughtfully. "What do you want to do, Your Grace?"

"You, Herbert, will remain with Princess Rowan tomorrow. First order of business is to ensure that she is given access to her people. After, you will go to the docks and assemble a new crew for the trader."

Herbert frowned and watched her closely. "Yes, Your Grace," he said after a moment.

"Peter," Elizabeth said. "Take the watch. Find the crew of that trading ship. Sean, you and I will go out as planned and attend to the farmers—and we need to send word to the king about our guests."

"Yes, Your Grace," Sean said.

"Then good night, gentlemen," she said.

"Your Highness. Your Grace," they chorused, bowing and backing out of the room.

Rowan eyed her coolly after they'd left. "Don't you think that you should be a good hostess and remain with me?"

Elizabeth raised an eyebrow. "I can't be in two places at once. My duchy will still be here long after you and your people are gone. Peter is perfectly capable of discharging whatever task I give him. Plus, given that you aren't interested in diplomacy, *and* you want my head on a silver platter, *and* I have a great deal to do before being able to fulfill your desire to see me swinging at the end of a rope, I'm not really sure what you're expecting my company to accomplish."

Rowan gaped and watched her closely for a moment. She finally shook her head and snorted a laugh. "Under other circumstances I'm sure we could be friends."

Elizabeth gave her a sad smile. "I'm sure we could." She took a deep breath. "I'm sorry, Your Highness, but if you want to leave you have to tell me when you intend to do it."

"May I call you Elizabeth?" Rowan asked.

"Of course."

"Then you must call me Rowan." Rowan tilted her head and regarded Elizabeth. "What's going on here?"

"What do you mean?" Elizabeth asked.

"You're not at all what I was expecting. Your house is a disgrace and you're a noblewoman sleeping on hearthstones. I am a foreign dignitary wounded on your soil, which I might add seems not under your control. Most nobles would be prostrate before me and begging for forgiveness, but not you. Who are you, Elizabeth St. John?"

"I apologize for the apparent disarray but I am building my new home. While this is true, I have nothing to beg you for forgiveness for. I didn't sink your ship and I didn't leave you on the beach to fend for yourselves. You're in my house and enjoying my hospitality, rough as it is. You have the run of my house. Personally, I think my manners, while I'm sure are much less than you're used to, are quite pleasant."

Rowan gaped at her for a moment and then burst out laughing. "Oh, Elizabeth, you really aren't a statesman, are you?"

Elizabeth felt her face heat and gave her a cautious smile. "That's what I told you."

"I'm not really a statesman either," Rowan said, tilting her head and studying Elizabeth long enough for her to want to fidget. "Perhaps I was a little hasty in rejecting diplomacy."

"Really?"

"Really," Rowan said. She gestured toward the hearthstones. "Why *are* you sleeping on hearthstones? What's going on here?"

Elizabeth hesitated.

"Come now," Rowan said as the silence played out. "You've given me free run of your house and city. I'm going to find out what's going on one way or another and quite quickly, I think."

Elizabeth glanced out of the window, and saw the deep blue of morning sky and the first golden corona of the sun on the horizon. "It's a long story and I don't have time to tell it to you right now." She gazed at Rowan, frankly studying her beautiful features. "I can tell you when I return."

Rowan returned her close scrutiny. "All right. You'll be back this evening?"

"I hope so. If I am, eat with me this evening. The accommodations are a little rough but I'm sure you've probably seen worse."

Rowan nodded. "I'll be there, Elizabeth of Manusk."

"And I'll be looking forward to it, Rowan of Welland," Elizabeth said, finding that it was true, much to her surprise.

CHAPTER 7

"GOOD MORNING AGAIN, Your Grace. How is Her Imperiousness holding up with the wretched hospitality?" Sean asked, holding the reins of Elizabeth's horse and bowing as she approached.

Guardsmen saluted and mounted their horses, then milled around to form two columns behind her.

She laughed, pulled on her riding gloves, and mounted her horse in a smooth, graceful motion. "She's not that bad, actually. She didn't complain about the bath water, nor did she mention my execution once."

Sean's grin slipped.

"Relax. I'm not going to let her arrest me. And if she tried it I'm sure Father would have something to say about it."

Sean nodded. "Yes, Your Highness."

"Right," Elizabeth said, nudging her horse into motion.

They rode out of the courtyard and down the city street through light foot traffic that hurried out of the way.

"Did you find out where the road block is?" Elizabeth asked.

"Harriet said that it is about half a day's ride from the western gate."

"Harriet seems to know *everything* doesn't she?" Elizabeth said.

Sean nodded. "That she does, Your Grace. I'm glad she's on our side."

"She's not exactly on our side but at least she's not against us." Elizabeth scanned the road and decaying buildings around them. She caught flashes of movement behind splintered doors and lights behind thick, ragged curtains. She turned her head to follow movement she'd seen out of the corner of her eye, but only saw bare cobblestones and shadowed corners.

"Are you joking, Your Grace?" Sean said. "You *own* her."

"No I don't," Elizabeth said.

"Yes, Your Grace, you do," Sean said. "You hooked her when you offered the good citizens of this godforsaken duchy food and reeled her in when you told those farmers that you'd help them. She's yours for the taking, Your Grace."

Elizabeth felt her face heat. "I didn't do anything any reasonable person wouldn't have done."

"Yes, Your Grace," Sean said.

"I didn't."

"*Of course* not, Your Grace."

"Sean."

"Yes, Your Grace?"

"I didn't."

"As you wish, Your Grace," Sean said, saluting.

Elizabeth sighed and shook her head. She glanced around, feeling an itch between her shoulder blades and seeing the expressionless face of the guardsman riding behind her.

"Is there something wrong, Your Grace?" he asked.

Elizabeth listened closely for a moment, but heard nothing besides the clatter of horses' hooves against the cobblestones, and saw nothing but ragged citizens going about their business. "No." She looked steadfastly forward. "How far are we from the Western Gate?"

"Another half hour," Sean said.

Elizabeth eyed the streets and the empty houses. "Peter has his work cut out for him."

Sean nodded. "Yes, he does."

"There are three gates, yes?" Elizabeth said. "Northern, Western, and Eastern? And the walls of the city are stone?"

"Yes, Your Grace." Sean glanced at her. "But as you can imagine, the stone is somewhat the worse for wear and the three gates are a joke."

"Do you know of any stonemasons working for us?"

"There were a couple. They've been sent to the Northern Gate to shore up the walls. Eastern leads to Sargay so the lieutenant and the captain decided to do that last."

"But the Western Gate is untouched?"

"Yes, Your Grace," Sean said.

"Why not, I suppose," Elizabeth said. "It's the best defended of all three."

"And if Sandcliff and Osk come from any direction it's most likely to be the Northern or Western gates."

Elizabeth nodded. "Agreed. Although, if they had any brains, they'd try and cut me off from the rest of my forces."

"Yes, Your Grace," Sean said. "But first they'd have to work out where your forces were hiding."

"They're not exactly hard to find. I don't seriously think Osk or Sandcliff would attack us. That would be foolhardy. My father would be furious and his army would tear them apart."

"Agreed, Your Grace."

They fell silent and Elizabeth watched the city streets carefully. Young men lounged on the street corners, eyeing men and women going about their business. They sneered when they saw her and her guardsmen. The men and women of Manusk saw her pass and stopped and stared, sometimes knuckling their foreheads, sometimes holding them in dumb regard, and still others rushed away.

"Did you find out about the deed to Jarrod and Rebecca's land?" Elizabeth asked.

"Yes, Your Grace," Sean said. "The land is owned outright by Jarrod. His taxes are up to date. The land is also still officially owned by him so he is dealing with squatters."

"That would be true regardless, I think. Any document not signed by me or the Steward of Manusk is illegal."

"Yes, Your Grace."

They fell silent again and watched the citizens of Manusk go about their business.

It felt like days later that Elizabeth rode through the Western Gates of Manusk, past a stonemason inspecting the outer walls.

Once out on the highway, they pushed their horses into a trot, careful to avoid walking people and slow moving farm carts bumping and swaying down the road.

The traffic became denser and Elizabeth slowed her horse to a walk, Sean slowing beside her. Her horse's ears went back and she champed at the bit. Elizabeth patted her neck, soothing her.

"Now we're stopped," Sean said, reining his horse in.

"No, now we finally reached the thieves unlawfully blocking the road and extorting honest citizens of Manusk," Elizabeth said coldly.

The crowd around quieted and stared at them.

Elizabeth focused on the column of people ahead of her, bumping and jostling each other. She felt a tug on her boot. She frowned and looked down. A dirty faced, ragged boy of about fourteen stared up at her, blinking.

"Yes?" she said.

"Is it true that Manusk has a new duke?"

"No."

"Oh."

"Not a duke," Elizabeth said with a grin. "A *duchess*."

The boy broke into a smile. "Is it true, what they're saying? That she's come to help us?"

"Oh, yes. That's certainly true." Elizabeth glanced at Sean. "Clear the way, Sergeant."

Sean nudged his horse forward, pushing people out of the way as gently as possible, to cries of *watch it, who do you think you are?* And *wait your turn, soldier.*

Elizabeth trailed behind him, straightening her shoulders and lifting her chin.

They finally stopped behind a pair of farm carts. Ahead of them were a row of men on horses. They wore unmarked armor and stared straight ahead, ignoring the angry cries from the farmers.

They have a master. They're too well disciplined to be mercenaries or thieves.

"Sergeant, dismount. Guardsmen, crossbows," Elizabeth said, sliding off the back of her horse and drawing her sword. Sean quickly followed suit and she heard the clatter as the guardsmen armed their crossbows.

She pushed through the crowd, ignoring ragged taunts and cries of indignation and outrage. She reached the front men, who were searching a farmer's wagon. The man, his wife, and two small children stood on the other side of the barrier, carefully watched by the mounted men.

"Take their goods. They are contraband," a pockmarked man said, sliding down from the back of the wagon.

Elizabeth rested the point of her sword on the ground between her booted feet. "No. *Do not* take their goods."

The pockmarked man glared at her. "Who are you to interfere with us?"

"Elizabeth St. John. Duchess of Manusk!" Sean called as loudly as he could.

The crowd instantly quieted and a wave of whispers started up.

Elizabeth St. John.

The Duchess of Manusk.

Her Grace.

It's true.

The rumors are true.

The pockmarked man signaled the mounted men and drew a long dagger. He roared and lunged toward her. Elizabeth neatly sidestepped him, brought her sword up, and sliced him open. He screamed and fell to his knees, clutching his destroyed midsection. Sean neatly impaled his companion and crossbow quarrels hissed through the air and thudded into the mounted horsemen.

Elizabeth pulled off her cloak, dropped it over the gutted man, and wiped her sword clean as quickly as she could. "Move the bodies. Quickly."

Sean saluted and the guardsmen moved forward, shielding the crowd from the fallen men.

The crowd watched them, deathly silent. Their eyes flickered to Elizabeth. Some were pale, some shocked, some dismayed, some resigned, some clearly relieved, and still others a mix of these emotions. They all watched her closely, tension evident in their rigid bodies.

"May I?" Elizabeth asked the farmer whose cart had just been searched.

His mouth worked and he gaped at her. He held his pale wife close and his children behind him. "Y-yes, of course."

"Thank you," Elizabeth said as she climbed into the back of the cart. She held up her hands. "I am Elizabeth St. John, the Duchess of Manusk. I am here because I was told you were being taxed along a public highway out of the city of Manusk. This is illegal according to the laws of Manusk and the King's Heartland." She folded her arms and eyed the crowd. "Good citizens of Manusk, I have been sent here to bring Manusk back under the lawful rule of the king. I come here to give you back your land and your freedom. No one who comes to me seeking help, comfort, or shelter will be refused. All I ask of you in return is to obey the laws of Manusk and to be loyal and true to her."

She jumped down from the cart. The crowd remained still, watching her.

"Sean, post four guards here. If Osk and Sandcliff return to rob people I want it made clear to them that their industry is not welcome in Manusk."

Sean stood at attention and saluted Elizabeth. "Yes, Your Grace." He turned away and began issuing orders to the guardsmen.

The crowd remained immobile. Elizabeth sighed, blinking her burning eyes. She felt exhausted.

"Let's go," she said to Sean. "We still have to go to Jarrod and Rebecca's farm."

"Your Grace," Sean said with a bow.

The mute crowd parted to allow him through and he returned a moment later with the horses. Elizabeth, uncomfortable, restrained a sigh of relief.

She took the proffered reins, and Sean nodded, his eyes cutting to a point behind her. She turned.

The farmer stood before her, shifting from foot to foot, eyes downcast.

"Your Grace?" he said softly, and fell to one knee. "I am Calvin and I am your man."

Elizabeth smiled, put a hand under his elbow, and helped him to his feet. "Calvin, I am pleased to meet you." She held out a forearm.

He stared at her proffered forearm and finally clasped it firmly. He turned to his wife and children and motioned them forward. "My wife, Hester, and our children, Calvin Junior and Hazel."

"I'm pleased to meet you," Elizabeth said as Hester gave her a clumsy curtsey. Calvin Junior stepped up next to his father, flushed and quickly shook Elizabeth's hand.

The crowd's paralysis broke and it looked as though every peasant was on their knees, curtseying or knuckling their foreheads. Elizabeth accepted their greetings and promises of fealty with a smile.

"We'll take care of the bodies, Your Grace," a grizzled old man said, nodding sharply toward the line of corpses by the side of the road. "It's the least we can do. Those men were pigs." He spat at them.

Elizabeth nodded. "Thank you, good sir."

The old man knuckled his forehead. Four other men joined him as Elizabeth mounted her horse.

"Manusk," a lone voice sounded behind her.

Another joined it. "Manusk!"

Elizabeth drew her sword and held it high. "*Manusk!*"

Sean and the remaining guardsmen also drew their swords. "*Manusk!*"

Elizabeth and her guardsmen saluted the crowd. They heeled their horses around to cheering and rode away on a wave of applause.

After they were clear of the crowd, Sean turned to Elizabeth and gave her a broad grin. "Nicely done, Your Grace."

"Thank you, Sean," Elizabeth said. "But everything I said was the truth."

"And that just makes it all the sweeter," Sean said.

Elizabeth nodded and they lapsed into a comfortable silence. She looked around. The fields were half overgrown and showed clear signs of neglect; grass and dying corn were interspersed with weeds. The dusty, dry road ahead of them had very little traffic, thanks to the bottleneck that Elizabeth had just cleared.

"We haven't passed the farm, have we?" Elizabeth asked.

Sean shook his head. "I don't think so, Your Grace. They did say it was the first farm after the soldier's checkpoint."

"Can you see a farm house in any of the fields?" Elizabeth asked.

Sean reined in his horse and peered all around. He scanned over to their left. "There, Your Grace." He pointed. "There. There's a farm there."

"That must be it," Elizabeth said, heeling her horse into motion again.

They went about fifty feet and a figure appeared from between two tall corn stalks. Elizabeth's horse snorted and took a step back. Her broad nostrils flared and Elizabeth patted her neck.

"I'm sorry, Your Grace," Jarrod said. "I didn't mean to startle your horse."

"Hello, Jarrod," Elizabeth said. "We've come to help you."

Jarrod bowed. "Thank you, Your Grace."

"Let's be about it, then. Who's on your land? Armed guards or civilians?"

"I think it's only civilians," Jarrod said.

"All right," Elizabeth said. "Where's Rebecca?"

"She's looking for Farrow and the other farmers in the hills."

"Good. She's safe."

Elizabeth nudged her horse forward, Jarrod beside her. They walked in companionable silence down the wide, dirt rode that led to Jarrod's farm. Elizabeth spotted a child starting at them as they approached the dooryard.

"Are your parents here?" Elizabeth asked as they drew closer.

The little girl stared owlishly up at them.

Elizabeth opened her mouth to speak again, but the girl gave vent to a bloodcurdling scream followed by shouts of "Mama! Mama!"

Elizabeth glanced at Sean. His eyes were wide with surprise.

"What?" she said.

"I have no idea," Sean said.

Jarrod stifled a snort of laughter beside them.

"Yes?" Elizabeth said, glancing at him.

"Nothing, Your Grace," Jarrod replied, smirking.

The door to the farm house opened and a woman spilled out, wiping her hands on her apron. The little girl tugged on her dress, seemingly determined to drag her across the dooryard.

"Can I help you?" the woman said, eyeing Elizabeth up and down. "Madam?"

Elizabeth frowned and studied her. She was roughly thirty, ruddy faced, and plump. Her brown eyes were cold. She swatted at the little girl who tugged at her.

"Good lady," Elizabeth said. "I am Elizabeth St. John, the Duchess of Manusk. I want to speak to you and your husband regarding this farm."

The woman huffed and gaped at her. "My husband is in the fields. He'll be back at sunset. You can talk to him—"

"*Now*," Elizabeth said, pinning her with a merciless stare.

The woman bent down and whispered into the little girl's ear. The little girl tore off into the fields as though the hounds of hell were chasing her.

Elizabeth raised her eyebrows. "Well." She glanced at Sean.

"Your Grace?" he said, grinning.

"Dismount," she said, sliding off her horse, the guardsmen following close behind her.

They stood out in the dooryard, staring at the woman, who stared back defiantly.

They stood awkwardly staring at her for another fifteen minutes until the small girl came back through the corn, tugging a weather-beaten man's hand.

He puffed, out of breath, and came to a standstill before Elizabeth.

"Gemma here tells me you're claiming to be the Duchess of Manusk," he said, staring into her eyes.

"I'm not claiming anything. I *am* the Duchess of Manusk. How long have you had this land for?"

"It's been in my family for generations," the man said coldly.

"That's a lie," Jarrod snarled, stepping around the side of Elizabeth's horse.

"You. Get off my land!" The man lunged at Jarrod, earning a kick from Sean. The man fell forward to his knees as Jarrod clumsily stepped out of the way.

The man began to splutter but quieted at the hiss of Sean's sword leaving its scabbard.

"Let's play nicely, gentlemen," Elizabeth said, glancing between the two.

Jarrod colored and looked away. The man stared at her, defiance mixed with fear in his gaze.

"Now, then," Elizabeth said, motioning Sean to pull the man upright.

Sean levered him to his feet.

"Now that we can see each other," she continued, looking him in the eye, "you have fifteen minutes to load up your cart and vacate this land. You're lying when you say this land has been in your family for generations. It's not yours at all. It belongs to this man. You're squatting illegally on his land." She folded her arms and stared into his eyes.

He remained silent and glared at her.

"*Well?*" Elizabeth said. "Have you nothing to say to the charges?"

"I will come for you," the man said. "When you least expect it."

Elizabeth gave him a small smile and leaned in close so she whispered directly into his ear. "Did you know it's a capital offence to threaten a noble like you've just done? I'm perfectly within my rights to execute you where you stand."

The man's head swung around. His mouth was set in a grim line but his eyes betrayed his fear.

"Fifteen minutes. Move."

Sean kept a tight grip on him. The tip of his sword dug into his neck. He spun the man around and shoved him toward his wide-eyed family.

"Move!" the man said, grabbing his wife's arm on the way past.

Elizabeth, Sean, Jarrod, and the guardsmen stood shoulder to shoulder, watching as they rushed into the house and began dragging out belongings.

"Keep a close eye on him," Elizabeth said to Jarrod. "Let us know if he drags out your belongings."

"Thank you, Your Grace," Jarrod said. "It's quite all right. We took everything of value when we left. We won't use what he leaves behind."

Fifteen minutes later, the man, sitting on weather beaten cart, pulled out of the farm. Their belongings had been carelessly tossed into the back. The woman sat beside him, rigidly straight, steadfastly refusing to look at them. The girl stared at them, wide eyed, and the man glared at Elizabeth with a breathtaking level of hatred in his eyes.

Elizabeth watched until the cart became a spec at the end of the dirt road. She turned to Jarrod. "Do you mind if we stay here tonight? I want to be sure he doesn't come back tonight."

"Of course, Your Grace," Jarrod said. "What's mine is yours. I'm not sure how much hospitality I can offer you, though."

"Well. Let's go and look." Elizabeth walked toward the house. "When do you expect your wife to return?"

"She's to return at sunset with Farrow," Jarrod said. "He's the leader of the farmers in the hills."

"Good," Elizabeth said. "I need you all to come and defend the land I give back to you. I'm sure our good farmer friend will return and he'll be with men wearing armor and carrying crossbows."

Jarrod nodded. "I hope you're wrong, Your Grace."

"So do I," Elizabeth said.

She put her hand on the door latch and Sean cut in front of her.

"My apologies, Your Grace," he said. "Better let me go first."

"Sean, I'm perfectly capable of defending myself," Elizabeth said.

"Your Grace, you're a straw target who can swing a sword," he said, pushing the door open and entering the house.

Elizabeth gaped after him. *I hadn't considered that. I could very well be a straw target for Osk and Sandcliff now.*

She went into the house and blinked at the lower lighting levels. She looked at Jarrod. "They were neat at least."

Jarrod nodded, and she followed his gaze toward the swept floor, the clean windows, and the polished table. The banister of the stairs that led to the upper floor looked as though it'd been recently replaced.

Jarrod looked sad as he gazed at it. "My grandfather would be sorry to see that."

Elizabeth nodded, not knowing what else to say. "My men and I will make ourselves comfortable in your barn."

Jarrod looked scandalized. "The Duchess of Manusk in my *barn*? Rebecca would kill me as a boor."

"And I would defend your honor, Jarrod," Elizabeth said. "Maybe you should accustom yourself to your house before we trample all over it. Besides, we'll need to leave early to return to the city tomorrow. I'll leave four of my guards behind. I have to send out an official with the record of who holds all the titles to the land in this area. You must all have a roof over your heads and food in your bellies."

Jarrod bowed low. "Thank you, Your Grace."

"Sean, take a guard and search the house from top to bottom. We'll bed the horses down."

"Yes, Your Grace," Sean said.

Elizabeth left the house with the remaining guards behind her. The horses hadn't strayed far and it was easy to round them up again and lead them toward the barn.

One of the guardsmen pulled the barn doors open, and Elizabeth led them inside.

"Plenty of hay, at least," Jarrod said, materializing beside her and peering into the barn. "Also plenty of places to put them."

The barn had ten horse stalls in it and a wide hayloft above. There was also a stall for a cow and a small opening in the wall for chickens to go into an outside chicken run. Both of the latter were empty.

"Make yourself comfortable, Your Grace," Jarrod said. "I'm going to go and get Rebecca and Farrow."

"Early?"

"I think my wife'd like to see her house in daylight," he said.

"I'm sure she would."

"Well," Jarrod said, giving her a bow. "If you'll excuse me, Your Grace, I'll take my leave of you." He straightened and looked at the guardsmen at her shoulder. "There's a well behind the barn for water and a yard if you want to stretch out and relax."

"Thank you," the guardsmen said, sketching him a quick salute.

Jarrod walked off into the corn fields, tossing off a careless wave in his wake.

"I'll take care of your horse," the guardsman said, gently extracting the reins from her hand.

Elizabeth smiled at him. "I could do that, you know."

"I know, Your Grace," the guardsman said with a quick bow. "But I like horses and I think yours is a beauty." He gently scratched the mare's nose and she nudged him. "Of course I'll give you something."

Elizabeth patted her horse's neck. "I can see she's in good hands." She shook her head at the mare nudging the guardsman again. "You're a little strumpet aren't you?" The horse turned and gave her a reproachful look. She held up her hands. "Sorry. I'll just leave you two alone, then."

She made her way toward the back of the barn, to the sunlight she could see outside the rear door. Outside was a wide, open area, covered in thick, green grass. A fire pit stood close to the middle with a long table with benches on either side. Easily twenty people could sit around it.

Elizabeth nodded and went back into the barn, almost immediately finding the ladder to the hayloft. She climbed up it and saw fragrant piles of hay and large, golden dust motes circling lazily in the warm air. For a few seconds her head pounded with exhaustion, and the heat of the day made her feel thick and heavy.

"Your Grace," a voice said from below her.

She looked down. The guardsman stood below her, holding up her saddle bags.

"I'll bet it's comfortable up there," he said as she came down.

"Like heaven," she said.

"Is there enough room for all of us?"

"More than enough," she said, taking her saddlebags off him, slinging them over her shoulder, and beginning to climb again. "Wake me up when Jarrod returns."

"Yes, Your Grace," the guardsman said.

As soon as she reached the loft, she dropped her saddle bags, tossed down the blanket, and collapsed onto it with an exhausted sigh. Drowsiness overtook her and she drifted off to sleep.

ELIZABETH FELT HER shoulder being shaken and she forced her gritty eyes open.

"I'm awake," she muttered. She peered up at Sean, blinking her stinging eyes.

"I apologize, Your Grace, but Jarrod and Rebecca are coming down the road. They have a group of . . . friends with them."

Elizabeth heard his hesitation and sat up, wincing at her pounding headache.

"Are you all right, Your Grace?" Sean asked, eyeing her, concerned.

"I'm fine. Just a little tired." Elizabeth forced herself to her feet, she made her way back toward the ladder, and climbed down it with Sean close behind her.

"Right," she said as she strode toward the front of the stables. "Time to go and meet them."

Sean followed her as she left the barn. She raised her eyebrows. Sean had not been exaggerating. Jarrod had brought a group of about twenty people with him, mixed men and women, young and middle aged, the oldest looking close to fifty.

They stopped before her. Jarrod and Rebecca bowed low, the others a second or so behind and more awkward.

A tall man, close to Sean's six-foot-five height, took a step toward her and held out his forearm. Elizabeth studied him for a moment before taking it. He had dark eyes and a weather-beaten face, with deep creases carved into the grey stubble around his mouth. His hair was dark but lapsed into iron grey around the temples. His old shirt was clean and neatly patched.

"Duchess Elizabeth," he said in a deep and melodious voice. "I am Farrow. Beside me you see my daughter, Mia, and my wife, Heather."

Mia and Heather curtseyed.

Mia was almost Elizabeth's height with her father's dark eyes and her beautiful mother's blonde hair. She eyed Elizabeth up and down, lingering on her eyes, her face, and then her breasts.

Elizabeth felt her nipples stiffen and struggled to remain expressionless. *Oh, she's a lovely little thing. Very tasty.*

Heather also eyed Elizabeth, but her gaze was more speculative and skeptical.

"Well met, Farrow," Elizabeth said. She smiled at Mia and Heather. "Well met to you both as well."

"We have brought some food with us," Farrow said, and one of the men beside him held up a string of gutted and skinned rabbits. "Let's eat and talk."

Elizabeth smiled at him. "With pleasure."

Farrow handed the string to Mia, and she disappeared toward the farmhouse, with one last quick, interested look at Elizabeth. The younger women quickly followed her.

"Let's go and make ourselves comfortable in the yard," Jarrod said, taking Rebecca's hand. She resisted a moment but he gently pulled her closer to him. "Come," he murmured. "Please."

Rebecca nodded and they silently went through the barn and out into the shadowed grassy area behind it. They all assembled around the table. Elizabeth's guardsmen threw logs into the fire pit and lit it. They stayed around it, listening closely to the conversation at the banquet table.

Jarrod gestured for Elizabeth to take the head of the table but she shook her head. "I'm only a guest, Jarrod."

Jarrod gave her a genuine smile and sat down at the head of the table, Rebecca to his right and Elizabeth and Sean to his left. Farrow sat opposite them, together with Heather and the other farmers that had come back with him.

Mia returned from the farm house with pitchers of cool, clear water. She leaned against Elizabeth, her breasts brushing against her shoulder.

"Would Your Grace like some water?" she asked.

"Yes," Elizabeth said. She lifted her cup and looked into Mia's dark eyes.

"Thank you," she said as Mia filled her cup.

Mia smiled. "You're welcome, Your Grace."

She filled everyone's cups with water.

Jarrod stood and held up his cup. "I propose a toast. To working our land again."

The others took up the toast. Elizabeth drained her cup dry, enjoying the sensation of the cool, sweet water trickling down her throat. Her cup was immediately refilled by Rebecca.

"This is magnificent," Elizabeth said, taking another deep swallow.

"It's only water," Farrow said, watching her.

"Water is life," Elizabeth said. "It's always better than the most expensive wine."

"You don't drink wine?"

"Not very often. Leading men into battle requires sobriety."

Farrow nodded. "Is that what you want us to do? Go to war for you?"

"No," Elizabeth said. "I want you to grow food to feed Manusk."

"And that's all."

"That's all."

Farrow studied her carefully. "My family and I have made a life for ourselves out in the hills. There are others with us and we are all free. We are a community and a family. Why would we want to come back under your control?"

Elizabeth thought for a moment, not having expected an answer like that. "Doesn't it bother you that your land was simply taken off you?"

"Of course it bothers us," Heather said exchanging a glance with Farrow. "But it's gone and we're not. Now, at least, we do not have to go hungry from the taxes forced from us."

"So you think I'm going to tax you to death, do you?" Elizabeth asked.

Farrow and Heather stared at her.

Elizabeth sighed. "All right. You realize you are all still registered as the owners of your land. If you really don't want it, I require you to sell it back to me so I can pass it on to new owners. I can't have these lands lying idle. I have a city of hungry mouths to feed."

"You never answered about the taxes," Heather said.

"I didn't think I needed to answer such a discourteous comment," Elizabeth said. "*Of course* I'm not going to tax you to death."

They stared at her.

"What would it possibly achieve? My guardsmen are paid by the king. I have no need for the latest fashions, to throw outrageously expensive balls or lavish gifts on favorites." She leaned forward and stared into Farrow's eyes. "I am an honorable person. I look after my own." She fell silent for a moment, trying to rein in her temper. "Now, I ask you again. If you don't want your land back then come to this farm in two days time and my land scribe will have you sign the deed over to me. You will be compensated."

Farrow stared at her. He glanced at Jarrod and gave both he and Rebecca a broad grin. "You're right, old friend. She *is* different." He turned to Elizabeth. "Not necessary, Your Grace. I am your man and I would appreciate your help in getting my land back."

Elizabeth allowed her heart rate to return to normal. She forcibly relaxed her hands that were resting in her lap. "Thank you, Farrow. I now have some further questions for you. First, where is your farm? We will go there tomorrow and take it back for you."

"My farm is the next one over," Farrow said. "Like this one, no armed guards. Just a man and his woman."

"We'll go at dawn."

Farrow regarded her. "You said you had two questions. What's the second?"

"Will you help me take back Manusk?" she asked.

Farrow and Heather exchanged a glance. She nodded and he turned back to Elizabeth.

He leaned forward with his forearms resting on the edge of the table. "What do you want us to do?"

"Do you know how to fight? With a sword? Or quarterstaff? Bow? Crossbow?"

Farrow snorted a laugh and a smile played about his lips. "My father was a guardsman in Manusk before he went to farming. He made sure he taught me his skills. I've been teaching those with me to do the same."

Elizabeth gave him a broad grin. "Excellent. I have a small problem, however. My guardsmen are spread dangerously thin and I am not as well able to defend the highways and the farms as I'd like. I have to bring in more troops, but I need the ones I have to do it."

"You want us to help take back the farms and watch over them?" Heather said. "Rebecca and Jarrod told us you want us to be your militia. Yes, Your Grace. We'll be your militia."

"Thank you," Elizabeth said, bowing her head. "I'll need regular reports from you on how the farm reclamation and your planting are going. I'll accept word, but you are always welcome in person at my table. I'm usually there at six o'clock each evening, in the kitchen of my house."

"*Kitchen?*" Heather said.

"My house is a disgrace," Elizabeth said apologetically. "It needs a great deal of work. But that doesn't matter. As long as we have a place to eat and sleep we're doing well."

Farrow, Jarrod, Rebecca, and Heather exchanged glances with the other farmers at the table. They all threw their heads back and slapped the table, roaring laughter as though they'd heard the best joke of all time.

"Did I say something funny?" Elizabeth asked, glancing from face to face.

"No, lass," Jarrod said, clapping her on the shoulder and refilling her cup. "It just sounds very familiar, that's all. When we were first cast out of our homes and began to gather together to make a new home for ourselves, that's what we said to each other."

"You can tell we're all from Manusk," Elizabeth said.

They all gave her a questioning look.

"A tent looks like a castle to all of us now."

They burst out laughing again, and held up their cups.

"Manusk!" they cried.

"Manusk," Elizabeth replied, grinning and taking another swallow of water that tasted better than anything else in her entire life

CHAPTER 8

ELIZABETH OPENED HER mouth in a bone-cracking yawn. "I'm sorry." She waved a hand. "It's been a long day." The sun had long gone down and they'd feasted on stew and fresh bread. She felt pleasantly full and drowsy.

"Nothing to forgive, Your Grace," Jarrod said. "And I know you have an early start tomorrow morning."

"Thank you," Elizabeth said, standing and bowing. "You set an excellent table, Jarrod and Rebecca."

Everyone around the table also stood.

"Thank you, Your Grace," Rebecca said with a pleased smile and a curtsey. She frowned. "You can't really be serious about sleeping in the hayloft? We could easily give you a bed in our house."

"It's fine. Your barn is heavenly, believe me. And I'm sure you want to sample your own clean sheets this evening."

Rebecca sighed blissfully. "I can't deny that, Your Grace."

"Good night, everyone," Elizabeth said, backing away from the table and heading toward the barn.

Most of her guardsmen had fallen asleep around the fire pit and no one had the heart to wake them and get them to their bedrolls. Sean volunteered to take first watch and was sitting with them.

Elizabeth went into the barn and climbed the ladder to the hayloft. She loosened the laces on her shirt and lay back on her blankets with a sigh. This was the softest bed she'd slept in since their last night on the road before entering Manusk.

She heard a rustle from the hay and turned around to track it.

A silhouette came toward her, Mia, and Elizabeth sat up.

Well, well, well. She eyeing Mia's curves appreciatively.

Mia put a gentle hand over her mouth and pushed her back down again. Elizabeth grinned.

A while later, Elizabeth, boneless, lay in Mia's arms for a few moments until she felt Mia shift and pull away from her. She watched as Mia sat up, pulled on her blouse, and straightened her skirt.

Mia flashed a smile, blew a kiss to Elizabeth, and quietly descended the ladder back down to the barn.

Elizabeth pulled on her shirt and breeches.

She felt wonderfully relaxed as she lay back down in the hay, and she fell deeply asleep seconds later, a smile playing about her lips.

"YOUR GRACE, IT'S time," Sean said, gently shaking Elizabeth awake.

Elizabeth opened her eyes, blinking. Her terrible, pounding headache had receded and her eyes felt heavy but didn't sting as badly as before.

"I'm awake, Sean," she said.

"Bucket waiting for you below," he said, backing away and climbing back down the ladder.

Elizabeth felt her face heat at her sudden memory of Mia. Even rudimentary bathing seemed like a good idea.

She straightened her clothing and slung the blanket over her shoulder. She followed Sean down the ladder.

Twenty minutes later, Elizabeth flicked her wet hair out of her face and mounted her charger. She held out her arm and helped Farrow to mount behind her.

"Thank you, Your Grace," he said as she nudged her horse into motion.

"You said you were the next farm over, yes?" Elizabeth asked.

"Yes, Your Grace," he said.

They lapsed into a comfortable silence as they made their way down the dirt road from Jarrod's farm. Jarrod and Rebecca stood outside, waving to them. Elizabeth and her guardsmen returned it with a grin.

"You also said there were no armed guards on your farm?" Elizabeth asked.

"No," Farrow said. "I don't think everyone's land is like that, though."

"How do you mean?"

"We saw a large number of armed men coming into and out of Felson's farm house about an hour's ride from here. That one's going to be hard to get back, although I didn't even know it'd been lost until we saw all the armor."

Elizabeth felt a warning bell go off inside her mind. "It's probably being used by the troops as a home base."

"Probably," Farrow said, sounding as unconvinced as she felt.

"Why did you think it hadn't fallen?" she asked.

"Felson is the master of that land and he and his haven't joined us."

"Is that something I should worry about?"

"No. Yes. I don't know."

"Why don't you keep an eye on the farm and let me know if I should be concerned about anything other than it being a base for armed troops."

"Yes, Your Grace."

They lapsed into silence.

Twenty minutes later they were riding up the dirt road toward Jarrod's homestead. The layout of the dooryard was similar to Jarrod and Rebecca's land but there any similarity ended.

The house looked as though it'd been covered in mud and dust. Paint peeled off it and the hinges on the door and windows leaked rust in a long, russet runner down the sides of the house. The barn looked worse. The doors were half off their hinges and held closed with a hank of fraying rope.

"Oh my god," Elizabeth muttered, wrinkling her nose. "What the devil is that stench?"

"I think that's coming from the barn, Your Grace," Sean said in a strangled voice.

Elizabeth looked at him. He looked pale and his jaw worked.

"What have they done to my damn house?" Farrow said, sliding off the back of Elizabeth's horse.

"I don't think you want to know," Elizabeth said, sliding off behind him.

She looked at Sean and then signaled one of the other guardsmen. She strode toward the house, straightening her riding gloves and breathing shallowly.

They reached the door and Elizabeth drew her sword. She pounded on the door with the hilt and the booming sound echoed throughout the house.

They heard running footsteps coming toward the door and enough cursing for Elizabeth and the guardsmen to frown at one another.

The door flew open and a dirty man stood in stained clothing, his slovenly wife cowering behind him.

He opened his mouth to speak, his breath wafting over to them.

Elizabeth held up her hand. "I am Elizabeth St. John, Duchess of Manusk. You are on this land illegally. Leave. Right now."

"You have no right," the man snarled.

Elizabeth jabbed the point of her sword into his chest, nicking it and drawing blood. "Out. Now."

The man opened his mouth again but as his eyes took in her expression, he closed it with a snap. Elizabeth growled and he ran out of the house and down the dirt road without looking back, his wife close on his heels.

Elizabeth watched them go and gestured at the remaining guardsmen. "Stay here. I'll send out the land scribe today. You can accompany him as he evicts more squatters."

She was greeted with a chorus of, "Yes, Your Grace."

She turned to Farrow. "I expect you won't be thanking us for this. Do you want us to burn all this down?"

"Tempting," Farrow said. "But I think Heather would kill me."

"I'm not sure she won't kill you for leaving it standing."

Farrow snorted a laugh. "I'm sure you're right, Your Grace." He held out his hand. "Thank you, Your Grace. You are welcome anytime you come this way."

"Thank you, Farrow," Elizabeth said. She headed back toward her horse, Sean straight behind her. "I have to go and find out what trouble the city has managed to get itself into while I was away."

"We'll see you soon, Your Grace," Farrow said.

Elizabeth mounted and tipped him a salute. She pushed her charger into a trot back toward the highway.

THE SUN HAD crossed the sky past its midpoint and was well on the way to setting again when Elizabeth and Sean finally reached the soldier's checkpoint. As they approached, Elizabeth noted with interest the extra blankets and rations that had accumulated around their fire.

"Corporal," she said as the guardsmen stood up and saluted her.

"Your Grace," the corporal said. "The road has been quiet and we've seen neither hide nor hair of any Osk or Sandcliff men."

Elizabeth nodded. "Good."

The corporal indicated their extra supplies. "These came from the good people of Manusk, Your Grace. They are pleased you're trying to help them."

Elizabeth smiled. "Excellent. What are they saying?"

The corporal exchanged a glance with his fellow guardsmen, some of whom were trying to smother smiles. Elizabeth raised an eyebrow.

"We've had people asking us if it's true you rode in with fifty of us and slaughtered every Osk and Sandcliff man, woman, and child within fifty miles."

"Bloodthirsty," Elizabeth said, rolling her eyes. Why did they invent such a ridiculous rumor when all she'd done was clear out an illegal checkpoint?

"Another question we've been asked is if you really rode in on a winged chariot and destroyed the checkpoint to demonstrate the wrath of the gods against Osk and Sandcliff."

Elizabeth gaped. *Just when I thought I'd heard everything.*

Sean snorted a laugh.

She fished for a reply as the men caught each other's eyes and began a deep belly laugh.

"Either way, we now have spare food and blankets to thank us for our protection of the good citizens of Manusk," the corporal said when their laughter died down.

"Very good, corporal," she said. "Please continue." She waved a hand.

They rode on to the city, passing travelers on the road who stared at them. After several hours, they finally reached the western gate.

She saw several figures waiting for them. As they got closer, she could see Peter, Mark, Marcus, and Daniel standing behind them.

"Peter, this is a surprise," Elizabeth said as she dismounted.

"Your Grace," Peter said, bowing.

"Is everything quiet in the city?"

"About as quiet as this place gets," Peter said, exchanging a glance with Mark.

Sean quietly took the reins out of Elizabeth's hand and they walked through the city toward her house.

"Were you waiting for us?" Elizabeth asked.

"Yes, Your Grace," Peter said. "I have some news for you."

"Good or bad?"

"I don't know," Peter said slowly. "Do you remember a few days ago the report that our guardsmen had been killed during the course of the incident with the signal fire?"

"How could I forget that?" Elizabeth asked.

"Well, in keeping with your orders to find the missing sailors, we've inspected the city prison and the hospitals. They're not there," he said. "While we were looking we ran into the bodies of the guardsmen that were killed. We don't recognize any of them, Your Grace. Neither does Captain Herbert."

Elizabeth frowned and thought for a moment. "You're certain they're not ours?"

"No, Your Grace, they're not ours."

"If they're not ours, whose are they?"

"We don't know, Your Grace."

"The uniforms. Are they from our guardsmen or are they forgeries?"

"I'm not sure, Your Grace."

"Then I suggest we find out. Take me to these bodies."

"The bodies have already been burned, Your Grace," Peter said. "But I think the uniforms have been removed. Standard practice."

"Do we normally keep the clothes from dead bodies, Peter?" Elizabeth asked with a grimace.

"Only if they have effects that need to be returned to their families, Your Grace. You know that."

Elizabeth nodded. "Where are the uniforms?"

"They're back in our makeshift barracks," Peter said.

"Well, we go there first, then."

They continued to the manor house and Elizabeth's mind churned. *If those soldiers weren't mine, then whose were they? The most logical choice is Osk or Sandcliff, but what's to be gained by extinguishing the signal fires? Unless they thought I'd come in by sea. Osk and Sandcliff could never be that naïve. My father sent me to take Manusk. The quickest route is by land and they have to know that. No, the extinguished signal fires weren't for me. Were they for Rowan?*

She turned that over in her mind for a moment. *That doesn't seem likely either. What's to be gained by killing the crown princess of a foreign nation that has no ties to the King's Heartland? It seems doubly unlikely because it'd mean that they'd have to have known Rowan would come into Manusk.*

That *was* likely, however.

If Osk and Sandcliff took the sailors from the trader, then perhaps they'd told their captors that Rowan would sail in if the trader went missing?

Elizabeth felt her blood run cold.

"Peter," Elizabeth said. "Do we know how often the signal fires weren't lit?"

"I don't know, Your Grace," Peter said after a moment's thought. "Mark? Do you know anything about the signal fires at the mouth of Manusk Harbor?"

"Yes, Lieutenant," Mark said. "It wasn't the first time. It's a problem that's been plaguing us for months. The merchants know when there's a valuable shipment due in for the King's Heartland. They go out, extinguish the signal fires and the ship is wrecked on the rocks. The traders send out their mercenaries to do some illegal salvaging and they sell what they find on the black market."

Elizabeth shook her head. "What happens to the people who survive the ship wrecks?"

"Who said there were any survivors?" Mark asked.

Elizabeth frowned. "Peter, please see that the signal fires stay lit." She felt some fleeting relief that ship wrecks weren't part of some larger conspiracy, but it was mixed with anger that innocent people had been slaughtered to satisfy someone's greed.

They reached the courtyard to the manor house and Elizabeth stopped and looked up at the roof in surprise. "Did someone fix my roof?"

"Yes, Your Grace," Peter said with a grin. "Her Imperiousness began hounding the carpenters yesterday. We're running out of space on the lower floors to house people." He gave her a sheepish grin. "It looks like your people are starting to actually believe we're here to help."

"As long as we can feed them I'm fine. Do you know where Her Im-*Highness* is now?"

Peter smothered his laugh with a cough. "I think she went to the North Gate this morning. She wanted to meet the city watch."

Elizabeth pulled him to a halt and looked him in the eyes. She raised an eyebrow. "Am I to believe that you're allowing a crown princess from a nation with no ties to us free run of our city? An unescorted stroll through places that could be *very* dangerous, not to mention ones we'd rather not have her see?"

Peter leaned forward. "Your Highness, I think you can trust her. She met with her people yesterday morning, as arrogant as the day was long, but come the midday meal, was as meek as a lamb. I think you'll want to speak to her and soon."

Elizabeth took a deep breath, shoving down irritation, and nodded. "I'll do as you suggest, Peter." She nodded toward the house. "I'll look at the uniforms tomorrow. What time is it?"

"It's close to five, Your Grace."

"All right. I'm going to go and bathe and change my clothes. Can you see to it that the land scribe comes to dinner this evening?"

Peter bowed low, Mark, Marcus, and Daniel following suit. "Yes, Your Grace."

He turned and walked away, Mark, Marcus, and Daniel in tow.

Elizabeth strode into her house through a foyer bustling with peasants and guardsmen, and up a new set of main stairs to the upper corridor. The doors to both rooms of survivors were open and she glanced in each one as she strode past. There seemed to be more people sitting up and some of the beds were empty. The servants in each of the rooms went from bed to bed attending to the needs of the survivors.

Elizabeth strode into her room, and Mara jumped away from the window.

"Hello," Elizabeth said, feeling a little surprised. "What are you doing here?"

"Princess Rowan asked that I return here at five," Mara replied with an awkward curtsey, refusing to meet Elizabeth's eyes.

"Oh, all right," Elizabeth said. "Look, while you're here, could you please ask Harriet if I could get some water for my bath and fresh clothes?"

"Yes, Your Grace," Mara replied, bobbing another of her awkward curtseys.

Elizabeth watched her scurry out of the room. *My presence upsets her a great deal. I'd have thought she'd be a little used to me by now.*

Elizabeth went to the window and looked out at Manusk Harbor. There were different ships at the dock, and it bustled with people and sailors. A cluster of people were gathered around the entrance to the import hall.

It looks like our enforced licensing laws are making things interesting for the harbor master. I must ask Richard how trading is going.

It'd only been a day since she'd put the guardsmen in place, but she hoped it was enough to stop the intentional scuttling of ships and the lucrative—and highly illegal—salvage trade that had been booming, unnoticed by the king, in Manusk.

I wonder how long it's going to take before Gilbert of Osk and Clayton of Sandcliff come knocking on my door? We must be ready for them when they do.

A knock sounded on the door.

"Enter," she called.

The door opened and Mara came in, leading a column of servants carrying buckets of steaming water. Elizabeth looked down at herself and sighed. *I wonder if Harriet will make good on her threat to bring frilly dresses? Could I legally execute someone for that?* She shuddered.

She sat on the hearthstones and pulled off her boots. She was untying the laces of her shirt as the servants filed out. She strode into the bathing chamber, shedding her clothes, and slipped into the water with a sigh.

It was warm and inviting and she leaned back, closing her eyes and letting her mind drift. *I just need to rest for a minute,* she thought, the warm water lulling her toward sleep.

She felt a hand gently shaking her shoulder and her eyes fluttered open. She fuzzily became aware of two things. First, her bath water was tepid. Second, Rowan's arms rested on the sides of the tub and her beautiful mouth was curved into an amused smile.

"Welcome back, Your Grace," Rowan said softly.

Elizabeth was suddenly uncomfortably aware of her lack of clothing and felt her face heat. "Your Highness."

"You know you're expected for dinner, Elizabeth?" Rowan said.

"I know," Elizabeth said. "I suppose I'd better get out of my bath then, hadn't I?"

"Yes," Rowan said. "I suppose you should."

Elizabeth stared at her for a moment, struggling to control her heated features. "Are you going to let me get out of my tub?"

"I'm not stopping you."

"Dammit, do you normally interrupt privacy or is this just for me?"

"It's just for you," Rowan said, with a smirk. She levered herself to her feet, winced, and clutched at her side.

Elizabeth got up and out of the tub, all thoughts of her state of undress vanishing. She caught Rowan before her knees could buckle.

"Sit down, will you?" Elizabeth said, pushing her clothes off the stool with a foot and guiding Rowan down. "You can tease me about all of this later."

She grabbed a towel and quickly dried herself, then pulled on her clean clothes and knelt to check on Rowan.

"Show me your stitches." She tugged at Rowan's shirt and Rowan pulled it out of her breeches, revealing her flat, muscular stomach. There was a wicked, half healed wound under her rib cage. It leaked blood.

"You really should have a bandage on this," Elizabeth said, touching the cool skin.

Rowan flinched back. "I know. I should. But I don't want one on there. It's restricting my movement."

"And what, exactly, were you planning on doing? Dancing? Climbing? Acrobatics?" Elizabeth said, exasperated.

"Sparring," Rowan said softly, glancing at her. "Sparring, if you must know."

"What in God's name for?"

"Someone has to teach your people to fight."

Elizabeth stared at her.

"The first of your farmers came in today, looking for you," Rowan said. "The only one of your officers available was Herbert. He told me what you'd promised your farmers. I helped him teach."

"Rowan," Elizabeth said softly. "I appreciate the help but I think it's a very bad idea for you to be involved in my problems. What will your countrymen do if something happens to you?"

Rowan's mouth tightened. "It won't be pretty." She sighed. "I have to ask you, formally, as the crown princess of a foreign sovereign power, if you would consider entering diplomatic negotiations with us?"

"You want us to talk about the treaty that you wanted before the disaster with both your ships began?" Elizabeth asked.

"That's exactly what I'm talking about."

"Why?" Elizabeth asked. "I can't formally accept, since I'm merely a representative of the king, not the king himself."

"You may not be able to sign the treaty but you can say yes to it. If you say yes we could honor it in principle by our law. It would be non binding by both sides at an agreed date. In the meantime, I would be legally able help you."

"Helping me is probably only going to be a death sentence for you," Elizabeth said quietly.

"I understand the risks, Elizabeth," Rowan said with some asperity. She gazed steadily at Elizabeth for a moment or so. "Let's talk after dinner."

"All right," Elizabeth said, helping Rowan to her feet. "We will."

Rowan stood for a moment, wincing a little and favoring her injured side. Elizabeth led the way back into the bed chamber and sat heavily on the hearthstones. She pulled her boots on. "I have to ask. What brought you into the bathing chamber anyway? Weren't expecting me back?"

Rowan sat on the window sill, gazing out. She turned back to Elizabeth with a smirk. "Maybe I was."

"Well, I'm here again."

Rowan was spared answering by a knock on the door.

"Enter," Elizabeth called.

Mara appeared in the doorway and dropped into one of her now familiar awkward curtseys. "You're expected downstairs, Your Grace."

"We're on our way," Elizabeth said with an encouraging smile.

Mara backed out and closed the door.

"Are you going to join us?" Elizabeth asked.

"I wouldn't miss this for the world," Rowan said, levering herself up with a wince.

"After you, Your Highness," Elizabeth said, opening the door and gesturing for Rowan to go through first.

"Thank you, Elizabeth," Rowan said.

Once they were in the corridor, Rowan offered Elizabeth her arm, much to Elizabeth's surprise. She took it.

"Is this a custom in your country?" Elizabeth asked, gesturing at their linked arms.

"I'll let you decide for yourself, Your Grace," Rowan said with a broad grin.

Rowan carefully led Elizabeth back toward the stairs, then down and to the kitchen.

Guests waited for them around the main table. Rowan brought Elizabeth to the head of the table and took the seat to her right. Isengard, with a bow to Elizabeth, sat beside Rowan. Herbert, Richard, and Peter sat to Elizabeth's left. A birdlike man with sharp eyes sat next to Isengard, and rough-looking peasants on the other sides of Peter and the man.

"Good evening, everybody," Elizabeth said with a cheerful grin. "I know some faces—Herbert, Richard, Peter, Princess Rowan, and Isengard, it's good to see you. You others I don't know." She looked at them with a politely raised eyebrow.

"My name is Petris, Your Grace. I am your land scribe," the birdlike man with sharp eyes said.

"Hello, Petris," Elizabeth said. "You're just the person I wanted to see."

"Thank you, Your Grace," Petris said, inclining his head. "I must admit I'm puzzled as to why you asked me here."

"I'll address your questions and concerns in a moment, Petris. I have a feeling that the other ladies and gentlemen at the table would also like to introduce themselves. I think they're especially pleased to see you, Petris."

The peasants finally seemed to break from the awkwardness they were afflicted with and quickly introduced themselves. There were four more farmers and their wives, a thatcher, and a tax collector.

"Have all of you been driven off your land by armed guards and had your land seized unlawfully?" Elizabeth asked when they were done.

"Yes—"

"Sandcliff bastards—"

"—in my family for generations—"

All the peasants talked at once, and Elizabeth held up her hand for silence.

"In a moment, in a moment. Petris," she said, and took a bite of the stew that'd been put before her. "The problem is this. As you've just heard, these ladies and gentlemen have had their farms seized because of unpaid taxes. The farms were given away by the state to other peasants."

"Which is entirely illegal," Petris said, daintily wiping the corners of his mouth. "However, I feel obliged to point out a small item of law. You realize that these farms have always been officially owned by the people you see before you? However, they haven't paid any *genuine* taxes since their land was seized. Therefore, they really *are* in arrears and the farms return to you, Your Grace."

The peasants paled and looked set to argue but Elizabeth again held up her hand. "I'm giving everyone's farms back, free of any alleged incurred debts. We're now in a period of amnesty, if this time needs a label." She turned to the peasants. "All I ask in return is a portion of your crops as taxes. Your taxes will be considered paid in full. New taxes will be discussed next planting season."

"Thank you, Your Grace, that would be wonderful," one large, hulking man said, his carriage stiff. He held onto his spoon as though he'd never used one before in his entire life.

"All right. In keeping with this amnesty, Petris, I need you to send out your assistant land scribes with proof that the seized land is owned by someone other that whoever is currently squatting on it. My guards will go out with your assistants and these farmers and they will enforce your word. Also, you'll find that my militia will be at each of these farms and they will also see to it that your assistants travel unmolested and in peace. I expect you'll need a day to organize yourself. I'll send Sean to you tomorrow morning with the first places I need you to go. Is this agreeable to you?"

Petris gave her a broad grin and she saw his sharp mind working behind his shrewd eyes. "Yes, Your Grace. I'm sure we can restore some form of order."

"Thank you. That would be wonderful." She turned to the farmers. "Now, gentlemen. Are all of you here from Jarrod?"

"We are," another narrow-faced man said. "He tells us that you're good with a sword, Your Grace, and that you wanted a challenge. We're here to cross blades with you."

Elizabeth smiled. "I always love a good challenge. Would tomorrow morning be good?"

"Yes, Your Grace," the man said, grinning at her.

"How much fighting experience have you had?"

"I used to be in the guardsmen of Manusk," one peasant said.

"So did I," another said.

"I'm good at brawling in inns," another man said and they all laughed.

"I'm good with a pitchfork," a younger man said.

"That's going to become useful if we have to sling hay at our enemies," Elizabeth said and they all laughed again.

The conversation became more spirited and the kitchen had half emptied out by the time the farmers took their leave of her. Petris followed behind them, as he had to prepare for his assistants' journey in the morning.

That left Richard, Herbert, Peter, Isengard, and Rowan still at the table.

"Richard," Elizabeth said, sitting back and sipping at a cup of water. "How is it going at the docks?"

"Well, first the good news, Your Grace. Your traders are now in the import hall. Osk and Sandcliff are held firmly at bay. I have been asked by the traders of Manusk to offer our thanks to you for your efforts." He inclined his head and saluted her with a cup. "Almost all of the traders are willing to work with you to rebuild Manusk. We still have some holdovers but they will be made to see reason by the end of the week. Trade is also proceeding briskly, so there are goods finally entering the city of Manusk for the citizens. There are also goods on the way to the King's Heartland, with only the small matter of the collection points on the roads to deal with, which we leave in your capable hands."

Elizabeth gave him a broad, genuine smile. "Thank you, Richard. That's excellent news. The roads are on my list of things to work out next. Is there anything you need for me to do in the next day or so?"

"I would like you to take some time out and tour the import hall, if you could," Richard said. "Your Sergeant Hunter is an excellent officer and a talented representative but he's not you."

"I'll stop by after I've spent some time with our new farmers," she said.

"We would love to offer you lunch, Your Grace."

"I'd love to accept, Richard."

"Then we'll see you at midday tomorrow, Your Grace." Richard stood and bowed. "If you'll excuse me, Your Grace?"

"Of course. Have a good evening."

"You too, Your Grace." He bowed to Elizabeth's officers and visitors and left the kitchen.

Rowan watched him go and turned to Elizabeth. "I need to speak to you alone."

Elizabeth frowned. "Of course." She turned to her officers. "Is there any further business?"

"No, Your Grace," Herbert and Peter said together, exchanging a glance.

"Then good evening. I'll see you tomorrow morning."

They bowed and left. Isengard watched them go, and then stood and bowed to them both. "If you will excuse me, Your Highness, I'm a little tired and I'd like to call it an evening as well."

"Of course, Isengard," Rowan said.

Isengard saluted and strode out of the kitchen with an energy that belied his grey hair.

"We're alone," Elizabeth said. "What do you want to talk about?"

"I'd rather be upstairs. I need quiet."

"All right. Let's go."

Elizabeth stood, held out a hand for Rowan, and helped her to her feet with energy she didn't have to spare.

Rowan led the way back upstairs to Elizabeth's bed chamber. Mara was in there, turning down the bed covers.

"Do you want some hot chocolate?" Elizabeth asked.

"What is that?" Rowan asked.

"You've never had hot chocolate? That's criminal. We must remedy that at once." She motioned Mara to come closer. "Mara, please go and get us mugs of hot chocolate." She looked at Rowan. "Both with cream, I think."

"Yes, Your Grace," Mara said with a curtsey. She scurried out of the room.

Rowan watched her go and shook her head. "I've never seen a servant like her." She grinned at Elizabeth. "You seem to scare her. She becomes clumsy around you."

Elizabeth shook her head and rolled her eyes. "I'm lucky she's not a nose picking, pox ridden wretch. I'll put up with what I have from her."

Rowan laughed and gestured toward the window sill. "There's plenty of room to sit. The moon over the water is a beautiful sight."

Elizabeth nodded and they sat on the sill.

Elizabeth gave Rowan an expectant look. "What do you want to talk about?"

"We have to talk about the treaty. And I think you should tell me the unvarnished truth about why you're living the way you're living." Elizabeth opened her mouth to protest but Rowan held up her hand. "I've been in your city by myself for two days now. I've spoken to my own people and I've spoken to the residents of your city. Do you want to know what I've been hearing?"

Not really. She nodded.

"My people say you spent the night ministering to them a couple of days ago. They didn't know you were the ruler of this city and were surprised to find out. You're very unusual for a noble. Yes, I know, you're going to tell me you're nothing but a common soldier." She smiled. "They've listened to what your servants have said about you and your servants are loyal to you. You have earned the favor of my people as a fair and even tempered ruler." She stared into her eyes. "Early days, though, Elizabeth. My people are jaded with nobles."

Elizabeth remained silent, watching her.

"There are many rumors flying around the city about you. Half of the citizens consider you to be a black-eyed demon, the other a black-eyed goddess. Now, I ask you, which of these are you really?"

"It depends on who you are," Elizabeth said.

"Fair enough," Rowan said. "From what I've been able to gather, listening to the gossip in your kitchen, you really were telling me the truth when you said you arrived a few days ago. You are trying to gain control over this city, against the wishes of something called Osk and something called Sandcliff."

Elizabeth shook her head and snorted a laugh. "It sounds so simple when you say it like that."

Rowan watched her.

"Since I have little control over this city it's in your best interests to leave before Osk and Sandcliff retaliate for my driving their activities out of the city."

"I can't do that," Rowan said. "It would mean leaving some of my people behind in something that may become an armed conflict. A shipwreck is one thing but knowingly leaving people behind to die is quite another."

"No one said they would die. I'm not a monster." Elizabeth winced. "I *do* see your point—but you could leave them under my care. I would care for them as I care for my own. I would keep them safe until you could return for them."

"Rowan as a leader and a crown princess can't do that." Rowan sighed. "Who are Osk and Sandcliff?"

"Manusk, Osk, Sandcliff, and Coral Bay are the four duchies that make up the Southern Holdings of the King's Heartland. My grandfather was the Duke of Manusk and he was a cruel, greedy man. He taxed the citizens of Manusk almost to extinction and they revolted. He called in his friends, the Dukes of Osk and Sandcliff, borrowing their troops to quell the rebellion. They did so, moved in, and completely took over after my grandfather's death, despite a steward being appointed for Manusk."

"The peasants managed to kill your grandfather?"

"No, he was killed by the Duchess of Eagle's Reach during a duel."

Rowan frowned and stared at her.

"A matter of honor," Elizabeth said. "Nothing more than that."

"Why wasn't his son or daughter appointed to be the ruler of Manusk?" Rowan asked.

"His son wasn't an appropriate choice."

"Why?"

It has to come out sooner or later, I suppose. "Because his son—my father—inherited the title of Crown Prince after my grandfather died, and he wasn't in a position to be both a duke and a king."

Rowan's eyes widened and then narrowed in anger. "That would make you a princess, wouldn't it? Are you the crown princess as well?"

Elizabeth shook her head. "No, I'm just a princess. My brother, Gareth, is the crown prince."

"Were you planning on telling me this at any stage?" Rowan asked.

"What difference would it have made?" Elizabeth said, beginning to get angry. "Who cares if I'm a princess? All *that* does is lock me into a life of frills and vacuous conversation. I much rather prefer the life I have now. The world is mine and I'm not nailed to one small patch of land."

"Settling down isn't such a bad thing, Elizabeth." The fight abruptly went out of Rowan. "I suppose this simplifies things a little. You can certainly treat with us on behalf of your father. If you say yes, as a member of the royal family, it would be legally binding, the same as a signed treaty."

"What are the terms of the treaty?"

"Mutual military aid and trading, like I mentioned."

Elizabeth gave it a bare second of thought. *My father would want this.* "I accept on behalf of the king."

Rowan offered her forearm. "To seal our bargain."

Elizabeth accepted it. "To seal our bargain."

Mara stepped between them and put the hot chocolate on the window sill.

Elizabeth nodded thanks and gingerly lifted her steaming mug. She blew on it and sipped it. "This is wonderful. Take a sip." She glanced at Rowan. "You look like I'm asking you to drink a vial of poison, Your Highness. You want me to turn this into a diplomatic incident?"

Rowan shook her head and gamely took a sip. Her face lit up in surprised pleasure. "You're right. This is wonderful."

Elizabeth grinned and turned her attention back to Mara who stood frozen beside them. "That's all, Mara."

"Yes, Your Grace." Mara glanced at Rowan. "Does Your Highness need her bandages changed?"

"No," Rowan said.

"Yes." Elizabeth turned to Rowan. "You need that cut bound. If you really insist on not wearing bandages, do it tomorrow." She gestured toward the door. "Go and fetch the doctor," she said to Mara.

"The last time I looked I outrank you, Elizabeth," Rowan said, watching Mara scurry from the room.

"Not while you're under my roof and my guest," Elizabeth said.

"Is that some strange law or custom in your land?"

"No, it's just me being a battlefield commander."

"Ah," Rowan said, a smile playing about her lips. She was silent for a moment. "What are your plans for tomorrow?"

"You heard most of them at dinner," Elizabeth said. "I have sparring with my farmers in the morning. Lunch with Richard and the traders. After that, I have to meet with my lieutenant."

"Do you mind if I go with you?" Rowan asked, her tone making it clear that argument would be an uphill battle that Elizabeth would lose.

"Of course not," Elizabeth said.

There was a knock at the door.

"Enter," Elizabeth said.

The door opened and the doctor came into the room, holding his satchel, his shirt sleeves rolled to his elbows.

He stopped before Elizabeth and bowed low. "Your Grace."

"Doctor," Elizabeth said. "Would you mind taking a look at Her Highness's stitches? She's bleeding a little."

"Of course, Your Grace," the doctor said. He turned to Rowan and gestured toward the bed. "Please lie down and lift your shirt, Your Highness."

Rowan glared at Elizabeth and Elizabeth gave her a bland smile and shrugged. Rowan stretched out on the bed, carefully lifted her shirt, and winced.

The doctor bent over her and examined the cut closely. He shook his head. "I'm going to have to stitch this again."

Rowan rolled her eyes as the doctor pulled powder, ointment, and a needle out of his satchel.

The doctor glanced at Rowan. "I'll try to make this as painless as possible."

Rowan sighed. Her muscles were tense and she had paled. Elizabeth sat down on the bed beside her and took her hand. Her hand was clammy.

"Squeeze as hard as you like," Elizabeth said softly.

"I'm not a coward," Rowan said.

Elizabeth gave her a reproachful look. "No one said you were. What happens in this room stays in this room." She glanced at the doctor and nodded.

The doctor sprinkled powder on the cut and Rowan turned her head toward the window.

"What's Welland like?" Elizabeth asked.

Rowan grimaced as the needle pricked her skin and she drew in hissing breath. "It's a lush, green place with mountains and snow in winter. The sky is always blue and looks so big it's almost like it's the whole world. When the snows come, the white and grey clouds come over and the air changes. Cold is the time of festivals, so the air feels alive and friendly. The Winter Solstice is my favorite time of year."

Elizabeth smiled. "It sounds beautiful."

Rowan's beautiful blue eyes showed pain and her hand tightened in Elizabeth's.

"What is the Winter Solstice like?" Elizabeth asked. "What do you do?"

"The Winter Solstice is a celebration of life. We give thanks for the end of the war. My father holds the winter games," Rowan said. "A sleigh race through the mountain pass. I won two years in a row."

"Your father must have been proud of you."

"He *is* proud of me."

"What of your mother?"

"My mother is dead. She died early in the war." Rowan's face shadowed in pain.

"Done," the doctor said brightly, carefully rubbing ointment on the wound. "Your Grace, if you could help Her Highness sit up so I can bandage the wound?"

Elizabeth nodded, slipped an arm around Rowan's shoulders, and helped her sit up. Rowan hissed in pain.

The doctor pulled strips of cloth out of his satchel and wrapped them around Rowan's midsection. "I'll come back to change them tomorrow." He tied off the ends.

"Can't Elizabeth do it?" Rowan asked, glancing between them.

The doctor looked at Elizabeth and she nodded.

"Yes," he said. "Your Grace, not too tight, like so."

Elizabeth looked at the bandages. "I can do that."

"Excellent," the doctor said, standing and repacking his satchel. He bowed to both of them. "Your Highness."

"Thank you, doctor," Elizabeth said as he left. She turned back to Rowan. "It must have been hard for you, the war."

Rowan's bright blue gaze turned inward and she sighed heavily. "Yes, it was terrible. I lost my mother early when my uncle deposed my father. She was killed when we tried to run. I was only five."

"How did you escape your uncle?"

"Do you normally ask so many questions?" Rowan asked, blue eyes flashing anger.

Elizabeth studied her. "I do. I must admit I find you interesting, Rowan of Welland."

"As interesting as I find you, Elizabeth of Manusk," Rowan said after a moment of frank study of Elizabeth. "You're very beautiful and I've never seen eyes as dark as yours. They're black, odd for someone with such fair skin."

Elizabeth felt her face heat. "You're pale. You should try and get some sleep."

"I am," Rowan said. "Are you going to stay on the hearth stones tonight? You don't have to. There's plenty of room in here."

Elizabeth smiled and shifted so she was on the bed beside Rowan. "Tell me about your father."

"My father is a wonderful man and a good father," Rowan said. "I love him dearly. Tell me about your family."

"My father's name is Vincent and my brother is Gareth. He's much older than me and we have different mothers. My mother died when I was young and my father and brother took care of me." She smiled, remembering herself as a little girl, running through the audience hall toward her brother—who looked as tall, dark, and strong as a mountain—who scooped her up with a grin and swung her around in a circle. "My brother taught me to ride and swing a sword. My father was horrified. My brother talked to him and convinced him to teach me how to be a good king."

"Does it bother you that you're not going to inherit the throne?"

Elizabeth raised her eyebrows. "*Of course* not. I like traveling from place to place. I can't think of any life more boring than to be stuck in a castle and pandering to spoilt nobles."

Rowan laughed softly. "I understand completely. It's not the life I want either and I'm lucky my father is happy for me to learn more about life and other countries before I settle down."

"Do you have any other brothers or sisters?"

"I have a younger sister. She's a brat," Rowan said. "Tell me more about your brother."

"My brother is as good a man as my father. I love him and I miss him. I'd like to see him after I have brought some stability to Manusk."

She heard a soft snore and looked down at Rowan. Rowan's face relaxed in sleep and as soon as Elizabeth tried to disentangle herself Rowan frowned and snuggled in closer to her.

Elizabeth settled back onto the pillows with a sigh. Her eyes closed and she drifted off to sleep.

CHAPTER 9

ELIZABETH SIGHED AS she slowly came to wakefulness, aware of warmth and light. She opened her eyes and sat up. She was still in bed and she was alone. She looked at the sunlight streaming in through the windows. The air still had the sting of cold in it, and she reasoned it was early.

She swung her legs over the side of the bed. *I can't believe I spent the night in my guest's bed, although I have to admit I feel the better for it.*

"Good morning, Your Grace," Mara said.

Elizabeth looked into the bright sunlight streaming into the window, framing Mara in a corona of light.

"Good morning, Mara," Elizabeth said. "Where's Her Highness?"

"She left at dawn and instructed me to draw your bath when you woke up, Your Grace," Mara said, bobbing a quick, awkward curtsey. "She said she'd be out in the courtyard if you were looking for her."

"Thank you," Elizabeth said, turning toward the bathing chamber.

Twenty minutes later she emerged, pushing her wet hair back over her shoulders and lacing up her shirt. Mara was gone.

Elizabeth headed down the corridor through the fragrance of fresh timber, by the soft footfalls of servants in the rooms housing the shipwreck survivors. The cries of soldiers drilling in the courtyard drifted through the open front door. She jogged down the stairs, feeling almost pathetic gratitude that the main staircase had been repaired. She heard Rowan's voice, her words indistinguishable, drifting toward her on the cool air. She followed the smell of rich stew toward the kitchen.

Her stomach rumbled and she went toward the cooking pots, nostrils flaring at the fragrance of cooking meat and fresh bread. She snagged a couple of thick slices of warm bread and a kitchen maid gave her a large slice of creamy cheese.

She murmured her thanks and looked out into the half empty tables in the kitchen. She frowned at the sight of two small figures hunched over at the end of the longest table. She grinned, headed toward them, and dropped down onto the bench beside one of them.

"Good morning, Benton," Elizabeth said, grinning at the girl.

"Hello," Benton said, eyes wary. She tensed as though ready to run.

Her hair and face seemed cleaner and Elizabeth smiled inwardly. "How are you doing, my little friend?"

Benton took a cautious, almost furtive bite of thick stew. "I'm good." She pointed a spoon at the boy sitting beside her. "This is my friend Thomas."

Elizabeth leaned back and held out a hand toward a small boy with bright blue eyes, a year or so younger than Benton. "Well met, Thomas. I'm Elizabeth St. John."

He stared at her, wide eyed, and hesitantly shook her hand.

"How are you enjoying your breakfast?" she asked.

"It's good," Thomas said, giving her a small smile. "Do you mind us eating here?"

"No," Elizabeth said, biting into her bread and cheese. "You are welcome in my house."

"You're not afraid we're going to steal anything?" he asked.

She shook her head and gave Benton a half smile. "I think we know where we stand on that, don't we, Benton?"

Benton nodded once. "Yes, Your Grace." She looked as though she wanted to say more but remained silent.

"I like your eyes," Thomas piped up. "I've never seen such pretty black eyes before."

Elizabeth gave him a broad grin. "I like yours too, blue eyes."

Thomas nudged Benton. "You're right. I like her."

Benton blushed furiously.

Elizabeth stood and gently patted her on the back. "You should come and join me for dinner some time, both of you."

Thomas gave her a broad grin and elbowed Benton. Benton, her eyes turbulent, looked into Elizabeth's eyes. She nodded once.

"I have to go. Second helpings are free!" she said as she strode from the hall.

"Thank you, Your Grace," Thomas said.

Elizabeth grinned to herself as she headed toward the courtyard, swallowing the last of her bread and cheese.

The guardsmen standing at either side of the door saluted as she walked out and she nodded in acknowledgment.

She headed toward the guardsmen clustered in a circle at the edge of the courtyard. She shouldered her way through the crowd and went to stand beside Peter. His eyes were riveted on the combatants in the center of the circle.

Rowan sparred with the large, hulking farmer, and each of his blows was hesitant and almost a second too late.

Rowan shook her head. "No, come at me as though you mean it. Your life is at stake!"

He shook his head. "I don't want to hurt you."

"You won't hurt me. Again. Keep your feet apart and your weight centered." Rowan took a step forward and swung her sword at him and he blocked her blow. Elizabeth caught the flicker of pain in her face as the muscles tugged on the injured side of her body. They stopped again.

"Peter," Elizabeth said softly, holding out her hand.

He gave her the wooden practice sword. "Your Grace."

Elizabeth strode into the circle. She bowed to Rowan, a grin tugging the corners of her mouth. "Your Highness, if I may?"

Rowan nodded, her mouth tight. "Your Grace." She bowed and moved back.

"Good morning," Elizabeth said.

The farmer bowed. "Good morning, Your Grace."

"Defend yourself, my good sir," Elizabeth said softly.

The man steeled his jaw and brought up his sword. He swung heavily toward her neck and she easily ducked under his swing, slipped inside his defenses, and kicked the back of his knee. His leg buckled and he stumbled. Elizabeth tapped the side of his neck with her sword.

She leaned forward. "You, good sir, just lost your head." She held out a hand and helped him to his feet.

He gazed at her with a thin gleam of anger in his dark eyes. "You took advantage of me."

"You think I should be more demure because I'm a woman?" she asked. "I'm a woman with a sword and won't hesitate to use it to take off your head."

He gave her a measuring stare and finally nodded once, sharply. "Again."

Elizabeth gestured for him to raise his sword and they danced around each other again. The match ended as abruptly as the first with her boot on his chest and the tip of her sword dimpling his throat.

"Don't get angry. Just watch the way I move. Keep your feet apart and stay balanced. When you move, make sure you can protect your body at a second's notice." She held out her hand and helped him to his feet. "Do you like fighting with a sword?"

"Honestly, Your Grace, not really. It doesn't feel right."

"Then let's try another. Quarterstaff?" she asked, signaling Peter.

Peter jogged to the practice staffs leaning against the wall. He tossed one to Elizabeth and to the farmer.

Elizabeth swung it easily in her hands, testing the balance and working her muscles. It felt good.

"This should suit you much better," she said, and demonstrated the basic moves of over, mid, and under attacks. The farmer blocked each of her attacks.

"Very nice," she said, about half an hour later.

The farmer rested his hands on his knees, breathing hard. He looked up and gave her a broad grin. "Yes, Your Grace. I like it."

"And you're good at it," she said.

"But how is that going to help me against an armored opponent swinging a sword?"

"Get good at using a quarterstaff and it is possible to almost always win," she said. "Watch. Peter!"

She felt a sword thrust into her hands and she swung as she casually tossed her quarterstaff to who she assumed was Peter. Rowan caught it easily, giving her an arch grin.

Elizabeth grinned back, watching a spark dance in Rowan's bright, blue eyes.

Rowan launched into an overhead attack that Elizabeth barely defended against. She danced back, looking for weaknesses in Rowan's stance, her combination moves and footing, but finding none. She launched an attack herself but Rowan blocked all her blows.

Rowan gave her an underhand blow. Elizabeth was too slow to defend against it, and her feet came out from under her. She crashed to her back with a grunt as the air exploded out of her lungs and yelped in pain as the end of the quarterstaff drilled her chest and nailed her to the ground.

"The match is yours, Your Highness," she said, accepting Rowan's proffered hand.

Rowan gazed at her, blue eyes turbulent, and hauled her to her feet. "You are a skilled opponent, Your Grace." She held Elizabeth's gaze.

"Not as skilled as you, Your Highness." She leaned forward and whispered into Rowan's ear, "Where did you learn to do that?"

"Civil war is a wonderful teacher," Rowan said softly, pulling back, her eyes flickering in remembered pain.

Elizabeth winced. "I'm sorry. I didn't mean to be insensitive."

"Don't be. You had nothing to do with it." Rowan gave Elizabeth a sad smile. "I don't mind sparring but I hate war. I don't want to do it anymore."

Elizabeth bit her lip. "All the more reason for you to leave. If you stay you'll be in one again, most likely."

"I can't. You know that." Rowan looked around, wincing as she saw their audience. She gazed at Elizabeth. "I think it's getting close to noon. We need to meet the traders for the midday meal."

"You want to come to lunch with me, then?" Elizabeth said.

"Thank you for asking, Your Grace. I'd love to," Rowan said with a broad grin.

Elizabeth snorted a laugh. "You did tell me that we were going to be sewn together at the hip. I welcome your company, Princess."

"Excellent," Rowan said. "I'm starved."

Elizabeth smiled and turned back to the farmer. His friends had joined him and were watching her closely.

She bowed. "I apologize, gentlemen. I have another engagement. My guardsmen would be happy to spar with you."

All the farmers bowed low.

"Thank you, Your Grace," her opponent said. "If you don't mind we'll be your guests for the rest of the week and then we'll go."

Elizabeth returned his bow. "Of course. Gentlemen." She turned to Rowan. "On we go."

Rowan nodded and they headed toward the city streets, Sean and Isengard falling into step behind them.

The streets were teeming with citizens, who parted when they saw Elizabeth approach. She felt their eyes on her, some friendly, some hostile, and some measuring. Most inclined their heads when they saw her coming.

She and Rowan remained comfortably silent until raised voices caught their attention.

Elizabeth scanned the road ahead of them, trying to catch the source of the disturbance. She finally saw a young man waving his fist and shouting at a woman standing in the doorway to a merchant's shop. A child darted out of the alleyway between two shops and raced up the street.

As they drew closer she was able to make out individual words.

"When I come back I will expect every last cent of your taxes. And the interest you owe," he screamed at the woman.

She stood in the doorway, pale as death but unwavering. "I owe you nothing. I pay my taxes to the duchess and you're not her legal collector."

Elizabeth felt Rowan stiffen beside her and she laid a restraining hand on Rowan's arm. Rowan looked at her and Elizabeth shook her head.

The young man raised his hand to the woman.

She cowered back. "Watchmen. Watchmen of Manusk."

Seconds later two uniformed men sprinted down the street toward the shop.

"What's going on here?" the older of the men demanded. Elizabeth recognized him. It was Daniel.

"This woman won't pay her rightful taxes," the young man said indignantly.

"You?" Daniel said, looking pointedly at the woman.

"He's not a tax collector for Manusk," she said.

Daniel stared at the young man. "Where is your identification as a tax collector for Manusk?"

The young man lifted his chin, but some of his swagger was gone. "I don't need documentation, you oaf. Ask Elizabeth of Manusk."

"Search him," Daniel said, seizing one of his arms. The other watchman seized the other arm and they pinned him against the wall.

Daniel searched through his pockets and pulled out coins but no paper. He inspected the coins. He gave a feral smile and waved a coin in the young man's face. "You have no official identification, and this is a coin from Sandcliff. That's your home, isn't it? You're not from Manusk, are you? You're merely impersonating a rightful official of Manusk."

The young man tried to rally but had lost all of his arrogance and merely sounded petulant. "I have a right to collect taxes."

"And I have the right to take you to the city jail until we can establish your true identity."

The young man struggled furiously until Daniel clubbed him over the back of the head with the hilt of his belt dagger. The young man sagged between them, unconscious. They dragged his limp body away.

"Thank you," the woman called and Daniel's companion turned back and sketched a quick salute.

Elizabeth smiled and Rowan frowned.

"Why did you let him do that to her?" Rowan said, holding her still.

"I won't always be around in these situations," Elizabeth said. "Manusk must learn not only to trust me but also to trust my soldiers and watchmen. My watchmen have to learn to trust me."

"She could have been seriously hurt."

"I would have stepped in if that was the case. It wasn't." Elizabeth walked toward the docks again. Rowan followed a split second later.

"You think you're going to die in the war, don't you?" Rowan said softly, pained.

Elizabeth looked at her and saw the turbulence in her eyes. "Not necessarily. There's no reason to assume this will come to war. *If* it does—*if*—I may live or die but that's for the future to decide. The odds are in favor of my surviving. I've been well trained in the art of fighting and war."

Rowan hissed and winced. "Aren't you sick of this?"

"It is what it is. I am to bring stability to Manusk. There's no guarantee there'll be armed conflict despite current appearances. If there is, I'm prepared. If there isn't, I'm content."

"Don't you want more?" Rowan asked.

Elizabeth was spared an answer by their arrival at the docks, heralded by catcalls and jeers from the crowd. The merchants' guards pulled together and held the surging crowd back.

Cries of *bitch, war monger,* and *murderer* tumbled out of the crowd in a cacophony of sound.

Elizabeth steadfastly ignored the barbs and snuck a quick look at Rowan. Rowan's face was rigid with tension and her mouth tightened with displeasure. She glanced back at Elizabeth, her eyes flickering between anger and resignation. Elizabeth took her hand and gently squeezed it.

Rowan opened her mouth to speak but two merchants guards materialized out of the crowd and flanked them.

Sergeant Hunter followed close behind and bowed low. "This way, Your Grace." He gestured ahead of them.

Elizabeth nodded and followed him through the crowd. She drew in a breath as a rock flew out of the crowd and hit her arm, tearing a small hole in her shirt.

The merchants' guards crowded in closer, pulling Elizabeth and Rowan along until they were behind the barrier of mixed soldiers standing outside the hall.

The taller of the merchants' guards, wearing Richard's colors, bowed low, his gaze flickering toward her torn shirt and the thin ribbon of blood that colored the edges of it.

"I apologize, Your Grace," he said. "I should have foreseen that."

Elizabeth looked at her arm and shrugged. "I don't think either of us saw that coming. I should have brought guardsmen with me." She looked at Rowan. "You, Your Highness? Are you all right?"

Rowan's mouth was set in a thin line of displeasure and she frowned. "I'm fine."

"Diplomacy, Your Highness, diplomacy." She grinned.

"Then I'm just *wonderful*, Your Grace," Rowan said with a flourish. Her eyes showed her lingering anger.

"Better," Elizabeth said. She gestured toward the door. "Under the circumstances it's probably a good idea if I go first."

"Fine."

Elizabeth sighed and pulled Rowan to a halt. She looked deep into her eyes. "Don't be angry. They're all just angry at me because I've taken away their ability to rob my people blind. They mean nothing."

Rowan's shoulders sagged. "I know. But that doesn't make it right or easier to deal with."

"It *does* make it easier to deal with. They don't like me. Not everyone in this world does. So what? I have other concerns, like making sure my people have homes and food in their bellies. My people come first, not harsh words from thieves."

Rowan colored. "You're right," she said after a moment. She looked as though she wanted to say something else but remained silent.

Elizabeth nodded and walked into the trading hall.

The front desk was empty.

"Where's Lawrence?" Elizabeth asked.

"In the city jail," Sergeant Hunter said. "He was dealing with the traders from Osk and Sandcliff under the table."

Elizabeth nodded. "Is he of Manusk?"

"No," Hunter said. "That's the main reason we had for being able to remove him."

Richard came out of the inner hall with a number of traders tagging along behind him.

"Your Grace," he said with a flourishing bow.

They all bowed low.

"Gentlemen," Elizabeth said. She held out a forearm. "Richard. How's your trading going today?"

"It's going well, Your Grace," Richard said, clasping her forearm and giving her a friendly grin. He gestured ahead of them. "In the hall. There's a banquet room about midway down the hall to your left." He turned toward Rowan and bowed low again. "Your Highness. This is an unexpected pleasure."

All of the traders followed his lead and bowed as low as he did.

"Thank you, Richard of Manusk," she said.

"This way," Richard said, leading them into the trading hall. It was empty of people except for some guards milling about. Only ten of the tables showed any signs of use, while the rest were empty, gathering dust.

"I had no idea we had that many traders not of Manusk in the hall," Elizabeth said to Rowan. Rowan nodded.

"I told you things were bad when you got here, Your Grace," Richard said.

"Are there enough of you for all the inbound ships?" Elizabeth asked.

"Barely, Your Grace," a new voice said.

"Captain Delmarco," Elizabeth said with a broad smile, holding out her forearm. "How are you?"

Delmarco took it and bowed. "I'm well, as is my little ship. I'm happy to be making money." His gaze flickered over Rowan. "Things are better for us now that we can unload more quickly."

"Your goods are always welcome in the hall," a sharp-eyed man with his beard oiled to a careful point said. Elizabeth fleetingly wondered if he'd ever accidentally stabbed himself with it.

"Thank you, Raphael," Delmarco said with a flourishing bow toward the trader.

Richard led them into the room. It held a finely made wooden table surrounded by sturdy benches, worn smooth and gleaming from frequent use. Torches flickered around the room, heating the air and casting warm light.

Richard escorted her to the end of the table and Rowan took the seat to her right, Delmarco to left. Richard sat at the other end. The other traders took their places around the table and they all sat.

A servant moved discretely between them, heaping their plates with meat and a thick potato stew. After the last man had been served they all dug into their meal.

Elizabeth allowed herself a few moments of enjoyment, and then looked at Richard. "My compliments to you all. This is an excellent meal."

"Thank you, Your Grace," Richard said and tipped his goblet toward a trader sitting halfway down the table. "This is courtesy of Damien."

"Thank you, Damien," Elizabeth said. "Where did you get this food from?"

Damien, a small, clean shaven man with dark, intense eyes, gave her the ghost of a smile. "Our former colleagues feared a shortage of food in Manusk. They took care to amass some of it against times of need."

"How good of them to have left some of it for us, then," Elizabeth said with a fleeting smile, stifling a stab of irritation.

"We have organized for the bulk of it to be shipped to your kitchen, Your Grace," Damien said. "As a gesture of thanks."

Elizabeth nodded appreciatively. "I and mine thank you, gentlemen. This is an unexpected courtesy."

"It's the least we could do, Your Grace," Raphael said. "Business has certainly been looking up since you came in."

"When trade is good, Manusk is good," Elizabeth said.

"That it is, Your Grace," Raphael said.

Elizabeth snuck a look at Rowan. The princess seemed engrossed in her food, but her sharp eyes scanned the room, briefly studying all the men sitting around the table.

"I have to ask, though," Elizabeth said. "To what do I owe the pleasure of this good food and company?"

The traders exchanged a glance.

"You're right, Richard," Raphael said with a laugh. "This one is a direct one, isn't she?"

Richard glanced at him, a small smile playing about his lips, and continued to eat with relish.

"All right, Your Grace," Raphael said. "It has come to our attention that you're looking for the sailors from the trader at the docks, and the sample of cargo from it." He took another spoonful of stew and carefully ate.

Elizabeth felt Rowan shift and shifted so their knees were touching. Rowan looked at her in surprise, her blue eyes bright and intense. Elizabeth met and held her gaze, willing her not to speak.

Rowan looked away and played with her stew.

Elizabeth waited for another moment. "Did Richard tell you about our bargain?" she asked the room in general.

The traders and Delmarco exchanged glances and shook their heads.

"I am here to bring Manusk back under the king's banner," she said. "And if, at the conclusion of this business, you want me to continue as your Duchess, I will stay. If you want me to leave, I'll leave."

"Is that a promise you can honor?" Raphael asked.

"I can do it," Elizabeth said easily. "The king is my father and if I really don't want to stay I'm sure he'll let me go." She smiled briefly. "What happens after that is entirely up to him."

Damien shot her a penetrating stare. "I like her."

The traders around the table exchanged glances and each nodded.

"All right," Damien said, eyes fixed on Richard. "There is some news we can give you on this, but I warn you we really know precious little. We were virtually kept in cages over the past few weeks."

Elizabeth frowned. "Why only weeks? I was under the impression you'd been under the thumb of Osk and Sandcliff for years."

"Oh, we have," Richard said, putting down his spoon, his dark eyes boring into hers. "We've been virtual prisoners here, forced to give an honorable face to thieves. It was dangerous for us, you understand?"

Elizabeth nodded.

Rowan shifted beside her. Her knuckles were white. Elizabeth reached under the table and gently squeezed her knee. Rowan glanced sharply at her, and forced herself to relax. She put down her spoon. Elizabeth forced herself not to start at the sensation of Rowan's calloused hand covering her own.

"A week or so ago we saw guards in unfamiliar livery on the docks," Raphael said. "The crest was a black rose entwined around a sword."

"That's mine," Elizabeth said. She felt every nerve ending spring to attention, and forced herself to relax as Rowan's fingers tightened around hers.

"Not quite," Richard said. "We saw when you arrived that the background of your standard is pure white. The crests they wore were not on a brilliant white background. The background was off white."

"So soldiers masquerading under my standard took away the sailors?"

Richard nodded, looking embarrassed. "I'm sorry, Your Grace. It wasn't until you posted your guards at the docks a few days ago that we realized the markings were wrong. We thought they belonged to you."

And that's why you were hesitant to deal with me. She felt a hot bolt of anger and pushed it back.

"Is that the first time you've seen them?" Elizabeth asked.

"Y-yes, Your Highness," Richard said. He looked pale.

"I'm not angry at you, Richard, or any of your friends." Elizabeth glanced around the table at the other traders, who studiously avoided her eyes. "Thank you for telling me this." She looked at Rowan. The princess's eyes glittered with anger and her mouth was set in a straight line of displeasure.

"I apologize, gentlemen, but I find myself with a distinct lack of appetite." Elizabeth stood and the traders hastily stood. She bowed and they bowed back.

"Thank you for the excellent food," she said. "It was a pleasure to meet you. You are all welcome at my table for dinner whenever you choose to come. Captain Delmarco, it was a pleasure to meet you again."

Delmarco held out his forearm. "And you, Your Grace."

Elizabeth took it.

Rowan bowed to the traders and they left the room.

As soon as they entered the trading hall Richard's guards fell into step around them, a silent Sergeant Hunter led them from the hall and into the sunlight. They made their way back through a sea of insults from the savage crowd.

Rowan remained silent until they were on the street that led to the manor house. She pulled Elizabeth to a halt.

"I'm sorry, Rowan," Elizabeth said. "I really don't know what to say."

"Elizabeth, I'm at your mercy," Rowan said. She took a deep

breath and her jaw worked. She turned and studied the harbor for a moment. She turned back and her eyes were cool and measuring. "I have to ask, you understand. Did you have anything to do with what happened to my people?"

Elizabeth suppressed a wince. The question caused her an unexpected stab of pain. "No, I didn't." She turned and began walking. After a moment she turned around to ask if Rowan was coming, but the princess had disappeared.

CHAPTER 10

ELIZABETH HEADED BACK to the barracks, feeling irritated and strangely alone without Rowan's quiet warmth by her side. She was troubled by what the traders had told her, and her mind kept coming back to the insult of her crest used in the kidnapping of the Welland traders. It bothered her that Rowan had actually asked if she'd had anything to do with it.

What do you expect? she asked herself as she blindly made her way through the city streets, absently dodging citizens. *She doesn't know the first thing about me. All she knows is that she woke up in my bed and at my apparent mercy. How must this all look to her?*

She took a deep breath. *She's heard so many different things about me over the past couple of days, and I'm not even sure what half of it was.* She snorted. *It probably wasn't good, though. Everyone knows I'm my father's war hammer.*

She stopped by the side of the road and looked up and down it, at the open merchants' shops, the quiet tavern across the road, heard voices raised in conversation and children's cries of joy as they played hide and seek in the alleyways.

She shivered. This wasn't an open battlefield and these people weren't trained soldiers. They were simply helpless people bullied by cruel nobles—and her presence made it worse for them.

What on earth is wrong with me? Why don't I feel right?

She forced herself into motion again.

"Your Grace?" a hesitant voice asked from beside her.

Elizabeth looked up. "Hello, Harriet."

Harriet fell into step beside her, casting a worried glance in her direction. She opened her mouth several times and closed it again.

"Is there something wrong?" Elizabeth asked.

Harriet pursed her lips, and then gave her a small smile. "I was going to ask you the same question, Your Grace."

Elizabeth stopped and looked at her. She saw the lines around

Harriet's mouth, her furrowed brow, and her wrinkled hands. Her eyes were a guarded, watery blue.

"Do you think I should leave, Harriet?"

Harriet blinked and for a second her eyes showed her confusion. "I don't recall having a say in the matter, Your Grace."

"Now you do. I ask again. Do you think I should leave, Harriet?"

"If you left now you'd be a coward," Harriet said slowly. "You've started something here. Manusk is starting to believe in you."

"What do you think I can do for you?"

Harriet tilted her head and regarded Elizabeth with some amusement. "I think you're already doing for me what you're supposed to be doing. For the first time I see people walking with their backs straight and with some measure of pride." Her smile dropped away. "Don't you understand, girl? You *started* something here. You give people hope for the future and then take that away from them. Manusk will collapse completely if you do. Osk and Sandcliff will take it all, the Kingdom will eventually fall and we will all be with the devil." She grabbed Elizabeth's shirt and gave her a brisk shake. "Grow up, Elizabeth. We need you." She snorted and strode away without a backward glance.

Elizabeth stared in shock at Harriet's retreating back. A jumble of images flew through her mind. The crowd of hungry people at the door to the kitchen; Jarrod's smile as his farm was given back to him; Richard's guards leading Rowan and her through the crowd to the trading hall.

God, how do I do this? I want to stay here.

She felt her mouth tighten as she strode up the road in Harriet's wake. Memory took her back to the evening with Rowan when the surgeon stitched her cut and bandaged her wound. She remembered the pain in Rowan's voice and her eyes as she spoke about her home and the civil war.

She glanced around the courtyard. Guardsmen stood in neat ranks, drilling against each other. There was ragged peasant's clothing nestled in their ranks. She smiled as her officers shouted encouragement or recommendations on their techniques.

"Your Grace," Peter said, materializing by her side. "I was expecting you this morning."

"I'm sorry, Lieutenant," she said. "I was drilling with the farmers and ended up having lunch with the traders. I want to see those uniforms."

Peter's mouth tightened. "They're not uniforms, Your Grace. Not ours. They're supposed to be but they're bad copies."

"Show me," Elizabeth said, as he led her across the courtyard into the main hall.

Off duty guardsmen playing at dice or simply lounging around quickly got to their feet, stood at attention, and saluted her.

"As you were," she said. She looked at the back wall and saw a few neat rows of beds, a portion occupied by injured guardsmen. She nodded toward them. "I want to see the injured. I already know the uniforms are a forgery. It can wait for another few moments."

"Yes, Your Grace," Peter said.

She wondered if he was confused by her scattered behavior but his ruggedly handsome face remained pleasantly neutral.

He gave her a slight bow and gestured toward the beds. "This way, Your Grace."

They went to the beds and Elizabeth knelt beside the first. A grizzled veteran lay still and unmoving, his chest heavily bandaged. His face was pale and his breathing was shallow.

"Will he live?" Elizabeth asked softly, glancing at Peter.

"Only the gods can help him now, Your Grace," he said.

The man in the next bed watched them with fever bright eyes, his hair wet with sweat. "Water," he gasped.

Elizabeth looked around and saw a cask with a dipper resting on top of it. Peter made a move toward it but she pushed him back down. She scooped cool, clear water from the barrel and took the dripping dipper over to the man. He tried to sit up, and she put an arm around his hot shoulders, and held him as he gulped at the water.

"Thank you. Thank you." He sank back onto the bed and his bloodshot eyes closed. His breathing evened out as sleep took him. Peter took the dipper off her and she went to the next bed.

The man lying in it was conscious and watched her intently.

"I apologize, Your Grace, I'd like to salute but I can't," he said with a grin.

"I think I can let that pass," Elizabeth said, returning his smile. "How are you feeling?"

"I'm almost healed, Your Grace." He cocked his head. "May I ask you something?"

Elizabeth nodded.

"Is the farmland here as good as they say it is?"

"Yes," Elizabeth said. "And there is room for you, Guardsman."

He smiled blissfully. "That's good." He looked at her sharply. "Is there any place I can see the water from my new land?"

Elizabeth laughed. "I think we can find something for you to grow old on."

"I look forward to it. I think my wife would like that."

"I'm sure she will."

They passed a few more minutes in idle conversation, and then Elizabeth moved on to the next bed. This one held a man with a broken leg, and he was a fisherman, glad to be by the sea again. The next was a stonemason and he had ideas on the form her rebuilt manor house should take.

After an hour, Elizabeth had visited every sick man in the barracks. A few were not expected to survive and she felt helpless. There was nothing she could do for them. The others balanced out her mood. Each of them spoke as though there were a future and it lightened her mood. Peter silently followed her, waiting patiently for her to finish.

"Now," she said, turning to him. "Show me these uniforms."

"Yes, Your Grace," he said, gesturing for her to follow him into a small antechamber behind the main hall.

It was dark and smelled musty. A smoky lamp burned in a corner, supplementing the light that came in from the main hall. A small desk and chair stood in the middle of the room, and a stack of folded uniforms in a corner.

Elizabeth went to them and pulled a dagger from her boot. She picked up a hastily made tabard and rubbed her fingers against the coarse cloth. She quickly found the crest—a rose entwined about a sword. She cut it out with a few deft strokes of her dagger and studied it in the warm light. The surrounding looked yellow, and she glanced at the door.

I need better light. She strode back out into the main hall, toward the large windows. Late afternoon sun streamed through and she stood in a pool of light, studying the crest closely, Peter at her shoulder, almost forgotten.

Richard was right. This crest is almost perfect. You'd have to look closely to notice the stem is too long and a leaf is missing. The background is wrong, though, and that's obvious. It's almost beige.

"You wouldn't know it wasn't white if you saw it in lamp light," Peter said quietly. "Everything looks yellow in lamp light."

Elizabeth nodded. "I agree. It means these uniforms were never meant to be seen during the day." She looked sharply at him. "Our uniforms are being copied, and now whoever is doing it has the real thing, thanks to our missing patrols."

"Yes, Your Grace," Peter said with a grimace. "The real question is why. Why is your crest being copied?"

"No mystery there, Peter," Elizabeth said. "Someone wants to pass themselves off as one of my guardsmen."

"To what end? There's no point in pretending to be a guardsmen when all Osk or Sandcliff has to do is walk into a shop or onto a farm and simply threaten the inhabitants."

Elizabeth nodded. "That's what I think. This is personal. Someone is doing something in *my* name. What's going on here? What have we missed?"

Peter shook his head in frustration. "I don't know."

"We're going to have to double the watch," Elizabeth said. "All uniforms need to be accounted for. We need to remove the crests of everyone else's uniforms. The guardsmen are to go out unmarked."

"Do you want them to dress as peasants?"

"No, they need to be in unmarked armor. The last thing I want is for our men to be picked off one by one because they're only half dressed. We don't have enough men as it is. Do you know each of the guardsmen that came with us?"

Peter nodded. "Yes, Your Grace."

Elizabeth nodded. "Good. Ask the same of all the other officers. We need to send for reinforcements. Something is coming and I don't like it."

"Yes, Your Grace." Peter nodded. "I'll send Martin to Captain Callas. He's known to Callas."

"Yes. And make sure he's given a marker and that Callas sends the marker and confirmation of his orders before the reinforcements arrive."

"At once, Your Highness," Peter said.

"Meet me at the city jail when you're finished," she said. "Bring Sean with you. Quickly, Peter."

"Yes, Your Grace," Peter said with a quick bow. He headed to a junior guardsmen, giving orders as he approached.

Elizabeth watched him, feeling uneasy.

She went out into the courtyard and scanned it for any sign of

Rowan. There was none and she felt disappointment. She hoped to see Rowan. She wanted to explain but wasn't sure exactly what.

"Your Grace," Sean said, appearing by her side and saluting her.

"Sean," Elizabeth said. "We're going to the city jail. Do you know where that is?"

"Yes, Your Grace," Sean said and walked back out into the street, Elizabeth by his side.

Ten minutes later they arrived at the jail.

Elizabeth strode in and peered around. The foyer was a lot like the trading hall— a high desk overlooked the front doors and locked iron doors to each side of the hall.

The watchman stood and saluted when he saw them. "Your Grace."

"Corporal," she said. "How long have you been stationed in the jail?"

"For a week, Your Grace," he said.

"Were you one of the first guardsmen here?" she asked.

"Yes, Your Grace."

"Were there prisoners here when you got here?"

"Yes, Your Grace." He pointed to the door to their left. "In those cells. They were teeming with people. The ones to the other side were all empty."

Elizabeth exchanged a glance with Sean. His brow was furrowed. "One side was overcrowded, the other empty?"

"Yes, Your Grace."

"Are there any prisoners in those cells now?"

He nodded. "No, Your Grace." He paused for a moment. "The cell they were in has been empty since they left."

"Can we search the cell?"

He nodded and gestured behind them, then stepped away from the desk and hunted for keys on his belt.

Elizabeth and Sean turned and saw the guards appear in from the shadows behind the doors.

"Some soldiers we are," Elizabeth muttered.

Sean snorted a laugh.

The corporal gestured for them to follow him and quickly unlocked the door with practiced ease. Elizabeth stepped in front of Sean and followed the corporal down the wide corridor. It was dimly lit by two spluttering lanterns hung high on the wall at the far end.

"There are more lights if there are more prisoners, Your Grace," the corporal said, glancing over his shoulder at them.

Elizabeth nodded.

"Here," the corporal said. He stopped in front of the cells half way down the corridor. He gestured at them. "Here."

Elizabeth nodded again and accepted the lantern he offered her. He rifled through the keys, selected one, and opened the lock with a solid click.

"Your Grace," he said with a bow and stood aside.

"Thank you, Corporal," Elizabeth said and entered the cell.

It was about ten feet square, with a cot chained against the back wall and an empty slop jar in the corner. Elizabeth sniffed, but only caught the background stinks of unwashed prisoners, distant human waste, and fresh straw. She felt a moment of confusion. She looked at the back wall of the cell. The mortar between the bricks looked new and she ran her fingers along it, feeling for imperfections.

The light became brighter as Sean peered over her shoulder at the wall.

"You see, Sean?" she asked, glancing at him.

He ran his fingers along the bricks and nodded. "The bricks are clean." He blew out a breath. "Someone cleaned up this cell after the prisoners left."

Elizabeth nodded. "Yes." She went to the cot and lifted the mattress. "Even the chains are new. Someone's gone to a great deal of trouble to hide something, haven't they?"

"But I think they missed something," Sean said, bending over the cot.

He held the lantern close to the chain link that held the mattress. He pointed to a dark spot on the chain and then scratched at it with his fingernail.

He held it up for Elizabeth's inspection. "Blood."

Elizabeth bent and studied the dried red under his nails. She nodded. "Blood." She straightened with a sigh. "We knew this was coming."

"What I don't understand is why, Your Grace," Sean said. "Why go to all the trouble to capture foreigners and then harm them? Didn't it occur to the people who did this that they'd be missed?"

"You're assuming they're dead. But I see your point and I agree." Elizabeth turned back to the corporal, who was watching them with interest. "Did you hear anything about this when you came into the town prison?"

The corporal shook his head. "No, Your Grace."

"Do you remember seeing anything?" Elizabeth asked.

The corporal thought about it for a moment. "No, Your Grace. But in all honesty there was chaos when we arrived. Most of the traffic into the city comes in from the western gate. My guess would be that if they were taken from the city they went that way."

"Thank you, Corporal. That will be all," Elizabeth said, gesturing for Sean to follow her. He inclined his head and they followed the guardsman out of the wing back into the main hall of the city prison.

Once they were out in the sunshine, Elizabeth stopped for a moment, a feeling of nagging unease tugging away at her belly.

"Are you thinking of that farm, Your Grace?" Sean asked.

"Huh?" Elizabeth asked.

"The farm. Close to Farrow's farm. That had all the guardsmen."

"Interesting idea, Sean," Elizabeth said. "Where else would be the perfect place to hide a group of foreign dignitaries?"

"If they're alive," Sean said.

"If they're alive you could ransom them and blame me for it," Elizabeth said.

Sean's jaw tightened. "That you could, Your Grace."

"I think it's time we went out to see what's at that farm," Elizabeth said.

Sean nodded.

Elizabeth walked toward the manor house. The streets teemed with people and most of them gave her a wide berth.

I really don't want to tell Rowan about this but I don't know how not to. I suppose I could always keep my mouth shut until we know for sure what's happened to Welland crew.

"When was the last time we checked in with the army on the plains?" Elizabeth asked.

"I don't know," Sean said. "You would have to ask the captain or the lieutenant."

"Go and get them and meet me in my room," she said.

"Your Grace," Sean said, bowing and backing away.

Elizabeth continued on toward the manor house, absently returning the salutes that the city watch gave her as they patrolled the streets. She finally entered the courtyard and glanced around at her drilling soldiers, but didn't see Rowan. She suppressed the strange feeling of loss that accompanied the observation.

As she strode through the doors, she felt the ghost of fingers brushing her breeches.

She glanced down and saw Benton lurking in the shadows, almost indistinguishable from the door.

She opened her mouth to speak but Benton immediately put her finger over her lips for silence. She darted across the foyer toward an alcove beneath the main stairs.

Elizabeth followed her, curious. She stopped in the alcove, towering over Benton. Benton looked up at her.

"What can I do for you, Benton?" Elizabeth asked softly.

Benton's jaw worked and she peered anxiously at Elizabeth.

Elizabeth knelt before her, concerned. "Whatever's the matter?"

"Charles is going to be mad at me," she said.

"Why?" Elizabeth asked.

"Because I'm talking to you."

"I won't tell if you won't."

Benton studied her.

Elizabeth watched her closely, struck by the weariness she saw in the young eyes. "I told you I would take care of you if you worked for me. That offer stands. I can find something for you to do."

"I like the job you gave me first. It's easy to do."

Elizabeth tilted her head. "You mean to listen, don't you?"

Benton nodded once, sharply.

"What have you heard?" Elizabeth asked.

"*I* didn't hear it. *Thomas* heard it," Benton said after a moment. "We were in the alley the day before yesterday and we heard two men talking. They weren't from Manusk." She fell silent.

"What did they say?" Elizabeth asked after a few moments.

"They were talking about a farm and some foreign men." She leaned forward and beckoned Elizabeth closer.

Elizabeth leaned toward her, felt the whisper of Benton's breath against her ear.

"They said the men were dead and they were at the farm," Benton whispered.

Elizabeth widened her eyes and she felt dismay. "Do you know which men they meant?"

"The men from the trader." She pulled back and looked at Elizabeth anxiously. "Is that what you wanted us to listen for?"

Elizabeth nodded, studying her. Fear lurked in Benton's eyes and

Elizabeth waited for a barrage of child's questions, none of which came.

"That's good. Very good. That's what I asked you to do." She smiled. "Don't worry. I *will* take care of you."

"And Thomas?"

"And Thomas," Elizabeth said. "Have you eaten?"

Benton shook her head.

"Why don't you and Thomas go and get something from the kitchen? And you can sleep here tonight if you want to."

Benton shook her head. "I have to go to Charles."

"You don't have to stay with him."

"I know." Benton darted out of the shadows before Elizabeth was able to add anything.

Elizabeth sank back on her haunches and sighed. She couldn't wait anymore. She had to go to the farm now and see what Osk and Sandcliff were hiding. If the ambassadors from Welland had been murdered she had to tell Rowan and put herself at her mercy.

What did it all mean? A Welland trader had been waylaid in the harbor just before her men arrived. They'd been taken away by men masquerading as her guardsmen and murdered practically under her nose. Another Welland ship had broken up on the rocks, the signal fires extinguished by Osk and Sandcliff and troops wearing her insignia but unrelated to her. They were found dead near the ashes. It was clear she was supposed to bear the blame for sinking Rowan's ship and for the death of the Welland ambassadors.

The question that niggled and gnawed away at her was how Osk and Sandcliff stood to gain by killing Welland sailors and sinking their flagship. Why would they do that?

Frustrated by an understanding that felt out of her reach, Elizabeth stood and shook her head. Her first order of business was to reinforce the city with troops from her army on the plains. Her soldier's sense of danger was pinging for all it was worth and she knew through bitter experience not to ignore it.

She looked out from under the stairs and emerged without drawing any attention to herself. She made her way up the stairs, every step a millstone around her neck. She dreaded the idea of telling Rowan what she'd found out. Rowan would be devastated and it would crush their tenuous attempt at diplomacy.

She made her way down the corridor, steeling her jaw and squaring her shoulders. She opened the door with a decisive push.

Mara, standing by the bed, squeaked in shock and jumped. She bobbed an ungainly curtsey when she saw Elizabeth.

"I'm s-sorry, Your G-Grace," she stammered.

Elizabeth waved her away.

Rowan sat on the window sill, her long legs stretched out in front of her, watching the foam flecked sea in the bay.

Elizabeth slowly approached her and knelt beside her. She felt sick.

Rowan turned and looked at her, her eyes sad and measuring.

"Rowan, we have to talk," Elizabeth said.

"You found my people, didn't you?"

"I'm not sure. I think I may have. I'm going to go and look. I think they were taken to a farm outside of the city. We thought it was being used as a barracks by Osk and Sandcliff but now I'm not so sure it's that simple."

"They're dead, aren't they?"

Elizabeth felt sad. She looked directly at Rowan and remained silent.

Rowan held her gaze for a long moment and then sighed. "I thought so."

"I'm so sorry, Rowan," Elizabeth said, sitting on the window sill beside her. "I know this has destroyed any semblance of peace there ever could have been between us. I will submit to your justice on behalf of my father and his people." She was silent for a moment. "I think it's best you take your remaining people and leave. You have my word that I'll come to you, but I have to honor my father's orders and take back Manusk for him." The words felt like a knife twisting into her heart.

"There will be justice for what has happened to us, mark me. But it won't come from you." She turned to Elizabeth, a trace of anger in her eyes. "That's *not* what I want, Elizabeth." She swung her legs off the window sill and sat so they were looking into each other's eyes. "I don't want to hurt you, Elizabeth. I *know* you had nothing to do with any of this."

"Then what *do* you want?" Elizabeth asked. She felt herself relaxing.

"I want *not* to be the guest of a charming woman ruling a duchy on the brink of civil war. I *want* all of my people to be alive. I *want* us both to turn old and grey in a land of peace." Her voice broke and she blinked away tears. "I'm sick of war and leading troops into battle. I'm sick of knowing people for the final few days of their lives." Her jaw tensed as she turned to look back out to sea.

"Rowan," Elizabeth began.

"Don't *you* want more? Don't you want to sit by your beloved's side watching your children as you turn old and gray?"

"I am a woman that no man can tame." Elizabeth pulled Rowan into her arms and Rowan sobbed in earnest. "My father's orders were to take and hold Manusk. I am the duchess here for better or worse and he doesn't want me to leave. I was always frightened of settling down but now I'm not so sure. I don't like being thought of as a bloodthirsty butcher or as my father's war hammer. I don't like looking at my troops and knowing some of them won't be alive to enjoy the evening meal with me." She took a deep breath. "When I agreed to do this for my father, I knew there was a good chance we would fight. It's a duty that hangs around my neck like a leaden weight. No matter what happens, this will be my last mission. I promise you that."

"Come with me to Welland," Rowan said pulling back and looking into her eyes. Her arms tightened around Elizabeth. "Come with me when I leave."

Elizabeth nodded and smiled. "I would love that."

There was a knock on the door and Elizabeth released Rowan with a sigh. "Enter."

Herbert, Peter, and Sean entered the room.

"Gentlemen," Elizabeth said. She looked at Mara, almost forgotten in her position by the door. "Mara, fetch us some tea."

Mara bobbed her lopsided curtsey and hurried out of the room.

"It seems the sailors from the trader were taken to a farm outside of the city. I am going to leave for the farm as soon as we are done here."

Herbert frowned, Peter looked shocked, and Sean nodded his head.

"How do you know this, Your Grace?" Herbert asked.

"I have eyes and ears in the city," Elizabeth said.

"Your little urchin?" Sean asked.

"Who requires protection, as do her friends," Elizabeth said. "Make sure you're a friendly face, Sean."

Sean nodded. "Yes, Your Grace."

"If I may ask, Your Grace?" Peter said. "Who's this urchin you're talking about?"

"Sean and I had a run in with our little street thieves a day or so ago. They seem to have switched allegiance to me," Elizabeth said.

Rowan stared at her. "Very good but a little cold, Elizabeth. They could easily get hurt doing what you're asking them to do. They're just children."

"They're anything but," Elizabeth said. "They are safer sinking into shadows than they are living at my house, although that's what I think they're going to be doing from now on."

Mara bustled in again with a tray loaded with steaming tea. "Your Grace?"

"Thank you, Mara," Elizabeth said, scooping up a cup and handing it to Rowan.

Herbert, Peter, and Sean also helped themselves to a cup, and Elizabeth took a sip of the last steaming mug.

"Good," she said as Mara backed away. "Herbert, I think it's best if we call for reinforcements for the Manusk garrison. Send a runner to General Arnett and have him send two companies. Do you know where Osk and Sandcliff troops are camped?"

"There are no signs of troop movements from either Osk or Sandcliff," Herbert replied. "We don't know where they're hiding."

Elizabeth stared at him and felt her blood run cold. "How can you lose an army?"

"Technically we haven't lost them since we never found them to begin with."

"Are you trying to tell me you're afraid of a phantom army?" Rowan asked, her flickering blue gaze traveling between them.

"I don't understand, Herbert," Elizabeth said, feeling her head pound with anger. "Why didn't you tell me this straight away?"

"The uniforms, Your Highness," Peter said softly.

Elizabeth nodded. "Yes, I agree—and we've been feeding them the real thing."

"What?" Herbert asked. He glared at Peter. "What uniforms?"

"It seems that we have soldiers masquerading as guardsmen in our midst," Elizabeth said.

Herbert gasped and Elizabeth nodded.

"Sir," Peter said, steeling his jaw. "We found dead men wearing the princess's insignia at the signal fire."

"And imposters took my people from your city prison," Rowan said. She had gone pale.

"And I'll bet that by now half of my army on the plains isn't loyal to me," Elizabeth said archly.

She spat out a venomous curse, anger pulsing through her body. She swung around to Herbert.

"And you've been sending out search parties for missing patrols and then—" She tilted her head. "Captain Herbert isn't that incompetent, but then you're not Captain Herbert, are you?" She drew her sword from its scabbard with a quick hiss.

Rowan looked alarmed, backed away from them, and fumbled for a phantom sword at her waist. Peter and Sean, grim faced, drew their own swords and circled him.

The man calling himself Captain Herbert snarled and threw himself forward onto her sword. He went rigid as it pierced his heart and let out a sigh as the life fled from his body.

Elizabeth cursed and caught his dead weight as he sank to the floor. She quickly felt for his pulse but there was none. Grim faced, she pulled her sword out of him as Peter tore off a section off Herbert's cloak and handed it to her. She cleaned her sword, mind whirling. *How could I have been that stupid? Why didn't I question him more closely about the missing companies of scouts?*

She felt Peter's, Sean's, and Rowan's eyes on her. Her face heated with humiliation.

"Do any of you recognize this man?" Rowan asked after a moment.

Elizabeth shook her head. "He's not one of mine. He's Gareth's. I'd never seen him until we got here. I took him because I needed an experienced advance commander and Gareth assured me he was virtually a military genius."

"You?" Rowan asked, looking at Peter and Sean.

They shook their heads.

"I'm sorry, Your Grace, I never served under Captain Herbert," Sean said. "I thought you knew him."

"Wonderful," Elizabeth said. "Peter, as the most senior officer in the garrison, you're now promoted to captain. Sean, you're his new lieutenant." She turned to Rowan. "You must really think we're all stupid by now, mustn't you?"

Rowan shook her head. "No, I don't. I think there's something larger going on here that you only just stumbled on. I believe you have been cut off from your army and are about to be overrun by your enemies. Accordingly, Welland honor now stands with yours. Any hostilities against Manusk and the King's Heartland will be seen as hostilities against Welland. We will stand with you and fight. If I may make a suggestion, Elizabeth?"

Elizabeth nodded, shocked by Rowan's declaration that they would stand together. Yet the words had only been spoken in that room amongst them. No one knew of their new and binding alliance and she, Peter, and Sean could agree to remain silent about it. She could still force Rowan out of Manusk.

"You and I will go out to the farm with Isengard. I *know* he's an experienced battle commander. Peter and Sean must make preparations for battle." She gave Elizabeth an apologetic look. "I *have* to know what happened to my sailors."

"And I *have* to clear that farm out so we aren't hit on that flank when Osk and Sandcliff attack us. I don't think there's any more question of that, do you?" Elizabeth said, eyeing Peter and Sean.

"No, Your Grace," they chorused with a bow.

"Peter, Sean—find out what's happened to the army, if we have any loyal men left. We also must send word to Captain Callas and General Arnett to send in reinforcements. Double time them to us if they must. We *must* have my army within these city walls as soon as we can. Send word to Coral Bay for help and also to my brother."

"Yes, Your Grace," Peter said, who still looked as though he was in a fog.

"Get rid of him," Elizabeth said without preamble, nudging Herbert's body with her boot. She looked at Rowan. "We're going to the farm. Right now."

"Yes, Your Grace," Peter, Sean, and Rowan said.

Elizabeth felt sick as she strode from the room, Rowan in tow as Peter and Sean gathered up the corpse. She absently noted Mara's shaking figure in the corner and suppressed a flinch. So many innocent lives depended on her. Had she managed to avert disaster? Was any of her army still alive?

CHAPTER 11

"ISENGARD," ROWAN CALLED without preamble as they entered the courtyard.

Isengard broke away from his discussion with the corporal standing before Elizabeth's assembled company of guardsmen. He trotted to her and bowed.

"Your Highness," he said. "I'm glad you came. The corporal there was just telling me Duchess Elizabeth intends to ride to a farm outside the city. I suggest I go with them."

"Do you now?" Elizabeth said, folding her arms and staring at him. She looked pointedly at Rowan. "I'm not convinced it's not in your best interests to leave right now. It would be much safer for you."

"We've covered this ground already, Duchess Elizabeth," Rowan said coolly. "I'm not going anywhere. If your suspicions are correct then *I* owe it to *my* father to remain and determine justice for Welland." She turned to Isengard. "Get the men ready to ride."

Isengard saluted and backed away.

"You are the most stubborn woman I've ever met," Elizabeth said, throwing up her hands. "This isn't really your problem."

"Willingly or not I'm now in the center of your civil war. Honor demands I remain with my friends until the bitter end."

"Are we friends, Rowan?" Elizabeth asked softly. "Really?"

Rowan looked at her for a long moment, her face unreadable. "Do you really need to ask me that? You know what I think. I think you are the most remarkable woman I've ever met."

"As are you, Rowan. Not many people would stand by a virtual stranger the way you stand by me." She felt her face heat and bit her lip. "I . . . I . . . can't . . . don't know how to say . . ."

Rowan nodded and smiled. "You don't need to say anything. I understand perfectly."

Elizabeth nodded and cleared her throat. "Well, then. We should get moving."

A groomsman materialized beside them, handing them the reins to their horses. Elizabeth and Rowan mounted and Rowan's mount pranced.

Rowan patted his neck soothingly. "Good boy."

Elizabeth smiled. "I haven't ridden him for a few days and he's anxious to get out."

Rowan smiled back. "So I see."

Elizabeth heeled her horse around. "Isengard. Move out." She looked at the column of men and saw a small force of Welland nestled comfortably at the back of her guardsmen. She raised an eyebrow.

"Not one word, Your Grace," Rowan said softly.

"I hadn't planned on saying anything," Elizabeth said. She turned her horse and rode out of the courtyard, Rowan by her side, Isengard behind them both.

"Manusk," a man called out from behind them.

"Manusk stands," Elizabeth called.

"Manusk stands!" a few more voices called out.

As they left the courtyard, the cry became a roar as a hundred voices joined in. *Manusk!*

As they rode through the city streets, the call became louder as ordinary townsfolk stopped to watch Elizabeth, and to take up the cry.

Manusk! Manusk!

Elizabeth's back straightened as they rode through city streets, the cry coming to them on waves all the way to the city gates. The sentries emerged from the gates and saluted them.

"All's well," the officer of the watch called.

"Carry on, Corporal," Elizabeth called back.

They rode through dusk down the road, peasants and tradesman making way for them. After a while, Rowan broke the comfortable silence between them.

"This is a beautiful place," she said, waving an arm to encompass golden fields and a foam flecked sea bathed in the red sunset. "I can't remember a time I haven't ridden out like this into battle." Her tone was sad.

Elizabeth gave her a wry grin. "You know what I'm going to say to that don't you?"

"Don't say it. I'm here by my choice and as my duty."

Elizabeth nodded. "I won't. I think I've spoken the words often enough." Her smile faded. "How old were you when you began to fight?"

"I was fourteen. Until then, the most responsibility I was ever given was to be back at my parents' table for dinner at sunset. I spent my time playing with my friends in the fields."

"What of your friends?"

A sad look shadowed Rowan's beautiful features. "They are all gone. Everyone I knew in my childhood is gone. My friends were all the children of noble families loyal to my father. When my uncle took over, he purged the land of everyone who was loyal to my father."

"How did you survive? How did your father regain his kingdom?" Elizabeth asked, feeling her own sense of loss over the friends she'd had over the years who were now in the grave.

"My mother hid me. She took me during the coup and we ran. My uncle hunted us down and shot my mother with so many crossbow bolts it was a miracle she was still alive, let alone running with me. She finally collapsed and hid me beneath her. When my uncle found us, he knew he'd killed her and thought he'd done the same to me because of all the blood." She gave Elizabeth a humorless grin. "My mother's blood saved my life." Her jaw worked. "I hid for days in the fields until one of my father's soldiers found me. I was half starved and mad with grief for my mother. He took me back to my father and my father showed me how to fight. He showed me how to never be afraid again. Over time I became one of my father's generals. My father and I fought the final battle that captured my uncle and brought Welland back to us." She glanced at Elizabeth. "Twenty years. Twenty years of slaughter, Elizabeth. Twenty years of blood and death. After that, a year of peace and returning prosperity, and now more blood."

"I'm so sorry, Rowan," Elizabeth said. "I never meant for you to be caught up in this. I will keep you safe for as long as I can, but you *have* to leave. You shouldn't feel compelled to stay here. You owe me no debt and the one the King's Heartland owes you will be paid by me. I will come to you and answer to what has happened to your people."

"I know I should leave," Rowan said in a subdued voice. "I *know* I should." Her jaw worked and Elizabeth saw the sheen of tears in her eyes. "It's *you* I can't leave." She watched Elizabeth closely for a few moments, and Elizabeth saw the terrible battle raging inside her as she tried several times to phrase more words.

Elizabeth felt shocked. "What are you saying? Are you afraid I'm going to die?"

The tears brimming in Rowan's eyes finally spilled over, starlight catching them as diamonds on her cheek. "I can't. I just can't," she whispered, so softly Elizabeth almost missed her words. She slowed her horse and fell back beside Isengard.

Elizabeth gave a deep sigh of sadness. *Fourteen. Fourteen years old. That's a cruel introduction to the world. Twenty years of war? It's a wonder she's not locked up screaming in a cell. No wonder she almost cries whenever she sees me. I must be a terrible reminder of a life she thought she'd left behind.* She stilled the urge to turn and gaze at Rowan. *No more, Rowan. No more. Once we are done here, I will send you back out to sea and to your people. I swear to you I will do this. You deserve better than this.*

She rode on ahead of them, sighing. Her heart ached for Rowan. She simply couldn't understand why she stood at the center of the storm that seemed to be raging inside Rowan. They were from different lands and very different backgrounds, yet they seemed to meld together seamlessly. She dimly realized that it had never really crossed her mind *not* to trust her. Rowan and her sailors had free run of the manor house and the town and were free to take up arms. Rowan was unquestionably one of her inner circle of advisors. Was it because they were so similar? Was it because Rowan was clearly well versed in the arts of war? Or was it because they really *were* friends despite their differences?

God. Dear God in heaven, what is the matter *with me?*

She forced her scattered mind to focus on more immediate dangers.

Thanks to the interference from the impostor Captain Herbert, there was no telling how much of her army remained on the plains, assuming he'd been telling the truth. Elizabeth felt her blood run cold. There were reports that Osk and Sandcliff had marshaled in the vicinity of ten thousand men in their combined army. Hers was a force of eight thousand well-trained men, less than half of her father's force, veterans of more than one war. She couldn't afford to lose any single one of them.

She'd divided her force into the sixteen hundred who'd come with Herbert, a fifteen hundred of which were still on the plains on the outside of the city, ready to serve as reinforcements to her handpicked guardsmen; the guardsmen she'd brought with her, all four hundred of them; and the six thousand that were following behind. It took much more time to move a force of six thousand, so they were a week's march behind them.

Osk and Sandcliff had something planned but Elizabeth still couldn't quite fathom what it was.

"Halt," a man called from the darkness.

"At ease, guardsman. It's Elizabeth St. John." Elizabeth turned around and looked at the party. "And some friends."

"Your Grace," the guardsman said, approaching her in the darkness. "We weren't expecting you."

"I know," Elizabeth said. "Have you got anything to report?"

The guardsman, a grizzled veteran, approached her horse. "Not much, Your Grace. The militia reports there are soldiers gathering at Felson's farm. We wanted to check the rumors, but Captain Herbert has withdrawn half of my force so we are barely able to keep the road safe." He glowered.

"Captain Herbert is dead," Elizabeth said. "Your orders come from Captain Peter and Lieutenant Sean now."

The guardsman gasped. "May I ask, Your Grace?"

"He was a traitor. God knows how many of our men are still loyal to us."

The guardsman bowed low. "*We* are your men, Your Highness."

"Thank you, guardsman."

"I don't mean to interrupt the pleasantries, Your Grace," Isengard said, pushing his horse forward beside Elizabeth. "If I may inquire as to how big the force is at this Felson's farm?"

The guardsman looked at him, his face an impassive mask although his mouth tightened.

"You may answer freely, guardsman. This is General Isengard and behind him Princess Rowan. They are friends from Welland." Elizabeth glanced back at Rowan and Rowan pushed her horse forward to the other side of Elizabeth.

The guardsman bowed low. "General, Your Highness. Welcome to the Duchy of Manusk."

"Thank you, guardsman," Rowan said with a brief smile. "Now, if you could please answer the general's question?"

"It's a force of about twenty with more coming in by day."

Elizabeth glanced back at her party. There were twenty guardsmen and six from Welland. The odds were in their favor.

"I will leave some men with you when we come back this way." Elizabeth leaned down and looked him in the eyes. "I need eyes and ears on the highway. I need to know of these troop movements and keep a sharp eye out for our own men. I want to know who passes, where and when. Understood, guardsman?"

The guardsman pulled up and gave her a crisp salute. "Yes, Your Grace. I understand. We will report directly to you."

"Excellent. Carry on, guardsman."

He bowed and stood back to allow Elizabeth and her group to pass.

Rowan rode alongside Elizabeth. "Penny for your thoughts, Your Grace."

Elizabeth glanced at her. "You mean you still want to talk to me?"

Rowan gave her a reproachful look. "If it means hearing that lovely voice of yours more often, yes, I want to talk to you."

Elizabeth felt her face heat and fished for a witty reply.

Rowan's quiet laughter surrounded her. "You are at a loss for words, Your Grace? *You?*"

"I'm assuming that's not one of your traits, *Your Highness?*"

Rowan laughed harder.

"No wonder your father hesitated to send you out on a diplomatic mission, Your Highness. I'm sure that beautiful face of yours has been slapped more than once," Elizabeth said.

"As has yours I'm sure."

Elizabeth laughed softly. "Perhaps but *never* for my diplomatic skills."

They both laughed.

"Seriously," Rowan said. "What's going through your mind?"

"My mind keeps circling around the false insignia and the deliberate destruction of one ship."

"You want to know what *I* think?" Rowan said softly.

Elizabeth regarded her for a moment. "I realize it's to blame me for something, the destruction of your ships would be an accurate assumption, but the *why* of it escapes me."

"Are you interested in my thoughts on this subject?" Rowan asked.

Elizabeth nodded. "Of course."

Rowan took a deep breath. "This is what I think and you can call me paranoid if you like. They are more likely than not trying to kill you. Your duchy is the main port for the King's Heartland and Osk and Sandcliff have been in control of it for at least fifty years and are unlikely to give up such a prize on the king's whim. They will fight you for it. The easiest way to remove you from the equation is assassination. A simple way to achieve this would be to have you killed by one of your own men—or by us. They would have their hands clean at the end of it and they would also keep control of Manusk as your father is hardly likely to do something as dangerous as send in your brother to avenge your death."

"If they wanted to kill me, all they would have to do is march into the manor in Manusk and slit my throat as I slept. My guardsmen may object but I'm guessing half the city won't complain. They are a little lethargic." Elizabeth gave a rueful grin. "I don't doubt for one second there's a price on my head, though. No, that's a given. What I don't understand is why your ship was wrecked on the rocks. That doesn't fit with the assassination theory. Were the men at the signal fire there to extinguish it or defend it? We—or you—were meant to find the uniforms and insignia on the bodies. Osk and Sandcliff have your sailors. They had to know you were coming, and that you would logically think I'd sunk your ship."

"They may have known we were coming but not when," Isengard broke in. "One possibility is for us to blame you, Duchess Elizabeth, for their capture. Another equally likely possibility is that sinking the ship was an attempt to keep us from finding out about the sailors. Perhaps we were simply in the wrong place at the wrong time."

"I don't think it was to prevent you from finding out about the sailors. That seems unlikely. Why go to the trouble to make false uniforms if they hoped a wreck on the rocks disposed of all of you? Why not just kill you when you landed and then scuttle your ship?" Elizabeth said, shaking her head. "No, I think you were meant to blame me. We are now full circle and come back to the question of *why*." She sighed. "So far, the facts, as we know them, are these. Imposters masquerading as my men took your sailors. Imposters acting as my men were at the signal fire. So, to the outside world, it would look like I kidnapped ambassadors, and then tried to kill more Welland sailors who were trying to sail into Manusk, presumably to look for the first lot. The city of Manusk has been cut off from the real men who are loyal to me and there's no way to tell my father about the Welland diplomatic mission. I have also had a spy working as my captain of the guard, so I think you're not so safe either, Rowan. Osk and Sandcliff by now know that you're alive and well, and that you know they've been sinking ships to steal cargo and your ship accidentally got caught in their trap. My father won't know any of this. He's just going to assume I'm going on my merry way retaking Manusk for him. I no longer control information to the King's Heartland."

Rowan nodded. "Yes, I think we can all agree on this." She was silent for a moment. "There's no reason to assume I'm a target. They have no reason to assume I'm not going to drag you out of Manusk in chains. They don't know if I believe your story about forged uniforms."

"No matter what, I'm in the same position I was in when I first rode into Manusk," Elizabeth said. "I have a target painted on my back."

"You won't come to any harm if I have anything to do with it," Rowan said softly.

Elizabeth felt her heart warm and gave her a brief smile. "Thank you, Rowan."

They lapsed into silence.

Elizabeth held up her hand and reined in her horse. The guardsmen stopped and Isengard gave her a questioning look.

"This is as far as we go. The farm is across those fields." Elizabeth nodded in the direction of Felson's farm.

They dismounted quietly.

"Corporal," Elizabeth said. "Secure the horses and ready the men. I'm going to go ahead and take a look at the farm."

"I'm going with you," Rowan said, giving her a cool look that brooked no room for argument.

Elizabeth nodded. "All right, *we're* going to scout out the farm."

"With me," Isengard said. "I won't allow the princess into harm's way without me by her side."

"Thank you, old friend," Rowan said with a fond grin.

Elizabeth rolled her eyes. "All right." She turned to the corporal. "Give us one hour."

The corporal saluted and took the reins to her horse.

"Ready?" she asked Rowan and Isengard.

They nodded.

"Let's go," she said.

They walked into the tall corn stalks and angled toward the house. They had not gone more than a few feet when they heard rustling coming from their right. Elizabeth immediately halted, Rowan and Isengard stopping with her.

"Who's there?" a man demanded in a loud whisper. "We have you surrounded."

"Who are you?" Elizabeth demanded.

"Your Grace?" the man asked, immediately sounding contrite.

"Yes," Elizabeth said. "Show yourself."

A shadowy figure of a man stepped out from between the corn stalks. "It's me, Farrow."

"Farrow," Elizabeth said. "What are you doing here?"

"Waiting for you," Farrow said.

"How did you know I was coming?" she asked.

"I knew you'd turn up sooner or later. We left word with the roadside watch that there was a buildup of forces at Felson's farm. We knew you'd come," he said, and the men around him nodded.

"Did you tell them anything about a grave?" Rowan asked.

Farrow's brow furrowed. "Grave? No."

Rowan, Isengard, and Elizabeth exchanged glances. Elizabeth could understand the news of the buildup of forces not reaching her, given Herbert's interference, but it begged the question of how Benton had found out about the mass graves. That was assuming Benton was correct and it wasn't simply a ruse to get her out of the city.

Well, no help for it now. No matter what we stand and fight and clean up the farm.

"I think we came here by coincidence," she said. "Your message never reached me. We had a traitor in our midst, Captain Herbert."

Farrow and his men exchanged another glance. "That doesn't surprise me, Your Grace. Your sentries along the road have been complaining about the strange and senseless orders they've been given, and also having manpower stripped away from them."

"What kind of senseless orders?" Rowan asked.

"The kind that send men to oblivion," Farrow said. "The patrols that've been ordered out normally don't return."

Elizabeth shook her head. "That won't be happening anymore. Now, you take your orders direct from me, Peter, and Sean. Yes?"

Farrow bowed. "Yes, Your Grace."

"All right." Elizabeth nodded toward the farm. "It's time to take back that land, Farrow. How many do you have with you?"

"There are twenty with me," Farrow said.

Elizabeth raised internal eyebrows. *That's a lot of displaced farmers.*

"All right. My men are by the road. Send your people to them. We're going to take the farm and it's better if you stand behind armed men and help them. You yourself will need to come with us. We need your eyes on the land."

He bowed, his teeth flashing in a grin. "Yes, Your Grace."

"Let's go." Elizabeth, Rowan, Isengard, and Farrow slipped silently through the corn field as the others headed back toward the guardsmen by the road.

They reached the wheat field, and Elizabeth and Farrow crept forward on their hands and knees as Rowan and Isengard split off and headed toward the rear of the farm.

There were no signs of armed men watching the road but they heard the sounds of laughing men in the distance.

Very arrogant. They seriously think we're going to leave them sitting here so they can do what they want.

Farrow nodded toward the house. The light from the windows spilled out into the dooryard, casting soft shadows. The door was open and they could see figures shifting around inside.

Laughter and catcalls sounded from inside, and Elizabeth listened carefully for the voices. She glanced at Farrow. He held up seven fingers. She nodded.

She saw shadowy figures in the distance. They crept out of the cover of the trees near the barn and toward the open door. More light spilled out of the barn and a horse neighed restlessly.

Elizabeth felt her heartbeat pick up. *What does Rowan think she's doing? She's going to get caught.*

Elizabeth felt her heart leap to her throat as a man emerged from the house and walked for the barn. Rowan slipped around the side, but the man stopped dead and tilted his head toward her disappearing figure.

"Hey," he called.

Elizabeth cursed and began to stand but Farrow quickly drew her back down into the field. He stood and lurched toward the man.

"Here!" he slurred, wavering unsteadily on his feet. "Innkeeper! Where's my horse?" He stumbled toward the man, waving his fist in an exaggerated manner. "A man goes out to use the privy and look what happens. His horse gets stolen."

He made to grab the man by the lapels but the man stepped back with a cry of disgust. "Get your hands off me, you skunk." He kicked at Farrow.

Rowan and Isengard slipped away from the barn and back into the shadows.

Farrow collapsed back with a grunt, cursing. "Whatcha do that for, you pig?" He attempted to roll back onto his feet. "What kind of establishment are you running here?"

"This isn't an inn, you wretch." The man shoved Farrow back down again.

"If it's not an inn then what is it, you bloody liar?" Farrow said, attempting to get back to his feet again.

More men emerged from the house and Elizabeth cursed again.

"Are you all right, Mason?" a taller man said, coming to stand beside the first, Mason.

"I'm fine, but this accursed wretch is convinced he's at an inn," Mason said, tilting his head toward the second man.

"Really?" the second man asked. "Then how about we let him sample our hospitality?"

Mason laughed, dragged Farrow to his feet, and slammed a fist into Farrow's stomach.

The breath exploded from Farrow as a solid grunt of pain.

Rowan and Isengard crept up beside Elizabeth.

"Go and get help," Elizabeth said shortly. "I'm going to get Farrow."

"No," Isengard said.

"Now," Elizabeth snarled, shoving him.

"Go, Isengard," Rowan said. "Elizabeth, let's go and get your man."

She got to her feet before Elizabeth had a chance to respond. Elizabeth followed a split second behind her, heart hammering in her chest.

She's going to get hurt. Elizabeth pulled her sword from its scabbard. She snarled and ran toward the men, overtaking Rowan and slashing at Mason. Farrow barely had time to roll out of the way as Mason drew his sword and blocked her blow. The concussion rang all the way up her arms and her muscles screamed in protest as she pulled back and slashed at him again. He blocked her blow again and slashed back at her.

Rowan parried and slashed at the second man and they soon found themselves back to back, fighting more men as reinforcements poured out of the farm house. Elizabeth was dimly aware that Rowan was faltering behind her, hampered by the injury to her side. Then she felt the sting of a sword against her own side as a man thrust forward and slipped beneath her defenses to nick her.

Just then, an arrow thudded into one of the men before her. He went down with a yelp, clutching at the arrow sticking out of his chest.

"Down!" Elizabeth yelled as archers fired at the men in earnest.

She felt Rowan duck behind her, and more arrows thudded home. Soon the men were scattering and pulling away from them.

Elizabeth risked a look at the fields behind them and saw a line of archers marching toward them. The men at the farm ran for better cover and the archers made short work of them.

Soon the dooryard was littered with dead and injured men.

Isengard, looking grim, ran toward them, the corporal and two peasants behind them.

"Your Grace? Your Highness?" the corporal said, skidding to a halt before them. "Are you all right? What happened? Weren't you supposed to wait for us?"

Elizabeth glared at Isengard and Rowan, still squatting in the dirt. She shook from the aftermath of adrenaline pounding through her system.

"Yes, Corporal, we were," she said. She knelt beside Rowan. "What were you thinking, Rowan? You could have gotten yourself killed."

Isengard and the corporal withdrew, looking everywhere other than at Elizabeth and Rowan. Isengard quickly knelt beside Farrow, who was sitting on the ground and groaning. An arrow jutted out of the meaty part of his biceps.

Rowan stared at Elizabeth, blinking. She was pale.

As the silence stretched out, Elizabeth put a gentle hand on her shoulder. "Why don't you let me have a look at the wound in your side?"

"You're bleeding." Rowan peered at Elizabeth. "You got hurt, didn't you?"

Elizabeth smiled wryly, despite herself. "It *was* a sword fight, Your Highness. These things are to be expected."

Rowan stared at her, ashen faced.

"I'm fine, I can assure you," Elizabeth said softly. "Now, then, let me look at that wound on your side."

"Please, Your Highness," Isengard said, appearing beside them. He knelt beside Rowan.

Elizabeth reached for her but Rowan slapped her hands away. Elizabeth stared at her, shocked.

Rowan glared at her. "Isengard will do it. Go and find out what happened to my sailors, *Your Grace*."

Elizabeth slowly withdrew, stung by Rowan's anger and the fury evident in her icy blue eyes. "Yes, Your Highness," she said coolly and bowed.

She stood and walked away, stiff backed.

She saw the corporal and several peasants kneeling beside Farrow. She joined them awkwardly, giving Farrow a tired grin.

"Your Grace," he said. "You've got blood on your shirt."

She looked down at her shirt and saw the thin smear of blood around the edges of a slice through the fabric.

"And you have an arrow sticking out of your arm," she replied.

Farrow snorted a laugh and hissed in pain. "That I do, Your Grace." He winced. He looked at one of the peasants. "And Vance here can explain why to my wife and daughter."

The man standing beside the corporal blushed and shifted slightly. "Sorry, Farrow. Those men moved around a little and I couldn't see well."

"Yes, and the result is meself as a pincushion, lad," Farrow replied, not unkindly.

"Corporal," Elizabeth said. "The men holding the farm?"

"All you see here are dead. We are bringing the injured into the barn. No losses on our side."

"Well done, Corporal," she said.

"Thank your militia," the corporal said dryly. "This would have gone much worse without them."

A man jogged from the barn. "Corporal!"

"Excuse me, Your Grace, gentlemen," he said with a bow and withdrew.

"Vance, is it?" Elizabeth said to the boy who'd shot Farrow. He seemed in his late teens, the shadow of acne still on his face.

Vance nodded and gave her a clumsy bow. "Yes, Your Grace."

"That was good shooting," she said. "The *flesh wound* Farrow is moaning about is hardly lethal."

"You aren't the one with a bloody arrow sticking out of your bloody arm, lass," Farrow said archly. "This bloody thing hurts."

"Let me look," Elizabeth said.

She leaned in and looked at the wound. The skin on the side of his arm bulged and she could see the arrow had pierced his arm cleanly.

"You want me to pull it out? I can snap the arrow and pull it through." She looked at him. "It's probably going to hurt, though."

Farrow nodded. "I believe it is. No need to worry, though. Heather will see to me, as will Mia." He looked at the arrow glumly. "She's going to kill me for the shirt, though."

"Where is she? We can take you to her," Elizabeth said.

"She's close," Farrow said. He gave a sharp whistle.

Figures slipped from the shadowed stand of trees on the other side of the farm house.

One of the figures picked up her skirts and jogged toward them, closely followed by another.

"Farrow," Heather said.

Mia stopped just behind her, sparing a quick glance at Elizabeth.

"Heather," he said. "Vance shot me."

Heather's mouth tightened and Vance blushed, his glance darting around. He looked as though he wished he could be anywhere else.

"Oh, he's fine," Elizabeth said.

"I'll be the judge of that," Heather said archly. She inspected the wound and clucked her tongue.

"I'll break it and we can pull it through," Elizabeth said. "Guardsman."

The ringing of steel against steel erupted from the barn.

CHAPTER 12

ELIZABETH CURSED AND jumped to her feet, distantly aware of the feel of a hand slipping along the outside of her shirt.

She ran for the barn, sword in hand, a guardsman behind her.

The barn had erupted into a furious melee of fighting. She saw a trap door lay open in the center of the floor and about ten men—with more emerging from the hidden room—poured out and engaged her guards in combat.

She quickly engaged the closest one and helped a guardsman push him back into the barn.

Her world became a raw, instinctual collage of thrust, slash, and parry as the armed men engaged them in earnest.

It felt like hours later that the battle finally came to an end. Elizabeth's sword was coated with blood and she sweated freely in the stuffy barn.

A group of disarmed men knelt close by the empty horse stalls, the militia watching them carefully for further signs of hostility. Guardsmen were pulling the dead into a row outside the barn and tending to the injured. Elizabeth grabbed a section of shirt from one of the dead and cleaned her sword.

"Corporal?" she asked.

"Yes, Your Grace," the corporal, looking disheveled, said as he came up beside her. "You're bleeding, Duchess Elizabeth."

Elizabeth felt the stinging of the sword cut in her side and waved it away. "I know. Probably just needs a stitch or two." She glanced around the barn, looking for Rowan, who was not there. "Please get Princess Rowan and Isengard."

The corporal saluted and jogged out of the barn.

Elizabeth slowly approached the kneeling men, studying them closely. They were clean and well fed and had the lean, muscular look of fighting men.

"Which one of you is in charge?" she asked.

The men looked resolutely forward and remained silent.

"No one, hmm?" she said. "None of you?"

She turned in time to see Rowan striding into the barn, looking every inch the royal princess. Isengard followed a correct pace behind her, his back straight.

"Ah, Your Highness," Elizabeth said with a bow. She turned back to the men. "Since you have no officer, how about your own tongues? What are you doing on this farm? You occupy it unlawfully."

The men remained silent but some of them shifted uneasily.

Elizabeth let the silence play out. "Let's try this again. It is a capital offense to attempt assassination of a royal. As you know, I am not just the Duchess of Manusk, but also Princess Elizabeth St. John. I can—and will—string you up for your little prank of attacking my men and me in the barn. Talk or I begin executing you. It's your choice."

The silence became almost pressurized.

"All right," she said. "Since no one's willing to talk, I'll begin hanging you. Corporal, please fetch some rope."

The corporal saluted and hurried off. Elizabeth turned back to the men.

"Where are my sailors?" Rowan said coldly.

Elizabeth snuck a glance at Rowan and flinched. Rowan's bright blue eyes burned with rage.

"Elizabeth," Rowan ground out before Elizabeth could utter another word. "Are you going to let these . . . garbage dwellers . . . hold silence while my men lie in graves on foreign soil?"

"Well, we were getting to that. I suppose now is as good a time as any." Elizabeth turned back to the men. "If you answer the princess's question I will let you go."

The men, some of whom were whey faced, exchanged glances. One of the men closest to her cast a black look at his companions. They all shifted and avoided his gaze.

"You," she said to him. "Even if you're not an officer, you seem to be in charge. Are you willing to talk?"

He glared at her and slowly shook his head.

The corporal re-entered the barn and Elizabeth waved him over. She pointed to the grim-faced man. "Hang him. Now."

The corporal saluted and gestured toward a guardsman. They dragged the kicking and struggling man from the barn.

Elizabeth turned back to the group of captured men, most of whom looked terrified as well as shocked.

She heard the sound of a neighing horse, and the terrified cries of a man, cut off by a brisk snapping sound.

"Anyone?" she continued.

Silence.

"They're in the field behind the barn," a man blurted out.

"Thank you," Elizabeth said. She gestured for one of her militia. "Take as many men as you can find and search the field behind the barn."

"It's dark outside, Your Grace," the man said. "The chances of us finding something are slim."

"If you see nothing now then we'll look by light of day," Elizabeth said. She turned back to Rowan. "Do you have any further questions you want to ask?"

"Who do you answer to?" Rowan said. "Who is your master?"

The men shrugged.

"We are of Sandcliff," the one who had already spoken said.

"Did you kill my sailors?" Rowan said.

Silence.

"Live or die, gentleman. Take your pick," Elizabeth said.

Silence.

She pointed to the man who had spoken. "Him. Hang him next."

"No," the man blurted out. "For the love of God, no. It was Mason. Of Osk. And all of his Osk companions."

"The dead men outside?" Elizabeth asked.

The man nodded so hard his head seemed in danger of falling off.

"What did they tell you?" Elizabeth said.

"They were from a place called Well . . . Wellard . . . somewhere and were an advance trading mission. Their fleet was ten days behind them and they had to report back to them by then."

Elizabeth backed up and stood beside Rowan. "Is it enough for you?" she asked softly.

Rowan nodded. "It's enough. But they must come to Welland justice. You must keep them alive."

Elizabeth nodded. "I'll have them brought back with us and put into the city jail. Fate will take them from there, or you, whichever catches up with us first."

"Chain them as the chattel that they are and see they are taken to the city jail," Elizabeth said to the corporal. "You can keep them in their hole until we leave."

Elizabeth turned and strode from the barn, leaving Rowan inside.

She approached the closest tree by the barn and sank down into the darkness against the rough bark of the trunk. She leaned back and sighed. She was tired and her side hurt. She put her hand against the cut and it felt wet and stung badly. She pulled her fingers back.

She felt exhausted, exhausted enough to fall asleep sitting up.

She slowly became aware of a feminine form beside her and she looked up, her lips quirking into a grin.

"Your Grace," Mia said softly, dropping to her knees. "My father said you'd been injured." She leaned forward, her soft breasts pressing into Elizabeth's arm.

"I think you've earned the right to call me Elizabeth," Elizabeth said softly. "Thank your father for me."

Mia's fingers found Elizabeth's shirt and gently pulled it up over the cut. "I'd love to call you Elizabeth but you're always going to be Your Grace to me." She gently probed the cut.

Elizabeth sucked in breath and her muscles tightened as Mia hit a sore spot.

"Always?" she said.

"Always," Mia said. "You're too dangerous a woman for a simple girl like me, Your Grace."

"I'm not offering marriage, Mia."

"I wouldn't accept if you were. We're too different," Mia said, quickly stealing a kiss.

Elizabeth felt her body heat and she moaned softly. "I know. It wouldn't work."

"You take my breath away, Elizabeth," Mia moaned. "You're so beautiful."

"I could say the same to you," Elizabeth said as Mia tore herself away and tended to Elizabeth's wound.

Elizabeth sighed and a grin tugged about her lips. "How's it look, Mia?"

"Shallow," she said, sounding firmer. "I don't think you need stitches. I'll clean it out and bandage it."

Elizabeth shifted and Mia cleaned the wound, applied salve, and a bandage.

"Lean back," she whispered when she finished.

Elizabeth, feeling heavy with exhaustion, leaned back into Mia's embrace. Mia massaged her shoulders, drawing a deep groan of contentment from Elizabeth.

She was almost asleep when a sharp voice cut into her haze.

"This is a charming scene," Rowan said.

Elizabeth opened her eyes to see Rowan's hot gaze shifting between Mia and her.

"Rowan," she said. "Have you been seen to?"

Rowan's blue eyes spat fire. "Yes, although not as well as you."

Elizabeth glanced at Mia guiltily. Her guilt instantly vanished as she saw Mia's eyes spitting the same fire as Rowan's.

"Her Grace is the Duchess of Manusk," Mia said coldly. "She has earned our respect. Remember that, *Your Highness*. If she wishes to sleep under a tree then so be it."

Elizabeth cleared her throat. "It's fine, Mia."

Mia gave her a pointed look. "With Your Grace's permission?"

Elizabeth nodded. "Yes. Of course."

Mia gathered her things, flounced off, and cast another vicious look at Rowan as she left.

Rowan glared at her retreating back. She turned back to Elizabeth. "Are you having fun with your playthings?"

Elizabeth shot to her feet, hands shaking with rage. "She is a free woman, *not* my *plaything*. I am much more honorable than that. Second, who are you to judge me? You know nothing of me or about me."

Rowan held her gaze, fight gone out of her. Her eyes held the same glimmer of sadness as they had before. "Yes. I'm sorry. I shouldn't have said that." She gestured toward the tree. "Do you mind if I sit for a while?"

Elizabeth felt exhausted. She waved to the ground next to her. "Yes. Sit."

Rowan sat beside her and Elizabeth studied the silhouette of her perfect profile. "What's on your mind?"

"My sailors."

"Ah. Of course."

Rowan glanced at her. "No, not quite like that. It's what the men said to you. They said my sailors told them we'd be in Manusk Harbor ten days after them. That's not right. Our agreement was *seven* days."

Elizabeth nodded. "All that proves is that they wanted your ship to surprise the men at the docks."

"My ship was lost at seven days."

"Your ship being lost was as per expectations. They'd been

extinguishing the signal fires to break up traders on the rocks to steal their cargoes." Elizabeth shifted and hissed in pain as the cut in her side stretched.

Rowan shifted so she was sitting behind Elizabeth. "Lean back." She pulled Elizabeth back into her arms. "Rest. Is that comfortable?"

Elizabeth sank back into Rowan's embrace, surrounded by her warmth and spicy scent. "Yes."

"Something about all of this bothers me," Rowan said, her breath tickling Elizabeth's ear. "The uniforms indicate that we're to think you're the blame for the unlit signal fires. Do you know when the false uniforms began to appear? Was it the time you were due in Manusk or before?"

"I have no way of telling. Herbert was there before me and he never told me the truth."

"Herbert. We'll get to him. If it was the same time, what would normally happen if a foreign dignitary was almost killed in your land?"

"We assume it would be seen as an act of war by the foreign power. If the king didn't stand behind the act of aggression it would mean that the king would depose the noble who committed the act of aggression."

"What if all of this was done in a duchy not under the king's control?"

"The nobles that committed the act of aggression would stand between the foreign dignitaries and the king. It would mean they would have a stranglehold on the situation. They could play either side. They could tell the foreigners that they were innocent and the king was guilty. They would need the help of the foreigners to bring the king to *justice*. The foreigners would end up unwittingly supplying them and they would be free to wage war against their rightful ruler. It would come to civil war." Elizabeth opened her eyes and she felt suddenly wide awake as adrenaline coursed through her system.

"Very good," Rowan said. "I think this situation is much worse than either of us thought."

"I have to get back to the city. I have to pull together my army and get word to my father."

"What you need to do first, is get some rest," Rowan said, shifting so that her strong hands kneaded Elizabeth's tense shoulders. "We need to strategize and plan. Civil war is an ugly thing and we have to minimize loss of innocent lives."

"I've been a complete idiot," Elizabeth said. "Could I have been more stupid and arrogant?"

"Relax. You walked into a trap. Now you see it before you, and you must decide if to spring it or if it's best to escape first." Rowan sought out the knots in Elizabeth's shoulders and worked them away. Elizabeth relaxed.

"What do you need to do?" Rowan asked softly.

"I need to pull together my army and send word to my father. I have to fortify the city and evacuate as many civilians as I can."

"And all of that can wait until tomorrow, can't it?" Rowan said.

Elizabeth gave a bone cracking yawn as days of weariness and stress caught up with her. "I should start now."

"You can't do anything," Rowan whispered. "You're in my arms under a tree. There's plenty of time to leave later."

Elizabeth felt her eyes slide closed. Despite herself, she slept, nestled in the security of Rowan's arms.

"YOUR GRACE?" A male asked.

Elizabeth opened her eyes, blinking, trying to push back the vestiges of sleep. Her eyes felt gritty and tired. She still felt safe and warm, snuggled in Rowan's arms, and looked up into Rowan's beautiful, sleepy blue eyes. Her perfect mouth twitched with a smile. Elizabeth gave her the ghost of a grin.

She turned to the corporal who was kneeling patiently before her.

"Yes, Corporal?" she said, disentangling herself from Rowan with a distant feeling of loss.

"It's dawn," he said. "We couldn't find anything in the field during the night, so we're going out now to search."

"Why didn't you wake me earlier?" she asked.

"Isengard wouldn't let us," he said, coloring.

"Since when do you take your orders from Isengard?"

"He's the ranking officer, as he reminded us when we suggested waking you. He wasn't pleased with the idea."

Elizabeth sighed. "All right. We will discuss discipline and the chain of command later. In the meantime, begin your search."

"Yes, Your Grace," the corporal said with a bow.

"And corporal?" she said to his retreating back.

He turned to her.

"Thank you." She smiled.

He grinned, gave her a quick salute, and continued on his way.

Elizabeth turned to Rowan. "Who *is* Isengard, anyway?"

Rowan's laughter chimed out into the dawn stillness. "He's my bodyguard. He was a general in my father's army and the soldier who found me in the field."

Elizabeth gave her a lopsided grin. "Then he's welcome to boss my guardsmen around." She leaned back and whispered in Rowan's ear. "And remind me to thank you some time."

Rowan smiled.

Elizabeth got to her feet and held out a hand to help Rowan up. Rowan took it and Elizabeth pulled her to her feet. Rowan gave her hand a quick squeeze before releasing it.

"That smells like breakfast," Rowan said, nostrils flaring as she sniffed the early morning air.

The scent of roasting meat wafted out of the open kitchen door. A cluster of guardsmen and militia waited outside, glancing at the door and talking quietly amongst themselves.

The men parted as Elizabeth approached them, Rowan and Isengard behind her. She went to the door and stuck her head in and saw Heather, Mia, and a small group of women moving purposefully around the kitchen preparing food.

Heather looked up and saw Elizabeth in the doorway and her face creased into a broad grin. "Good morning, Your Grace."

"Good morning," Elizabeth said with a return smile. She nodded toward the cooking pot. "That smell is driving me wild. Any chance to beg a bowl off you?"

Heather laughed. "Of course. Mia." She gestured for Mia to serve Elizabeth, Rowan, and Isengard.

Mia silently laded some stew into a bowl, following it with a chunk of thick bread. Elizabeth murmured her thanks at the bowl thrust in her direction. Mia looked everywhere but at her.

Rowan and Isengard both accepted their bowls with polite thanks and backed out of the house to eat leaning comfortably against the house.

"After we've eaten we'll go to the bottom field," Rowan said. "I want to see how the search is progressing."

Elizabeth nodded. "A good idea."

They devoured their stew and put the plates back into the kitchen. Heather waved away Elizabeth's thanks, and they left the house again. Farrow was standing outside, his arm heavily bandaged.

He bowed when he saw them. "Your Grace."

"Farrow," Elizabeth said with a grin. "You look much better without the arrow."

"I *feel* much better without the arrow," he said. "Now, then, I expect you'll be wanting to go to the fields?"

Elizabeth nodded. "Yes, please."

"I've been waiting for that," he said. "Come with me."

They followed him across the dooryard and across the wheat fields behind the barn. Early morning sunlight bathed the trees that bordered the fields ahead of them.

Elizabeth took a deep breath of the clear air and smiled. "This land is beautiful."

"Yes, it is, Your Grace," Farrow said. He looked around at the tall stalks of wheat. "I suppose it could have been much worse. At least there's going to be a harvest this year."

"I hope so," Elizabeth said.

Farrow glanced sharply at her. "Why, lass? What's the problem?"

"I don't know yet," she said. "War is coming. You should take yours and get out while you can."

Farrow pulled her to a halt and looked at her. "My family has farmed our land for centuries. I don't intend to turn tail and run. Especially since you're counting on your militia to keep your farms safe."

"Yes, I need you as my militia, Farrow," she said. "Make no mistake about that. But it's much better for you to stay alive. I can't guarantee your safety and I certainly can't guarantee Osk and Sandcliff will leave you alone."

"Easy, lass," he said. "Osk and Sandcliff have never been friends to the men of Manusk. We have always kept to ourselves and taken care of our own. Town politics mean nothing out here."

"You're now in the middle of town politics," Elizabeth said. "I've brought you into it and for that I'm truly sorry."

He shook his head. "Nothing to be sorry for. For the first time in generations we have pride in our land and our duchess. You were the first who tried to give us back our hearts. For that you have our thanks, lass. Your militia will stand behind you until the last."

She clasped forearms with him. "I don't know what I've done to deserve your loyalty. But you have my thanks for it." She paused, looking at the birds wheeling in the early morning sky. "Stay away from the city if you can. If you see any of my guardsmen by the road tell me and take them in. They'll fight with you."

Farrow nodded.

They turned and continued walking.

"Those birds," Isengard said, pointing at the crows wheeling in the sky. "Are they carrion eaters?"

"Yes, they are," Farrow said slowly. "The bastards *did* desecrate Felson's farm."

They broke into a jog and headed toward the cluster of guardsmen and militia they could see just beyond the tree line.

"Corporal," Elizabeth called as they got closer. "Have you found something?"

The corporal looked pale and grimaced. He nodded. "I think so."

"Show me."

The corporal stood aside and gestured at the ground.

Elizabeth dropped to one knee and studied it. A bloody hand stuck out of the ground, bone showing in places that the crows had pecked away the flesh. The air stank of rot.

She put a hand in front of her face and backed away. "Dig it up."

The corporal's mouth tightened but he saluted. "Start digging," he said to three pale and grim-faced guardsmen standing close by.

They gouged the ground with their hands and Elizabeth joined in with them. The first body they uncovered was filthy from the earth and blood that seemed to cover it. It was bloated and showed signs of heavy bruising.

"His teeth are missing," a guardsman said in a high, tight voice. He turned around, fell to his knees, and expelled the contents of his stomach.

Soon the stench of vomit joined with rotting flesh and Elizabeth held her hand in front of her face.

"Is he yours?" she asked Rowan.

Rowan looked at the body, nodded, and then turned away, breathing shallowly and clenching her jaw. Her eyes were hot with rage.

Isengard knelt by the corpse and studied it carefully. "He was tortured."

Elizabeth bit back a sarcastic retort and shook her head. "Dig the rest of them up." She turned to Rowan. "Are they to be buried? Are there any rituals that you require to be performed?"

"Prove to me you didn't do this, Elizabeth," Rowan said, turning to her.

Elizabeth stared at her in shock. *She can't possibly believe I did this?*

"What about this?" the corporal said, eyes flashing with anger.

He pulled the corpse's head back and pointed at the jaw.

Elizabeth held her breath and took a close look at the bruising. It formed the vague shape of a sea bird.

"That looks like it was done with a ring, doesn't it?" she said.

The corporal nodded.

"Whose family crest is a bird?" she asked.

"Eagle's Reach is an eagle. Brandywine is a swallow. Osk is a tower and Sandcliff is a seagull," the corporal said.

"It's a seagull, not an eagle or a swallow." Elizabeth turned to Rowan. "The mark is from Sandcliff."

"Can you prove it?" Isengard asked.

"I will bring you Duke Clayton of Sandcliff's ducal signet as proof," Elizabeth said.

"Thank you, Duchess Elizabeth," Isengard said with a low bow. "We would accept that as proof."

"Will you allow us to bury your men?" Elizabeth asked, looking at Rowan.

Rowan turned to her and gave her a sad smile. "We will burn the bodies."

Farrow and the guardsmen gathered firewood as other men of the militia took the remaining bodies from the ground.

Rowan and Elizabeth stood shoulder to shoulder as Isengard carefully lined up the battered corpses. Each one was a testament to the brutality they had been subjected to. They were all covered with bruises, had missing teeth and fingers, and torn flesh.

"That was seven of them," Rowan said, turning to Elizabeth. "What happened to the other three hundred on the ship?"

"They have to be in either Osk or Sandcliff," Elizabeth said. "I don't think they're here. Not even Herbert could hide that number of prisoners."

"We have to get them if they're alive," Rowan said.

"They will be freed as soon as we are able to leave Manusk," Elizabeth said.

"I want Duke Clayton of Sandcliff's head," Rowan murmured. She turned to Elizabeth. "We came in peace and were killed for our trouble."

"Justice will be served, I can promise you that," Elizabeth said. "Even if I'm not around to deliver Clayton, my father and brother will gladly give him to you."

Rowan flinched and nodded.

They silently watched as the men built a rough pyre.

The corporal came over to them and at Elizabeth's nod turned to Rowan.

"May we place the bodies on the pyre or must we wait?"

"Place them on the pyre," Rowan whispered. "Please."

The corporal saluted and the men quickly lined the bodies up neatly on the stacked wood.

"Fire when I give the signal," Isengard said and the corporal nodded.

Rowan took in a deep breath and began to sing. Isengard joined in a moment later, his tenor melding seamlessly with Rowan's contralto.

They listened for long moments to a melancholy song sung in a foreign language. Elizabeth gazed at the ground, acutely uncomfortable. *Why couldn't Rowan and I have met later? When Manusk was under the control of my father? Why?*

The song finished and Rowan spoke a brief sentence in her own language. Isengard repeated it and they put their hands over their hearts.

"It is done," Rowan said to the corporal. "Start the fire."

The corporal gave her a low bow. "By your command, Your Highness."

He signaled a guardsman who held a blazing torch. He held it against the dry wood and soon a finger of flame wound around a single twig. It spread to the other twigs and within minutes the entire pyre was completely aflame.

They stood and watched as the bodies burned to ash. When the ashes finally cooled a little the sun stood more than halfway across the sky. Rowan and Isengard each took a scoop of ashes and tossed them onto the field.

Elizabeth, the guardsmen, and Farrow helped spread them into the earth.

When they were finished, a somber Elizabeth and Rowan took their leave of Farrow.

Elizabeth held out her forearm. "Well met, Farrow."

Farrow clasped her forearm. "Well met, Your Grace. Don't forget about us when you town business is done. Come and see us." His eyes looked sad.

That's an easy promise to make. "I will."

ELIZABETH AND ROWAN finally mounted their horses to begin the trek back to the city of Manusk in the afternoon.

The ride back to the city was silent as each was immersed in her own thoughts.

As they approached the city, Rowan turned to Elizabeth. "Do you know what you're going to do?"

"I'm going to proceed more carefully than I have," Elizabeth said. "I've been rash enough without any further indiscretions to add to our poor tactical position."

They rode through the gates to the cry of *Manusk* from the watchmen standing above the gate.

Elizabeth grimaced. It was a catch cry earlier but now it sounded more like a death knell.

The late afternoon traffic in the city was heavy and Elizabeth and the guardsmen slowed to a walk. The children—the thieves—of Manusk darted in and out of the alleyways, ostensibly playing. Elizabeth spied Benton darting out of the shadows, grinning wildly, Thomas behind her. Benton stopped dead and the smile fell away from her face at the sight of Elizabeth.

Elizabeth stared at her and offered a small salute.

Benton stared back, blank faced.

They rode on.

As they approached the manor, there was a bustle of activity in the courtyard, and Sean jogged up to them.

"Your Grace." He pointed to the group of tattered guardsmen milling in the courtyard. "Look who we found outside the city."

Elizabeth got off her horse, Rowan and Isengard close behind.

"Who's your officer?" she asked, approaching them.

The guardsmen dropped to one knee.

"Your Grace," one of them said. "We don't have one. We're ordinary guardsmen."

"All right, then," Elizabeth said. "Who *was* in charge?"

"Lieutenant Calvin," the guardsman said. "Up until a few days ago. He was killed in an ambush."

"Don't you mean Kelvin?" Elizabeth asked smoothly.

The guardsman looked up with a penetrating stare. "No, I mean *Calvin*, Your Grace."

Elizabeth drew her sword. "I don't have a Calvin who reports to me."

The guardsman drew his sword and they circled each other. The guardsmen who had been kneeling pulled away, giving them more room, and others jogged over and circled them.

"Has Her Grace lost her mind?" the guardsman asked coldly. "Calvin was promoted from corporal for his actions at the Battle on Sonder Hill. He charged into a nest of archers with a group of five men after being cut off from the army. He himself took an arrow for you. Don't you remember? You gave him a commendation and General Arnett himself gave Calvin his stripes while he was lying on his cot yelling about getting an arrow pulled out of his arse."

"I think you mean chest, don't you?"

"I mean arse. Left cheek. He couldn't sit on that side for a week."

Elizabeth lowered her sword. "At ease," she called to the guardsmen watching them carefully. She held out her hand. "Easy, guardsman. Yes, I do remember that event." She grinned. "Including the blood and cursing from the tent."

The guardsman looked at her for a long moment and then nodded warily. "Yes, Your Grace."

Elizabeth beckoned to Sean, who approached her carefully, looking at her as though she'd lost her wits.

"Clean up, guardsman, and get some food and sleep." She turned to Sean. "See to it they have beds. You might consider promoting that man to sergeant if he's really as good as he seems."

Sean saluted. "Yes, Your Grace." He hesitated for a moment. "May I ask as to what's on Her Grace's mind?"

Elizabeth leaned forward. "Not out here," she said softly. She stood. "Meet us in my chambers in an hour, Sean. Bring Peter with you."

"Yes, Your Grace," Sean said, saluting and backing away from her.

Elizabeth turned to Rowan and Isengard, who were both watching her carefully.

"I'm off to have a bath and get some food," she said. "I'm hungry."

She headed into the house, Rowan and Isengard in tow.

"I find it interesting your officer is missing," Rowan said as they headed toward the kitchen.

Elizabeth nodded. "I really want to know how they got here, and what happened to Lieutenant Calvin."

"I suppose it's a clever move, killing your officers," Isengard said. "It robs you of valuable leadership and battle skill."

"I know," Elizabeth said as they entered the kitchen.

"Your Grace," Harriet said, running up to them. "I heard about Captain Herbert."

Elizabeth nodded. "I'm sorry. He was a spy."

"I'm so sorry, Your Grace," Harriet said, putting her hand on Elizabeth's arm. "I didn't know."

"Neither did I," Elizabeth said, patting her hand. "Not to worry. We'll recover."

"I told him everything," Harriet said.

"And he told me nothing," Elizabeth said. She took a deep breath. "After I've had my dinner and a bath, my officers are going to meet with me. Perhaps you should join us. It's about time I knew some of the things he was privy to."

"You aren't angry?" Harriet said with uncharacteristic hesitation. She clutched her skirts convulsively.

"No," Elizabeth said. "I can be angry later when we have more time. At the moment I'm more interested in securing the city than casting blame on people. I'm as guilty of poor character judgment as you seem to think you are. The damage is done."

Harriet nodded. "I suppose so. I'll join you in your chambers in an hour, then, Your Grace."

"Thank you, Harriet."

"I wonder how much she told him?" Rowan whispered into Elizabeth's ear.

"I'm sure she didn't tell him anything more than he already knew," she said softly. "I think he knew more than either one of us."

"I'm sure Osk and Sandcliff know all about the intricacies of your supply situation," Rowan said.

"I know," Elizabeth said. "And I suppose I'm going to be the last one to really know what it is. That's not good."

They got their food and sat down at Elizabeth's now accustomed table. Richard joined them five minutes later.

He bowed to them. "I trust Your Grace is well? We haven't seen you for a little while."

"I have news, Richard," Elizabeth said slowly. "I will share it with you but not in so public a forum. I need your help yet again."

Richard wiped at his lips and put down his spoon. He gave her a penetrating stare. "You can count on my help and the help of the rest of the merchants."

She gave him a genuine smile. "Excellent. Eat, and when we're done we'll adjourn to my chambers."

Richard nodded.

They ate in silence and when they were done, Elizabeth stood up from the table and looked at the others. "It's time. Follow me."

They all stood and followed her out of the kitchen. As they approached the main stairs, Elizabeth saw a flash of Benton's face.

"Go ahead," she said to the others. "I'll be with you in a moment."

"Is everything all right?" Rowan asked, looking curiously at her.

"Fine." Elizabeth smiled. "Really."

Rowan studied her carefully for a moment. "All right. For now."

Elizabeth waited for them to go and then looked around to make sure no one else was watching her. A few guardsmen moved around the foyer and a distracted-looking servant walked by. The guards at the door stared resolutely into the courtyard, relaxed and alert.

She went into the alcove, satisfied no one was paying attention to her.

"Benton?" she whispered.

"Shh," Benton whispered, a shadow amongst darker shadows. "Your Grace."

"We're alone," Elizabeth said, going to one knee so she could see into Benton's dark eyes. "Your secret is safe."

"My secrets aren't safe," Benton said. She tilted her head and studied Elizabeth. "Did you go to the farm?"

Elizabeth nodded. "Yes, I did. Rowan's sailors were there. It was as you said."

Benton drew in a watery breath. "I don't want to play this game anymore."

Elizabeth wanted to tell her it was too late. She wanted to say she would look after Benton if anything happened. She wanted to say Benton would be one of the first to leave the city, but she didn't.

"Yes. I understand. You don't have to play this game anymore. But you are always welcome at my table, daughter of Manusk."

Elizabeth could see beads of moisture on Benton's cheeks. "What's the matter?"

"You're betrayed by someone close to you, Your Grace," Benton said in a wavering, watery voice. "I don't know who."

Elizabeth wiped the tears from her eyes. "I know about my captain of the guard."

"It's not him," Benton said.

Elizabeth felt her blood run cold.

CHAPTER 13

I SHOULD REALLY ask her if she has any ideas at all of who it is. But I can't. This hurts her too much. I should never have asked her to listen at keyholes for me.

"I'll find out who it is," Elizabeth said.

Benton's eyes were wide and aware and wet with tears. She looked as though the weight of the world was on her young shoulders and she couldn't carry it anymore.

Elizabeth felt her heart twist. She held out her arms and Benton was in them, crying for all she was worth.

"Shh," Elizabeth said, stroking her back. "Don't trouble yourself with my problems. I've asked too much of you. You don't have to play this game anymore."

"I can't help it," Benton said, her body shaking with her silent sobs. "I'm sorry, Duchess Elizabeth. I'm so sorry."

"There's nothing to be sorry for," Elizabeth said. She pulled back, smoothing Benton's unruly hair away from her forehead. "Go and eat. Sleep well by the fire. Go out and play with your friends in the alleyways tomorrow. Come and say hello to me every now and again. I like you just for you."

Benton's arms tightened around her neck. "I like you too, Your Grace. I'm one of your proud daughters of Manusk."

Elizabeth smiled. "And we are lucky to have you. Go and get some sleep."

Benton pulled away from her, wiping the tears from her eyes. She darted to the entrance of the alcove and quickly slipped back into the foyer and was gone.

Elizabeth felt her gut twist. *Something's very wrong with Benton. Why is she so upset? And who's the new traitor in our midst?*

Elizabeth stepped out into the foyer, glancing around to see she was still unobserved. She jogged up the stairs, idly marveling at the new wood of the risers and hand rails and then jogged along the corridor to her rooms. It seemed darker than it normally was and she looked up.

The carpenters have replaced the ceilings. I must thank Harriet. I never thought I'd ever get any repairs done. The woman is truly amazing.

She entered her chambers and saw Peter, Sean, Harriet, Richard, Rowan, and Isengard waiting for her. Mara stood unobtrusively by the door.

A table and chairs had been hastily erected in the room and when she entered they all bowed and took their places at the table.

"Mara, tea," Elizabeth said.

Mara bobbed her self-conscious curtsey and scurried out of the room.

Elizabeth took a deep breath. *Where to begin?* "A few things have come to light over the past days that have cast into sharp relief our perilous grasp on the Duchy of Manusk."

"You mean we're in trouble, Your Grace?" Peter asked with the ghost of a grin.

Elizabeth gave him a rueful grin. "I think it's probably worse than that, Captain." She told them what had happened at the farm.

Mara quietly came in and gave them tea.

"Thank you, Mara," Elizabeth said. "That will be all."

Mara massacred another curtsey and fled the room.

"I've been very stupid," Elizabeth said. "I think, Peter, that your disquiet about the counterfeited uniforms and sigils is well founded. I think we've walked into a trap. Osk and Sandcliff captured the Welland trader and tortured and killed part of her crew. The rest are in Osk by the admission of the men at the farm. I don't think Rowan's sunk ship was done by accident. I think it was a deliberate attempt to goad Welland into helping Osk and Sandcliff wage a war against my father. By shifting the blame to me, Welland would almost certainly seek vengeance against my father. I don't think they counted on survivors of the shipwreck and that we would pick them up."

"Do you have any proof of any of these theories?" Richard asked after a long silence.

"We have the confession of the men at the farm and we have the bodies of the sailors. We also know there are prisoners in Osk, again by their admission."

"You realize that Princess Rowan and the other Welland survivors are now targets, don't you, Your Grace?" Peter asked.

Elizabeth looked at him. "Go on."

"If Her Highness and the other survivors rejoin the Welland fleet, then Welland won't supply Osk or Sandcliff because Welland will know they're staging a coup. If I were Gilbert of Osk and Clayton of Sandcliff, I would do my best to ensure no one survived. That way, when the rest of the fleet comes looking for their princess, the only story they'll hear is the one told by Osk and Sandcliff."

Rowan grimaced. "I had realized that." She held up a forefinger to forestall Elizabeth. "Before you tell me again I should leave—and this time I'm inclined to agree with you—I'm telling *you* I'm *not* going to do it until the last minute. I'll not leave my friends to face starving wolves without me."

Elizabeth smiled. "Thank you for your loyalty, Rowan." *It means the world to me.* She looked at each grave face in the room. "I thank you all for all the loyalty you've given me. Richard and Harriet, war is going to descend upon us. It's inevitable now. I'm giving you the choice to leave if that's what you want to do. You've done enough for me."

Richard cleared his throat. He exchanged a glance with Harriet. She pursed her lips and shook her head. He smiled and turned back to Elizabeth. "We're not leaving. We're staying." He took a deep breath. "We of Manusk always thought the king didn't care about us. We were wrong. He sent in his daughter to help us, and that you have, Your Highness. You've done it with honor and compassion for the people of Manusk. There is food, coin, and self respect for us. We would be proud to stay with you, daughter of Manusk, for as long as we are needed."

"Yes," Harriet said. She opened and closed her mouth several times as though she wanted to add something, but finally settled on a sigh.

Elizabeth was at a loss for words. "I don't know what to say, other than to thank you. Truly. From the bottom of my heart."

Richard smiled.

"For Manusk," Harriet said softly.

"Yes," Peter said. "For Manusk."

"For Manusk," Elizabeth said, nodding. "All right. This is what we have, then. My advance force is scattered on the plains, thanks to Herbert's treachery. They must be brought into the city and the city reinforced for battle. My father must be told of what has happened here, and what is going to happen, and the rest of my army on the plains brought in to hold Osk and Sandcliff at bay until my father and his army arrive. The civilians in the city must be evacuated, and the militia must hold our farmland and disrupt supply to the Osk and Sandcliff armies. They can also keep an eye on those troops and report troop movements to us."

"How do you plan on evacuating the civilians?" Sean asked. "If the roads start to see an increase in traffic, Osk and Sandcliff are going to know that we've discovered their plan."

"They won't be going by road," Rowan said with a grin, eyeing Elizabeth carefully.

"By sea?" Richard asked. "I doubt we have enough traders to help us and where would we send them?"

"The Welland trader you have in your harbor will easily hold three hundred people," Isengard said.

"And I can bring in my fleet, unload and carry more people out," Rowan said.

"That would take days," Isengard said. "I'm not convinced we have that much time."

"What if it's a short hop to Coral Bay?" Peter asked. "Duke Carter is an ally."

Richard shook his head. "Coral Bay is shallow. That's why Manusk is the main sea port into the King's Heartland. Any traders that go to Coral Bay have to anchor in deep water and barges are sent out to unload cargo. That's a time consuming process. Only ships with non perishable cargo are willing to go to Coral Bay."

"The only other option is the smaller seaport of Sargay," Sean said. "But that's really at the mercy of tides."

"We have no real choice," Elizabeth said. "If civilians want to leave Manusk they should be freely able to do so. We can send word to Earl Remus of Sargay and Duke Carter of Coral Bay and ask if they can take our people."

"This plan of yours relies on the merchant seamen in the harbor granting passage to the civilians who want to leave," Rowan said. "I can almost guarantee you that prices will rise sharply once the captains realize that the people have no real choice in their method of escape."

"Richard, can you ask Delmarco if he can help?" Elizabeth asked.

"I will, Your Grace," Richard said. "May I make a suggestion?"

"Go ahead."

"I think Princess Rowan is correct in her assessment of greed," he said. "Perhaps we could suggest a system of barter whereby the citizens given passage on a trader will also help load and unload the trader?"

"You think they'll agree to that?" Elizabeth asked doubtfully. "Isn't that what their crews are for?"

"I think they will once Captain Delmarco sets an example for them." Richard grinned. "Besides, a sailor's job is to sail a ship. I'm sure they won't mind if that's all they have to do and not unload cargo."

"And I'll reinforce this with a ducal decree barring the merchant traders from gouging the general population," Elizabeth said.

Richard winced. "They're not going to like that."

"Nor will they like not having a major sea port to unload cargo, which is what *definitely* will happen if they don't try and help me." She smiled. "All right, ducal decree it is, then. Richard, Harriet—I'm sure rumors of invasion will start flying any day now. If you can, spread word about evacuation after the decree comes out. Richard, Peter will give you the decree for the docks when we are done here."

"As you wish, Your Grace," Richard replied, inclining his head.

"All right," Elizabeth said. "Next, the troops. Peter, where the devil is my army?"

"We have seven hundred guards in the city. A few hundred of these are from the plains outside the city. Reports from those hundreds are that there are small detachments of armed troops ambushing them. The strikes are coordinated and have detailed knowledge of our troop positions."

"That makes sense," Rowan said. "Your guard captain was a traitor."

Peter nodded. "Yes, Your Highness. Also, it seems that the strikes target officers. There was a campaign two days ago that we didn't hear about that left six hundred dead. I'm unsure how many we have left, Your Grace, but I think we're now close to our full contingent of guardsmen."

Elizabeth grimaced. "We have seven hundred left to defend Manusk."

"That's not enough to guard the walls, Elizabeth," Rowan said.

"We can still do damage with the troops we have," Elizabeth said. "Do we have a map of the city?"

Sean smiled and bowed. "I thought you might ask, Your Grace. So I brought these." He pulled a roll of maps out from the floor beside him and unrolled them on the table.

"This is a map of the city." He pointed to the second one. "The first is a map of the Duchy of Manusk."

"Excellent. Thank you, Sean." Elizabeth moved the two maps so they were side by side. She ran her finger in a circle around the northern plains. "These," she said to Isengard and Rowan, "are the northern plains. The Duchy of Manusk encompasses the main highway to the King's Heartland. My father changed the boundaries when he found out Osk and Sandcliff were still in Manusk. To the left lies Osk, the right, Sandcliff. My troops came down the main highway and stayed on Manusk soil."

"That corridor of land is obviously where Osk and Sandcliff have cut you off," Rowan said.

"Yes," Elizabeth said. "The jaws of the trap. We expected them to take the land when we came down it. That's why," she pointed to the western section of Manusk, "we've concentrated on keeping this land clear. It's deep in Manusk territory and leads to the border of the Duchy of Coral Bay. Coral Bay has good access to the King's Heartland, as does Manusk."

"What about the rumors we've heard of Coral Bay being without its duke?" Sean asked.

"If Coral Bay was taken," Rowan said, "you don't have enough troops to guard that side of your own duchy. It's already a loss."

"And if the rumors are true, then it means Osk—which borders both Manusk *and* Coral Bay—is pushing down to cut us off from the west."

"What about this side?" Isengard asked, pointing to the east. "Sargay?"

"Sargay is a small holding on the marshes," Elizabeth said. "It's not big enough to give us any military support. Remus is a good man but he can't help us. It's going to take all the troops he has to remain neutral. If the rumors about Coral Bay are true, then I'm sure Sargay is holding off Sandcliff troops. The only military aid we can rely on will be from the King's Heartland."

"What about your General Arnett?" Rowan asked. "Where's he?"

"Above Osk and Sandcliff lies the Princedom of Callipsys, under my brother's control. My troops are normally stationed there. They guard the border of Callipsys against Osk and Sandcliff to the south, and Grimm and Piper to the east. Shay's Canyons and Harper's Wells to the west border the King's Heartland and I have troops patrolling those borders, as well as Fotheringill and Eagle's Reach to the north. Normally the majority of troops are stationed to the south to guard against Osk and Sandcliff since relations with the other duchies are either neutral or good."

Rowan gave her a measured stare. "So you put the bulk of your troops above the cork of the bottle you find yourself in?"

"No," Elizabeth said. "That's what the sixteen hundred troops with me were for. To guard the border of the highway against Osk and Sandcliff."

"But thanks to a traitor in your midst most of them are now dead."

Elizabeth sighed. "Exactly. But even that may not be a complete loss. We have messengers that regularly report to Arnett. If any one of them does not report in at a designated time, Arnett must assume the worst and send down the army to find out what's become of us."

"Do you have regular messengers or do you change them all the time?" Isengard asked.

"We change them so Osk and Sandcliff can't detect a pattern," Elizabeth said. "Normally it's a good system, but this time I have to assume we've been compromised. Captain Herbert would have received a response back from Arnett and would have asked about it I'm sure."

"Or, if he really wanted to be devious, he'd kill any messengers you sent out and replace them with one of his own," Rowan said. "That's what I would do. I'd send Arnett the message to stay in place."

Elizabeth nodded. "Certainly. So I'm going to need another volunteer to go out to Arnett and bring him in."

"Osk and Sandcliff will be on the lookout for a lone traveler," Rowan said. "They'll need a better disguise than that. How many peasants still use that road?"

"Peter?" Elizabeth asked.

"Not that many," Peter said. "They mostly travel to the east and west where the majority of farmland is, but I'm sure we could make it look as though a small group was headed toward the King's Heartland."

"Excellent," Elizabeth said.

"If I may suggest one of my own people?" Rowan said.

"Why would you want to do that? I thought you were leaving," Elizabeth said, giving her a sharp look.

"I have an expert in infiltration and spying with me. She was meant to be a handy addition to this trading expedition. She will go through where others can't." Rowan grinned.

"Does this lady have a name?" Elizabeth asked.

"You've met her, I believe. Kellen."

"Garvin. That's the boy with the broken leg? His friend Kellen?"

"That would be the one."

"But she can barely speak our language."

Rowan's eyes danced. "That's what you think. I can assure you she can speak it better than I. She's a trained diplomat and an expert at blending in. Plus, she can look after herself."

"She's a harmless little thing."

"That's as far from the truth as you can get," Isengard said. "I'm sure the princess told you I'm her bodyguard and that's true, but Kellen is truly her protector."

I feel like such a witless idiot. How on earth could I have missed this much going on around me?

"Don't feel badly, Elizabeth," Rowan said. "None of this was supposed to have happened. Under normal circumstances, Kellen would have stood by my side, learning your customs and language so trade between our nations went more smoothly."

"And it's entirely normal for a duchess to rely on her guardsmen to handle military matters while she sees to the governance of her duchy," Peter said. "I've been happily blabbing like a fool to Herbert and I'm sure I'm in no small part to blame for the decimation of our guardsmen."

"And I've been following orders without complaint, no matter how idiotic they may seem to me," Sean said.

Elizabeth gave them both a rueful grin. "Thank you, gentlemen. I suppose none of this really matters now. What matters is that we realize we've made some terrible mistakes and we're trying to fix them." She nodded at Rowan. "All right, we'll send Kellen to General Arnett. I'll give her my ducal signet ring as proof that the message is from me."

"Yes, Your Grace," Peter, Sean, Isengard, and Rowan chorused.

Elizabeth smiled, despite herself. She grabbed her cup of tea and found it empty. "Harriet, would you please send for Mara to bring us more tea and some food?"

"Yes, Your Grace," Harriet said, heading to the door.

"Next order of business is defense of the city," Elizabeth said.

They bent over the second map of the city.

"How sound are the city walls?" she asked.

"All of the main gates have been repaired," Sean said. "So they are in good condition. The walls on either side of the gates have also been repaired and can withstand a siege. The rest of the walls are unsound. They need repairs and in some cases rebuilding. They wouldn't withstand catapult assault for very long. The builders say it will take a few months to repair them properly."

Elizabeth looked at him.

"I know," he said. "We don't have months. Days perhaps, but not months."

"It's certain they're going to get into the city," Rowan said. "But you can control *how* they get into the city and *where* they go."

"What do you mean?" Elizabeth asked.

"Look," Rowan said, bending over the map. "You have three major streets that go into the city. From the north, the east, and the west. They will be coming in through the northern gate. At the southern end of the city is the port of Manusk. It's a natural wall for them. If you can force them all down to the port, my ships will be waiting for them."

"It's a good idea," Elizabeth said. "But you can't fire on the city. We don't know how many civilians will be left and the cannon fire will destroy everything."

"I think she's right," Peter said after a moment. "We stand a much better chance of winning if we take them from behind. No army wants to fight in a city, so as soon as they enter they'll destroy as much as they can to minimize their own losses. We can apply the same tactics to them as they are to us. Once they're in the city we can cut them off from their supporting troops. By that time, our army should have arrived to pin their supporting troops outside the city."

"Too risky," Elizabeth said. "It would mean that the troops going behind the force in the city potentially have a battle on two fronts." She stared at the map.

Harriet entered the room, carrying a large tray filled with thick sandwiches, pitchers of water, and more tea.

"Thank you," Elizabeth said, accepting a sandwich from her and taking a sip of a cup of water. "And you're just the person I wanted to see. You've spent a lot of time of late talking to the citizens of the city of Manusk, haven't you?"

"Yes, Your Grace," Harriet said.

"What is the state of repair of the buildings of Manusk?" Elizabeth asked. "Are they as much of a disgrace within as they are without?"

"If it were up to me, the entire city would be condemned and rebuilt."

"Wish granted," Elizabeth said.

There was a collective gasp of shock.

"Callous as this sounds, the part of Manusk that most people care about are the docks," Elizabeth said. "We have to hold and keep those at all costs."

Richard nodded. "And the warehouses."

"And the warehouses," Elizabeth said. "The rest of the city is secondary to those. We can rebuild the city with the help of my father but trade for the entire kingdom will suffer a severe blow if we lose the ability for trading ships to load and unload cargo." She looked down at the map and bit her lip. "What that means for us is that we'll use the city as much as we can to kill as many Osk and Sandcliff forces as we can. We won't deliberately destroy buildings but we won't keep them standing at all costs." She looked up at the others. Isengard, Peter, and Sean looked grimly determined and nodded.

Rowan gave her a look of quiet understanding.

Richard and Harriet looked a little shocked and sad.

"We have to keep their forces confined to the ground," she said. "We can use the upper floors of the buildings to fire arrows into the guardsmen. We can pin them down and use ground forces to clean up the rest. We also need to confine them to as few streets as possible. We can't have them spreading out. We need to use the side streets ourselves to move troops around."

"But our guardsmen don't know the city of Manusk as well as those who have been here for generations," Peter said.

"We will need the thieves of Manusk to help us," Elizabeth said.

"They're just children, Your Grace," Harriet said, sounding horrified.

"Not all thieves are children," Elizabeth said. "And all they have to do is lead troops to streets of our choosing. They'll be too valuable for fighting. That will be up to us."

Harriet looked slightly mollified. "I suppose you'll be needing to speak to the Master Thief, then."

"Yes, I will," Elizabeth said. "Do you know who that would be?"

"Charles," Harriet said. "His name is Charles."

"Benton's Charles?" Elizabeth said.

Harriet nodded.

"How do I get an audience with Charles?" Elizabeth said.

"You don't," Harriet said. "You'd have to ask a thief to bring you to their master, or to bring him to you."

Elizabeth nodded. "I'll ask."

"I'm not clear on this," Rowan said. "What are your plans for the city? What are the thieves for?"

Elizabeth grinned. "It's very simple. We have potentially a large number of troops coming into the city. We have to break them into small groups so that the odds favor our smaller number of troops. The thieves will create diversions and as larger groups splinter to follow the thieves, we attack the smaller groups."

"I like that idea," Rowan said with a grin.

"And we will keep them to the outer walls as well as we can."

Rowan nodded.

"The merchants guards will hold the docks as well as they can," Richard said.

"Yes. I don't want to use them," Elizabeth said. "They're going to be our last line of defense."

"We will stand with you at the docks," Rowan said.

"Thank you. All right. So we have the beginnings of a plan for defense of the city. We will reconvene tomorrow and make further plans." Elizabeth leaned her hands on the table and sighed. "Everyone go and get some rest. We will be busy tomorrow."

They all stood and bowed to Rowan and Elizabeth. Peter, Sean, and Richard, talking quietly amongst themselves, left the room. Isengard trailed behind Harriet, who stopped to clean up the remnants of their snack.

Rowan turned to Elizabeth after they all left and studied her closely.

"There's something you didn't tell them, isn't there? The reason you were a few moments behind us up here?" she said, her blue eyes intense.

"I can't hide anything from you, can I?" Elizabeth asked, shaking her head. "When did I become so transparent?"

Rowan took up her accustomed place on the windowsill and smiled at her. "That's not it. You're tense. I can tell. Why?"

Elizabeth sat opposite her with a sigh. She studied Rowan's beautiful face. "You have very beautiful eyes. They're very kind and gentle. Did you know that?"

Rowan smiled. "I've been told that on occasion. Just as I'm sure you've been told you cut a very beautiful figure with your long black hair and incredible black eyes."

"I look like my grandmother," Elizabeth said.

"And I look like my mother."

Elizabeth nodded. "She must have been a very beautiful woman."

"What troubles you, my friend?" Rowan said softly after a moment of comfortable silence.

Elizabeth expelled a deep breath. "Benton came to me again. She told me that I have a traitor in my midst. I told her I knew, that Captain Herbert had been discovered, but she said it wasn't him. I have *another* traitor with me."

Rowan groaned.

"Have you ever seen the Duke's Garden?"

Rowan shook her head.

"Let's go. It's too fine a night to be stuck in here."

CHAPTER 14

"THIS IS IT, I think," Elizabeth said, pointing to an iron studded wooden gate set into an overgrown wall bordering the rear of the manor's overgrown gardens. "It's the entrance to the duke's garden in Manusk. Off limits to everyone except the duke and the duchess. I seriously doubt anyone remembers it's here."

Rowan eyed the dark, overgrown path that led to the rickety gate. "I doubt anyone would know to look for it. How did you know it was here?"

"I studied maps of the city before I left Callypsis. Of course, the real thing is nothing like the maps. They must be extremely outdated." She pushed down the path, holding onto tree branches so they would not hit Rowan.

"Have you ever been in here before?" Rowan asked.

Elizabeth snorted a laugh. "No. I got here when you did, remember?"

"This ought to be interesting," Rowan muttered and Elizabeth laughed.

"Ready?" Elizabeth said with a grin, her hand against the aged, wooden gate.

"Yes," Rowan said.

Elizabeth pushed it and it gave a little. She glanced back at Rowan. "Just a moment."

She shoved the gate with her shoulder and it gave way with a rusty, earsplitting squeal. She overbalanced and tripped into the garden.

Rowan followed her, bent slightly, and held out a hand to lever her up.

"Lovely, Your *Grace*," she said, grin twitching her lips.

"Always ready to please," Elizabeth said, accepting the hand and allowing herself to be pulled to her feet. "Thank you, Your *Highness*."

Rowan's teeth flashed in a full grin. She rested her hands on her hips and looked around. "In all honesty, with a little attention, this garden could be absolutely spectacular."

It was hard to tell in the darkness, but Elizabeth felt inclined to agree. An overgrown path led to a wild hedge with a tiny gap. She went through it, Rowan close behind, and gave a low whistle of appreciation. They stood at one side of a circle enclosed by hedges. A stone path stretched out to the left and right, bordering the hedge. It also cut a cross through the circle. At the intersection of the cross was an enormous fountain.

"Look at that," Elizabeth said, intent on the fountain.

She carefully made her way through the overgrown grass to the fountain, and could see gaps in the long undergrowth. She went to one of them, and saw it was an ornate stone bench, almost overtaken by the grass. The gaps were at even intervals around the crumbling fountain, and she guessed they were other benches.

"Smell that," Rowan said, taking a deep breath. "Aren't those what you call roses?"

Elizabeth took a deep breath and the perfume of roses filled her lungs. "Yes, although I can't really tell where they are."

"Neither can I. They're lovely." Rowan gestured toward the stone bench. "Your Grace."

Elizabeth took her hand and allowed Rowan to draw her toward the bench. She sat carefully and almost breathed a sigh of relief as it showed no signs of wanting to collapse under their combined weight.

They drank in the quiet night air for a moment.

In the distance, they could hear the watch cry out, *Manusk stands*, and the answering calls from the other watchmen in the city.

Elizabeth shivered. *How does Benton know I've got another traitor? Who could it be? I don't think it's Harriet or Richard. It doesn't make sense for it to be either of them. And Peter and Sean have been with me forever. We know each other too well to hide such a deception.*

"Penny for your thoughts," Rowan said. "Or perhaps I shouldn't be paying so much. You have treachery on your mind, don't you?"

"What else?" Elizabeth said. "I feel like I've lost control of what's going on around me."

Rowan was silent for a long moment. "The war was a terrible time for us. Not only was there constant bloodshed, but our people were starving, we had no homes and we'd been driven almost into extinction in a series of caves on the bluffs overlooking the Markand Sea. I'd had a terrible day. I'd led on a routine patrol and we'd been attacked by my uncle's soldiers. Only one soldier and I survived the massacre." Her mouth twisted and she shook her head. "As I went through the camp, I felt everyone staring at me. I felt their disappointment in me. It wasn't until I spoke to my father that I found out I was the intended target of the attack. The soldier with me—my best friend—was the one who'd given away our position. My father was angry and I was humiliated. He finally finished yelling at me for my youthful arrogance and irresponsibility when I couldn't hold back my tears. He took me into his arms and held me and told me something important that I've always carried with me. Do you want to know what that was?"

Elizabeth nodded.

Rowan smiled. "He told me that I was my own worst enemy. Trust and leadership only exist in a group when they exist in you for yourself. You must always know and understand your limitations. If you can't keep your own secrets, who could you possibly trust with them?"

Elizabeth thought it over for a moment. She nodded. "I think I understand what he meant. I've relied too much on my people, haven't I? And I've been spewing out all kinds of information without paying attention to the ears around me."

"Good," Rowan said, nodding, after studying Elizabeth's face for a moment. "I have one further observation, if I may?"

Elizabeth nodded.

"It's clear you're *not* new to battle but *are* to being a ruler. And you've never had to do both at once, have you?"

Elizabeth felt her face heat and was glad of the darkness. "No. I haven't."

"I have," Rowan said. "And I've have to deal with all the same kinds of problems you have now. I would like to help you with the civilian population of Manusk. Would you let me?"

"Like what?" Elizabeth asked.

"I could oversee the day-to-day operations of your duchy. I will see to it that your people are fed and housed and I will see to it that they are able to leave when the time comes."

What harm can it do? I'm being torn apart because I can't give my full attention to both problems. I was fine when battle was only a possibility but now that it's upon us I have to give it my full attention or we're all dead.

"All right," Elizabeth said slowly. "I agree to this. But I want to know what you're doing. Not to hover over you, but to understand what is best for my people. I want them to come back when Manusk is ours again. I *want* them to live here in peace."

Rowan's teeth flashed in a grin and she gently laughed. "Of course, Elizabeth."

"May I ask you a question?" Elizabeth asked.

"Yes," Rowan said.

"Why are you here? Why are you staying? I can see how weary you are. Don't you have anyone to go home to?"

"I'm here because I wanted to see more of the world. I wanted to meet new people and to see a world that wasn't rebuilding after a stupid war. And no, there's no one at home for me. My heart doesn't lie there." She shifted on the seat. "You? Why are *you* here?"

"I've been around armed men my whole life. I've never done anything different. It's always one more patrol, one more battle, one more mission. I don't really have a home. Yes, I have a room in my father's house but it doesn't suit me. I think my father finally looked closely at me and didn't like what he saw. He told me to take up my grandfather's mantle of duke. He meant me to stay here." She sighed. "For a while I thought I couldn't do it. I like traveling too much. But I see that there's something here I can care about." She nodded. "This will be my last battle. It will end here."

"So there's home and hearth in your future. Do you intend to share it with your farm maid?"

Elizabeth felt her face heat and glanced at Rowan in surprise. She bit off a teasing reply and instead settled on the truth. "Mia is a lovely girl but neither of us would be happy for long. She likes home and hearth and I like to *come back* to home and hearth."

Rowan nodded and her full lips curved into a gentle smile. She stiffened and turned.

"Wha—?" Elizabeth began.

Rowan immediately brought her finger to her lips, silencing her. She cocked her head, listening.

Elizabeth frowned and focused her attention on the night sounds.

The crickets were quiet and a gentle breeze stirred the grass.

It shouldn't be this quiet. The crickets were certainly making enough noise when we came in here. And, come to think of it, it's a still night. There's no wind.

"Watch! To me!" she screamed, drawing her sword and swinging her legs over the bench.

Three men in the grass broke into a dead run toward her. She could make out their silhouettes and saw the raised swords. She felt Rowan shift behind her and heard the hiss of her blade as it cleared her scabbard.

The three men were on them and she blocked a vicious downward swing and twisted the sword out of her opponent's hands. She thrust her sword at him and heard the grunt as it penetrated his gut.

"Watch! To me!" she screamed again.

She heard a yelp of pain from Rowan and turned to see both men darting in and slashing at her with their swords. She clutched her shoulder and her sword hung limp in her hand. The second swordsman drew his sword back to ram a killing blow to her heart. Elizabeth felt her own heart stop for one blinding, terrible second. She swung her sword as hard as she could and decapitated him and dealt the first swordsman a deep cut to the cheek and neck. He screamed and faltered.

Blood fountained from the corpse and the body slumped to the ground, twitching.

Footsteps pounded across the deep grass behind them, and Marcus was there, wrestling the injured man to the ground.

Elizabeth bent over him, her sword cutting deep enough into the man's neck to draw blood.

"Who sent you?" she said.

The man groaned.

"I'll tear the skin off your face with my bare hands unless you answer me."

The man mumbled something made incoherent by the blood and his swelling face.

"Take him away," Elizabeth said coldly. "I'll see him tomorrow. Ask the doctor to patch him up so he can talk."

The watchman saluted and dragged the man away.

"I'll have someone clean this up," Marcus said, indicating the two dead men.

Elizabeth nodded, distracted by the sight of Rowan sitting in the grass and cradling her shoulder. She knelt by her and tore off a piece of her shirt to use as a bandage.

"I'm fine, Elizabeth," Rowan said, hissing in pain as Elizabeth pushed the wad of cloth onto the open wound.

"You're hurt," Elizabeth said softly, cursing her shaking hands.

Rowan covered Elizabeth's hand with a warm hand and gave it a gentle squeeze. "Really. I'm fine. It's a little painful but I'll live."

"I'm so sorry," Elizabeth said. "I should never have brought you here."

"I don't regret it," Rowan said. "I like the garden and the evening was lovely right up until now."

Elizabeth helped Rowan to stand and led her from the garden. *I'm not going in there again until it's been restored. What about Rowan? She could have died in there if I hadn't accidentally slashed the second man.*

"Come," Rowan said softly. "Let's go up to your chambers. I think I'd better lie down and get some rest."

Elizabeth looked at her shoulder more closely as they approached the kitchen and the light from inside revealed the damage. Her shirt sleeve was blood soaked, as was the makeshift bandage she had pressed to the wound.

"Oh, Lord," Harriet said, rushing to them as they entered the kitchen. Her eyes widened at the blood. "What's happened?"

"We were attacked in the duke's garden." Elizabeth helped Rowan onto a bench in a corner. "Could I trouble you to send someone for the doctor? I need him now."

"I will," Harriet said. She gestured for a serving girl, who came at a run. Harriet spoke quickly to her, gesturing at Elizabeth and Rowan. The girl looked at them with wide eyes and then lifted her skirts and ran from the kitchen.

"Come into the pantry. There's a little office and it's much more private than out here." Harriet glanced at the room at large. Elizabeth followed her gaze. Men and women were either openly staring at them or trying to show they weren't looking.

"Good idea," Elizabeth said, helping Rowan to her feet.

Rowan hissed in pain. "Anything just to get this cut stitched up." Blood ran down her knuckles.

Elizabeth helped Rowan through a small door hidden in an alcove near the corner of the kitchen. They found themselves in a large pantry, filled with salted meat, cheeses, preserves, baskets of vegetables, and several casks of oil. In the center was a small desk, the chair pulled out behind it.

Rowan dropped into the chair with a grunt and a sigh.

"This is quite a scratch, isn't it?" she said, pulling her hand away from the wound with a grimace. Fresh blood flowed down her arm.

"That's quite a deep cut," the doctor said, sounding out of breath. He turned to the serving girl. "Bring the lantern a little closer, please."

Rowan pulled her shirt away from her shoulder with Elizabeth's help. The serving girl, holding the lantern, paled and shook. Harriet quickly rescued the lantern from her unsteady grasp and dismissed her. The girl fled the room.

"It's deep but missed everything vital," the doctor said, peering at the cut. "However, it will require stitches, Your Highness." He looked at her and she nodded.

The doctor sprinkled herbs onto the open wound and Rowan grimaced and hissed in pain.

Elizabeth took her hand and slid an arm around her waist. "You can hold me as tight as you like. I can take it."

"I know." Rowan nodded, burying her face into Elizabeth's neck.

The doctor quickly threaded his needle with catgut and got to work. Rowan remained silent during the entire operation, but her hand tightened almost painfully in Elizabeth's and Elizabeth could feel the wetness of tears against her neck.

The doctor worked quickly and efficiently. He finished and sprinkled more herbs onto the cut and bound Rowan's shoulder with a makeshift bandage Elizabeth handed to him.

He pulled out a small bag of herbs and gave it to Rowan. "Steep these in hot water and drink when the pain becomes too much." He bowed to Elizabeth and Rowan. "Your Grace, Your Highness, with your permission?"

Elizabeth smiled at him. "Of course, Doctor. And thank you for your help, as always."

The doctor smiled at her and saluted. He turned smartly and left the pantry.

"Let's get up to my chambers," Elizabeth said to Rowan. "We should get you into bed so you can get some rest."

"Bed sounds wonderful," Rowan groaned.

Elizabeth nodded and helped her to her feet. She helped Rowan back into her bloodstained shirt and stayed close to her as they left the pantry.

As they crossed the kitchen, Elizabeth spotted Benton and Thomas. They peered at her with wide eyes. Benton bit her lip.

"One moment, Rowan," Elizabeth said. She beckoned Benton closer.

Benton hesitated and came over to her. She peered up at Elizabeth, blinking.

"Benton," Elizabeth said. "I want to meet Charles. Will you bring him to me at twelve tomorrow?"

Benton bit her lip again and was silent for a moment. She nodded. "I'll tell him to come or you'll send in your soldiers."

"Good. That's the truth." Elizabeth hesitantly smoothed Benton's unruly hair away from her forehead. "You need to brush and cut your hair, young friend." She smiled. "Get a good night's rest and I'll see you at breakfast tomorrow."

Benton nodded.

Elizabeth stood. "Let's go," she said to Rowan.

They made their way along deserted corridors, up the stairs, and to Elizabeth's chamber.

Mara waited for them inside, her eyes widening when she saw Rowan.

"Your Highness, you're alive," she said, bobbing a half competent curtsey.

"I'm not sure by whose definition," Rowan muttered. She glanced down at her shirt. "I want a bath before I climb into that nice, clean bed."

"So do I. Bathwater," Elizabeth said to Mara.

Mara wobbled another curtsey and scurried from the room.

"I'm going to need some help," Rowan said, blushing.

"I know," Elizabeth said with a grin. "I'll help you."

Rowan's uncharacteristic blush increased.

"You've nothing I haven't seen a hundred times before, Your Highness," Elizabeth said with a grin.

"That's what I'm afraid of," Rowan muttered and Elizabeth laughed, despite herself.

Elizabeth led Rowan to the bathing chamber and helped her strip of her boots, breeches, and shirt as Mara and the servants filled the tub with streaming, fragrant water. When they were finished, Elizabeth helped Rowan into the tub.

She tried not to stare at Rowan's body.

She's so beautiful. She wanted to circle Rowan's narrow waist with her hands as she nibbled Rowan's full breasts. Her creamy skin almost begged for the touch of Elizabeth's lips. *Keep your hands to yourself,* she silently chanted.

They bathed and dressed in robes laid out by the bath servants.

Elizabeth took Rowan to the bed and slid in beside her. Rowan slipped into her arms with a sigh.

"I'm exhausted," she said with a yawn.

"I know you are," Elizabeth said. She stroked Rowan's long, golden hair.

"That feels so good," Rowan murmured, her eyes fluttering closed.

Elizabeth thought she would be awake for most of the night but she fell asleep, moments later, Rowan's deep, even breaths tickling her chest.

ELIZABETH AND ROWAN entered the kitchen together the next morning. Elizabeth felt rested despite her few hours of sleep. Rowan looked tired and worn and she moved stiffly.

"Sit down," Elizabeth said. "I'll get you something to eat."

Rowan nodded. "And some of that hot coffee if you have any."

"I'm sure Harriet can find something for you, Rowan." She went to the pots with stew that seemed to be eternally simmering over the cooking fires. She grabbed a couple of bowls, hesitated a moment, and filled both with vegetable stew. She saw Harriet pass by.

"Harriet, good morning," she said.

"Good morning, Your Grace," Harriet said, stopping and wiping her hands on her apron.

"Do you have any coffee this morning?" Elizabeth asked. "I can't see the pot."

"Yes, I'll get you some," Harriet said. "I'll be back in a moment."

Elizabeth nodded and headed back to her usual table. Rowan sat near the head, Thomas on one side of her, Benton opposite her. Elizabeth smiled.

"Good morning, everyone," she said, depositing the bowl in front of Rowan and at her place. "I'll be back in a moment."

She jogged to the cooking pots and snagged some fresh, warm bread, cheese, and beef broth. There were two cups of steaming coffee waiting for her when she returned to the table and she groaned in pleasure at the first sip.

She halved the food and put it between their places. She grabbed a slice of bread and dipped it into the beef broth and took a spoonful of the vegetable soup.

"How are you this fine morning?" Elizabeth said to Benton. "Did you get enough sleep?"

Benton gave her a brilliant smile. "Yes, Your Grace. I slept well."

Elizabeth inclined her head. "That's excellent, Benton."

"Can I go now?" Benton asked.

"Of course," Elizabeth said. She held out a slice of bread. "Why don't you snack on this later?"

Benton nodded and took it from her. Thomas looked pointedly at Elizabeth and Elizabeth flashed him a grin as she handed him her other piece of bread.

Elizabeth and Rowan watched Thomas and Benton run from the kitchen.

Elizabeth shook her head. "Children."

Rowan grinned. "You have two wonderful children, Elizabeth."

"They're not mine," Elizabeth said.

"Yes, they are," Rowan said. "You own them now. She's probably happy because you're going to take Charles off her hands."

Elizabeth felt a shot of anger she struggled to suppress. "I'm going to teach him to play nicely with other children." She took another spoonful of soup. "What do you have planned for today?"

"The first thing I'm going to do is go down to the docks and ensure your decree banning price gouging is enforced so we can begin evacuating people. Then I'll plan out the evacuation with Richard and Delmarco."

Elizabeth grinned. "I'd pay good money to see that."

Rowan gave her an arch smile. "How much?"

"How much do you want?" Elizabeth cursed her mouth for running away without input from her mind.

Rowan leaned forward and gave her a saturnine smile. "*Everything, Elizabeth. I want everything of yours.*"

Elizabeth studied her for a moment, and saw her blue eyes dancing with mirth. "I see. We can discuss terms of payment *after* this is all over."

"When you're on your way to Welland with me," Rowan said softly. "Promise me you'll return to Welland with me."

Elizabeth smiled. *It's an easy promise to make. I'm sure father is going to insist I go with them after all the horror stories they're going to bring back with them.* "I promise."

Rowan gave her a broad, genuine smile, although her eyes became sad. "I'll hold you to that." She spooned up the last of her soup and clasped Elizabeth's hand. "Why don't we meet back here for dinner?"

Elizabeth gently ran her thumb along the back of Rowan's hand. "I'll be looking for you."

Rowan stood up and turned away, about to leave.

"Rowan?" Elizabeth said.

Rowan turned to her, raising an eyebrow in question.

"Rest if you get tired."

Rowan grinned and sketched a salute. "I'll see you later."

Elizabeth nodded and watched her retreating back.

She signaled to a guardsman who was just finishing his breakfast. He stood and bowed. "Yes, Your Grace?"

"Escort Princess Rowan to the docks and wait for relief."

The man blinked and bowed. "Yes, Your Grace."

He jogged out of the kitchen, straightening his tabard as he went.

She sighed and turned her mind to more immediate matters. *I have to find Peter. I want to see those walls for myself and I want to see what kind of cover we have in the city. I also want to inspect the guardsmen. I also have to find out what the state of our armory is, and I need to talk to Jarrod, Rebecca, and Farrow.*

She got up and almost collided with Sean.

"Your Grace," he said with a bow.

"Good morning, Sean," Elizabeth said.

"Captain Peter sent me to get you. He suggested you would want to see the city walls today."

"I do," she said, following him from the kitchen. "And I also want to meet with Jarrod and Rebecca. Send word for them to come in."

Sean bowed. "I will, Your Grace." Sean led the way up the corridor, and then pointed at a new door set on the wall opposite Benton's alcove under the stairs. "This is your new study, Your Grace. The captain also suggested that perhaps we should have a more private location to talk."

Elizabeth studied the door, feeling at a loss. *I never noticed a door in that wall before.*

"Before you ask about the door, Your Grace," Sean said. "I feel honor bound to point out that was a wall before the carpenters removed the outer paneling. It's an office that looked like it hadn't been used for years. We cleaned it up a bit so we could use it as a headquarters."

"I definitely approve," Elizabeth said, running her fingers along the new oak paneling.

She turned the handle and pushed the door, half expecting the hinges to squeal and groan in protest. The door opened in almost ghostly silence onto a large room with bay windows to the left and a solid wall of flat paneling to the right. The paneling held maps of the Duchy of Manusk and the city of Manusk, as well as a close-up map of the docks.

In the rear of the room, in front of an old, ornate fireplace, was a large, plain desk that looked as if it had been rescued from storage, oak chairs, and a large table that could seat twenty people.

"The desk is quite solid, Your Grace, as are the chairs," Sean said, following her gaze. "The carpenters repaired them."

"This is magnificent, Sean," she said. "I'm suitably impressed and quite thankful."

Sean smiled and bowed. "We thought you'd like it."

"I do." She went to the desk and sat in the chair. It was surprisingly comfortable and wonderfully sturdy. "I like this. All right. To business. Please get Jarrod and Rebecca into the city. We need to talk about the militia. Second, Benton is going to bring Charles here at noon. Have someone notify me as soon as he arrives. Make sure he has a large number of well-armed escorts with him. Do you know where Peter is?"

"Yes, Your Grace," Sean said. "He's at the Northern Gate."

"Good. I'm going to see him there."

"The captain suggested you would want to. He's assigned me as your bodyguard."

"Thank you, Sean." *I'm sorry, old friend, but I have other plans for you.*

Sean bowed and went to the door. He beckoned for a guardsman and issued a rapid stream of orders. He turned back to Elizabeth. "When Your Grace is ready."

"There is one more thing, Sean," Elizabeth said, indicating that he should sit.

Sean sat opposite her, watching her warily.

"I suppose you and Peter know about the attempt on Rowan and myself last night in the duke's garden."

Sean's eyebrows rose. "No, Your Grace, I didn't know."

Elizabeth frowned. "It was the watch who came to our assistance. How do you not know this?"

"The watch reports directly to Peter," Sean said. "I think he probably knows by now."

"I'll address that when I talk to Peter," she said. "But it's actually other things that concern me. No one knew where we were going. I didn't know myself until we got there. We were followed into the gardens and a deliberate attempt was made on our lives."

Sean gave her a sharp look and she waved her hand. "I'm fine. Rowan caught the brunt of the attack. If that was an assassination attempt, and I'm going to assume so, it wasn't aimed at me; I think it was aimed at Rowan. She was attacked by two of three armed men and stabbed through the shoulder."

"I agree, Your Grace," Sean said. "Are any of the men alive?"

"One is. The other two are dead." Elizabeth stared at him intently. "I can't have this anymore. Peter left you orders to guard me. I'm countermanding them. Go and guard Rowan. At all costs, understand, Sean?"

Sean nodded slowly. "I understand, Your Grace." He was silent a moment. "Why do you think it was done?"

"Simple," Elizabeth said. "If Rowan and our other Welland guests are dead, and *I'm* dead, Osk and Sandcliff can tell the rest of the Welland fleet what they like. And I'm sure they'd like to tell Welland that I'm a traitor and that I killed their princess. Welland would logically attack my father for that and there would be no one to stop them."

"My thinking exactly, Your Grace," Sean said.

"Good, then you'll understand why I asked you to guard Rowan at all costs. When she leaves Manusk, go with her. Guard her with your life. Rowan is our most valuable asset. Even *I* am secondary to her."

Sean's eyes widened but he nodded and firmed his chin. "I understand, Your Grace. What are you going to tell Captain Peter?"

"Exactly what I just told you. And I really don't need a bodyguard. I am perfectly capable of looking after myself. Rowan is at the docks, Sean. There is a guardsman with her waiting for you to relieve him. Go."

Sean stood and saluted, but hesitated a moment. "You need a bodyguard, Your Grace. Without you there's no Manusk to really fight for."

"That's where you're wrong, Sean," Elizabeth said. "We're not fighting for my father's seaport anymore, although that's still part of it. We're fighting for our homes and the King's Heartland. We are holding civil war at bay and that *is* much bigger than all of this, even the docks."

Sean was silent a moment, and then straightened to attention and gave her a crisp salute. "With Your Grace's permission?"

She nodded. "Dismissed."

Sean turned and strode from the room.

Elizabeth followed behind him, and as soon as she got out into the hallway she saw the guardsman that came in the previous day, that she'd sparred with. She beckoned him over.

He came over and stood to attention.

"What's your name, guardsman?" she asked.

"I'm Walter, Your Grace," he said.

"Do you trust the other men in your company? Are they good men? You came in with ten men, didn't you?"

He gave her a curious look, and then nodded. "They're all good soldiers and men, Your Grace."

"Good. Gather them together and take them upstairs to the rooms of the Welland survivors. From this moment forward, you're to guard them with your lives. This is your duty unless otherwise specified by me and me only. You are promoted to sergeant."

Walter saluted. "Understood, Your Grace. We are to guard the Welland survivors to the last man or until you tell us this duty is concluded."

Elizabeth nodded. "Carry on, Sergeant Walter."

Walter bowed and backed away.

Elizabeth went out into the courtyard and watched a group of farmers drilling with her guardsmen. They looked much better with swords than the last group. She watched with interest as another couple shot arrows into a straw dummy exactly where the heart would be. She made a mental note to congratulate Farrow and Jarrod with the training they'd already given to their people.

She signaled for her horse and mounted as soon as the groom gave her the reins. She walked her mare out into the city streets, and then pushed her into a trot toward the northern gate.

The streets were busy with pedestrian traffic and they stopped and stared at her as she passed. They eyed her intently and they all seemed to be in a hurry. The air felt thick with tension. *Harriet and Richard must have let the cat out of the bag about the evacuations.*

A young woman stepped out in front of Elizabeth's horse and Elizabeth halted.

"Your Grace," the woman said with a quick curtsey. "May I ask you a question?"

Elizabeth nodded. "Yes. You may."

"Is it true? Will there be war?"

"I hope not but I fear so."

"Are the traders really offering passage for trade to leave Manusk?"

"Yes," Elizabeth said. "Take your family and go while there's still time. If anyone wants to leave they can."

The woman went pale and trembled.

Suddenly Elizabeth felt as though she was surrounded by a thousand hands, all grasping at her boots and horse. Her mare snorted and pulled back.

"Silence!" Elizabeth called.

The crowd stilled and drew back a little and her horse quieted again.

"That's better," Elizabeth said, raising her voice. "I am Elizabeth St. John, the lawful Duchess of Manusk. War is coming to us and you should leave. While I and my guardsmen live, we swear to protect Manusk and everyone in it. That means you and yours. Until the last of us is dead and gone, Manusk stands. Manusk!"

She pushed her way through the crowd, and she heard the whispers begin. *Manusk. Manusk stands.*

She kneed her horse into motion and pushed her into a canter once she'd left the crowd. Citizens quickly got out of her way as they saw her coming and more than one saluted or knuckled their foreheads. She blindly pushed through the city streets until she reached the northern gate.

She dismounted almost before the mare finished moving and handed the reins to a guardsman who jogged up to her.

"Keep her handy," she said. "I may have to leave in a hurry."

The guardsman saluted and led her horse away.

She strode through the light pedestrian traffic into the guard house.

"Peter," she said, approaching him as he bent over a table with a guardsman wearing the insignia of a corporal.

"Your Grace," he said, looking up and bowing. "Good morning."

"Good morning," she said. "I suppose you heard about last night."

"I did," Peter said. He waved the corporal away, who strode out of the building. "The third man was found dead in his cell this morning. He'd committed suicide."

"Did he say anything of use before he was left alone?"

"No. Neither he nor his friends had any identifying marks on them." Peter gave her a humorless grin. "I think we know who sent them but we'd never be able to prove it."

Elizabeth nodded. "I agree." She sat down at the table opposite him. "I have countermanded your orders to Sean and diverted ten of your guardsmen. Sean is with Rowan and *Sergeant* Walter is with the Welland survivors."

Peter nodded. "I half expected you to do that. I suppose you tossed out the idea of a bodyguard for yourself, Your Grace?"

Elizabeth smiled.

Peter shook his head and looked exasperated. "We can't afford to lose you either, Your Highness."

"If you do, you still have Rowan."

"Permission to speak freely, Your Grace?"

Elizabeth nodded.

Peter leaned forward and looked into her eyes. "You think quite highly of Princess Rowan, don't you?"

"What are you suggesting, Peter?" Elizabeth said, frowning at him. She felt a spark of anger ignite inside her.

Peter smiled and leaned back. "Nothing, Your Grace. She's easy to care about and she herself seems to care about us."

"She does," Elizabeth said, suddenly eager to change the subject. "I didn't come here to talk about Rowan. I'm here to see the city walls and fortifications."

"I thought you might want to do that," Peter said. "I'm just waiting for Isengard and Kellen to join us."

"You trust them?" Elizabeth asked.

"I trust Isengard," Peter said. "He's an experienced commander and the guardsmen like him."

"What have you been doing with him?" Elizabeth asked.

"He's been drilling with the guardsmen and the militia. He's a good teacher and he offers leadership that listens to the younger recruits. I'm almost sorry we can't have him fight with us."

Elizabeth shook her head, sad. "I know. But they have to go. We can't afford to risk their lives by being here with us. What news do you have of troop movements, Osk and Sandcliff?"

Peter opened his mouth to reply but the door opened. Isengard entered the room, holding a bloody sack, and Kellen in tow.

"Good morning, Your Grace," Isengard said with a bow, Kellen following suit behind him. "I have a *gift* for you from an Osk trading caravan that was just denied entrance to the city."

Elizabeth took the sack from him. It was surprisingly heavy.

I already know what this is without looking, she thought with a sinking heart.

She put the sack on the floor, opened it, and took a step back. She felt a moment of lightheadedness from the stench of death that came out of it in a dull wave.

It was a severed head.

CHAPTER 15

ISENGARD AND KELLEN gasped. Peter stared at it grimly, his jaw working.

Elizabeth reached out a miraculously steady hand and lifted the bloody rag of her torn insignia to reveal the gory and fly blown features of a guardsman.

"Do you recognize this man?" Elizabeth asked, looking at Peter with a raised eyebrow.

"Robert," Peter said. "That was Robert. He was the last messenger we sent out for Arnett."

Elizabeth shook her head. "Guard," she called, putting the sack back around the head.

A guardsman came in and saluted.

She pointed to the sack. "Take that and burn it."

"What is it, Your Grace?" the man asked, gingerly lifting it.

"That's all that remains of Robert," she said. "Please treat it with respect. We lost a brave guardsman."

The guardsman bowed, took the sack, and carried it as gently as he was able to.

"We're about to play host to Osk and Sandcliff troops," Elizabeth said. "Now we're cut off."

"I think we can still get through," Isengard said. "Kellen?"

Kellen stepped forward and bowed deeply to Elizabeth. "Your Grace. Isengard tells me you have a task for me. You want me to deliver a message to your General Arnett, at the Princedom of Callypsis?"

"Yes," Elizabeth said, studying her closely.

She moved gracefully and with almost snake like speed. Her sharp eyes shone with anticipation for the journey ahead. Elizabeth suppressed a shudder.

Elizabeth reached around her neck and took off her necklace. She removed her ducal signet and royal signet rings and threaded them through the chain. She handed it to Kellen, feeling as though she had torn off a part of her body.

"The ducal signet goes to General Arnett and the message is *come at once. We are under attack.* Tell him who you are and who's in Manusk with you."

Kellen nodded and the jewelry disappeared into the folds of her peasant dress. "I'm to see General Arnett and tell him to come at once. We are under attack. Who do the other ring and necklace go to?"

"You can give them all to Arnett. He'll give the other ring and necklace to my brother and father."

Peter looked sharply at her and Elizabeth studiously avoided his eyes.

"Do you have a map?" Kellen asked.

"Yes," Elizabeth said. "It will take you two days to get there. Ask for General Arnett and make sure you show the sentries the ducal signet, or they will shoot first and ask questions later."

Kellen nodded. "I understand, Your Grace."

Peter had a map of the Duchy of Manusk on the table and Elizabeth quickly showed Kellen borders and where the Princedom of Callypsis was. Kellen pointed to some areas on the map and nodded. "I have it." She looked at Peter. "Do you know where your enemy forces are?"

"Robert came back to us from the highway to the King's Heartland," Peter said. "According to the soldiers who've come in over the past few days, the forces have gathered into a large army that marches toward us down the center of the plains. There are also scattered companies sweeping the sides of the plains."

"I'm to march through an army?" Kellen said, laughing.

Elizabeth felt a chill run down her spine at the sound. She nodded.

"I will be back in five days," Kellen said. She turned to Isengard and saluted.

Isengard returned her salute. He rattled off a few words of their language and Kellen returned them. She left the room, suddenly looking exactly like a silly, peasant girl.

Elizabeth shook her head and restrained the urge to feel for the missing chain around her neck. Her hands felt bare and she balled her fists.

She looked at Isengard. "You're telling me she'll make it where an armed man can't?"

Isengard nodded. "Yes."

Elizabeth shook her head. "I'm not even going to pretend to understand how."

Isengard gave her an enigmatic smile.

She turned her attention back to Peter. "Are the reports you have of troop movements accurate?"

Peter nodded. "They are. The army is marching toward us and if we are lucky we have at most three days."

"Siege engines?"

Peter nodded. "And catapults. Not that it's going to take that much to knock down these walls."

There was a knock at the door.

"Enter," Peter called.

The door opened and a guardsman entered, saw Elizabeth and bowed low. "Your Grace."

"Yes, guardsman?"

"You are requested to return to the manor. Charles has arrived, as have Jarrod, Farrow, and Rebecca."

"I'm on my way." She turned back to Peter and Isengard. "I'll be back in a couple of hours."

She left without waiting for acknowledgement from them.

ELIZABETH GALLOPED INTO the courtyard and pulled her horse to a stop. The mare's hooves slid on the cobblestones and Elizabeth cursed.

She slid down off the horse, blindly handed the reins to a stable boy, and strode into the house.

She found Rowan waiting for her outside her new office.

"Rowan," she said, genuinely pleased. "What are you doing here?"

"I came here to see if you were all right," she said.

"I'm going to ask you the same thing," Elizabeth said. She gently stroked Rowan's shoulder. "How's your shoulder, Your Highness?"

"You see?" She gingerly moved her shoulder and a flash of pain crossed her beautiful face. "It's sore but it's fine. I'm looking forward to getting a good night's rest."

Elizabeth leaned forward and whispered in her ear, "See that you do. We are expecting to see the first of the enemy troops in at most three days."

Rowan drew back and stared at her in shock. "So soon?"

Elizabeth nodded sadly. "So soon."

"I know it's not easy," Rowan said. "But try to stay safe. I don't . . . I don't . . . I don't want you to forget your promise. I want you to come back to Welland with me. After." Her jaw worked and then firmed. Her chiseled face was pale and her expression strained.

"You have to go. Tonight," Elizabeth said softly.

"I won't go until I have to. And tonight I stay with you. You are a friend."

"And you are one to me." Elizabeth let out a deep, tired breath. "I won't have much time tonight."

"I'll take whatever you can give me," Rowan said softly.

Elizabeth nodded. "All right. Come with me." She felt a pain in the middle of her chest and her emotions were in turmoil. She could scarcely sort through the riot of feeling tearing through her. *God, what's the matter with me? It's just another battle. Maybe it's the thought of facing my father and admitting how badly I've made decisions. Where has my head been?*

She sighed and strode into her office, Rowan's comforting presence behind her. Four guards encircled a boy in his teens, two of them with cocked crossbows pointed at his back.

She stared at him for a moment, fleetingly noticing Benton perched unobtrusively on one of the chairs around the large table.

Charles still had acne and he had the hard, wiry look of a half-starved peasant. His features were even and well proportioned but the expression in his eyes was icy cold and they darted all around the room, before finally resting on her. Then they became calculating and greedy, roaming up and down her body, resting on her breasts.

She felt Rowan shift behind her.

"You're Charles?" she said.

He gave a sharp nod.

"You're a thief, aren't you?"

He gave her a brief smile. "That's a strong word."

She tilted her head and regarded him, aware of his insolence and lack of respect for her. "But true."

Charles remained silent.

Elizabeth snorted. "I'd hoped to ask you to do something for me for the good of Manusk."

"Why would I do that?" he asked, snorting a laugh. "It doesn't matter who thinks they're in charge of this city because I *own* it."

"Charles," said Benton hesitantly. "Don't you want—"

"Shut up," Charles snarled. His head swung and he pinned her with a predatory stare. "No one spoke to you. We will discuss this later."

Benton shrank back, bit her lip, and twisted her fingers together.

Elizabeth watched her and felt a spark of anger. She took a step toward Charles and motioned to her guards.

The two unarmed guards grabbed him and slammed him to his knees. One grabbed his neck and held him in place.

"You don't own Manusk," Elizabeth said. "I simply haven't until now gotten around to dealing with you. I will find you again, and I won't be as nice to you then."

"I won't be here," Charles ground out. "You stupid get of a diseased bitch, don't you know knowledge is worth more than coin?"

Elizabeth glanced at Benton. Benton was white and trembling. She bit her lip again, tears swimming in her eyes.

"What have you done, Charles?" Elizabeth asked, leaning toward him.

Charles snarled and tried to wrench his arms free of the guardsman's grip. He roiled like a snake and the guardsman gasped at his suddenly empty hand. A dagger swiftly appeared in Charles's hand and he lunged toward Elizabeth.

"Elizabeth," Rowan cried, shifting behind her, as Elizabeth took a step back.

Suddenly Benton was in front of her, slipping under Charles's defenses. She cried out as she sank her own dagger into Charles, then stumbled back and sobbed.

"You've killed me, you ungrateful brat," Charles whispered, stilling and staring at the blood on his hands from the dagger sticking out of his heart. His knees gave out and he fell onto the floor.

Elizabeth nodded toward the guards and they dragged his body from the room, leaving a trail of blood behind.

Benton knelt on the floor, great sounds of misery erupting from her small body. She shook. Elizabeth knelt before her, put her arms around her, and pulled her in close. Benton struggled for a moment, punching at her and wailing, but Elizabeth tightened her grip, shushing her and stroking her back. She finally stilled, crying and burying her face into Elizabeth's shirt.

Elizabeth felt Rowan kneel beside her and put a tentative hand on Benton's back. She said a few words in her language and kissed Benton's head.

Serving maids hastily cleaned the floor behind them by the time Benton shed her last tear. She turned red and swollen eyes toward

Elizabeth, blinking. "Charles is gone. What did I do? What are we going to do now?"

Elizabeth scarcely knew how to answer. "Trust me, Benton. I'll take care of you. You *and* your friends."

Benton peered up at Elizabeth, blinking uncertainly. "But I killed someone. I'm a murderer."

Elizabeth flinched inwardly.

"Protecting your duchess isn't the same thing as murder, is it?" Rowan asked.

"Duchess Elizabeth can take care of herself," Benton said.

"Then why, Benton? Why did you do it?" Rowan asked softly.

Benton was silent for a moment. "I *hated* him," she said with a vehemence that made her seem years older. "He *wanted* to hurt her. He *did* hurt her."

Rowan and Elizabeth exchanged a glance.

"Me?" Elizabeth asked.

Benton nodded.

"How?"

"He was talking to a woman," Benton said. "He gave her coin for her secrets."

"What kind of secrets?" Rowan asked.

"You wanted to use the thieves of Manusk to confuse Osk soldiers."

Elizabeth felt the shock flow through her system. *There was someone listening at the door. Who? Or was it Harriet?*

"Do you know who the woman was?" Rowan asked.

Benton shook her head. "I haven't seen her in the kitchen before."

It's not Harriet. Harriet is no traitor. Who, then?

"Would you know her if you saw her again?" Rowan asked.

Benton was silent for a moment, and then nodded.

"We'll find her," Elizabeth said. "And if you see her you tell me, yes?"

Benton nodded. "Are you mad at me?" she asked in a small voice.

"No," Elizabeth said. "Why would I be angry at you?"

"For not telling you."

Elizabeth shook her head. "No, I'm not angry at you for that. You should be angry at me. I asked you to do things no woman should ask a child to do. I'm sorry. I shouldn't have asked you to spy for me."

"Don't say sorry," Benton said. "You were always nice to me

even after I said I wouldn't help you. You're a good person, Duchess Elizabeth. You're my friend." She tightened her arms around Elizabeth and a few more tears came.

"And you're mine, Benton." Elizabeth pulled back and cupped Benton's chin so they were looking eye to eye. "Go and wash your face. Find your friends and bring them here. I'll ask Harriet to find you somewhere to sleep. Rest. You've done enough for me."

Benton gave her a tentative smile, a small gleam of hope in her eyes. She attempted a curtsey and blushed at her clumsiness. "Thank you, Your Grace."

"I'll see you later," Elizabeth said as Benton ran from the room.

They watched the door close behind her and Elizabeth turned to Rowan and sighed. "Wonderful."

Rowan gave her a rueful grin. "At least you know your spy is a woman and she heard your plans."

"It's not Harriet," Elizabeth said. "It can't be her. It's got to be someone else."

"Nor is it your kitchen staff although I'm not sure how many of them Benton can recognize by sight."

Elizabeth gestured to a chair as she took a seat at the table. "I don't think it matters who the traitor is."

Rowan stared at her in shock. "Elizabeth, you have to find out who is giving away your secrets."

"I know," Elizabeth said. "But now we have to prepare for war. I have to worry about evacuating the city and my troops. I will find the traitor when I can."

Rowan shook her head. "I think that's a mistake."

"Understand, please. I care very deeply that someone has sold information to the enemy. We have some time. Now Charles is gone, and I think it was Charles who actually gathered the coin for it. Our traitor has no way to contact Osk and Sandcliff to tell them what we plan. We're safe." She paused and looked into Rowan's sad eyes. "We will catch her, mark my words. She won't escape. But I can't afford to divert resources to questioning panic-stricken civilians as they try to save their own lives. I have to get them out of the city if they want to leave." She smiled. "Now that you're here and I have your undivided attention, can you tell me how you are doing at the docks?"

"You've always had my attention, Elizabeth," Rowan said softly, her blue eyes lighting up with a smile. "Your proclamation was delivered this morning and word is spreading. You can feel the tension in the air and people are short tempered with one another. They're gathering at the docks. Richard and I spoke to Delmarco—he's a good man, Elizabeth—and he's agreed to talk to the traders. He'll report back to me by sunset. He himself is prepared to begin pulling people out of the city tonight. Even if Coral Bay and Sargay can't take them, they can still go to those cities and seek life elsewhere." She smiled. "My trader is ready to sail. Half of my people are well enough to travel, and we've found some Manusk citizens who are willing to sail with us back to my fleet." She leaned forward and put a hand on Elizabeth's knee. "If we go, it will take me four days to return here with the rest of my ships. We are anchored a day out of port but we must go by Coral Bay and leave those that want to remain here. Do you think you can hold off Osk and Sandcliff for so long?"

Elizabeth shook her head. "I don't know. Peter told me we have *at most* three days before the enemy arrives. We could be fighting tomorrow already. No matter what, we have to gain time so people can flee."

"What about you?" Rowan stopped and stared at her intently. "You don't intend to leave, do you?"

"I can't," Elizabeth said. "If I leave we lose the docks of Manusk and won't easily be able to get them back."

"Which means civil war for your father," Rowan said. "What about if we gave you support from our ships? You could fight from sea rather than land. You'd still be able to get the docks back if you had to abandon them."

That's not a bad idea. We could use the ships as our final fallback if we're driven into the city.

"But we'd have to buy four days, wouldn't we?" Elizabeth said.

Rowan thought for a moment. "Yes. I don't think I can make it back any sooner. And we can't leave with an empty ship. That would be cowardly."

"I appreciate your sense of honor," Elizabeth said with a genuine smile. She leaned forward and took Rowan's hands into hers. "I don't think I've ever thanked you for everything you've done for us . . . for *me* . . . since you got here."

Rowan gently squeezed her hands. "You are a remarkable woman, Elizabeth of Manusk. It is an honor to ally with you. I don't think as many of our allies have your strength." She grinned. "Or your beauty." Her beautiful face became still. "I care a lot about you."

"And I, you." Elizabeth looked deep into her eyes. "I think *you* are a remarkable woman, Rowan of Welland." She cupped Rowan's face. "I wish I could take away your pain, but all I seem to do is add to it. I see you look at me and you look so sad." She gave a rueful grin and it fell away at the sight of the tears that gathered in Rowan's eyes. "I promise you, this will be my last battle. I will settle down and start the family that you seem to think I deserve."

"I want to be there for it," Rowan said, taking a deep, watery breath. She pulled back and wiped the tears from her eyes. "Some princess and ambassador I am, aren't I?" She waved a hand, indicating the room and the city outside. "You'd think I'd never seen this before." She turned to the windows and her shoulders hitched.

"You have and that's why it pains you," Elizabeth said.

She went to Rowan and put a tentative hand on her shoulder, turned her, and opened her arms. Rowan was in them in a heartbeat and Elizabeth could feel her silent tears on her neck.

"I promised you I would come to Welland. I will. I promised you I wouldn't fight any more battles. I will. Now you must make a promise to *me*, Rowan of Welland."

"What?" Rowan asked. "Anything."

"Come back after the battle is over. Meet me in the duke's garden. We will plan our voyage to Welland. You and I. I want to see the fields and sky of your home."

Rowan pulled back and gazed into Elizabeth's eyes. "I promise."

Elizabeth smiled. It hurt to look at Rowan and see the lingering pain in her eyes.

They turned at the sound of booted feet coming toward the door and a second later there was a knock.

"Come," Elizabeth called, pulling back as Rowan stood and moved toward the window.

The door opened. Farrow strode into the room, stopped before Elizabeth, and bowed deeply.

"Your Grace," he said.

"Farrow," she said with genuine pleasure. "You're here quickly."

"Your men reached me as I was on the road," he said. "I was coming to tell you. Our scouts in the hills see a large army of men with catapults coming toward the city."

"I expected them. How far away are they?"

"I think it will take them three days to get to the city. They're moving slowly."

"How many?"

"Thousands, Your Grace. I am thinking Gilbert and Clayton brought their entire armies."

Ten thousand men, then. "As expected. How many are in the militia, Farrow?"

"There are four hundred men and women," he said.

"That many?" Elizabeth said.

"Once people heard that the Duchess of Manusk wanted them, and that she was helping us, they began to come in droves. More come in every day. Not all are good with weapons, though," he said with a frown.

"I don't need them to be," Elizabeth said. "You're not a fighting force. You're my farmers and tradesmen, and I need your hunting skills."

Farrow raised an eyebrow and gave her the ghost of a grin. "You want us to interfere with their supply lines and their reinforcements. You want us to slow them down."

Elizabeth smiled at him. "Exactly."

"We can do that. My people are at ease in the fields."

Elizabeth laughed. "That's where I want them."

Farrow bowed. "As you wish, Your Grace. With your permission?"

Elizabeth nodded. "Yes. But before you go, I have a final question for you. Have any of you seen Coral Bay and Duke Carter?"

Farrow looked surprised. "You haven't heard?"

Elizabeth frowned. "Heard what?"

"Duke Carter is dead. He was killed in a *hunting accident.* Rumor has it that he was mistaken for a stag while standing in the town square of a village on the road to Manusk. His fourteen-year-old boy, Henry, holds the mantle of duke."

Elizabeth sighed. "When this is over, I will send my condolences. Duke Carter was a good man. How is Duke Henry?"

"Under siege. Osk holds Coral Bay. Half of Gilbert's forces are in Coral Bay."

"So we are only faced with about seven thousand men. That evens up the odds nicely." Elizabeth looked sharply at Farrow. "How do you know all of this, anyway?"

"Captain Garamond," Farrow said. "He was with Carter when they were *hunted.* He had a hundred men with him."

Elizabeth nodded. "Is he going back to Coral Bay?"

"He will go back to Coral Bay himself," Farrow said. "He was the one who told us that Osk and Sandcliff were on the march. He was coming to you for help but knows there's none to be had from this quarter."

"Stop him. Tell him to wait for my army. We will help him take Coral Bay back. I will send forces with him when they come to us."

Farrow bowed. "You're a brave woman, Duchess Elizabeth."

Elizabeth snorted. "Hardly brave. I have my own army at my back. All I have to do is send word to them." *I hope Kellen can sneak through the lines. If she doesn't we're all dead.*

"Send word quickly, Your Grace," Farrow said softly.

Elizabeth nodded. "Go, Farrow. Make Gilbert and Clayton wish they'd never gotten up this morning."

Farrow gave her a broad grin. "I will hurry to carry out Your Grace's commands." He bowed low and backed out of the room.

"You seem remarkably calm," Rowan said from her place by the window.

"I can't panic," Elizabeth said. "No use panicking. When Kellen gets through the lines and reaches Arnett, my army will be on the march."

"How long before they get here?" Rowan asked.

Elizabeth inwardly flinched. *I can't tell her it won't be until after she gets back.* "They will be here before you arrive."

Rowan gave her a half smile. "I'd say you're lying."

"And if you did you'd be calling my honor into question and you don't want to do that, do you?" Elizabeth asked.

Rowan shook her head. "I wouldn't dream of it."

They regarded each other for a moment.

"I won't be back to the manor," Elizabeth said. "I'll be on the city walls."

Rowan's jaw tensed and she nodded.

"Come and see me tonight. Sean can bring you."

Rowan nodded again. "Yes. I'll come. I want to."

Elizabeth nodded. She felt as though something was missing. She fought back the impulse to pull Rowan into her arms again.

Rowan took a hesitant step toward her, her eyes intense, but stopped.

They stared awkwardly for another moment at each other, and then Elizabeth turned and left. She tried to erase the image of Rowan standing before the window gazing at her, but it refused to go.

CHAPTER 16

ELIZABETH STRODE INTO the guardhouse, finding Peter deep in conversation with Marcus. They were bent over the map and Peter looked up when the door opened. She sat down.

"Your Grace," Peter said with a bow.

"Peter," Elizabeth said.

Marcus looked up and bowed.

"Marcus," Elizabeth said. "How many watchmen are under your command?"

"There are a hundred of us," Marcus said.

"Take as many men as you can and go down to the docks. I think we'll be dealing with a mob down there if there isn't one already."

"Your Grace? Won't you need us for the wall?"

"I will but I need you to ensure order at the docks," Elizabeth said.

Marcus bowed. "Yes, Your Grace."

After he left, Peter and Elizabeth regarded each other.

"We had another spy in our ranks," Elizabeth said. "It was a woman."

Peter shook his head. "Wonderful. Do you have any idea how much of our plans she was able to pass on?"

"I have no idea. We have to assume she told them everything. We have to come up with another plan. Farrow also reported that there is an army headed toward us—no surprise there—in the order of seven thousand men, including catapults."

Peter sat down in the chair behind the desk. "If I know you, Your Grace, you've already asked the militia to help."

Elizabeth grinned. "Harry supply lines. The usual." She turned more serious. "Coral Bay was taken by Osk. Duke Carter is dead. We'll have to ride to them once we've secured the city."

"So we're going to have to hold out for a week?" Peter asked.

Elizabeth nodded. "I think it would be a good time for you to show me the walls and the gate."

"Yes, Your Grace," he said, standing and indicating the door.

He led the way out and into the courtyard. They stood beside a pair of new, wooden gates, reinforced with steel. The brickwork holding them was also new and looked solid.

"This follows the old design of the walls." Peter pointed to the brickwork. "The walls were very sturdy when they were first built. They're a double layer of stone. There's a walkway all along the top that encircles the entire city and we can station archers and crossbows all along the top." He led her up two flights of stone stairs to an upper walkway. They dodged guardsmen piling arrows and crossbow bolts at intervals along the wall.

"That's quite an assemblage of ammunition," Elizabeth said.

Peter nodded. "The armory is well stocked and the fletchers have been working non stop for days. We have enough arrows to shoot each soldier as they approach us. All we have to do is aim properly." He grinned.

"Good," she said. "What about oil? Do we have enough to make their lives interesting as they try to scale the walls?"

"Very little, Your Grace," he said. "We might get in perhaps a day of fires but no more."

"We have none on hand at the docks?"

Peter shook his head. "According to Richard, Osk and Sandcliff merchants have been siphoning it away for months."

Elizabeth shook her head and went to the outside of the wall. She leaned over and looked down. Half of the brickwork was new and it patched into old, crumbling brick and mortar. "That doesn't look like it's a hard climb." She glanced at Peter. "How do the inner walls look?"

"Much sturdier than the outside walls," Peter said. "If we're lucky they might hold."

"We have to last a week," Elizabeth said. "It will probably take Kellen three days to reach Arnett if she doesn't rest much. If Arnett sends the reinforcements straight away, the first of our troops should begin engaging the rear of the army four days after that."

Peter nodded. "My calculations exactly, Your Grace."

Elizabeth straightened and they walked further along the wall. The walkway was spotlessly clean and every guardsman they passed was well armed. The lookouts stood at intervals along the walls, eyes trained toward the horizon.

"Any signs of dust or the enemy?" Elizabeth asked, stopping beside a sentry.

"No, Your Grace," he said. "Traffic into the city is at a steady stream."

"What kind?"

"Mostly farmers loaded with their possessions, Your Grace," he said.

"Running ahead of an army?" Elizabeth said, glancing at Peter.

"Now some of them are starting to say that. Before it was quiet."

"Thank you, guardsman," Elizabeth said.

She turned to the inner wall and looked out over the city. She saw a panorama of city streets, broken and whole roofs, and wood smoke curling from scattered chimneys. She could see the docks in the distance and fleetingly thought of Rowan. She felt a stab of pain and pushed it aside.

"We have to hold the walls," she said. *If they have catapults they will fire at the city. We'll be trapped between swords and a wall of flames.*

"I know, Your Grace," he said.

"How much pitch do we have?"

"That we have more of, Your Grace," Peter said. "Richard and the other traders have been instrumental in getting us as much as they can."

"I'm glad Richard is on our side," Elizabeth said with a grin.

Peter nodded, returning her grin. "Yes, Your Grace."

BY THE TIME ELIZABETH returned to the guardhouse, it was dark and Rowan was waiting for her. Sean stood unobtrusively to one side, quietly engaged in conversation with Peter.

"Elizabeth," Rowan said with genuine pleasure. "You look exhausted."

You are a sight for sore eyes, pretty lady. "So do you."

"Have you eaten?" Rowan asked.

"No," Elizabeth said. "There's a tavern close to the gates that I think is still in business. Are you interested in something to eat?"

Rowan's stomach growled. She blushed. "It would seem so."

"Let's go," Elizabeth said with a laugh.

She led the way back out into the city streets. She saw the herald quietly talking to one of her guards. "Herald. Call *Manusk stands*. Do it every night until Manusk is gone."

The herald turned, looking annoyed. His irritation vanished when he saw who had spoken. He immediately bowed. "Yes, Your Grace." He waved to the guard and began to walk the city streets, his cry of *Manusk stands* echoing in the dusk.

"Feeling optimistic?" Rowan asked.

"No. Just trying to give everyone some hope," Elizabeth said.

"Is it in short supply with you, then?" Rowan asked.

"No. There's always hope. Are you ready? We have an engagement to keep." Elizabeth offered her arm. "Your Highness?"

Rowan took her arm. "Thank you, Your Highness."

They spotted an open tavern, a sign proclaiming it to be The Singing Sheep. They exchanged amused glances.

"How many sheep have you heard sing lately?" Rowan asked as they headed toward it.

"None," Elizabeth said. "And if we're lucky we won't be hearing it any time soon."

Rowan laughed as Elizabeth held the door open for her.

The room was crowded, almost half of the clientele her guardsmen. The common room was noisy and smoky. The publican and serving maids rushed about refilling tankards of ale. Elizabeth headed to a table by the window, quickly vacated with a bow by two of her guardsmen.

The publican, sweating profusely but cleanly dressed, approached their table.

"What can I get for you, Your Grace?" he asked, giving her a quick bow.

"Two tankards of ale and some of your mutton stew," she said, looking at Rowan, who nodded. "When does your music start?"

"Now," he replied with a smile, indicating the musicians who were just sitting down before the fireplace, tuning instruments.

"Excellent." Elizabeth turned back to Rowan, who was staring at her with amusement.

"Why are you in such a good mood?" she asked.

"Today is for today, tomorrow is for the gods and fate to decide," Elizabeth said. "I want an evening of entertainment before tomorrow."

"I'm leaving tomorrow so tonight has to be good," Rowan said.

"It will be," Elizabeth said as a serving maid hurried over to them with their food and ale.

She leaned over Elizabeth, her breasts maddeningly pressing into Elizabeth's shoulder. "It's good to see you, Your Grace," she whispered into Elizabeth's ear.

Elizabeth glanced at the cleft of her breasts and beckoned her closer. "It's good to see you, too," she whispered back.

The serving maid blushed and rushed off.

Rowan stared after her, her expression cool.

"Dig in and enjoy your stew," Elizabeth said, taking her own spoon in hand. "Enjoy yourself. Please."

Rowan took her spoon in a white knuckled grip. "I will."

The thick stew was well spiced and they quickly ate it. Elizabeth swallowed a mouthful of ale when she'd finished eating, enjoying the flavor.

"This is good," she said.

Rowan smiled at her. "It is." She gestured toward the room. "Why all the merriment when you all know what's coming?"

"Why not?" Elizabeth said. "Who knows when we'll be able to enjoy it next?"

Rowan opened her mouth and closed it again. Elizabeth waited patiently for her to speak, but the band began playing.

Elizabeth grinned. "Have you finished eating? Did you enjoy your stew?"

"Yes, I did and I enjoyed it," Rowan said and drained the last of her mug of ale.

"Good," Elizabeth said. "It's time for you to work it off, Your Highness."

She grabbed Rowan's hand and dragged her out into the middle of the other dancers. Rowan began to protest, but Elizabeth hooked an arm around her waist and spun her around the floor. Rowan pulled her in close and they danced until the band broke for drinks.

Rowan, breathing hard, took Elizabeth's hand and pulled her to their table, where the publican had left ales for each of them. They collapsed into their seats, brought their mugs together with a click, and drank deeply.

"I didn't know you could dance," Rowan said, grinning.

"I can certainly do it when the occasion calls for it and enjoy it when it happens."

A serving maid came over and bent to refill Rowan's glass. She gazed at Rowan, lingering at her breasts, and gave her a slow smile. She bent and whispered something in Rowan's ear and Rowan smiled and shook her head. Elizabeth felt like tearing the jug out of the girl's hands and smashing it over her head.

God, what is the matter *with me?*

The band started playing and this time the song was at a much slower tempo. Rowan took Elizabeth's hand and led her out on the floor. She pulled Elizabeth in close and they danced again. She ran her hands up and down Elizabeth's back, and Elizabeth tightened her grip. Elizabeth breathed deeply of Rowan's scent and smiled.

The song ended and they paid the publican and walked out into the night.

"There's so much I want to say to you but I don't know where to start," Rowan said.

"I understand," Elizabeth said. "And I find myself wanting to spend every waking moment in your presence."

Rowan's breath caught. "Do you really mean that? She bit her lip, blushing.

"Yes," Elizabeth said. "Yes."

"I want the same thing," Rowan said. "I wish we—"

Elizabeth's finger went to her lips. "No. No wishes. You don't need those. We will be together again in a week and then we will have time."

"You'll be busy rebuilding your city again."

Elizabeth shook her head. "No. No, I want something just for me and it's to spend time with you. Life is so short. I'm not going to waste it anymore."

"I will come for you, Elizabeth."

Elizabeth looked deeply into Rowan's eyes, almost seeing her soul laid bare in them. Rowan wanted her to believe.

"I will be waiting for you, Princess."

Rowan's face lit up into a smile. "I see the truth of it in your eyes, Your Grace."

Elizabeth smiled and the world fell away from her.

"What was your favorite thing to do as a child?" Rowan asked after a moment of peaceful silence.

Elizabeth gave her a half smile. "I liked lying in the fields at night and staring at the stars."

Rowan nodded. "So did I. I also like staring at clouds. Now I'm much more careful about how I do it. Do you want to find a field to lie in and stare at the stars?"

"I'd love to but I can't," Elizabeth said, pained at her words and desperate for Rowan to understand her refusal. "I have to get back to the city gates."

Rowan did look disappointed but she smiled and gently cupped Elizabeth's face. "I understand. Can I interest you in exactly that when we next meet?"

"With pleasure," Elizabeth said, holding the hand against her face. "I'll be back."

"And I'll be waiting for you."

They slowly released each other, and Elizabeth watched Rowan until she disappeared into the darkness with Sean by her side.

I wish things were different. I wish I had more time to get to know the very beautiful Rowan of Welland.

She walked back to the guardhouse, feeling as though millstones were tied to her ankles. She could not stop herself from turning back and looking down the darkened street. She felt as though Rowan had taken part of her with her.

"YOUR GRACE, YOU'RE back," Peter said as Elizabeth entered the guardhouse.

"What?" Elizabeth asked.

Peter looked surprised at her tone. "Our sentries have spotted a glow on the horizon."

"Campfires?"

Peter nodded. "We think so."

"How arrogant," Elizabeth said, clenching her jaw. "Muster the troops."

"Very good, Your Grace," he said.

"I'm going up to there."

"I'll go with you."

"No, you stay back. I need my experienced officers to give orders with an eye for the battle. We'll need cool heads when the fighting breaks out. Also to keep the men calm before."

Peter's sour expression spoke volumes about his views on her orders.

Elizabeth smiled gently at him, got up, and squeezed his shoulder. "I know you don't like it, old friend. But that's ducal privilege."

Peter's mouth opened and closed in outrage. "Don't expect me to be happy about you sticking your neck onto a chopping block, Your Grace. If you get hurt you answer to me, understand?"

Elizabeth laughed and saluted. "Yes, sir." She left the guardhouse and jogged up the stairs to the walkway. She saw something sticking out of an alcove and slowly approached it, shaking her head.

It's a cannon.

"Can I help you, Your Grace?" a guardsman asked, appearing from the right hand side of the muzzle.

"No. Aim well, guardsman."

The guardsman gave her a salute. "Yes, Your Grace."

She continued walking. A cannon wouldn't help them much against siege engines unless they were within its range, but it would stop the infantry and the less foot soldiers they had to deal with the better.

All along the wall the soldiers sat and waited as they looked out through the crenellations and fidgeted, eager to engage the enemy.

God, there are so few of them and they all look like children. Did I remember to recruit anyone who could shave?

Two of the soldiers close to her scuffled, nerves frayed with tension, and she put restraining hands on each of their shoulders. "Easy, guardsmen. Save yourselves for the enemy."

The first one gave her an angry stare until he realized who it was. He blushed and bowed. "Yes, Your Grace. I'm sorry."

She pointed at the discarded dice at their feet. "You only have to apologize if you lose. Did you?"

He blushed again and remained silent.

She leaned forward and whispered in his ear, "Come and see me after this is over and I'll show you how to roll dice, guardsman."

The guardsman gaped at her. "Yes, Your Grace."

Other soldiers rested against the wall, sleeping. *Good idea. Never turn down sleep when you can get it.*

As she walked toward the far sentries, she began to sing the anthem of the King's Heartland. One baritone voice joined hers, then another and another, until finally all the soldiers who were not sleeping were singing for King Vincent.

A hand clapped her on the back as the final notes ended, then another and another. Finally the men let up a cheer and Elizabeth saw that the tension had lessened. She began another song, to the gods, asking for victory and an honored place in the afterlife. More voices joined in.

She finally reached a point half way along the wall, where the brickwork was at its worst, and stood by the sentry, watching the orange glow on the horizon. *It looks like the entire army is here, not just some advance scouts.*

She went to the opposite wall and looked out over the city. The street lights were lit and they gave her an overall view of the city. The docks were in the distance and she could see the mob of people down there, with more streaming in by the moment.

She imagined Rowan down there, restoring order to chaos, and felt sick at the thought of any harm coming to her. She hoped the Welland survivors were there, safely tucked inside the trader.

She forced her mind and heavy heart away from Rowan and turned it to the more pressing matter of the city. It was constructed on a large grid pattern. One major road led directly down to the docks. The rest were side streets and some of them went all the way down, some only to the east west road through the city.

They had to concentrate on killing as many of the enemy infantry as they could before they reached the walls. They simply didn't have enough troops to hold the city if the wall was breached. If it was, the best they could do was fire at the enemy from the rooftops of the houses. There would be no way to contain them because they didn't have the manpower to barricade the side streets that joined onto the main roads.

Elizabeth sat down with her back to the wall, leaned her head back, and closed her eyes. She was exhausted in both her heart and her mind. *The sleeping soldiers had the right idea*, was her last thought before she fell into a deep sleep.

She dreamed.

In it, she ran down the city streets, screaming Rowan's name. She was chased by Osk guardsman and they had her cut off from the docks. She stumbled through the lines, only to see Rowan taken prisoner. They were just tightening a noose around her neck when the world began to shake.

"What?" she said groggily, trying to push back the nightmares that made her feel sick.

"Dawn, Your Grace," the sentry said. "They're coming."

Elizabeth slowly stood and tried to stretch out the kinks in her body. She could not resist a glance back over her shoulder, to the harbor of Manusk. The berth occupied by the Welland trader was conspicuously empty.

"Goodbye, Rowan," she whispered.

"Your Grace?" the soldier asked, watching her intently.

"Nothing," she said, shaking her head.

She looked over the wall out onto the northern plains. Groups of men marched toward the city, siege engines bringing up the rear of the companies. There looked to be four trebuchets and belfries heading toward them. They also had a battering ram.

She turned to the soldier by her side. "Ready the pitch. We have to destroy the siege engines. Hot oil for the battering ram as it approaches the gates. Do not fire until you are given the order from me." She took a step back. "Seal the gates. Seal the gates of Manusk."

Soldiers took up her cry, calling orders down to the soldiers at the gates and the cannons on the walls. Archers readied their arrows to fire flame at the enemy.

They waited for an hour for the army to approach Manusk, and when it got closer, they saw the command tents of Gilbert of Osk and Clayton of Sandcliff in the rear.

The army finally came to a halt on the plains, and the enemy soldiers prepared the trebuchets. Elizabeth watched them carefully.

"Your Grace?" the soldier asked, his tension showing in his short, restless movements.

"We won't fire until they fire first. If we do, this engagement becomes civil war started by me. We wait for them to fire first."

The soldier saluted. "Yes, Your Grace."

Elizabeth watched the command tents. There seemed to be a flurry of movement all around, and two figures galloped through the troops toward the gates of Manusk.

"I'm going down there," Elizabeth said.

The soldier saluted.

Elizabeth jogged along the wall, calling encouragement to the men and urging them to stay calm until given orders to fire. She went into the guardhouse.

Peter and her other senior commanders stood in the room, rigid with tension.

"Your Grace?" Peter asked.

"It's time, Peter. Gilbert and Clayton are galloping toward us. No one is to fire until the order is given by me."

"Your Highness," Peter said. "I'm not going to stand back. I'm coming with you."

"All right," Elizabeth said. "Come."

They left the guardhouse.

Elizabeth made her way with her shoulders straight and her head held high, Peter at her right shoulder. They approached the gate.

"Open," Elizabeth said.

The guards quickly opened the gate and Elizabeth and Peter walked through followed by twelve soldiers who took up positions behind them. The gate shut behind them.

Elizabeth watched Duke Gilbert of Osk and Duke Clayton of Sandcliff gallop toward them and then rein to a halt.

"Your Graces," Elizabeth said with a bow just short of insulting.

"Elizabeth," Gilbert said, a florid, flabby man with the cold eyes of a snake. "Explain yourself."

"What do you want me to explain?" Elizabeth asked with a relaxed smile she didn't feel.

"Why you've been imprisoning citizens of *my* duchy. And executing them." Clayton snarled, as tall and thin as Gilbert was short and fat.

"Rubbish. You could care less about your people. Don't pretend. It's unbecoming. I know about your plan for Welland and my father," Elizabeth said. "Don't pretend you know nothing about it. You're guilty of treason and I will tell my father, *after* I've defeated the mob of choir boys you call an army."

Gilbert looked surprised for a moment, while Clayton eyed her coldly, unfazed by her response.

"You pathetic bitch," Clayton said coldly. "*I'm* not the one sorely outnumbered. I'm going to take your precious Manusk. When you're gone there won't be anyone to tell the king anything."

"Over my dead body," Elizabeth said.

"That was my intention," Gilbert said. He turned to Clayton. "War."

Clayton nodded. He turned to Elizabeth. "You have one minute to return to your precious city or I'll kill you where you stand."

Gilbert and Clayton turned their horses around and galloped away.

Elizabeth wasted no time and jogged back toward the gate with Peter by her side.

"Your Grace," Peter said. "That little nose tweaking you gave him will be the death of us."

"We're dead anyway," Elizabeth said sadly. "We can't hold the city. Not even long enough for the army to get here. All we can do is finish what we started when we entered the city."

The doors opened and they trotted into the city. Soldiers rushed to close and reinforce the doors.

"Remember," Elizabeth said. "You must hold the docks of Manusk to the last man."

"Yes, Your Grace," Peter said. He stood to attention and saluted. "Good hunting."

"You too," Elizabeth said and jogged toward the stairs.

She raced up the stairs, two at a time. She burst out onto the walkway as the archers pulled back on their bows.

She looked over the crenellations and in the distance she could see the trebuchets pulling back their slings. A soldier lit the ball of pitch in the cup and they released the slings.

"Fire at the siege engines! Fire at the belfries!" Elizabeth screamed, ducking for cover as the balls of flaming fire crashed into the walls of the city. Some unfortunate men, now living torches, screamed in agony. Their cries were silenced by their fellow soldiers.

The ground shook, knocking her off her feet, and bricks tumbled from the walls.

"Return fire!" Elizabeth screamed as the archers fired arrows at the mob of soldiers running toward the walls.

"Put that out!" an officer yelled, peering over the inside merlons at the burning city.

A knot of men ran toward a crumbled section of wall that had not survived a direct hit from the trebuchets. Enemy soldiers poured toward the wall and Elizabeth ran toward it, drawing her sword.

Archers stood above the breach, firing with methodical precision into the crush of soldiers. The cannons roared. Soldiers climbed the rubble.

Thank God they've only breached the outer wall. She swung her sword and beheaded a nimble Osk soldier who had managed to climb up the rubble to the railing. Manusk guardsmen quickly followed her and the slaughter began.

Her world became a cacophony of the screams of angry men, some fighting, some dying, and the crimson splatter of freshly spilt blood.

Belfries rolled toward the breach, bringing more men, and the archers fired at the soldiers running toward them. The air filled with smoke as the wind blew the fire from the city back to the walls.

Elizabeth's eyes teared and she blinked, barely blocking a large man's sword. His face was a grimace of hatred as he tried to smash through her defenses. She scored a nick to her eyebrow for her trouble and her eye stung. Her face felt wet from the flow of blood from the cut.

In the distance, the trebuchets reloaded and fired at the city again. As the flaming balls flew toward the city, there was an explosion from a burning trebuchet.

A cannon. A cannon ball hit it.

More soldiers poured into the breach and Elizabeth settled into a comfortable rhythm of defend, attack, slash, and parry.

They fought for hours, Elizabeth and her soldiers refusing to give inches to the climbing soldiers. The wall became slick with blood and the corpses mounted, adding to the ladder over the wall.

By dusk of that evening, Elizabeth was exhausted. The enemy soldiers withdrew and everywhere exhausted soldiers fell to their knees, breathing deeply, nursing wounds, and calling for water.

Elizabeth sat a small distance from the breach, beyond the reach of spilt blood, and called for water. A grim-faced boy rushed up to her with a dipper and she drank deeply. She gave him back the dipper with a smile.

She levered herself to her feet. "Throw the bodies over the outside wall. Let them tend to their dead," she said to the closest guardsman.

She got up and looked over the crenellations to the plain.

Hundreds of bodies lay on the grass, most unmoving. Some cried out softly in pain. The remains of the trebuchets lay splintered on the ground, the land surrounding them ashes. Small figures moved amongst the fallen, tended to or taken by figures moving around the battle field. The belfries lay in splinters at the base of the wall.

Guardsmen walked along the walkways, collecting their own dead and putting them in a neat row. She did a quick count.

Of her thousand soldiers, only fifty were dead.

The advantage of higher ground. The cannons were an excellent idea.

Bodies lay all along the pitted and blackened outer wall, and some men lay back against the railings, blood flowing from fresh wounds. A young man she didn't recognize walked amongst the wounded, helping as best he could.

"Where is the doctor?" she asked.

"Killed during the day. I'm his apprentice." The man peered at Elizabeth. "You have a cut over your eye that needs tending."

Elizabeth felt worn out. *I'm going to miss the doctor. He was an honest and honorable man. I liked him.*

"There are others here who are worse," Elizabeth said. "Tend to them first as best you're able."

She looked over the merlons into the city. Collapsed and blackened roofs, still giving off tendrils of smoke, lay on ruined houses. The blazes hadn't gone any further than the first couple of city streets. It looked as though The Singing Sheep had also burnt to the ground. She grimaced and hoped that the publican and his serving maids had escaped.

She could see light down at Manusk Harbor, and a larger crush of citizens trying to flee the city. Two- and three-masted schooners, barques, brigantines, yachts, and fishing vessels were vying for space at the docks. She smiled briefly. Delmarco, Rowan, and Richard had done their jobs well.

"Ready your weapons and set the watch," Elizabeth called as she walked toward the stairs that led to the guardhouse. "Let me know immediately if soldiers appear on the plains."

A guardsman covered in ash and dried blood saluted. "At once, Your Grace."

Elizabeth let herself into the guardhouse and slumped in the chair across from Peter. Peter was engaged in conversation with three of his lieutenants.

"Your Grace," he said, bowing low. He looked profoundly relieved.

"Peter," Elizabeth said. "How bad is it? I saw that the fires in the city were put out and we have one breach on the weakest part of the wall. I passed fifty dead guardsmen and double that injured."

Peter nodded. "We have breaches in two other places along the wall. Of those, the inner wall was also damaged. It won't stand another direct hit from a catapult. A battering ram attempted to come through the gates but was stopped with boiling oil and fire."

"Excellent," Elizabeth said. "I know the trebuchets were destroyed during the day."

Peter nodded. "We managed to kill in the order of a thousand of the enemy last night, and according to our counts we have about eight hundred serviceable men remaining on the walls. The rest are either dead or too badly injured to fight."

"And we lost the doctor last night."

Peter nodded. "Yes, Your Grace. His apprentice was almost ready to take his final exams to certify him as a physician, so all isn't lost." He sighed. "We also lost Lieutenant Davidson last night. He led the defense of the worst breach."

Davidson. He was a good soldier and a good man. "He won't be the last," Elizabeth said. "How many men were diverted to put out the fires?"

"The watch came up from the docks. The trader's guards are taking their orders from Sergeant Hunter at the docks. Hunter sent the watch up as reserves." He looked at Elizabeth. "They're good fighting men, Your Grace."

Elizabeth nodded. "I know they are."

Peter looked at his lieutenants and then dismissed them.

Once they were alone, he took a seat on the other side of the table.

"I think you're right, Your Grace," he said.

"About what?"

"We can't hold the city long enough for either Princess Rowan to return, or for Arnett to come and reinforce us. We simply don't have enough men to keep the entire wall."

"That's why I need you and my other officers here. *You must protect the docks of Manusk at all costs,* do you understand, Captain?" She leaned back in her chair. "We must keep that for my father. Osk and Sandcliff think they've cut me off from the rest of the King's Heartland and my father's army. Perhaps they have, perhaps they haven't. That's for fate to decide."

Peter's jaw tensed.

"Speak up, Peter. You disagree."

"Yes, I disagree, Your Grace," Peter said, the anger in his voice carefully controlled. "You're setting yourself up as a straw target on the walls when we need your leadership the most down at our last line of defense at the docks."

Elizabeth gritted her teeth. "I *will not* hide down at the docks like a sniveling coward."

"No one said you were, Your Grace," Peter said. "But have you ever considered that perhaps that's where you're needed the most? When the soldiers come pouring into the city and the people see you at the docks ready to protect them, they might pick up a sword and help us."

"It's *not* me the people gather around, Peter," Elizabeth said. "It's *us*. *All* of those men and women who march under the banner of Manusk to stand and fight. Has it occurred to you that the panic will be even worse when the civilians see soldiers armed to the teeth marching down to the docks? They're going to think the walls have been breached and we're invaded. There will be *chaos* if we do that."

Peter smiled. "You're so wrong, Your Grace. It *is* you the people look up to, not us." He was silent a moment. "I can't change your mind, can I?"

Elizabeth snorted. "No. You can't."

Peter shrugged. "I thought not. But as a personal favor to me, Your Grace, try and stay alive, will you?"

Elizabeth smiled. "Of course."

"Manusk stands!" a hoarse voice called from the street below.

CHAPTER 17

DAWN OF THE second day found an exhausted Elizabeth lined up with her guardsmen at the walls, watching a wall of armored men marching toward the city. They held ladders. Small knots of soldiers broke away in groups, heading toward the damaged section of wall.

"Stand fast," Elizabeth called. "Archers take aim!"

The archers lined up in a neat rank and nocked their arrows.

"Fire!" Elizabeth called, her command echoing up and down the walls.

The archers fired and a row of enemy soldiers either dropped like stone or fell to the ground wounded.

"Fire at will! Fire the cannons!"

The world became a cacophony of roaring and booming as the cannons fired into the soldiers. They were knocked over like skittles, some torn apart by the cannon balls, and those that remained screamed battle cries and ran toward the walls.

Elizabeth and her guardsmen tensed, waiting for the inevitable round of soldiers climbing the walls. She glanced up and down the wall, seeing the widely spaced men, feeling every death and injury that her small force had gotten the previous day.

I wonder what Rowan . . . she thought, viciously cutting it off. Rowan was gone.

A ladder swung up the wall in front of her and she lunged toward it, ready with her sword. A head appeared and she stabbed at it, wounding the soldier. He screamed and tumbled back down the ladder, taking some of the men climbing after him with them.

One large soldier bent his back, the wounded man bouncing off him. He looked up, spotted Elizabeth, and snarled. He raced up the ladder with remarkable agility, considering his size, and dived over the wall at Elizabeth. She took a step back at the last second, avoiding his tackle, and swung her sword at his head. He rolled and caught it and she kicked him as hard as she could in the face. He howled as his nose exploded and sprayed blood. His hands slid away from her blade and she swung her sword at his neck, severing his fingers and biting deeply into his neck. Blood spurted out of the wound and he fell, bleeding out, as another man came over the wall and shoved her backward with all his might.

Elizabeth skidded backward, off balance, and barely managed to parry his sword. She engaged him in earnest, cursing as he shielded the extra men climbing up the ladder and over the wall.

Guardsmen rushed to her aid and they engaged the men on the wall.

Elizabeth felt the sting of the man's blade as a young man carrying a bucket slipped though the fighting. One of the enemy soldiers saw him at the last moment and lunged toward him, but the momentary lapse cost him his life as a guardsman killed him. The man fighting Elizabeth faltered for a second and it was enough for her to slip beneath his defenses and drive her sword home through his heart.

The young man carrying the bucket screamed, "Away!" and dumped boiling oil down the ladder.

Horribly burned men screamed in pain and let go of the ladder, falling off it and tumbling to the ground. One of them landed on his compatriots on the way down and the ladder snapped, throwing the rest to the ground.

Elizabeth and her guardsmen quickly dispatched the enemy soldiers on the walkway.

Men called for help a little further down at the breach and they ran into help.

The walkway became awash with blood as the bodies piled up.

As soon as a wave of soldiers slowed at one breach another started up further down the wall, so Elizabeth and her men were run ragged up and down the wall slaughtering soldiers that by some miracle had made it through a breach.

By the end of the second day, Elizabeth bled from a dozen nicks and cuts and she helped her exhausted soldiers toss bodies over the wall and onto the ground.

She walked along the wall, talking to her men and congratulating them on a good day's fighting as cries of *Manusk stands* began from the streets below.

Peter, looking ruffled, jogged up to her and gave her a tired salute.

"Peter," she said.

"The watch spent the day combing the houses, evacuating

civilians," he said. "We've managed to get most out. The city is safe for the moment."

Elizabeth nodded. "Good. If you will, do a head count. Let's see how many soldiers are still left."

Elizabeth walked back with him along the wall, inspecting the breaches. A stonemason joined her as they went to the largest breach.

The stonemason looked down. "That won't hold much longer." He shook his head. He led her to the other merlon and pointed down. "See the cracks? This whole section of wall is going to come down."

Damn. All we need is another three days.

"Peter, get me five of your best fighters. We'll hold the breach." She spoke with a confidence her exhausted heart did not feel.

"What are your plans for the rest of the men?" Peter asked as the stonemason bowed and backed away.

Elizabeth looked at him. "Pour pitch and oil over the walls at the ladders against the walls. Fire burning pitch at the belfries. Defend the breaches." She sighed. "There *is* no battle plan in a fight like this. We can't cut them off, they outnumber us and we're above them. That's our only advantage." She paused a moment, eyeing the carnage and rubble up and down the wall. She felt sick. "All they have to do is what they're doing. Put more and more ladders against the walls as our numbers dwindle. When we finally abandon the wall, we burn the city. That should hold them back but will trap us at the waterline. But hopefully it won't come to that."

Peter nodded. "My thoughts exactly, Your Grace."

"I'm going down into the city," Elizabeth said.

"I'll come with you," Peter said.

"No," Elizabeth said. "See to it that the men get food, water, and sleep. That's what they need the most now."

Elizabeth left him and headed back along the wall to the inner stairs that led down to the city. She was so exhausted she could barely put one foot in front of the other. She passed by a group of women she recognized from her manor.

"What are you doing here?" she asked.

"Your Grace," they said, bobbing a curtsey. "We're here with food." She held up a basket of bread and dried meat.

"I'm sorry," Elizabeth said, mustering a smile. "I didn't see. Please, continue."

The woman hesitated a moment. "If you don't mind my saying

so, you need to eat. You look exhausted." She pulled bread and meat from her basket.

Elizabeth's neglected stomach rumbled. "Thank you," she said, accepting the food thrust her way.

She ate her bread as she put one foot in front of the other. She passed by a soldier curled up in a ball at the bottom of the stairs. He was so deeply asleep his chest barely moved.

She went out into the city street and saw dozens of makeshift cooking fires in the street, women preparing food for the soldiers and serving them as they filed past with empty bowls.

Some children stood back, watching them. She went to them.

"You shouldn't be here. You should go down to the docks. But since you *are* here, come, eat," she said. "The food is also for you."

The children looked at her carefully and then jogged up to the line and insinuated themselves into it. The men made room for them and helped them fill their bowls.

Elizabeth walked down the main street, past the smoldering ruins of houses, heartsick. *I want to see Rowan one last time.* She saw her manor and flinched. Garvin, on crutches, stood by the main gates, looking out into the street. He watched her approach.

"Garvin," she said. "You shouldn't be here."

"Want to stay. Me want to be farmer."

Elizabeth smiled. "You want to be a farmer in Manusk?"

He nodded, once. "Not go. Stay. Me Manuskman now."

Elizabeth nodded. *If there's even a Manusk left after this.* "If that's what you wish. Does Princess Rowan know you're still here?"

He nodded. "She know. She give blessing and ask us to watch over you."

Elizabeth barely suppressed a flinch. It hurt to think of Rowan.

"Tell her I said thank you when you see her," she said, half saluting as she continued on her way down to the docks.

The docks were packed with people shoving and yelling, trying to storm ships leaving Manusk.

She forced her way to front of the crowd gathered outside the import hall.

"Silence!" she screamed and the crowd slowly quieted.

Richard's guards quickly flanked her. "Ships are coming back to take you out of here. They will be here soon!"

"Easy for you to say!" a man shouted back. "You're not the one standing here waiting."

Elizabeth's temper snapped. "No, I'm not. I'm the idiot standing on the walls holding back Osk and Sandcliff. Damn you, I'm the Duchess of Manusk and we're dying to keep you safe!"

"You're not doing a very good job," another man said. "The city burned. People died."

"Where's your fabulous army?" a third yelled. "The magic fighting men you're rumored to have?"

Elizabeth growled and shook her head. She felt angrier by the second.

The crowd booed.

Richard came out of the hall. He stiffened in surprise when he saw her.

"Your Grace? You look exhausted. What are you doing here?"

"I came to see how *you* were doing," Elizabeth said. "And also to find out how the evacuation is coming along."

"Just in time, then," Richard said. He took a step back. "One hour! One hour and the ships return!"

The crowd looked slightly mollified and began to thin out a little.

"How do you know that?" Elizabeth asked.

"We've had a couple of days to get it right," Richard said. "Delmarco has divided the ships into two groups. One comes in as the other goes out. We sent out the entire fleet this morning with survivors. Half will be back tonight. It should be enough to clear out most of this lot. We can hide the rest."

Elizabeth nodded. "That's magnificent. You've done a wonderful job, Richard. But what of you? The walls will likely fall in the next day or so."

Richard nodded and straightened. "You asked us to hold the docks. We'll do it to the last man. You can count on us, Your Grace."

Elizabeth smiled and clapped him on the arm. "And we'll buy you as much time as we can. We'll join you to hold the docks." *If there's anyone left alive.*

"Go and get some rest, Your Grace," Richard said, watching the crowd carefully. "You need your strength to fight Osk and Sandcliff."

"Thank you, Richard, for everything."

"You're welcome, Your Grace," he said, giving her a grin.

Elizabeth left the docks and headed back up to the walls. She could not resist a glance at the manor house, looking for Garvin, but he was gone.

She got back to the walls and crawled into the cot at the back of the guardhouse, asleep before her head hit the pillow.

DAWN OF THE third day brought a dreadful sense of familiarity as the guards—now only six hundred left—lined up on the walls, ready for battle.

Osk and Sandcliff troops marched toward the walls, carrying more ladders.

The day's slaughter commenced.

Elizabeth and her five defenders stayed at the breach, hearing the screams of wounded and dying men, their boots unsteady in the blood soaking the walkway.

They fought for hours, taking inches only to be forced into giving them back moments later as more soldiers stormed the breach.

One by one the men around her were torn to pieces by enemy swords and she felt the sting of blades herself as she fought two and sometimes three soldiers at once.

She was finally alone, hacking, slashing, and dispatching everything that her blade came in contact with. She felt the eyes of the dead on her, accusing her, as she faced down another three soldiers.

They attacked her, all together, and she slipped in the blood. She lost her footing for a second and felt a sword ram home in her shoulder. She cried out in agony, blood streaming down her damaged arm. The soldier brought up his sword, ready to separate her head from her shoulders.

It can't end like this. She shifted her sword to the other hand and swung wildly. He backed away from her blade as the others closed in on her. One of them suddenly stopped, looking down at the arrow sticking out of his chest, surprise clear on his features. He fell forward, dead before he hit the ground.

Arrows flew through the air around her, thudding home into the enemy soldiers. She fell to her knees, panting, blood soaking the left side of her body. Guardsmen streamed around her, engaging the enemy soldiers and forcing them back down the breach.

A figure knelt beside her. "Your Grace?"

Elizabeth wanted to answer him but couldn't get any words to come out. Her eyes rolled up in her head as she grayed out from the pain.

The guardsmen caught her, calling for a medic. A young man

appeared beside her, tore open her shirt, and staunched the flow of blood from the wound.

"Get her out of here," he said to the guardsman.

The guardsman nodded, picked her up and slung her over his shoulders.

The world exploded in agony from her injured shoulder and she passed out.

She opened her eyes what felt like moments later, to see a pale Peter bending over her.

"Don't move," he said, gently pushing her back down again as she tried to sit up.

She didn't offer much resistance. Her shoulder ached abominably and she felt weak and exhausted.

"It's dusk, Your Grace," he said. "You've been unconscious for most of the day. Here, eat. You need to keep your strength up."

Elizabeth nodded. "Thank you."

He helped her sit up to eat.

She took a few spoonfuls of the beef stew he gave her and her appetite roared to life. She gulped down the stew, bread, and cheese he gave her, plus the vegetable broth and milk behind him.

"What happened, Peter?" she asked.

"Manusk stands," Peter said softly. "Thanks to you. Did you know you were cut off from the rest of the guards? It took us a while to get to you."

Elizabeth nodded. "That doesn't surprise me. No one came to help us as we were cut down." She grunted in pain as she tried to move her arm.

"I know you're going up to that wall tomorrow." Peter put a gentle hand on her chest and pushed her back down onto the bloody cot. "I can't stop you. But if you do that, old friend, you should rest. Your shoulder is badly cut and we don't have a surgeon to sew you up anymore. They're all dead. Whatever people we've managed to find who know anything about medicine are on the walls seeing to the soldiers."

"How many?" Elizabeth whispered as sleep began to take her into its grasp.

"Four hundred. There are four hundred of us left," Peter said.

Come back, Rowan. Come to me, Arnett, Elizabeth thought as she drifted off to sleep.

DAWN OF THE fourth day found her on the walls again. Her arm ached and her movements were restricted from the tight bandage on her shoulder.

They waited for the soldiers to storm the walls again, watching closely for the tightly packed formation to march toward the wall.

This morning was different. The soldiers marched down the plains toward the city, Gilbert of Osk and Clayton of Sandcliff clearly visible, riding behind them.

"Arrogant bastards," Elizabeth muttered. "They think they've finished us and they've come to gloat. Well, they can go hang themselves. They can't have our city."

The guardsman next to her grinned. "Yes, Your Grace."

"What's that?" another man asked, staring off to the left.

"What?" Elizabeth followed the direction of his gaze.

She could see a mass of men and women marching over the hill toward the army. They carried all manner of weapons, from swords, bows, and quarter staffs to pitchforks, shovels, and clubs.

"It's the militia," the guardsman said. "What the devil are they doing? They're going to get killed."

"They're buying us time," Elizabeth said. "They know we're being slaughtered."

Elizabeth and her men could only watch as the militia screamed *Manusk* and raced toward the enemy as fast as they could.

The enemy soldiers at first seemed to think it was a joke and ignored them, but the militia held firm and continued to run toward them. The militia reached the soldiers and began to fight, pushing them into disarray. Arrows flew and soldiers fell. The militia swung their weapons and dispatched more. Osk soldiers turned to see the company of men dying and ran toward them, raising weapons.

More militia appeared in the distance, pushing cannons and a large catapult they'd clearly liberated from the Osk and Sandcliff forces.

The fight began in earnest.

Bodies fell to the ground, more soldiers than militia. The Osk and Sandcliff forces streamed toward the battle and the militia retreated, inch by inch.

"The catapult," the guardsman said beside her.

Elizabeth turned to the catapult and watched the militia fire it. A ball of burning pitch whizzed through the air and exploded in a dense knot of soldiers running toward the thick of the fighting. There was a tremendous thud and men were engulfed in flame, stumbling around, human torches. They screamed endlessly in agony until they fell, one by one.

A battle cry went up from Osk and Sandcliff and the troops engaged the militia in earnest.

"Archers! Fire into the soldiers!"

The archers obeyed her orders and fired into the soldiers, felling more of them behind and the enemy soldiers retreated, trapped on both fronts. The catapult fired again, hitting a knot of soldiers, burning and killing them.

An officer shouted orders and a group of soldiers broke away and ran toward the catapult. The militia had seconds to fire off another shot before the soldiers reached them. They quickly set fire to the catapult and ran toward the main battle.

The tide turned against the militia again, and they quickly began to fall.

"Get out of there," Elizabeth said. "Save yourselves."

The militia retreated as though they'd heard her soft words, and the march toward the city began again.

Elizabeth and her guardsmen braced themselves as groups of men poured toward the breach in the walls.

Elizabeth raised her sword, grunting in pain, shifted her stance, and waited for the first armored man to appear.

Moments later he did and she quickly dispatched him.

The battle began in earnest, much as it had for the past few days, yet this time the soldiers were clumsier and easily dispatched. They'd clearly been rattled by the engagement with the militia.

They fought steadily throughout the day, occasionally assisted by the militia harrying the sides of the enemy forces.

By the end of the day, Elizabeth was exhausted. She hung over the wall, watching the figures appear on the battlefield to take the wounded and dying. Over to the side she saw the militia appear on the field to remove their own wounded.

"Manusk!" she called. "Manusk!"

One man's voice joined hers, and then another. All the guardsmen still alive and well enough to make noise leaned over the railing and called to them, cheering.

The militia looked up at them, waved, and took up the call.

Peter appeared by her side. "They're the bravest people I've ever seen."

Elizabeth nodded. "They bought us another day. Have you heard any word from them?"

Peter shook his head. "I don't even know if any of them are still alive."

Elizabeth nodded. "I hope we're alive to thank them."

They stood, shoulder to shoulder on the railing, watching the brilliant sunset in the west and the movement of the helpers on the battlefield.

"Take care of the men," Elizabeth said, sinking down against the wall. "I need to close my eyes for a moment."

Her eyes were gritty with exhaustion and grey flowers bloomed in her vision. She was only distantly aware of Peter throwing his cloak over her to protect her from the night air.

ON THE MORNING of the fifth day, Elizabeth stood at the most damaged section of the wall, a corporal by her side, watching a catapult roll toward the city. She looked back over the rear wall to the harbor of Manusk. Each day she longed to see Rowan's standard flying over ships sailing into the harbor, and each day she was disappointed. On this morning, hope flared. It was the morning of the fifth day, and Rowan had told her she would return in five days.

"That looks like a good thousand men, Your Grace," the corporal said by her side, shaking her out of her thoughts.

Elizabeth nodded. "With a siege engine."

"They're going to breach the wall, aren't they?" the corporal said.

Elizabeth stared at the marching figures. "They're breaking formation to head to the breaches in the outer walls. Tell the commanders to hold the walls until there are no more men left."

The corporal took a deep breath. "Yes, Your Grace," he said shakily.

Elizabeth turned to him. He wasn't more than a boy, a very young man in his late teens. "We have an advantage in the higher ground. And the army is coming. The outcome of today's battle is not decided and won't be until dusk."

The corporal straightened his shoulders and firmed his jaw, but his pallor remained. "Yes, Your Grace," he said, sounding more confident.

Anything more that could have been said was abruptly cut off as the Osk catapult fired and the soldiers roared their battle cry. They hurtled toward the walls and Elizabeth readied her sword.

She felt the blood drain from her face from the pain of the wound to her shoulder.

Just a little longer.

The solid metal ball from the catapult smashed into the stone of the inner walls, shattering it into a million fragments. Elizabeth was knocked off her feet from the force of the blow, and she was momentarily deafened by the impact.

The wall was opened.

The enemy soldiers screamed in triumph and rushed toward the walls.

Elizabeth stumbled to her feet, staggered to the breach and engaged the first troops she could find in battle. Each sword stroke caused her pain and she yelped in agony but remained firm.

The corporal joined her, as did all the remaining men. They fought furiously to hold back the swelling tide of armored men.

A large man swung his sword under her defenses but stopped short of stabbing her with his weapon. His eyes widened at the sword sticking out of his chest. Elizabeth glanced around in a haze of pain. Peter stood by her side, grim faced, and pulled his sword free.

"Don't tell me to run, Elizabeth," he said.

"I won't, Peter," she ground out through gritted teeth. "Good hunting."

Peter nodded and joined the fight again.

They fought shoulder to shoulder as wave after wave of men poured through the breach. They fought back but gave in inch by agonizing inch. Guardsmen were butchered all around them, overcome by sheer numbers, and they found themselves in the city streets.

"Retreat!" Elizabeth called. "Retreat!"

She turned and ran toward the docks, Peter by her side.

At first the Osk and Sandcliff men gave chase, but finally Elizabeth and her remaining guardsmen—ten men—outpaced them.

Arrows rained down around them and Elizabeth felt the sting of metal as an arrow embedded itself in her back. She faltered, coughed, and spat out blood, but gamely continued to run.

Her chest felt as though it was on fire and it was more and more difficult to breathe.

Peter slowed with her.

"Come on! Run!" he screamed. "We have to get down to—"

His voice cut off as an arrow embedded in his throat. He clawed at it, wide eyed with shock as he sank to his knees.

"Peter," she wheezed. "No."

The life left Peter's eyes and he fell dead.

The pain of the arrow in her back and cut to her shoulder paled to the pain she felt deep inside at his loss. *He was my oldest friend.* She felt the sting of tears in her eyes.

A strong arm scooped her up under the armpit and tugged her up as another arrow sank into her back. She stumbled and the arm yanked her.

"Run, Duchess. Run!" a man screamed, dragging her along.

A second later he fell and she stumbled. She looked down the road toward the docks. They'd never seemed so far away. She tripped and fell to her knees. She dragged herself up and stumbled down the road, bruised, scraped, and bleeding.

A third arrow sank into her hamstring and she yelped in pain. She fell to one knee, dreadfully aware of the pounding feet on the road behind her. A young guardsman grabbed her damaged arm and slung it over his shoulder and she screamed in pain at the insult to her wounds. She tried to put pressure on her leg and screamed again at the gigantic bolt of pain from the arrow tip scraping along the bone of her leg.

An arrow thudded into the young guardsman's back and he grunted. Another struck her and the world went gray before her eyes.

She looked up, gathering herself and stumbling forward with him as best she was able. They slowly staggered toward the docks, toward a wall of armored men running up to greet them. They saw her, and their eyes widened in fury.

They ran faster, screaming, "Manusk! Manusk stands!"

The Osk and Sandcliff troops caught up to them and blade clashed against blade in a furious clang of steel. Elizabeth and the guardsman who helped her almost made it through the furious skirmish.

Elizabeth screamed as a furious arc of pain slammed through her belly. Her legs gave out and she fell to her knees, looking down with the guardsman at the sword sticking out of her midsection.

The pain was overwhelming and she felt the world gray out for a moment. When it passed, she felt weak. Weak and tired. She felt as though she wanted to go to sleep.

The battle raged around her and the armored men who had come to meet them pushed back the Osk and Sandcliff troops.

A small figure darted out of an alleyway toward her.

"Benton, you shouldn't be here," she whispered as she toppled down onto the road. *Look at those clouds. They're so beautiful. Rowan would like them.*

Benton flew at Elizabeth, her small arms encircling her neck, making her cry out in pain. "No," she wailed, tears raining down Elizabeth's bloody neck. "No. Don't leave. I don't want you to go."

I don't want to go either, Elizabeth thought. Or did she say it? She wasn't sure as the blackness swept over her in an unstoppable tide and consciousness slipped away.

CHAPTER 18

ELIZABETH OPENED HER eyes and blinked in confusion. She felt exhausted. Her leg and torso were covered in bandages and she was lying in a soft bed. She looked around the familiar room.

This is my *bed. How did I get here?*

Her room had changed while she'd been away. Now there was a rug and two chairs before the fire place, a small table by the window, and a canopy above the bed.

She slowly sat up, closed her eyes, and gritted her teeth against the dizziness that threatened to overwhelm her. She felt pain from her wounds but it was a dull, throbbing ache.

We won the battle. Kellen must have reached Arnett.

She lifted the covers and looked down at herself. She was bare, clean, and covered in bandages. She swung her legs over the side of the bed. The dizziness and black flowers in front of her vision increased and finally gave way. She felt weak as a kitten and hungry.

I want to eat. I want to know *what's going on.* She levered herself out of bed. Her mind gave her images of Rowan and she pushed them back. It was no use thinking about Rowan. She felt half healed; Rowan would have come and gone by now, if she'd even returned to Manusk. She glanced at the window but decided not to look out. *I can't bear the thought of looking at the harbor and not seeing the trader in its berth.*

She slowly and carefully limped toward the dressing screen in the corner. She found underwear, breeches, shirt, and boots. She slowly and carefully dressed and rested for a few moments when she was finished.

She limped across the room with a gait that bore only a shadow of a resemblance to her normal stride.

She sighed as she put her hand on the doorknob. She felt torn in two. Half of her wanted to go out and see what had happened while she'd been unconscious, the other half terrified of not seeing Rowan.

Don't be a coward, Elizabeth. You still have a home and you're alive. The rest will take care of itself.

She pulled the door open, stepped out into the corridor, stopped, and stared in shock.

Two columns of twelve people stood lining both sides of the corridor. They saw her, knelt, and bowed their heads.

One side was clearly distinguishable as the farmers of the militia of Manusk, headed by Jarrod and Rebecca.

The other, the Welland shipwreck survivors.

"Please, rise," Elizabeth said.

They all silently stood.

"It's good to see you all again," she said, looking at all of them. She turned to Jarrod. "Where's Farrow?"

"Dead, Your Grace," Jarrod said sadly. "Him, Heather, and Mia."

"Oh, no," Elizabeth said, feeling the sting of tears. She hesitated, unsure of what to say. Nothing seemed to be able to convey how much they'd meant. "They were good people."

Jarrod gave her the ghost of a smile. "Yes, Your Grace. That they were. They were Manusk to the core."

"Would you like to join me for something to eat? We will honor all those who gave their lives for Manusk."

Jarrod glanced at Rebecca and she nodded. "I would like that, Your Grace."

Elizabeth turned to Garvin, now out of bed and on makeshift crutches. He stared at her intently.

"You are looking better." She gestured toward his leg. "And I'm pleased to consider you and all of your people my guests. Would you like to join us as well?"

"Yes. Would like." Garvin tilted his head and studied her. "You look sick."

Elizabeth cleared her throat, distantly annoyed that she looked as weak as she felt. "I'm fine, Garvin."

He frowned. "No believe." He gestured with a crutch. "We follow."

"We walk together," Elizabeth said. "Always. But I understand what you're asking."

Garvin and the other Welland citizens glanced at each other and nodded. He gestured again with his crutch.

Elizabeth inclined her head and walked down the corridor. Welland and Manusk formed neat ranks behind her.

She looked around, amazed at the vast changes made in a small amount of time. There was a runner down the hallway and paintings on the walls. They were all seascape and mountain landscapes. She liked them.

They reached the head of the stairs and she slowly went down, wincing in pain as her leg tweaked with each step. She hung onto the balustrade, praying that she made it down on her feet rather than in an undignified, rolling heap.

They reached the bottom, and the room was suspiciously empty of people. She was used to the scurrying of soldiers to and from the kitchen and the great hall. Two guardsmen she did not recognize straightened when she approached, staring at her in surprise. They came to attention and watched the cavalcade pass by.

The corridor to the kitchen smelt of fresh wood, and was cleaner than she remembered. She wondered how Harriet had managed to get so much of her house rebuilt in such a small period of time.

The door to the kitchen was open as she'd always remembered it, and she walked through, regaining confidence with each step. As she went through the doors, she expected to see Harriet dashing between cooking pots, large tables with assorted civilians sitting around talking and eating with Manusk guardsmen.

The sight that greeted her stopped her in her tracks.

Harriet was gone; in her place was a plump woman with iron grey hair and an immaculate apron. There were still guardsmen—and not all of the liveried men wore the colors of Manusk—seated at the tables, but no signs of the citizens of Manusk.

The biggest surprise was the guests at the table she normally sat at.

The head of the table was conspicuously empty. A trim, white haired man with a well-groomed beard and immaculate linen sat to the left; to the right a large, muscular, black-haired man. To either side of them sat a woman with long, grey hair, and a young woman with jet black hair. Elizabeth approached the table slowly.

"Father," she said softly.

King Vincent whipped his head around at her soft voice. He stood slowly, trembling, came to her, and pulled her into his arms.

"Oh, Elizabeth," he said, his arms tightening around her. "Daughter."

"It's so good to see you," she said, her tears wetting his neck.

"I didn't think I'd see you alive again," King Vincent said, pulling back and cupping her face in trembling hands. "Gareth sent word that

Osk and Sandcliff had attacked and I feared the worst. We didn't hear anything."

"We all came with Arnett," Prince Gareth said, pulling her into his arms in a bear hug. He pulled back and grinned at her. "If you look out of your northern gate, you'll see the armies of the Northern Reaches here with us."

"If all of the Northern Reaches are here, then how come I'm only host to Eagle's Reach? Where's Fotheringill, Cayman's Leap, and Brandywine?" Elizabeth said as she accepted the motherly kiss of Duchess Sarah of Eagle's Reach.

"Gregory, Walter, and William weren't permitted entry to the city," Duchess Sarah said with a smile. "I'm sure they're spitting chips out there on the plains."

"Ahem," a voice said from beside her.

She turned and looked at the black-haired girl standing beside her. The girl's eyes were a startling shade of blue and they reminded Elizabeth of Rowan. She suppressed a quick stab of pain.

"Oh, Elizabeth, this is my daughter, Lady Katherine. Do you remember her? She is the heiress to the Duchy of Eagle's Reach. Lady Katherine, this is Princess Elizabeth St. John, Duchess of Manusk."

Lady Katherine took Elizabeth's hand—conspicuously bare of her rings—and bowed low. "It's an honor, Your Grace. I've heard so much about you."

Elizabeth felt a little overwhelmed. "You've grown a lot since I last saw you, Katherine." She smiled. "Do you mind if I sit down? I'm still a little unsteady on my feet."

"Of course," King Vincent said, as Prince Gareth ushered her to the head of the table and helped her sit. "We were beginning to think you wouldn't wake up."

"I need a moment, father," she said. "How long have I been unconscious for?"

"Three weeks," Prince Gareth said. "And we've been your guests for that time. Only us. We were only allowed small detachments of soldiers into the city, and we were the only ones. The others weren't allowed in."

Elizabeth's eyebrows shot up at this. "Who on earth told you that?"

"Our hostess," King Vincent said, grinning at the others. "Since you couldn't speak for your duchy." They exchanged a glance. "I expect she's in the duke's garden. She waits there every day."

Elizabeth's heart hammered. "Could you please excuse me, father? I have to see her."

King Vincent gave her an understanding smile. "I think you should. She's quite your defender."

"I know," Elizabeth said, flexing her hands to still their trembling. The nobles all stood and bowed.

Elizabeth turned to the militia and the shipwreck survivors. She beckoned them over. "Come. Eat. You must be hungry."

They all exchanged an uncertain glance.

"Come," Duchess Sarah said, patting the seat beside her. "We don't bite."

Garvin exchanged a glance with Jarrod and Rebecca. Jarrod gave a single nod and they all moved as a group to the table.

Elizabeth quickly left the kitchen and took the path that led toward the duke's garden. Her knees shook. She limped as quickly as she could up the path. She saw two figures, Isengard and Kellen, flanking the gate.

"It's good to see you, Your Grace," Isengard said as he opened the door. "It's good to see you up and about."

"I'm pleased to see you both as well," Elizabeth said, hardly pausing for a breath as she tore through the gate.

Chaos had given away to order in the garden. The lush grass was short and immaculately groomed. The paths had been swept and the fountain cleaned to snowy white. She jogged up the path to the opening in the hedge, burst through, and scanned the benches.

Rowan sat, shoulders slumped, on the bench they'd once sat on in the starlight. She was dressed in a long white gown, a simple golden circlet on her head. She studied the path intently. She looked pale and miserable.

"Rowan?" Elizabeth said softly, drinking in the sight of her.

Rowan straightened. Her eyes went wide at the sight of Elizabeth. She slowly stood, staring at Elizabeth as though trying to decide if she was an apparition.

"Rowan? It's me," Elizabeth said.

Rowan trembled. "Elizabeth?"

"Yes, it's me," Elizabeth said, her vision blurring as tears welled up in her eyes. Her heart ached at the sight of Rowan and the feeling of relief left her trembling. She ran as quickly as her limp allowed, launched herself into Rowan's arms and held on tight. She breathed deeply of Rowan's familiar, spicy scent as Rowan's arms tightened around her.

"God, it's so good to see you," Rowan said, pulling back and cupping Elizabeth's face. "I thought you'd never wake up. I was afraid. I came late." The words spilled out of her in a flood, and tears streamed down her beautiful face.

Elizabeth put a finger over her lips, trying to smile through her tears. "I was afraid I wouldn't see you again. I *wanted* to see you again. I wanted to say something to you. I love you, Rowan of Welland."

"And I love you, Elizabeth of Manusk," Rowan said, gracefully leaning down and claiming her lips.

Elizabeth wanted to crawl under Rowan's skin and stay there for the rest of her life. She poured all of her love into the kiss and when it ended, Rowan stumbled with her to the stone bench, pushed her down, and collapsed next to her. She pulled Elizabeth into her arms and gently stroked her back.

"I've never been so frightened in my entire life," Rowan said softly. "I saw you running down the road . . . armored men . . . a sword . . . I sent my men as quickly as I could but I was so afraid I'd gotten there too late. There was so much blood and you were so still."

"I don't remember much," Elizabeth said after a moment. "I hoped you'd come back but I didn't know. The last thing I remember is Benton telling me not to leave."

"Benton. She still wakes with nightmares." Rowan looked deep into Elizabeth's eyes. "So do I. You were so close, Elizabeth."

"I promised you that I'd settle down and start a family after the battle. I want to live the life I told you about, but I want that with you. I want to settle down with *you*." Elizabeth was terrified of Rowan's response. She felt naked, stripped bare.

"I want that with you, too," Rowan said, kissing her. "Will you marry me, Elizabeth of Manusk?" She bit her lip, her eyes showing her fear.

"Yes," Elizabeth said with a smile. "I'd love to marry you, Rowan of Welland."

She felt the tension leave Rowan's body. Rowan shifted her, pulled her into her lap, and held her close.

"We have to take care of Benton," Rowan said after a few moments. "She loves you. She's happy with me but she wants *you*. She refused to leave your side for the first few days after you fell. Her friend Thomas was able to coax her out of your room, but she still hates to be away from you."

"*All* the children of Manusk are mine now that Charles is gone. I'll take care of them." Elizabeth felt her face heat. "I know she loves me. I can see it. I think I can help her and so can my father and brother."

Rowan smiled. "Your father is a wonderful man and I like your brother. He signed the trading treaty I offered. I have to return to Welland and tell my father. Will you come with me?"

"Of course I'll come," Elizabeth said. *As if I wouldn't.*

"And we bring Benton with us?" Rowan asked. "She needs to be a child again for a little while at least."

"Yes," Elizabeth said. "If she wants to come she can come with us. Don't forget her friends. We can't bring them all. We have to ask her what she wants to do."

"I agree," Rowan said.

"When do you want to leave?"

"Before the week is out."

Elizabeth pulled back. "What about Manusk? We're still trying to recover from our unfortunate relations with Osk and Sandcliff."

"I spoke to your father and he's willing to let you go back to Welland with me. He's going to appoint a steward to take care of Manusk."

Elizabeth rolled her eyes.

Rowan grinned. "The choice is Lady Katherine of Eagle's Reach. Duchess Sarah will remain for a few months to ensure the transition is smooth."

"You've thought of everything, haven't you?"

Rowan grinned.

"I love you," Elizabeth said, stealing a quick kiss. She felt buoyant. "We have to go back to my father. I need something to eat. I'm starved." She looked at Rowan. "You've lost weight."

"I haven't really been hungry," Rowan said. "Although now I'm rediscovering my appetite."

"Good," Elizabeth said. She slowly got to her feet, grimacing.

"Are you in pain?" Rowan asked, sounding alarmed.

"Just a little stiff. I'm fine. I promise."

Rowan took her hand and they slowly walked back to the gate of the duke's garden. "If your wounds pain you, tell me."

"I will," Elizabeth said, pulling in close to her. "I wanted to ask you. Why didn't you let the other nobles of the Northern Reaches into the city?"

"I knew your father, your brother, and Duchess Sarah. You told me about them. I didn't know the others. I wasn't about to let any potential assassins close to my Elizabeth."

Elizabeth smiled. My *Elizabeth? I like the sound of that.* "They're safe. We can let them in."

"All right. This afternoon, we go on with the business of politics." Rowan pulled Elizabeth to a halt and looked into her eyes. "But tonight you're mine."

"Where are you staying?" Elizabeth asked, a little breathlessly.

"I'm staying in one of your guest rooms," Rowan said.

"Why don't you come back to our room with me? I miss you."

Rowan gave her a broad smile. "I'd like that." She was quiet for a moment. "I've missed you too."

They walked out of the duke's garden, Isengard and Kellen falling into step behind them.

"Where's Sean?" Elizabeth asked after a moment of comfortable silence.

"He's with Arnett. He's your new captain of the guard, since Peter is gone." Rowan looked at Elizabeth. "I'm sorry about Peter. He was your friend."

Elizabeth felt the sting of tears. Her mind gave her images of all the times they'd stood together in battle, in the barracks playing cards, visiting friends. "Who else, Rowan? Who else did I lose?"

"Sergeant Hunter, Sergeant Walter, Marcus, Daniel, and Mark are gone. Only ten of the guardsmen you brought into Manusk are still alive, almost all gravely injured. Half the militia is gone."

Elizabeth felt sick. "They were good people," she said around the lump in her throat.

"Yes. They were." Rowan pulled Elizabeth to a halt and cupped her face. "They were proud to serve you. They gave all of you your home back."

Elizabeth nodded. *She's right but it doesn't help. I want my people alive. I miss Peter.*

Rowan led her into the kitchen toward an empty table. King Vincent, Gareth, Elizabeth, and Katherine were gone, as were the militia and shipwreck survivors.

"You look pale," Rowan said, helping her into a seat. She sat beside Elizabeth, took her hand, and gently stroked it.

"I feel sick," Elizabeth said. "I just lost a lot of good, old friends and some new ones."

Rowan nodded. "I understand."

The woman Elizabeth saw when she'd first entered the kitchen appeared beside her.

"Your Grace?" she said, giving her a small curtsey. "Can I get you something?"

"I'd like a bowl of that delicious smelling stew you have on the fire, and some bread and cheese."

The woman smiled and nodded. "I'll just get it for you." She turned to leave.

"Wait," Elizabeth said. "What's your name?"

"I'm Florence," the woman said. "I'm your housekeeper."

"I'm pleased to meet you, Florence," Elizabeth said, trying to muster a smile. "Harriet is gone, isn't she?"

"No, Your Grace," a familiar voice said from behind her, sounding a little out of breath. "I'm still very much here."

Elizabeth got to her feet and pulled Harriet into a bear hug. "You're alive. It's so good to see you."

Harriet looked flustered and restlessly straightened her skirt. "I'm pleased to see you too, child. We were very worried about you."

"Well, I'm back on my feet now," Elizabeth said. "I have to ask, though, Harriet. How come you're not my housekeeper anymore?"

"My talents are needed elsewhere," Harriet said, a smile playing around her lips.

Elizabeth opened her mouth to beg her to reconsider when she was engulfed by a mob of about ten children. Benton was at the head, and she threw her arms around Elizabeth and squeezed her as hard as her childish strength would allow.

Rowan laughed and ruffled Benton's hair.

"You're alive," Benton said, tears in her eyes. "You're alive, Your Grace."

Elizabeth gently extracted herself from Benton's embrace and painfully knelt before her. "I'm very much alive and mending. And it's good to see you, too, young Benton."

Benton put her arms around Elizabeth's neck and kissed her cheek. Elizabeth felt her tears against her neck and tightened her arms around her. "You asked me not to go, and I won't. When I do, I want you to come with me. Do you want to come?"

Benton pulled back, gazing into her eyes, her expression dreadfully uncertain. "Do you mean it?"

Elizabeth nodded. "Yes, I mean it."

"Can Thomas come too?" Benton asked as Thomas slid up beside her and clasped her hand.

Rowan and Elizabeth exchanged glances.

"Who are you to Benton, Thomas?" Elizabeth asked.

Benton leaned forward. "He's my brother."

"Yes, he can come too," Elizabeth said, whispering in Benton's ear.

"She said you can come. She said you can come," Benton yelled, jumping up and down.

The group of children all cheered and patted Benton and Thomas on the back.

"What about us?" a small boy asked. "What will happen to us? Charles looked after us and he's dead now."

Elizabeth looked at him. He was under ten years of age and the expression in his eyes was dreadfully old. "What's your name?"

"Matthew," he said.

Elizabeth looked up at Harriet, who gave her a nod.

"Harriet's been looking after you, yes?"

He nodded.

"She's going keep looking after you. You're *my* children now. You're the children of Manusk."

Whispers of *the children of Manusk* swept through them.

"You're going to be like Charles?" Matthew said.

"No, I'm going to be like Duchess Elizabeth," Elizabeth said. "But I will care for you until you reach your majority."

They exchanged glances and whispered together. They broke, flocked to Harriet, and clutched at her skirts and hugged her.

Matthew turned to Elizabeth and bowed. "Thank you, Your Grace."

Elizabeth looked up at Rowan. "It's *our* pleasure," she said as Rowan nodded in approval.

"Come, now," Harriet said. "Let's go."

The children began a round of complaints.

Harriet herded them out of the kitchen, nodding sympathetically at their moans and groans of displeasure.

Sean entered the kitchen just as they left and his eyes lit up with pleasure at the sight of Elizabeth.

He crossed to her and saluted. "Your Grace is looking well."

"Sean, old friend," she said, clasping his forearm. "You're a sight for sore eyes."

"So are you, Your Highness," he said. "We were very worried about you."

Elizabeth nodded and gestured at his insignia. "That suits you."

He looked down at his insignia. "It's temporary. I just wish I wasn't wearing it. Peter was a good man."

"He was."

They were silent for a moment.

God I wish Peter was here with us.

"Elizabeth," Rowan said, sitting down at the table and gesturing at the steaming bowls of stew.

Sean bowed. "I have to go back to General Arnett. I came here to tell you King Vincent asks that you join him in your office in one hour."

"I will be there," Elizabeth said. "Thank you, Sean. Could you please have General Arnett send word to Walter, Gregory, and William on the plains to join us in the city? Their honor guard is also to be limited as per Rowan's instructions."

"Yes, Your Grace." Sean saluted and left the kitchen.

"Alone again," Rowan said softly, taking Elizabeth's hand and kissing her knuckles.

"Yes. With you by my side." Elizabeth looked down at her hand. "My rings. My royal signet and ducal signet. What happened to them?"

Rowan colored and held out her hands. Elizabeth grinned. Rowan was wearing the rings. "These belong to you, Your Grace." She slipped them off her fingers.

Elizabeth put her signet rings on and gazed at them appreciatively.

"I'm glad you got them," Elizabeth said, taking a spoonful of stew.

"It's all I had left," Rowan said, her eyes brimming with tears.

Elizabeth took her hand and gently brushed the back of it with her thumb. "You always had me. Always. Right from the second I saw you on the beach." She kissed the back of Rowan's hand. "You were so beautiful, even injured and unconscious. Then when you woke up and talked to me, I began to fall in love with you. I just didn't realize it until the serving girl fluttered her eyes at you in The Singing Sheep."

Rowan blushed. "You've held my heart since the moment I saw

your incredible black eyes. You really don't know how beautiful you are, do you? And Mia . . . I was ready to skin her alive because I knew she touched you the way *I* wanted to touch you."

"I think I knew then that I wasn't alone in noticing you," Elizabeth said.

"You were never alone on that one. Eat, Your Grace. You look like a ghost."

Elizabeth grinned. They demolished the meal before them.

"That was good," Elizabeth said when they were finished.

"It was." Rowan glanced at the clock in the kitchen. "We still have a little over half an hour before we have to see your father."

"I know where I want to go." Elizabeth stood and held out her hand. Rowan took it and Elizabeth slowly led her up to her room.

The upper corridor was deserted and they passed by the now empty rooms that had held the shipwreck survivors.

Elizabeth opened her door with a trembling hand. They went in and were barely in the room before she was in Rowan's arms, kissing her.

She nibbled Rowan's collarbones, feeling Rowan tremble and her hands running restlessly up and down Elizabeth's back.

Elizabeth felt her body heat and forced herself back. "Wait." She tried to get her breath back and her body under control. "We can't do this now. We don't have enough time."

"And you're covered in bandages," Rowan said, equally breathless. "Come."

Elizabeth's hand shook as she led Rowan to the window sill. They sat and looked down at the harbor.

Elizabeth flinched as she looked toward the berth that had once held the Welland trader. Her eyes widened at the massive warship tied up at the docks. High up on the main mast was the pennant they'd found on the beach, black with a red dragon on a yellow star burst.

"That ship's yours?" Elizabeth asked.

"The *Sea Sprite*." Rowan nodded. "Look closely at the import hall."

Elizabeth eyed the building closely. It looked the same as it had before, but without the angry mob held back by armed guards. Merchants, traders, and sailors walked there peacefully instead. She looked up at the three new flagpoles on the building.

The center flagpole held the standard of Manusk, a sea eagle on navy blue background; the second was the king's standard of crown and crossed swords; the third was her personal standard, a rose entwined with a sword.

Rowan smiled. "It was Richard's idea and the other traders went along with it. The trading guild standard has been permanently replaced by the personal standard of the Duchess of Manusk. They really are *your* people now."

Elizabeth was unable to speak. She felt pride in her people and overwhelmed by the simple courtesy of helping her take Manusk back for her citizens.

"Is Richard still alive?" Elizabeth asked after a moment.

"Oh, yes, he's still alive as well as the other traders."

"I'm glad. I like him."

Elizabeth shifted around so she was lying back in Rowan's arms, leaning against her on the window sill.

They stared out peacefully into the harbor, watching the choppy water and the seagulls wheeling in the air. The sounds of the streets below, the calls of vendors and cries of children and the clip clop of horses' hooves drifted up to them in the clean air.

Elizabeth, lulled by the warmth of Rowan's body and the movement of Rowan's hands on her stomach, drifted off into sleep.

Just as she nodded off, Rowan shifted and peered at her. "It's time to go and see your father."

CHAPTER 19

ELIZABETH PAUSED AT the door of her office and glanced back at Rowan. "Am I supposed to knock on my own door?"

Rowan laughed softly. "You could be imperious and fling the door open and stride through it."

"Or your big brother could just open the door for you," Gareth said as the door swung wide. "Leave it to you to keep Father waiting and to exasperate everyone sitting inside your study."

Elizabeth laughed. "And leave it to you to draw everyone's attention to my tardiness." She entered the office with Rowan by her side.

Vincent, Gareth, Sarah, and Katherine sat around the table, waiting for them.

"My apologies, Father," Elizabeth said. "I fell asleep."

"I think we can understand that, Elizabeth," Vincent said, his gaze swiveling between her and Rowan.

They took their seats, side by side, around the large table.

"Elizabeth," Vincent said. "There are some matters that need to be attended to before you return to Welland with Princess Rowan. They are your neighbors, Osk and Sandcliff, Coral Bay, and Sargay. There is the matter of kidnapped sailors sitting in prison in Osk. There is also the matter of the spy in your midst that you must decide. I have already taken care of the announcement about the stewardship of Manusk. Gareth?"

Gareth leaned forward. "We got word from Kellen that you were under attack from Osk and Sandcliff and we left at once to reinforce your garrison. We arrived just as they broke through the city walls. We defeated the army and accepted the surrender of Gilbert and Clayton. They will be hanged for treason and will trouble you no more. We thought you would want to talk to them when you woke up, so we've kept them in your city prison. Their sons—Martin of Osk and Oscar of Sandcliff—have taken up the mantle of duke in Osk and Sandcliff. Both are out of favor with the other nobles and it will be a while before they are able to cause trouble again, if at all. Martin is a coward and Oscar is a boor. Sean also told us about Duke Carter's unfortunate demise and the siege of Coral Bay. Coral Bay is now back in the rightful hands of her duke, Duke Henry. We also went to Remus and Sargay is no longer under siege."

Elizabeth shook her head, still shocked from the speed of the king's justice.

"Don't trouble yourself with sympathy for Gilbert and Clayton, Elizabeth," Vincent said. "Both were bad men. They held a city in terror for over fifty years, tried to murder a visiting dignitary, and almost started both a civil war *and* a war with a foreign nation. That magnitude of lives lost and for what? A squabble over warehouses on a dock owned by Manusk and *me*."

Gareth nodded. "Our army occupies both Osk and Sandcliff, and we have freed the Welland sailors. They've been back with their people for a couple of weeks now." He looked at Rowan. "And we can still only offer sincere apologies for this terrible act."

"Your apology was accepted weeks ago, Gareth," Rowan said. "My father will be shocked by all this but he is a good man. I can assure you if he were here he would also accept your apologies."

Vincent nodded and waved a hand. "If your father would like to meet in person, I am perfectly happy to travel to Welland to introduce myself and apologize in person." He turned sharp eyes to Rowan. "Princess? The spy?"

Rowan nodded. "It came as a shock to me but was not entirely unexpected. The spy you had in your midst was Mara. Benton made sure to point her out to me. She was still in the manor. I'm certain she was just waiting an opportunity to slip away once the fighting stopped."

Elizabeth growled, annoyed. "I knew something was wrong with her."

"So did I," Rowan said. "But if it's any consolation to you, it didn't occur to me that it might be her even though I thought she was the worst serving girl I'd ever met."

"All right," Vincent said. "Now. On to final business. I will remain in Manusk with Sarah and Katherine for the season. Elizabeth, you've done much to prove to Manusk that their king still cares about them, but they need to see me to know that I intend to keep watching over them. It will also cement Katherine's place as steward until you return."

Elizabeth wasn't sure how she felt. One half of her longed for Rowan, the other half wanted to stay behind and keep building a duchy with her people. She'd only just won their trust and was able to call Manusk home.

She nodded, heavy hearted. "I want to say good bye to some new friends before I leave."

"We'll go down to the docks tomorrow morning," Rowan said.

"Final business, if I may, Your Highness," Sarah said, glancing at King Vincent.

He gestured for her to continue.

"I believe, judging by Rowan's smiling face, that you accepted Rowan's marriage proposal. Don't look like that, Elizabeth. We all knew it was coming. Rowan very obviously adores you, and you her." Sarah smiled. "You have a wedding to attend tomorrow before you set sail for Welland."

Elizabeth felt her face heat and snuck a glance at Rowan. Rowan blushed furiously.

"Don't look like that, dear," Sarah said, clasping Elizabeth's hand. "Never turn down love and don't feel embarrassed by it." She sat back. "The king's chaplain will hear you take your vows tomorrow morning. All the legal documentation has already been taken care of."

"I suppose that's decided then," Rowan said, taking Elizabeth's hand.

Elizabeth squeezed it. "I don't mind. I like the idea."

Rowan grinned. "Good."

Vincent glanced around the room. "Does anyone have any further business?"

"No, Sire," Gareth, Sarah, and Katherine chorused.

"No, Father," Elizabeth said.

They stood and bowed.

Gareth headed toward the door. "I'm going to the northern gate. I have to talk to Arnett."

"I should do that," Elizabeth said. She thought of Gilbert and Clayton taking up valuable space in the city prison. "But instead I'm going to the prison to say farewell to our guests."

"I'll go with you," Vincent said with a cold smile.

"I'm coming too," Sarah said. She looked directly at Elizabeth. "Your duchy is in safe hands. We will take care of your people until you return. You have a lot to do in the next few days."

"Thank you, Your Grace," Elizabeth said softly. "For everything. And if it hadn't been for your kind instruction I wouldn't have been able to do any of this."

"All I did was give advice, dear. I'm glad you listened." Sarah patted Elizabeth's cheek.

Elizabeth looked at Rowan. "What do you want to do now, love?"

Rowan's eyes spoke volumes about her intentions, but her words were mild. "I'm going to go with you to the prison. After that, I think you should go down to the docks and see Richard and Delmarco. Both have been asking incessantly about you."

"We will go down to the docks after, then," Elizabeth said, offering her arm.

They went out into the courtyard and Elizabeth marveled at the changes weeks had made. The courtyard was clean and lightly trafficked. Gone were the columns of guardsmen sparring and the farmers learning how to fight.

The city streets seemed the same as they ever were. People still dodged horses and carriages in the streets, heading to their destinations without looking left or right. Vendors still cried out the highlights and qualities of their wares, trying to catch the eyes of passersby. The change Elizabeth saw were uniformed men moving amongst them. The patch on the chest of the tabard was the standard of Manusk.

"Who are the uniformed men?" Elizabeth asked.

"They're your watchmen. They wanted a uniform to make it obvious. I suggested the crest so everyone would know they were the watch."

Elizabeth shook her head. She'd never imagined that they'd ever want to wear the standard of Manusk.

People stopped and stared as they went past, and Elizabeth heard whispers behind her.

Elizabeth.

Duchess Elizabeth.

Elizabeth of Manusk.

A watchman looked sharply at them and his eyes widened. "Duchess Elizabeth! Your Grace!"

The people in his vicinity stopped and stared at her. To a person they went to one knee, murmuring, "Your Grace."

"Rise," Elizabeth said. "We are of Manusk. We don't bow and scrape to one another."

The people rose and stared at her.

"Duchess Elizabeth lives!" the watchman called. "Manusk stands!"

Slowly the people took up the cry. *Duchess Elizabeth lives . . . Manusk stands! . . . Manusk stands!*

Elizabeth bowed and then saluted them.

She turned toward the city prison, Vincent and Sarah flanking them, Katherine bringing up the rear.

As they got closer to the building, the crowd of people became thicker and the mood darker. Finally a group of watchmen jogged through the crowd, forcing them back so Elizabeth, Rowan, Vincent, Sarah, and Katherine could go through.

They entered the prison and an unfamiliar watchman got up from behind his desk and went to one knee.

"Your Highness," he said. "Your Grace."

They all looked at Elizabeth.

"I'm here to see Osk and Sandcliff," she said in a clipped voice, pushing down her temper.

He bowed. "This way, Your Grace."

He led them down a side corridor, the cells lining both sides empty of prisoners. He stopped before the last two and she heard shifting boots as the inmates got to their feet and approached the bars.

Elizabeth stood in front of the cells. Gilbert and Clayton were dressed in rags, purple with bruising and dried blood. They growled when they saw her.

"I thought you said she was dead, Gilbert," Clayton said.

"I thought she was. She looked like a porcupine and was yelping the last time I saw her," Gilbert replied.

Elizabeth felt Rowan shift beside her, and felt her father stiffen.

"And yet look at where we are now," Elizabeth said. "I'm standing out here with my father, who is very much alive, and you're contemplating swinging by your necks."

"You're pathetic, Elizabeth. You're a weak, sniveling incompetent who has no business being in charge of anyone," Gilbert said. "You were an accident born into privilege."

"I may be a *porcupine* and *pathetic* but I won the battle, gentlemen. Despite your best efforts."

"You don't deserve to live."

"Yes, I *do* deserve to live. What did I ever do to you? What have the people of my duchy ever done to you? You're a wretch."

"I quite agree with Elizabeth," Vincent broke in. "You tried to destroy a kingdom, you arrogant fool. And for what? Coin? Power? Prestige?"

"No," Clayton said coldly. "I did it because I am a *real* man who can lead this kingdom to greatness. *I* have control over trade. *My* duchy is richer than your kingdom. Why should I bow to a peasant like you? *I* should be on the throne, not a little boy like you who hides behind his daughter's skirts."

Pathetic pig. Elizabeth opened her mouth to speak but Vincent laid a restraining hand on her arm.

"Yet I'm still the king despite your best efforts," Vincent said. "It is *you* who are pathetic, Gilbert, and *you* Clayton. Neither of you is fit to be king. You gained wealth because you stole from everyone, including me. You are bloodthirsty bullies. You rule with fear and subjugation. Thousands of lives—including the lives of foreign ambassadors—were lost because of you. *You* are *an accident born into privilege.*"

"It's better than being a sniveling weakling," Gilbert said coldly.

"I've heard enough," Elizabeth said. She gazed at Vincent, who looked sad despite the simmering anger in his eyes. "You kept these men alive for me, didn't you?"

Vincent nodded. "I wanted to imprison them but as you can see that won't be possible. They'll always be a distraction to the people."

Elizabeth nodded. "You have a gallows prepared?"

Vincent nodded. "Technically it's yours."

"Then let it be now."

Vincent nodded and signaled for the wide-eyed watchman. "Get the guards."

The watchmen ran to obey Vincent's command and they continued to exchange vicious stares with Gilbert and Clayton.

The guardsmen came after a few moments and opened the cell doors.

"This isn't over, Vincent," Gilbert said. "We will take Manusk and we'll come for you. Your days are numbered."

"So are your minutes. You're in no position to threaten me." Vincent nodded to the guardsmen. "Take them."

The guardsmen dragged them from the cells and out toward the city street. They struggled and swore the whole way, raining insult after insult down on Vincent's head.

Rowan tightened her hand around Elizabeth's. "Are you all right?"

Elizabeth nodded. "I'm fine. I just want this nightmare over."

Citizens lined the streets, screaming and catcalling, hurling rotten fruit and sometimes more odious matter at Clayton and Gilbert as they were hauled to the town square.

In the center of it stood two large gallows and the smell of fresh wood, rotten fruit, and unwashed humanity pervaded the air.

The crowd screamed, furious, calling for their deaths.

"—You animals. You took my livelihood—"

"—should be boiled in oil, screaming for mercy—"

"—want to see your eyes pecked out of your bloated corpse—"

"—nearly killed Duchess Elizabeth—"

Vincent lithely jumped up onto the platform, flanked by Sarah and Katherine. Elizabeth stayed below in deference to her injuries.

"Quiet! It is time to deal with the matter of Gilbert of Osk and Clayton of Sandcliff." He turned to them, and they glared at him defiantly. "You have been convicted of fraud, extortion, mass murder, and high treason against the king, crimes punishable by death. If I could execute you for every life you took I would, but I can only do it once." He motioned the hangman. "Sentence will be carried out immediately."

"We aren't allowed last words, you coward?" Clayton asked.

"No," Elizabeth said coldly.

She painfully climbed onto the platform and approached Clayton carefully and stared into his dark, hate-filled eyes. She held his gaze and reached around the back of him to tear off his ducal signet. She did the same with Gilbert. She turned to the silent Rowan and held up the rings so she could see them. "For you, Rowan. I promised you proof of what was done to your sailors, and here it is. Clayton's ducal signet is a seagull." She turned back to Clayton and Gilbert. "Neither of you needs any parting words. The only thing you *should* be doing is begging for forgiveness but neither of you actually feels the need for it. I have no interest in listening to your poison anymore." She nodded at the hangman. "Hang them."

The crowd cheered as she carefully climbed back down to Rowan.

The hangman slowly and methodically put a noose around each silent man's neck, checking it carefully for frays or breakages.

"You have no right," Clayton said.

"I demand—" Gilbert began.

The hangman pulled the lever.

They fell through open trapdoors, their necks briskly snapping. Their bodies flailed and then swung limply as the ropes groaned and creaked.

The crowd went wild, surging toward the hanging platform, but were pushed back by the grim-faced guardsmen. The mood got uglier as the cries and insults increased in number and volume.

Rowan quickly scrambled up the platform and pulled Elizabeth with her. Elizabeth held up her hands.

One by one the men, women and children in the crowd looked up, and stared at her in wonder. They quieted in fits and starts.

"—the Duchess of Manusk—"

"—Elizabeth—"

"—Rowan of Welland—"

One by one they fell to their knees and bowed low.

They were now as deathly silent as they had been loud moments earlier.

"Rise," Elizabeth said. "We of Manusk do not bow and scrape to one another."

Slowly the crowd rose.

"Go in peace," she said. "And remember this for your children and your grandchildren. It is finished. Gilbert of Osk and Clayton of Sandcliff are no more. Manusk will *never* be bowed or broken while we walk in peace here! Long live King Vincent! Manusk!"

The crowd began to chant *King Vincent* and *Manusk*.

Elizabeth bowed to the people in the town square, and they bowed low in return. She got off the platform with Rowan, Vincent, Sarah, and Katherine close behind her. The crowd parted and allowed them through, bowing as they passed.

They'd got back out to the main street.

Vincent pulled her to a halt and stared at her. "You've finally found something you can really care about besides running around with the army, haven't you?"

Elizabeth nodded. "I have. I want to make this my home and try to be the duchess these fine people deserve."

Vincent nodded. "I'm glad, daughter." He gave her a quick hug. He pulled back and grinned. "I think I'll go up to the northern gate and see what trouble your brother has managed to get himself into."

"Mind if I tag along?" Sarah asked, and Vincent nodded.

"Thank you, Father," Elizabeth said, bowing.

"You're welcome, daughter," Vincent said. He turned to leave. "I'll see you later."

Rowan and Elizabeth both nodded as he walked away.

Elizabeth sighed and pulled Rowan into motion, a little rattled by the crowd at the square. *They were a bloodthirsty mob.*

"I'm glad that's over," Rowan muttered. "That ugliness was starting to become frightening."

Elizabeth nodded. "I know. I'm glad it's over too."

As they continued on down to the docks, the city behind them seemed to murmur, *Manusk.*

They finally reached the doors to the trading hall and saw the hulking figure of Richard's guard.

He started when he saw her and his scarred face creased into a broad grin. "Your Grace," he said, bowing low.

"It's wonderful to see you again," Elizabeth said with a matching grin. "Is your master within?"

The man nodded. "He is." He opened the door for her and Rowan and gestured for them to go in.

They passed by the scribe's desk, ignoring the stares and whispers as she limped by.

"Your Grace," Rowan said, holding the door to the main import hall open for her.

Elizabeth entered, feeling at peace. All of the tables were taken and sailors argued with merchants to get the best prices for their wares.

"Duchess Elizabeth," Richard cried, running toward her. "Welcome. Welcome back."

"Richard," Elizabeth said, clasping forearms with him. "I'm glad to see you."

"Our bargain," Richard said. "We don't want you to go. We want you to stay."

"Thank you, Richard," Elizabeth said.

"But I get her first," Rowan said.

Richard gave her a broad smile and bowed. "Understood, Your Highness." He turned to Elizabeth. "We will await your return. And we will come and get you if you stay away too long."

Elizabeth laughed. "I will always come back to Manusk, Richard." She held out her arm and they clasped forearms. "Thank you. You are a good man and I consider you a friend."

"I consider *you* a friend, Your Grace," he said.

"Tomorrow, we are having a wedding feast. We would consider it an honor if you and your comrades would join us," Rowan said.

"And I accept on behalf of myself and my fellow traders. We will be there." Richard took Elizabeth's arm and gently steered her toward the other traders. They all stopped what they were doing and stood to a man and applauded.

Elizabeth stared at them, wide eyed, overwhelmed by the good wishes from the traders.

"Thank you, everyone," she said when the noise abated. "I promise you that there will be no more interference in good and honest trade in Manusk. May the wind be at your back and may fortune favor you."

The men and women in the hall bowed low.

Elizabeth turned to Rowan. "Let's go. I think I might need some rest."

Rowan peered closely at her. "You look a little pale, my love." She took Elizabeth's arm and steered her from the import hall.

They made their way slowly back to the manor, passing by citizens who bowed and smiled at them. They passed by several lamp posts and notice boards that had an open invitation to their wedding nailed to them.

They finally reached the door to their room in the manor.

Rowan pulled Elizabeth to a halt. "I love you." She stared intently at Elizabeth. She was pale.

"I love you too," Elizabeth said, disturbed by Rowan's change in mood. "What's the matter?" She cupped Rowan's face. "Come. Let's talk."

Rowan nodded and Elizabeth took her hand and pulled her into the room. She led Rowan to the chair by the window and gently pushed her down into it. Her heart rate picked up, fueled by the dread she felt at Rowan's pallor.

"What's the matter, my love? Have you changed your mind about marriage?" Elizabeth forced the words out, bracing herself for Rowan's response.

"No," Rowan said. "I'll never change my mind about marrying you."

"Then what is it?"

"I saw your bandages, Elizabeth. I just . . . can't stand . . . the thought of losing you."

"I won't say I'm in perfect health, I'm not," Elizabeth said, taking her hands. "But I *can* say I'm feeling much better. I won't be leaving you any time soon because of my injuries, love." She gazed into Rowan's beautiful, blue eyes. "I promise you I will stay by your side. I'll ask my father to release me of my duties as his battle commander. I will be there by your side for years to come, watching our children grow to adulthood."

Tears brimmed in Rowan's eyes. "I'm so sorry. I just can't seem to get the picture of you lying on the road out of my mind. I keep seeing all the . . . blood . . ." She shook her head, tears spilling down her angular face.

Elizabeth slowly stood and pulled Rowan with her. She led Rowan to the bed and stopped her before it. She gazed into Rowan's eyes, and unlaced her shirt.

Holding Rowan's gaze, she pulled the shirt over her head and dropped it onto the floor. Her torso was covered in bandages and she looked down for the tie. Rowan's trembling hands found it and she slowly unwound the bandages and discarded them on the floor. Elizabeth felt relieved as they fell away from her. She looked down and saw the angry, half-healed cuts on her midsection and her shoulder. They didn't pain her, despite the way they looked.

She felt Rowan's eyes on her. They were turbulent and darkened with passion. Rowan opened her mouth to speak but Elizabeth put her finger against her lips. She slipped Rowan's gown off her broad shoulders and freed her full breasts. She gazed at Rowan, drinking in the sight of smooth muscle covered by soft skin.

Rowan knelt before her, pulled off her boots, and stripped away her breeches and underwear. She kissed Elizabeth's shoulder wound, pulled her in close, and traced the scars left by the arrow wounds to her back.

The brush of hair against her bare skin broke all of Elizabeth's restraint. She pulled Rowan down onto the bed, and Rowan settled herself down on Elizabeth, bare skin brushing against hers in an explosion of sensation that left her weak kneed and throbbing painfully. Rowan slowly and gently kissed each wound and scar she found, pausing in sweet torture at Elizabeth's breasts. She kissed and nibbled her way down Elizabeth's body, running her fingertips along the skin of Elizabeth's ribs and thighs, making her groan and beg for more. Rowan settled herself between Elizabeth's legs, tasting and teasing her to an intense release.

Elizabeth lay back for a moment as Rowan slid up beside her, kissing her breasts and nuzzling her neck. Elizabeth rolled over and claimed Rowan's lips, kissing her deeply, pouring all of her love and passion into the simple action. She broke the kiss and feasted on Rowan's silky, creamy skin, pausing here and there to lick and nip at old wounds. She feasted on Rowan's breasts until Rowan clutched the bed covers, begging her to end the torture. She took Rowan into her mouth, feeling her swell and stiffen as Rowan cried out her orgasm.

She slid up Rowan's long body into her arms and rested her head on Rowan's chest and drifted off to sleep.

They spent the remainder of the day and the night tangled together, alternating love making and sleep.

Dawn broke, and they rang for a servant and had their bath prepared. Bathing turned into another extended bout of love making, and when they finally emerged from their chamber they barely had time to dress for their wedding.

"WHO GIVES AWAY this woman?" the slightly out of breath priest asked. He looked expectantly at Isengard, standing behind Rowan.

"I do," he said with a nod.

The priest nodded. He looked back down at his book.

"We are gathered here today to celebrate the union of Her Highness, Princess Elizabeth St. John, Duchess of Manusk, and Princess Rowan Stonecypher, daughter of King Callas Stonecypher of Welland . . ."

Elizabeth snuck a look at Rowan beside her. Rowan looked radiantly beautiful and very happy. She squeezed Elizabeth's fingers and glanced at her, smile playing around her lips. Elizabeth felt at peace for the first time in what seemed forever.

"Princess Rowan, do you take Princess Elizabeth to be your wife, for better or worse, for richer and poorer, in sickness and in health, forsaking all others?"

"I do," she said firmly.

"You may place the ring on Her Highness's finger," the priest said. Rowan accepted the ring Isengard gave her. She took Elizabeth's hand and slipped it onto her ring finger.

The priest turned toward Elizabeth.

"And you, Your Highness? Do you take Princess Rowan to be

your wife, for better or worse, for richer and poorer, in sickness and in health, forsaking all others?"

"I do," Elizabeth said.

"You may place the ring on Princess Rowan's finger," the priest said.

Elizabeth accepted the gold band from Gareth and gently placed it on Rowan's finger.

"I now pronounce you married," the priest said. "You may kiss the bride."

Elizabeth turned to Rowan and kissed her. The crowd gathered in the church cheered and applauded.

"If you will follow me, I have some documents for you both to sign," he said.

They followed him into the vestry, followed closely by Vincent, Gareth, Isengard, and Kellen. They signed the marriage patent and the patents that made Rowan Duke of Manusk and Elizabeth a princess in Welland.

They left the chapel to cheering from the assembled citizens of Manusk and made their way to the town square. Citizens were already seated, waiting for them. Elizabeth saw Richard and the traders, the Welland survivors, and what remained of her militia at tables close to theirs. They stood and applauded, nodding approvingly as Rowan and Elizabeth took their places at the head of the table.

"Rowan," Elizabeth said as they sat down. "This is Duke Gregory of Fotheringill, Sir Walter of Brandywine, and Sir William of Cayman's Leap. They are the nobles of the Northern Reaches and our allies." Each of the young men bowed.

"Gentlemen, this is our new Duke of Manusk, Princess Rowan Stonecypher of Welland."

"Welcome," Duke Gregory said in a smooth baritone. He raised his glass and toasted the couple.

A finely dressed young man entered the square and came toward them. He trembled slightly, Elizabeth noted with interest.

He stopped before the table and bowed, a boy of no more than fourteen. He looked up, his eyes red rimmed from weeping. "Duchess Elizabeth. I am Duke Henry Delacourt of Coral Bay. I just wanted to say thank you for helping me."

Rowan and Elizabeth exchanged glances. He looked tired and unhappy. Rowan stood and took his arm. Vincent, seated by

Elizabeth's side, shuffled over and gestured for a servant to bring a chair and a new place setting. Rowan steered Henry over to the open space and he sat down.

"Welcome, Duke Henry," Elizabeth said. "I'm sorry for your loss. Your father was a good man and a good friend."

Fresh tears appeared in his eyes. Captain Garamond materialized beside him and put a comforting hand on Henry's shoulder as he blinked away his tears. Henry looked relieved by his presence and embarrassed by his own emotion.

"We don't stand on ceremony," Vincent said from beside him. "Cry your tears, lad. Your father really *was* a good man."

"Thank you, Sire," Henry choked out.

They looked away for a moment to give him time to compose himself.

"Thank you, Your Grace," he finally said in a thick voice. "My father was a good duke and he was a well-loved father. I'll miss him."

Elizabeth smiled. "I can see that he was." She paused while he collected himself. "I would welcome your company for the few days before we return to Welland."

He peered at her and gave her a tremulous smile. "I'd like that, Your Grace."

"Elizabeth," she said. "Call me Elizabeth."

"Elizabeth," he said awkwardly.

Duchess Sarah leaned forward and gave him a motherly smile. "You are amongst friends, Duke Henry. My daughter will be your neighbor while Elizabeth is away."

Lady Katherine gave him a friendly smile and waved. He blushed.

Rowan leaned toward Elizabeth. "I wonder if he knows Katherine is more interested in *you* than in him," she whispered.

Elizabeth glanced sharply at her. "She's not. Is she?"

Rowan laughed and patted her face. "You're spoken for. She knows that. Or she'd better know that if she knows what's good for her."

Elizabeth rested her head on her hands, shaking her head. "Oh God, you know you're going to start an incident if you do anything to her?"

Rowan laughed harder. "I know. But I also know she can see where your heart lies."

"You own me, Rowan. There'll never be anyone but you, my love."

"And there won't be anyone for me but you, Elizabeth," Rowan said, kissing her. "Let's go look at clouds in the duke's garden after this."

Elizabeth nodded. "I'd like that."

The crowd cheered and the celebration continued.

AT AROUND MID morning the next day, Elizabeth called for a council with the militia, the Welland survivors, and the nobles, including Vincent and Gareth.

Rebecca and Jarrod sat beside Harriet, Richard, and Garvin at the big table, surrounded by Vincent, Gareth, Sarah, Katherine, Duke Gregory, Duke Henry, Sir Walter, and Sir William.

Elizabeth sat at the head of the table, Rowan and Sean behind her. Isengard and Kellen stood discretely behind Vincent at the other end of the table.

"I wanted to talk to you today to discuss how we will proceed with the governing of Manusk while Rowan and I are away," Elizabeth said, looking at Jarrod, Rebecca, Harriet, Richard, and Garvin. "I know His Highness, King Vincent, has announced that Lady Katherine will take up the mantle of steward. But you, ladies and gentlemen, are equally my leaders and my friends in Manusk. She will rely on your support as she takes up the mantle.

"We all want Manusk governed by good laws and fair practices, ones that we established when we began to take Manusk back from Osk and Sandcliff. I want the trade guild to enjoy a place of respect once again, and I want the militia to continue to grow and prosper. You proved yourself an invaluable asset during the battle, one that we couldn't have done without."

She leaned back in her chair. "My question to you is if you are able to accept Lady Katherine as a steward? Can you give her your loyalty and support?"

Vincent remained expressionless but Elizabeth could sense and see his displeasure in the slight narrowing of his eyes.

Elizabeth held up her hand. "You asked me to give you back Manusk, Father. I did so. But I could only do it with the citizens you see sitting here. Richard leaned his guards for the safety of the import hall, Rebecca and Jarrod agreed to fight for me and did so—losing friends in the process. Harriet fed my people and helped me show them *you* cared about them. Garvin and his friends want to stay to be farmers amongst good people. These have shown themselves to be truly loyal to *me*—to *us*. You yourself taught me to cherish such loyalty. It does them a grave disservice to ignore their wishes in the matter now."

Vincent nodded once, sharply.

Jarrod, Rebecca, Richard, Harriet, and Garvin leaned back for a quick, quiet conversation. They separated after a few moments and Jarrod gestured for Richard to speak for them.

"We will accept Lady Katherine's stewardship if she will accept our counsel."

Lady Katherine, watching proceedings with interest, leaned back as her mother whispered in her ear. She looked sharply at her mother. Sarah pulled her in close again and whispered again.

Lady Katherine straightened. "Yes. I will do that. My mother will stay with me for a season and will help."

"You are known to be good and honorable by your people, Duchess Sarah," Richard said. "We gladly accept your presence and extend our hospitality to you."

Jarrod leaned forward and wagged a warning finger in Katherine's face. "And if you give us any lip, lass, I'll be the first to bend you over my knee."

There was a moment of shocked silence.

Elizabeth burst out laughing, followed by Rebecca, Richard, and Harriet at the outraged look on Katherine's face. Katherine finally laughed as well.

"Warning taken, Jarrod," Katherine said. "I'll listen."

Jarrod nodded and they all laughed again.

"Father," Gareth said. "I'd like to spend winter in Coral Bay, unless you have other plans for me?"

Henry brightened and grinned at Gareth. "That's a wonderful idea, Your Highness. We'd love to have you."

Vincent nodded approvingly. "I think the sea air will do you some good."

"Sargay is said to be beautiful this time of year," Duke Gregory said. "I think I should go and see Earl Remus. I haven't seen him for quite some time."

Sir Walter and Sir William exchanged glances. "We should really head home, I think. I prefer the mountain air. Do you mind if we stop in by Eagle's Reach and Fotheringill? Autumn is a beautiful season there."

"Of course," Sarah and Gregory said together.

"If you like, you can wait for my return," Sarah said.

"That's very gracious of you. We accept," Sir Walter said.

"Excellent," Vincent said with a smile. "We all know where we're going to go on holidays this year. However, someone has to rule the King's Heartland, so I'll be going home." He looked at Lady Katherine. "And I expect to hear from you often."

"Certainly, Sire," she said.

"Then let's be about our business," Vincent said. "I'd love to see more of Manusk. You have a beautiful home, Elizabeth."

They all stood and took their leave of Elizabeth and Rowan.

Sean remained behind after the others had left. "Your Grace?"

"Yes, Sean," Elizabeth said.

"May I join you on your voyage to Welland?" he asked. "I think I need a break."

Elizabeth smiled at him. "I'd welcome your company, Sean. Ask Delmarco if he'd like to voyage across the Markand Sea for new trade."

Sean smiled and bowed. "As you wish, Your Grace."

THE NEXT FEW days were hectic for Rowan and Elizabeth as they resupplied Rowan's flagship, *Sea Sprite,* in preparation for their voyage to Welland. They gathered together a company of Manusk guardsmen, headed by Sean, who was now officially promoted to captain of the guard.

Dawn of the day they sailed found Elizabeth and Rowan standing by the railing on the *Sea Sprite*, looking at the harbor city of Manusk. The now familiar cry of *Manusk stands* and *long live King Vincent* drifted to them from the city streets.

Onlookers, including Gareth and Duke Henry, stood on the docks, watching them and waving farewell. Elizabeth waved back at them, feeling slightly sad despite her excitement at seeing Rowan's home.

"Take us out," Rowan said to a uniformed sailor beside them.

Sean stood on the other side of him, watching them all with interest. Benton and Thomas were on the other side of Rowan, exchanging excited observations and pointing at everything.

"Up anchor and set sail!" the sailor called and the deck became a flurry of activity as the sailors rushed to obey his orders.

"Are you all right?" Rowan asked, peering anxiously at Elizabeth.

"I'm fine," Elizabeth said. "Why? Are you worried I'm going to jump ship and swim back to Manusk?"

Rowan nibbled her lip. "No, I just don't want to push you into doing anything you're not ready to do."

Elizabeth gently stroked her beautiful face. "Please, my love, don't worry about me so much. This is just the next adventure, as far as I'm concerned. Besides, I love you. I'd do anything for you. And going home with you is something I welcome. Where you go, I go."

"I'm sorry, you must think me very silly for being so insecure," Rowan said.

"No, I understand," Elizabeth said. "I don't think there's anything that will convince you besides me still being by your side as we both turn old and gray."

Rowan took a deep breath, her bright blue eyes filled with love for Elizabeth. "I love you, Duchess of Manusk." She put an arm around Elizabeth.

Elizabeth sank into her, feeling a deep sense of peace and contentment as the sun rose behind the city of Manusk. She bid a farewell to her city, content for the first time in a long time.

ABOUT THE AUTHOR

Jordan Falconer was born in Sydney, Australia, and from a very young age had an interest in ghoulies, ghosties and long legged beasties and all things that go bump in the night. After surviving Catholic school (twice!) she graduated from Sydney University with an honors degree in Psychology. She currently resides in Califorina with her other half and three small, demanding dogs.